MW01045743

WALLS OF WIND

J. A. MCLACHLAN

A SCIENCE FICTION NOVEL

J. A. McLachlan

Walls Of Wind

Copyright © J.A. McLachlan

ISBN: 978-0-9936306-4-4

For my daughter, Amanda
with my love and admiration

— a lifelong bond, as visible as my blood in your veins, as eternal as
the wind that blows over us both. My flesh yet separate, destined to
go places I will not, taking with you whatever passion and strength I
might impart before you begin your journey —
-Briarris, p. 23

Contents

Author's Note

On a world in which each species has only one gender, the very concept of gender could not exist; therefore, there would only be one pronoun used for sentient beings. Unfortunately, the English neutral pronoun, "it", has the effect of conferring object or animal status. Because there is no way to avoid gender classification without depersonalizing the characters, I have used the pronoun "he" throughout this novel; it is the more commonly used pronoun and will therefore be less intrusive.

Beyond the Wall

Briarris

I heard a low cough at our door. Of all the sounds on Wind, this was the one I was dreading. The window shutters were tightly latched so I couldn't see outside even if I wanted to, but I knew what waited at our door.

Perhaps no one else had heard. I looked behind me. Even that slight movement brought on a wave of nausea. The hot, heavy air of stillseason sickened me despite the rotating fans overhead.

A second cough, louder, from behind the door. My sibling, Ocallis, emerged from the back room. He didn't hurry to the door, but he didn't hesitate. He looked at me as he passed and I grabbed his arm.

"Don't open it," I whispered.

"It's Rukt'an."

"He is Ghen." I shuddered, feeling my nausea return. Ocallis laughed.

"Have you forgotten our last sight of Ghen?" I demanded, recalling the day we had sneaked down beyond the Ghen compound to watch them at their training. The growls and howls of their mock battle, the snap of vicious jaws and treacherous clash of spiked backs, the grip and rip of clawed fists, the slip of feet on dampened field… we fled in terror. I felt that same fear today.

"We aren't going to battle," Ocallis said.

I looked him in the eye and said no more.

A third cough sounded at our door. Matri hurried from the washing room, huffing at our rudeness as he passed us to open the door to Rukt'an. They stood there, swaying gently in unison so that each was the still point of the other's vision, their hands moving in signs that were meaningless to all but them. They were beautiful together and they didn't know it; some fundamental misunderstanding blinded them. I saw it for a moment, then it was gone and they were just Bria and Ghen once more, trying vainly to communicate.

Rukt'an extended and retracted his gruesome claws to complete the symbols our parent made with his longer, twice-jointed fingers. The Ghen larynx isn't designed to issue the high-pitched notes Bria use to communicate. Nor could Bria utter the guttural grunts and sub-vocal clicks and sighs of Ghen speech, or distinguish words out of those sounds and half-sounds. It had taken most of the five years they lived together for our parent and Rukt'an to learn to speak together, using gestures and signs that they developed between themselves. Pointless, all of it. How could I have imagined anything beautiful in it, even for a moment?

Matri stepped aside and Rukt'an entered. Through the open doorway I could see our city, absolutely motionless. I would have to walk through that deathly stillness beside Rukt'an. I turned and ran for the washing room and threw up into the waste basin. I leaned over it, waiting in case there was more, and closed my eye. The storyteller's chant from my childhood came back to me:

Bria are often sick during stillseason. When the wind dies it takes with it the dance of slender trees and tall grasses. When the wind dies the billowing clouds disappear, leaving only the ghostly Sphere inert upon our sky. The fluttering streamers upon our buildings, lampposts, and fences all hang limp and still. When the wind dies our single, unmoving eye loses perspective. The world flattens itself upon our retina in lines and colors like a drawing on a wall with only our own movement to give it substance. We stumble half-blind into our houses, groping to close window shutters and gulping in the fabricated breeze of our tightly-wound overhead fans. For one month every year the city must run itself. Street lamps hang still and dark while house lamps alone illuminate the city from dusk till dawn.

When the wind dies we are reminded that we must trust all things to the Creator Wind, who moves through our lives as invisible and as substantial as the wind.

I did not appreciate the reminder today.

Ocallis burst in on me. "Stop throwing up. It's time to go."

I opened my eye. "I don't know why we have to live with Ghen."

"You want to mate with a Ghen you don't know? Without even being joined?"

My ears twitched with embarrassment. "No," I said quickly. "It's just... pointless to have to live together a full year before we mate."

"It is civilized."

"It isn't civilized; it's expedient. A trade, nothing more."

"A trade without which neither Ghen nor Bria can survive."

"I know my duty." But I don't have to like it, I thought, staring down into the bowl of vomit.

"Why do you dislike Ghen so much?"

"I don't trust them."

"So don't come. You don't have to be joined if you don't want to." His scornful voice stung me. I looked up at him, leaning against the wall, as beautiful and self-possessed as the mythical Dayannis.

"What if there *are* Broghen?" I said, to rattle him. Stories of the mythical Broghen, Ghen-like but born of Bria—huge, mindless, devouring monsters—are so deeply embedded in both our species' barbarous pasts that at one time Bria refused to mate altogether. Until the Wind spoke to Dayannis, womb-parent of our races, bidding him to join with Heckt'er, the mightiest and wisest of Ghen. According to the story Dayannis bore no Broghen, but the customary two Bria and single Ghen, and every Bria since has done the same.

Ocallis laughed at my barb. He was my twin in appearance, but unlike me he was eager to join with a Ghen for future mating.

"Even if there really were Broghen," he replied, "I would take the risk in order to have children." He meant it, and I was grudgingly impressed. If there had been a real Dayannis, he would have been much like my sibling.

"I *want* to carry my Ghen mate's child as well as my own," he continued. "Don't look so shocked. It's not as though I'm going to exchange my fur for scales, or puff up twice my size, or grow a second eye, a heavy jaw, a set of claws…"

I threw up again. Above the sound of my retching, I heard Ocallis laughing.

That is the last of that, I thought. I stood up, wiping my mouth with finality.

"Why are you doing this to yourself?"

"You know I have to be joined to sit on Council." I washed my hands in the water basin.

"There are other careers."

"Not for me."

I swept out of the washing room, passed Matri without a word, opened the door and walked outside. Rukt'an followed me at once. We waited for

Ocallis, who doubtless remembered to blow gently on Matri's face and receive his breath in return before stepping into adulthood.

I would have gone back to do so also, but wasn't certain I could force myself outside again. If I had not already thrown up, I would have done so now. Ocallis, when he reached us, looked equally ill. We stumbled forward, each of us clutching convulsively to one of Rukt'an's arms, trying to deny with our minds the message of our confused, disoriented eye, trusting that Rukt'an would not let us walk into the trees, buildings and lampposts that reared at sudden angles as we moved, and receded, step by halting step, immediately before us.

I had never been outside in stillseason. My skin itched and sweated with the weight of my fur in the hot, still air. I gulped for breath, my lungs laboring to suck in the oxygen that normally blew freely into my nostrils with the friendly wind. Eventually I closed my eye, having to depend on Rukt'an anyway, and the nausea receded, allowing me to concentrate on breathing.

By the time we reached Festival Hall I was dizzy and disoriented, ready to surrender myself to the first Ghen who approached me and hating myself for my weakness.

Rukt'an opened the door. A gust of air blew across my face. I gasped in pleasure. Even so I hesitated, while Ocallis marched in boldly. It takes more strength to do what you must than to do what you wish, even when the task is equal. I forced myself to enter.

Rukt'an led us to two of the chairs that circled the huge hall. They were Bria chairs, slender and softly padded, with high, straight backs to lean against and armrests at both sides. I saw only a few of the solid, backless Ghen stools with their single armrest attached to the left side (as though a Ghen must always be ready to reach for his hunting knife!) The few I saw were unoccupied; Ghen are more comfortable standing.

Ocallis and I sank into the chairs, crossing our legs modestly and drinking in the fan-blown air, blinking in relief at the dance of streamers from every wall and all across the ceiling. We stole quick glances at the throng of Ghen swaying or walking in courteous, continuous movement about the hall. Half of them were our age, six years; the other half were five or six years older, here for their second joining. At least Bria only have to go through this once.

Ghen music filled the room and already a few Bria had risen to sway to its hypnotic rhythm. I saw one or two Ghen watching me, taking in the delicate planes of my high cheeks and narrow nose, my wide blue eye and sleek, blond fur. I tapped my left foot, a nervous habit, until I noticed several Ghen turn to stare at the rhythmic movement of my long blond thigh. I stopped tapping at once, feeling the heat of embarrassment rush over my face, dilating my eye…Merciful Wind, this just got worse! The Ghen nearby were all staring at me now. For once I was grateful not to be able to read their expressions. I looked away, and saw the door, and considered it…

A low guttural voice made me look back. He was small for a Ghen, not much taller than me. He was looking at the other Ghen, who at his words stopped staring at me and moved away, as though he had reprimanded them. Of course this was a foolish notion, but I was glad, nonetheless, to be left alone. I watched him thoughtfully, but he didn't so much as glance my way.

I tried to regain my composure but like all Bria I was thrown off-kilter by stillseason and the strong mating scent being emitted by the unjoined Ghen. Most were nearly two heads taller than any Bria and their heavy, gray scales only emphasized the cords of muscle that bulged on their legs and across their stocky bodies. I rose and walked among them, feeling as fragile as crystal between rock, keeping as much distance as possible in the crowded room.

I don't like feeling diminished. Annoyance began to overcome my timidity, followed by a familiar, grim resolve. Then I saw what I was looking for.

He was standing in a corner, talking with another Ghen. The two of them were so intent upon their conversation they were barely moving, and had forgot to look for potential mates. In one it was self-assurance. He was tall even among Ghen, as solid as a house, as casual as though he knew he could turn and choose any Bria in the room. His confidence was compelling. He was a natural leader, I felt it even where I stood.

The other Ghen was small, about my height; muscular as all Ghen are, but less certain. He spoke earnestly, punctuating with large gestures the guttural sounds that came from his throat, but there was a hesitancy about his stance, a diffidence in his refusal to look about the room. I glanced back to where Ocallis sat, looking at the roomful of Ghen and biting his delicate underlip in indecision.

I crossed the room toward him and told him that I'd found the best of the Ghen, but he must choose between us. Ocallis laughed softly.

"If you wanted him, Briarris, you wouldn't let him see me."

"Better he see you now than later, and regret his choice," I said. "Capture his attention and then let him choose."

Laughing still, Ocallis headed where I'd pointed, swaying in satisfaction when he saw him. Ocallis moved sideways, then closed in at an angle, never again glancing at the two conversing Ghen but stopping where they would catch Ocallis's profile, where the gentle movement of Ocallis's long legs could not help but distract them from their conversation. Seeing his purpose, I stepped forward, my back toward the conversing Ghen, preventing other Ghen who quickly gathered around from obstructing their line of vision. Ocallis continued to move with the music but slowly, languorously, arching his ears with interest at the Ghen who eagerly approached him, accepting from one a drink, from another a small appetizer, showing delight at its wild flavor, even reaching delicately for a second.

When the large Ghen broke off his conversation, Ocallis's ear twitched almost unnoticeably. When he approached, Ocallis barely stopped himself from preening. The Ghen stood quite close, just out of Ocallis's range of vision, watching him intently, waiting for him to turn. Ocallis ignored him.

At that, the large Ghen grimaced in laughter, and then Ocallis cocked his head, looked sideways at him, bright-eyed with amusement. Holding his gaze, Ocallis reached sideways to the tray of appetizers, lifted one to his open mouth and slowly bit down into its juicy center.

The Ghen stopped laughing and took Ocallis's hand but Ocallis withdrew it and beckoned to me as he had promised. I turned, almost holding my breath as the Ghen looked at the two of us standing side by side. Then he called something over his shoulder to his friend. I let my breath out slowly.

Was he calling the smaller Ghen because he offered no competition, or because he was worth more than he appeared? Who could fathom a Ghen? Igt'ur shuffled forward looking awkward, even a little frightened. Igt'ur, who would never have approached me, the second prettiest Bria in the room; who would surely have noticed me turning down Ghen after Ghen until only he was left, but who now knew only that I gave a slow blink as though to say "what difference?" and let him take my hand.

We presented ourselves to Council Chair and Chair Ghen, who stood within an arch of fluttering streamers beneath the most powerful fan in the room. Our names were recorded in both Bria and Ghen registries and we were assigned a co-joining pair. Then Council Chair said, "May the Wind blow over you and strengthen you and make your joining fruitful." Chair Ghen grunted something to Igt'ur and Mant'er, Ocallis's chosen Ghen. In my mind I translated it as "mate quickly and serve the Ghen again soon."

Igt'ur should then have led me to the new house I was to share with him. I watched as he went to Rukt'an for directions and knew that I had chosen well when he accepted what Rukt'an had to tell him.

Then Rukt'an helped me to my new adult home. Had Igt'ur insisted on his rights I would have refused him after all, rather than let him see me blind and helpless in the streets of my city.

By the time Igt'ur arrived, pulling the cart of his belongings, I had wound the overhead fan and mastered my nausea enough to arrange my things about the house. Its door was on the south wall, which meant the two main windows faced east and west. The more expensive homes were on adjacent streets, with windows opening to admit the stronger north winds.

It was an older house, and modest, as befit a councilor. It had seen thirty stillseasons already. I hoped by the time I was a senior councilor, I could have it torn down and rebuilt in a more modern style. I'd thought of moving into one of the new developments down-peninsula, near the Symba River, but this location was more convenient to Council Hall.

My house had only two interior walls, one dividing the large front room from the two smaller rooms behind, and another between the room for washing and elimination, and the room where our children would one day sleep. I decided to hang my lifedance on the long front wall, where the brightly-dyed strips of cloth could flutter in the breeze.

I was standing on a chair, pounding a spike high up into the wall dividing the main room from the back two, when I heard a quiet cough at the door. I continued pounding, a little louder, until I was satisfied. Then I stepped down and reached for my lifedance. Again the cough.

I mounted the chair and placed over the spike the taut rope stretching from end to end of the four-handspans-long pole that held the fabric wallhanging—similar to a work of fabric art, but no one would call a lifedance art; especially not in front of a real fabric artist.

My lifedance, like my life, was only one-third finished and hung at an angle until I slung over the unfinished end the two cloth pouches, loaded with pebbles and joined by a length of rope, to balance it. Just before stillseason I'd added, beside the long, narrow strips of fabric that represented my childhood, a strip of gray to represent my joining with a Ghen, and beside it a deep russet piece, the color of my first cappa-wood house with its bright, sap-oil finish. I adjusted the pouches, removing a pebble from each, until I was satisfied that my lifedance hung straight.

My parent had begun my lifedance for me, sewing on the first long, slender strip of fabric, the color of his pelt; beside it a gray, the shade of the Ghen that quickened my seed in my parent's womb; and beside that, a tawny blond that matched my own pelt, with a second the same color beside it to represent Ocallis. Up to this point, our lifedances were the same.

There were half a dozen more strips from my early youth—dark, ruberry red for the time I ate myself sick in a patch that was barely ripe, a bright turquoise-blue for the time I fell into the Symba, and beside it an exquisite piece, eggshell-beige delicately speckled with a deep russet. I'd gone with my matri to pick the turquoise strip the day after the river incident, and fallen in love with the speckled fabric.

"But it has no significance for you," Matri said.

"I eat eggs," I protested. "I eat them all the time!"

"We all do, Briarris," he smiled. "This is for someone who chooses to work on a farm. When you're old enough, if you make that choice, I'll get it then."

"No, now!" I cried. "Look how it goes with the turquoise." Already I had an eye for beauty. Then I had an inspiration. "There were fish-eggs in the river. I saw them. They were under the water, where you couldn't see."

"Fish-eggs are this color." He pointed to a midnight blue.

"Not the ones I saw! They were like this."

"I'll take it," Matri said to the cloth dyer.

"It doesn't belong beside Symba-turquoise," he said, being a conventional artist who demanded rigid order. I knew when to hold my tongue, and I held my breath, too, for good measure. I even sucked in my belly, as Matri often urged me to do.

"This is a lifedance, not fabric art, as are yours," Matri answered him mildly.

"You're encouraging him to lie."

Matri bent down and looked me in the eye, close enough that I could feel his breath. "Fish-eggs are midnight blue, Briarris. I'm buying this to signify that you are now old enough to be responsible for choosing the fabrics in your own lifedance."

"I'm sorry I lied, Matri," I said gravely. "I won't ever again."

℘

A third cough interrupted my reminiscences. Ignoring it, I stepped down to admire the effect of my lifedance, with its bright strips of fabric fluttering in the movement of air from the fans. I'd considered not adding Igt'ur's gray to it, but I was a councilor now and had better means of altering traditions.

From outside there came more coughing, becoming a little scratchy—was his throat tiring? I gave one last look around. My feather mattress and head-roll lay on the sleeping ledge that jutted out four handspans above the floor at the base of the wide west window, where the breeze could ruffle my fur all night. The east window extended two handspans from the ceiling to a hand-span above the floor, where Igt'ur would roll out his sleeping mat.

I replaced the Bria chair I'd been standing on beside the other two, along one side of the heavy, low table. Igt'ur could put the two Ghen stools he brought on the other side. The dishes my parent had given me as a joining gift were neatly stacked on the shelves beside the cooking oven, built against the south wall under a smaller window to the left of the door. The house was sparse of both furniture and decorations, but it would suffice. Finally, I opened the door.

Igt'ur came in and offered me the ritual salted meat, as though I would ever touch it; I turned away in distain. I did not need a Ghen to bring me food, especially not Ghen food. He put it in the cold food box and began to place his possessions about my home. When I could stand it no longer I went to my sleeping ledge and lay down, praying to Wind to blow down upon us soon and end stillseason, to free me from the confines of this Ghen-shared house.

℘

That night I dreamed of Rukt'an. In my dream I was perched upon his shoulders, shrieking with glee as he strode about the house. He'd put a rushmat across his back to protect my legs and buttocks from his rough scales. I was

9

very young, my fur had not yet grown in thick enough to cover my tender skin. My small heels drummed happily against his huge chest as the walls of the room swayed wildly around me. I was dizzy and exhilarated with the power of being so tall—I could have touched the ceiling if my arms hadn't been engulfed in his strong palms, holding me secure.

My sibling, Ocallis, had already had his ride, but Rukt'an's child followed at our heels, clamoring for his turn. When Rukt'an stopped I cried in protest. He lifted me easily over the huge bony crest that rose above his forehead, despite my struggles to retain my perch. His wide jaws opened, lips curled back, in that breezy, fang-studded grimace that was his laughter. He lowered me to the floor and reached for Durt'an.

As he lifted Durt'an, the mat slid from his back onto the floor revealing the sharp gray scales angled toward the hard ridge of his spine all the way down his back. The thick, tough leather of his arms, chest and underbelly was safe for me to lean against but too high for my reach. Nor could I grab onto his large, scaled legs as Durt'an had; my hands and arms would have been crisscrossed with bleeding cuts in minutes. I stood weeping as Durt'an rose into the air away from me and Rukt'an stepped back, back, his movements slower and slower until he was as motionless as stillseason, until he and Durt'an were only an outline, a shadow, a memory...

I awoke weeping, but quieted at once for fear Igt'ur might hear. I heard the rustle of scales on his mat and held my breath, but he did not rise or approach me. After a few minutes I relaxed and lay in the darkness, remembering.

I had dreamed this same dream often the year after Rukt'an left, when I was two.

"Make him come back!" I'd demanded of my matri.

"He is Ghen, Briarris," Matri explained patiently.

When I persisted, he said, "Ghen leave. Ghen return to their compound as they should. Rukt'an and I are no longer joined; his child is weaned. Now Rukt'an is needed on the wall."

"But you can speak to him."

He looked at me sternly. That was a private matter.

"You can, you can!" I insisted, barely preventing myself from adding, I've seen you.

"We will no longer," he said. "All that is over."

How weak I felt, how helpless and small, when all Rukt'an's strength and power had gone away.

When we were five, we studied government in school. In the Bria-Ghen Council I sensed another power, the power of the councilors who rule our city. To ride the shoulders not of a single Ghen, but of the entire community of my fellow Bria!

I knew at once that I must be a part of it. Who need fear anything while directing the mighty intellect of the Bria? What could not be accomplished from such a height? I longed to serve my city in this way.

When I reached my specialization year, I chose administration and government. I passed head of my class and was offered the first year seat on Council.

But first, I must be joined. Only joined Bria and Ghen could sit on Council. And those who sat on Council were joined for life.

This was the price of serving my city and leading my people into a new age of enlightenment, unfettered by the fears of the past. I knew the price and I accepted it, despite my dislike of Ghen, who hide their yen for violence under laughter and lies and breakable ties.

What are these ugly, two-eyed Ghen that they should live off us? Bria manage the city. Ghen may help to build our homes, but Bria create the oil lamps and swinging fans that brighten and make them livable. Bria sow and reap, raise and cook the food in ovens Bria make. Bria bear and rear and educate our children. Bria make and enforce the laws that maintain Bria civilization.

Meanwhile the Ghen lounge, arrogant and indolent, within our lovely city. They are flesh-eaters, hunting and killing their food; the blood sport sustains them as much as the meat itself. Ghen teach their children warfare and use their useless training in constant vigilance along the wall, guarding the industrious Bria against imaginary monsters. They claim the wall at the northern perimeter of our city was built to hold back Broghen. That may be true, our ancestors were very superstitious, but why should we put up with such nonsense now?

I planned to wield my council seat against the Ghen, to evict them from our city into the forest with the wild beasts they so loved to stalk; or further south, beyond the farms and woodlands to the tip of our peninsula, where they do their bog-ore mining. To take from them the undeserved luxuries of the civilization that we supplied, that we maintained, and allow them access only to Festival Hall during stillseason when mating must occur.

So my thoughts ran in the first night of my joining, until at last I slept.

やる

Council opened as soon as stillseason ended. Council Hall had just been re-built, fashioned into a series of rectangular rooms surrounding a large court-yard. It was the most impressive building in the city, not only because of its modern style but also because Council chamber, which occupied the entire front section, was twice as high as any other structure, in order to accom-modate tiered seating in the audience section and two oversized windows at either end. Covered verandahs wrapped around both the outside and the in-ner courtyard side, with doors to every room opening onto them, so that the verandahs served as external hallways leading from room to room.

I walked slowly up the wide stairway onto the outer verandah, brushing my hand like a caress over the ornately carved railing. Passing through the huge double doors, with glass windows set into them to symbolize the transparency of all governance proceedings, I entered the Council chamber.

The wind blew freely through the huge north-south windows at either end of the hall. The wall ahead, facing the courtyard, held two more large win-dows, also open, on either side of the door to the inner verandah. In the mid-dle of the hall, in front of the courtyard windows, stood a long U-shaped table.

Facing each other around this U were the twenty-six Council seats for thir-teen Ghen and thirteen Bria. I walked forward and took my place in the first-year Bria chair.

Beside me was an empty Ghen bench, then the second-year Bria, Perallis, and then another empty bench. Ghen regulations required them to do two years of duty on the wall before they served on Council, so Perallis's and my mates would not sit beside us until we each reached our third year on Council. However, in an emergency, Chair Ghen could temporarily set aside that regulation. Of course, this never happened.

Twenty-six seats plus two, ornate and raised, placed just above the open end of the U for Council Chair and Chair Ghen. My back was to the front door, on either side of which stretched the public gallery, which occupied the rest of the room, rows of benches at graduating levels. This location pleased me. I wouldn't be tempted to glance at visitors when I should be focusing on the

Chair and my fellow councilors, but the slightest turn of my head to face the Chair and I could cock my left ear to catch every sigh the audience made, while my right ear remained tuned to Council.

Chair opened session and welcomed me to Council. I almost wept for love of my city then, and for the great things I would do. But perhaps it was also with relief at the empty bench beside me. I had to live with Igt'ur and the adjustment was hard.

I found his constant presence in my home oppressive. I resented his gaze as he sat watching me. Sometimes I would sit very still, deliberately insulting him, but he could see me easily even then. It felt like an invasion of privacy. Whenever Igt'ur ceased to move, after a few minutes I became unaware of him. That's Bria perspective, of course; the two-eyed Ghen don't need motion to see. Occasionally I wondered if he minded retreating into the background of my vision as much as I minded never being out of the foreground of his.

I said very little in Council in my first few months. I was watching the play of councilors; who supported whom, who spoke up on which issues, who translated for their joined Ghen and who did not. I spoke only in support; when I opposed a motion, I cast my ballot in silence. I worked diligently to understand each issue, asking Perallis, across the empty chair between us, any questions I might have. I hoped to make him my ally. And I watched the Ghen, as they watched Chair Ghen.

Council Chair's fingers were never still. Although only Chair Ghen understood his signs, he translated everything. Often councilors waited to speak while he finished signing a previous speaker's comment, but none watched his hands except Chair Ghen. Language between a joined pair was private; it bound the two together. Only once did Chair Ghen raise his hand and grumble in his gutteral language to the suddenly watchful Ghen. The discussion concerned a repair to the wall, hastily done and in need of further work. Ghen business.

I watched and planned my strategy. Here was my battle ground; here I would gain victory over the arrogant Ghen.

***

I trembled as I rose to make my motion, hiding the tremor in a courteous sway. I had prepared painstakingly and I began by calling attention to the empty seats of year one and year two Ghen and the frequent absences of year six Ghen, preoccupied with the training of his offspring.

From the problem of attendance I moved on to the language problem, referring to the fact that every comment had to be translated by Council Chair to Chair Ghen, and then by him to the other Ghen councilors. How slow and drawn-out this process was, lengthening Council meetings so that, more often than not, Chair Ghen refrained from translating and entire meetings passed without a single word being understood by the Ghen.

"This might make sense if the Ghen were involved in city administration," I concluded, "but running our city is Bria work, and no concern of Ghen!"

I addressed my speech to the Chair, as was proper, but I kept my ear turned to the audience. I had hinted of my motion to groups of single Bria who I knew would be sympathetic and the gallery was gratifyingly filled. At my proud words stamping broke out across the rows of the audience, long and enthusiastic.

My ears twitched with pleasure and I swayed more confidently in its rhythm. When the cheerful noise died down I urged my fellow councilors to eliminate Ghen from Council and sat down, pleased by the applause that rose again at my back.

There was a heavy silence. The other councilors could think of no rejoinder to my arguments! Finally, one of the older Bria councilors rose to say he did not mind the time taken by Council Chair, in order to include Ghen in the process of running our joint city. Another rose and moved the immediate dismissal of my motion, but it had already been duly supported by Perallis. An angry muttering and stamping of feet across the tiered rows of the gallery prevented further suggestions of discharging the issue precipitously.

I listened attentively as the uneasy debate continued into late afternoon, almost twitching with eagerness to join in. Their arguments were pitiful. Tradition, that was what it amounted to—a stupid reason to do anything. But this was my first year on Council and I would not be expected to speak twice on an issue.

Despite the support of my audience, I could tell it was going badly. The turning point came when Chair Ghen, translated by Council Chair, rose to speak. He moved only slightly. Representing all Ghen, he pointed out their critical defense of the wall. Without Ghen on watch there would be no city.

The walls did not protect us; we protected them, guarding them for our safe-ty—only the ignorant thought otherwise.

I opened my mouth. Council Chair glanced at me. I shut it, grinding my teeth.

Did not Ghen refrain from comment on all matters pertaining to city ordinance? Chair Ghen continued, as if he had not seen me. But it was their right, no, their duty, to be present at Council when issues involving city defense arose.

The wall again. How much time is wasted on that antiquated wall! Somehow I must move my people to think beyond the wall. I rose to speak despite the disapproving glance of Council Chair.

"We don't need Ghen to guard the wall!" I cried. "No Broghen has been seen in all our lifetimes. Bria birth only Bria and Ghen infants, and have since Wind first spoke to Dayannis!"

I sat down amid thunderous cheers from the gallery. I thought the religious reference would appeal to the older Bria on Council, but every Bria coun-cilors' face, except those in years two and three, was still and pale. I'd gone too far. I had insulted their faith, I realized then, by using Dayannis's name to undermine traditions he set up.

When the vote was taken it was merely a gesture to formalize my mistake. The second-year councilor, Perallis, and even the third-year Bria councilor, big with his unborn infants, voted with me. All of the older Bria, and of course the Ghen, opposed.

When Council adjourned, the Bria in the gallery gathered around me to show their support and encouragement; but I had failed to convince the councilors and nothing else mattered. I expressed my gratitude and eased away to be alone.

Alone! Where could I be alone? Igt'ur was waiting for me at home, per-haps a greater symbol of my defeat than even the vote had been. I walked street after street, watching dusk fall upon my city. My Bria city, which I had failed today.

As far back as I remember, I have loved my city; loved the long, low lines of the buildings hung with brightly-colored streamers that tossed in the wind and caught the sun, throwing patterns of color to dance upon the walkways. I loved the slender green fronds of the tall ugappas that waved above us and the quadruple leaves of the shorter, broader cappas that shook like the wide belly of a laughing grandparent. I loved the silver grasses that rippled like a whispered melody underfoot, as soft as walking on the wind.

Even the wall, useless bit of antiquity that it is, encircling the northern half of our city like a generous hug, with its small, triangular pennants snapping in the breeze above it; even the wall I loved because it defined our city, divided it from the dark forest of the mainland above our secluded peninsula.

What pleasure could I take in the sight of my city this evening? Its very beauty was a reproof to me now.

It was almost dark by the time I reached the Symba. Normally I hated the darkness, as all Bria do, but tonight I welcomed it. I peered across the river at our farmlands. I could barely make out the tall grains swaying in the wind and beyond them at the edge of my vision the southern woods, so black they appeared still, as still as death. I took a step toward the river, and toward the blackness beyond.

How could I ever go back, after such a defeat? I stared down into the water, so dark and still, and its stillness called to me. I was hesitating on the bank when the street lamps were lit.

Reflected in the water I saw my city, shining in the night. I turned. The large oil lamps, hanging high upon their posts, swayed in the wind, so that from the riverbank the entire city seemed to be alight, dancing in the darkness. So beautiful, my city, beckoning me back. Wearily, I turned toward home.

Igt'ur was waiting for me. At my touch on the door handle he threw the door open, pulling me inside. Seeing my slumped posture, the weary droop of my head, he placed his hands more gently on my slim shoulders. I stood, head bowed, stiffening only slightly at his touch.

He spoke softly in his gruff tongue, leading me to a chair at the table. To my surprise, he brought a steaming bowl of vegetable stew and set it before me. Ghen hands are short and thickly padded, with straight fingers that bend only where they join the palm. My cooking pots and ladles all required the grasp of double-jointed fingers. I was touched despite myself at the effort that had gone into this bowl of stew.

I ate it because I needed it, and because I was too polite to refuse his gift. But every spoonful choked me. I did not want his stew, or his presence in my home, or his species in my city. I soothed my conscience by remembering that I would give him a child before evicting him. Even so, I dreaded the approach of stillseason and my first mating festival. But a little less, after that bowl of stew.

☙

Just before stillseason my breasts began to seep. The thick, sticky secretion disgusted me, but it was inevitable, the result of living in close quarters with a Ghen as stillseason approached. Igt'ur's heavy mating musk filled the house.

Suriannis and Barn'ar, our co-joining couple, were a year older, about to have their second mating. Soon they'd be coming to my house so that Suriannis and I could rub the fluid from each other's breasts over the painful rashes that had appeared on our abdomens. I'd been told about this but nothing could prepare me for the extreme discomfort of that rash. Waiting for Suriannis to arrive, I was tempted to rub my own breast fluid over it.

The idea shocked me. How could I think of such an unnatural act? I remembered a classmate in my first year of school teasing another child with the words, "Your parent soothed with his own fluid when he was carrying you!" Admittedly, the teased child was stupid, but that only made the taunt more cruel. I didn't understand it at the time, not being raised in a vulgar home. I chuckled now, despite my misery, to imagine my parent's distress when I'd asked him to explain the jibe.

When Suriannis arrived on Barn'ar's arm, I could barely wait for him to catch his breath after walking through the hot, sluggish streets to my house. I touched my breasts, massaging them into fresh seepage and gently applied the fluid to the angry red rash across Suriannis's lower belly. At first he winced at my touch then, as the fluid soothed his tender skin, he relaxed. His breathing eased and he began to work his own breasts, releasing the liquid that would bring me relief. We did this several times a day for two days, until our rashes disappeared.

Igt'ur and Barn'ar led us through the motionless streets to Festival Hall. The stillness of my city seemed a dreadful thing—or was it just an echo of the dread I felt? I closed my eye to combat the nausea, willing myself to be invisible in the empty streets. How appropriate, I thought, that our mating should occur when the wind, which is sight and life to us, has died.

17

But mating was not as I feared. I was disoriented as always by stillseason, thrown at the mercy of new sensations by the betrayal of my normal senses, and open to the mesmerizing influence of Igt'ur's mating scent. I would have been terrified had we not lived a year together. Instead I was excited. No, much more: inflamed by his scent and even by my own helplessness. The music in the hall was frenzied, ecstatic, meant to escalate our delirium. Soon the throbbing beat was inside us, part of us, no longer music, but need.

It was Ghen music, wild and pounding. I could see at the far end of the hall the sweating drummers; beside them, the vocalist, swaying to the mysterious, passionate words of his song. Igt'ur and I were intoxicated, frantic for each other. The experience was so intense I barely noticed when Barn'ar stepped in for his co-joiner's mating with me.

"May you bear a strong hunter," he intoned afterwards.

Although I couldn't understand his words, the ritual had been explained to me, and I responded with the expected gesture, bending my fingers claw-like and pretending to rake them across my belly. Then he was gone and Igt'ur returned to me. Again and again Igt'ur and I submerged ourselves in the sensations of our bodies until we emerged not only mated, but changed.

I wanted to understand him now. Where I had previously ignored the attempts he'd made to communicate, I now initiated them. It was impossible to reconcile my high Bria warble with Igt'ur's low, guttural rumblings, which all sounded alike to me. I tried to remember the gestures I'd seen my parent make, but they would be meaningless to Igt'ur. Instead, we pointed to objects about the house, inventing signs to represent them, often forgetting or changing the signs the next day until we dissolved in laughter.

I found I could soon differentiate the sounds Igt'ur made when he was happy from those that indicated weariness, or sorrow, or hunger, or farewell for his duty on the wall. That was the one word that needed no translation. Pitched at the lowest octave of a Bria's vocal chords and the highest note of a Ghen's, "wall" was the single bridge between our tongues. I did not miss the irony. Nevertheless, I looked forward to the time when I could argue that duty with him. How could he consent to waste so much of his time with no evidence of its needfulness?

The spell of our mating diminished in time. I was still determined that Ghen had no place on Council, though I was more tolerant of them living in our city, if only they could be convinced to find some useful work.

When Council resumed after stillseason, a young Bria named Rennis was introduced as the first-year Bria and I moved over into the second-year seat. Rennis was shorter than I, with a thick pelt which was a lovely dark charcoal color. At the end of the meeting, he pulled me aside to tell me he'd been in the audience the day I made my motion against having Ghen on Council and he was in complete agreement with me. I liked his openness, although I wondered if he might change his mind after his first mating.

Rennis was a lively Bria and very sociable. The first thing he did was move his chair so that we sat together with the empty benches for our Ghen mates on either side. Why hadn't I done that? Perhaps Rennis felt more comfortable with me, knowing we shared an opinion, than I had felt with Perallis, who was now the third-year Bria and was sitting beside his Ghen mate.

Rennis talked to the older Bria about how lonely it was for us, how intimidating, being young and new to Council and sitting all year beside empty chairs. He claimed that it made him feel alienated from the rest of Council, after he'd looked forward to working with them as a team. Then he proposed the elimination of the first- and second-year Ghen seats, in order to align Council positions more closely with Ghen regulations. Why have a Council seat for a Ghen when he wasn't allowed to occupy it? Council should support, not undermine, Ghen regulations.

We had worked it out together and decided it was best for Rennis to present the motion, but it was a victory for us both when it passed.

୧୨

Rennis returned from his first mating and I from my second, both a little changed. Suriannis and I had soothed our abdominal rashes with each other's breast fluid once more, but there was no need for Barn'ar to mate with me again. The ritual of strength having been performed at first mating, I could spend all my time at festival with Igt'ur this stillseason.

Later, Rennis and I laughed at the temporary madness of the experience. We discussed our increased interest in our own mates, but our sustained scorn for Ghen as a species. Then we began to mention in Council the need for unjoined Bria to be represented, in preparation for a motion to add an unjoined Bria seat.

Rennis's Ghen, Saft'ir, was not as easy-going as Igt'ur. He read Chair Ghen's translations after every Council meeting, and although he could not yet tell Rennis his opinion, he made his displeasure known in cold glances and deliberate stillnesses. It was bound to get worse in another year when he came on Council, but Rennis persevered.

Rennis had nothing to fear. No Ghen would hurt a Bria. Furthermore, he was carrying Saft'ir's child. But it was unpleasant in their home and Rennis regretted upsetting Saft'ir, for all that he was Ghen.

"They only need a little push," I consoled him. "Once they can no longer live on our endeavors, they'll have less time to play their battle games. They'll build their own city nearby and run it as they wish, instead of playing at running ours. We're helping them advance themselves, not hurting them."

We planned our motion well, and single Bria throughout the city filled the public gallery the day we spoke for them.

"Bria have a right to live unjoined," I touched my growing belly, "just as you and I, councilors, chose to join. All Bria have a right," I looked in turn each councilor in the eye, "to fair and unbiased representation on the Council of their city. Can any of us here, joined for life, truly speak to their issues? One seat to represent them, one seat to keep us from forgetting them, one single seat to acknowledge their contribution to our city!"

Once again I felt the appreciation of my people rise like a fresh wind at my back. Being in a minority, and often criticized, the single Bria were especially grateful to us for speaking on their behalf. When the stamping finally stilled, I made my motion and Rennis supported it.

There was little debate. Who would deny their people representation? Even those who saw what we were doing, garnering sympathetic Council seats, could hardly argue against a single seat before a gallery full of cheering Bria. Rennis and I walked home through our city victorious, escorted by a throng of Bria chanting our names and thanking us with elaborate praise before each turned aside to his own home.

That was the last time I saw Rennis smile.

The next morning, Saft'ir was found against the city wall, dead by his own hand. The single Bria seat went to Rennis.

We made no more motions together, Rennis and I. He retreated into bitter silence, repulsing all my efforts at solace. I was approaching my third and final mating; what could I say, about to induce the birthing of my babes, to one whose infants now must die within his womb? I only hoped that time would heal his grief.

That year Igt'ur and I didn't go to Festival Hall. I was nauseous enough without being led through the hot, dizzy streets in stillseason. Igt'ur took me gently in our house, murmuring reassurances.

The kicks and movements of the unborn infants increased rapidly after our mating. I began to remember childhood stories of Broghen, the monster within. I knew they were only tales to frighten children, but one has irrational fears just before childbirth.

I was terrified. But everywhere I turned, I received the same answer: Igt'ur would take care of everything when my time came. He knew what to do.

Igt'ur, like all joined Ghen, had been trained to deliver young. Trusting a Ghen, even Igt'ur, with whom I had lived for three years, went against all my principles, but I had no choice. It was unthinkable for any but Igt'ur, or in his absence another Ghen, to attend my birthing, and I dared not attempt it alone.

I was desperate enough to broach the subject to my parent and his sibling. Neither relented but I saw something in their eyes, some dark and fearful memory, before they changed the subject, so that I was almost glad they would not speak. Ocallis and I speculated in whispers, bolstering one another as we waited.

"It must be painful," I offered, wishing it were over.

"Very few infants die at birth these days," Ocallis said.

I placed my hand before my mouth, touching my breath to indicate agreement, but I was not consoled.

I began to regard Igt'ur in a new light. Despite my misgivings, I had to rely on him, and therefore I began to see him as necessary and capable. Certainly he appeared to exhibit no qualms about the approaching event, but how could I be sure?

I wished I'd worked harder at learning to communicate. I longed to voice my fears to him and understand his reassurances. When the infants gave particularly strong kicks and he saw me stiffen, he patted me gently, as one would soothe a frightened toddler who was only beginning to understand words.

Once again I dreamed of Rukt'an, wondering why these distant memories troubled me now. More and more I turned to Igt'ur for reassurance as I neared the time when I would give birth. He would not fail me willingly.

છ

A high-pitched scream filled the darkness. I awoke bathed in sweat. My abdomen was heaving as though a battle were raging inside my womb. I screamed again, my eye fixed in terror upon my writhing middle. Igt'ur hurried across the room but I took no notice. My concentration was riveted on the fiery agony within.

Igt'ur placed something heavy on the floor beside my sleeping ledge. I glanced sideways briefly. It was a cage, small but solidly built, the top open. A spasm of pain tore through me, forcing my attention back to my abdomen. It rose and shuddered in angry convulsions and I grew hysterical, imagining what might lie beneath my skin, waiting to enter the world.

"No!" I screamed, closing my eye as though to block the thought, "Nooo!"

A cup touched my dry lips; Igt'ur's voice resounded in the distance, loud and insistent, but I took no notice. My concentration was fixed upon my writhing body. He slapped my face lightly, breaking through my glassy terror. I looked at him in shock. He had never done such a thing to me. Again he urged the drink on me and numbly I swallowed.

Setting the empty cup aside, he clasped my shoulder briefly, reassuringly, and muttered something in Ghen. His voice was gentle but I could hear the urgency behind it: he wanted me to trust him. I closed my eye, but another spasm of pain urged it open. My terror returned with the pain, but both were more distant, dulled by Igt'ur's drink. I could endure it now, could allow Igt'ur to birth our children.

Distantly I felt him pulling my legs apart, rough in his haste. I was helpless to aid or resist him, could only pant for breath between contractions and stare at the nightmare movements of the battle inside me. I gasped as he plunged his arm between my legs, felt it withdrawing and turned my face, afraid to look.

A thin, high squeak. Bria!

I reached out eagerly. Igt'ur handed my infant to me, frail, elongated skeleton with tiny veins clearly visible through the gauze-thin, nearly furless skin, trailing the cord that had nourished his fragile life. I cradled the scrawny newborn, gently wiping clean his face and nostrils.

"Youngling," I whispered, savoring the term of endearment reserved for one's own infants. It implied so much—a lifelong bond, as visible as my blood in his veins, as eternal as the wind that blew over us both. My flesh yet separate, destined to go places I would not, taking with him whatever passion and strength I might impart before he began his journey.

I watched, enthralled, as he opened his eye for the first time and blinked groggily at the world he'd emerged into. Gently I blew my life's breath over him. How little prepared I was for the intensity of my emotions! Joy and terror struggled within me as Igt'ur once again reached into my womb.

Another diminutive Bria he handed me; another tentative miracle, clinging to life. I carefully placed my firstborn against one of my upper breasts and took this second baby. The potion Igt'ur had given me made it possible for me to nurture life into these precious scraps of being despite the torment of my still-heaving abdomen.

At least I was birthing Bria and Ghen. I sweated and I groaned, but I was no longer afraid. I had my Bria children, safe and sound; the last was his.

I heard them before I saw them; the tiny growl, several octaves higher than Igt'ur's but unmistakably Ghen, and the wild, crazed screech of the other. I opened my mouth to scream at the sight of the writhing body of a monster. The sound froze in my throat. A Broghen! I had borne a Broghen!

It was neither Bria nor Ghen, but a misshapen horror covered in Igt'ur's gray scales, with here and there tufts of blond fur. Its half-opened eyes were already searching for prey, oversized jaws snapping, scaly tail lashing with a fury impossible to reconcile with its newborn dimensions. The infant Ghen, bleeding from a dozen tiny scratches, instinctively gripped the monster from behind, to avoid its gaping jaws. Also, I realized with a start, to keep it from my fragile Bria younglings.

Igt'ur's fingers closed tightly about the Broghen's jaws. Gently he extricated the struggling little Ghen from the Broghen's claws and handed the exhausted newborn to me. Without hesitation I took him from Igt'ur, wiping his bleeding wounds and whispering my gratitude for his infant valor. He blinked at me wearily.

I tried to ignore the shrieks of the Broghen as Igt'ur cut the cord with which my body had traitorously nourished it and dropped the hideous thing into the open cage.

I stared down at the cage. He knew all along that I would bear four infants!

In that instant I, who had never known hate, hated Igt'ur. He'd put that hideous monster inside me, along with his infant! In innocence and trust, I'd allowed my body to breed such a thing. I was numb with shock as I finished my administrations to the newborn Ghen and placed him against my third nipple. He suckled greedily, absorbed in his first hunger.

My womb was still now and Igt'ur was gently applying an ointment to the abrasions I had sustained.

The desperate howls coming from the cage increased in volume. I peered down at the creature inside. The infant Broghen no longer seemed an object of horror, but piteous, now that it could not harm me or my infants. It opened its gruesome mouth and I heard the unmistakable wail of a hungry newborn. Instinctively, I stretched out my arms to it.

"Let me feed it." My fourth nipple wept in response to its cries of hunger.

"No," Igt'ur signed. "It wants meat, not milk."

I shrank away, repulsed. The caged infant screamed, hideous and pathetic.

"What will we do with it?" I signed. The thought of anyone knowing I'd borne a Broghen horrified me, even as I despised myself for such a shallow concern. "How could you do this to me?" I wailed, and the little Broghen keened in hideous counterpoint to my sobs.

"This is the way of our births."

I read his signs through a blur of tears. "Others have had a Broghen?" My fingers shook as I signed.

"Every birth bears a Broghen."

The magnitude of the revelation stunned me. My parent—the older councilors—all of them? They all knew?

"I don't believe you," I signed, turning my face to the window. "Go away!" The thing in the cage howled. "Take it away!"

Igt'ur rose and lifted the cage, but when he reached the door I cried out.

"Where are you taking it?" I signed when he turned.

He spoke the one word that I knew: "the wall."

Then I understood. Our terrible fourth offspring would live. Neither Ghen nor Bria could destroy their own. It would grow, in the dark, wild forest beyond the wall, into a terrible creature, howling at the edges of our civilization, a civilization as fragile as the three newborns at my breasts.

And there, at the perimeter of our city, between it and the ravages of bestiality, stood the Ghen. They built the wall, they walked the wall, they were the wall, holding back the nightmares of creation so that Bria and Ghen together might rise above savagery to create the order and the beauty of our city.

Council Relations

Briarris

The situation wasn't as dramatic as I'd imagined. The Broghen weren't raging right outside our walls, with Ghen dying daily to defend us. In fact, the Broghen were taken so far south they were rarely seen again. And the only Ghen I knew who'd died on the wall was Rennis's mate, Saft'ir, who killed himself after being attacked by a courrant'h. So we were told. I wondered now, but I didn't ask. I'd had enough revelations.

Even if it wasn't accurate, my idealistic vision helped me get through the shock of the birthing. I was back at work long before most new Bria parents. It also prevented me from falling into the complicated mix of guilt and blame that lay between most Bria and Ghen after their birthing. Igt'ur and I remained friends.

During my brief convalescence, Savannis, the Bria Voice of Wind, came to visit me. I'd never had much use for his advice, but I listened without comment as he explained to me the reasons for keeping the Broghen a secret from young Bria.

"How could you have mated and borne children if you had known?" he asked. "Our silence is meant to protect young Bria, not harm them."

For the sake of my city I agreed to keep the secret, like every Bria parent before me.

I don't know whether it was a tribute to my popularity or a punishment for stirring up the single Bria, but I was directed to handle Council Relations. I soon found myself in a meeting with Anarris, a Bria two years younger than I, who'd helped me raise supporters to attend Council for each of my motions.

"We've begun to organize ourselves," he told me. "We call ourselves Single-By-Choice."

The very name asserted their right to make a decision so widely disapproved of. I fidgeted in my chair. No wonder he was here looking to me for support; I'd started this. I could hardly tell him now that I'd changed my mind.

"We thought you might talk at one of our gatherings," he continued, "about being forced to join against your will, in order to sit on Council."

Breath of Wind, why had I spoken so openly?

"You're a public figure, a respected leader of our people. What's more, you always say what you really think. A rare trait in councilors."

I wished it were more rare.

"We offer support to young Bria who are intimidated by the pressure they're under to be joined."

"Bria shouldn't have to mate if they don't want to," I said.

But I was finding my younglings more delightful than I'd imagined, and didn't really know what I still believed. I needed time to think it out, statement by statement: what felt right, what no longer did. What I could still say and stand by.

"I'm finding parenthood very compelling, right now," I told Anarris. "I'm not sure I regret mating any more."

His movements stilled. I knew what he was thinking.

"You can't expect me not to love my younglings. But those who don't want to join shouldn't be made to feel they must." Yes, that much I still believed, although I hoped he wouldn't ask about councilors. Even if Ghen left Council, I could see now why Bria councilors had to be joined. I hadn't even known what the real issues were before I birthed a Broghen. I was tempted for a moment to tell Anarris everything.

But there was a stubborn look about his face that reminded me of myself. I know what I would have done with that information; I'd have used it to further my case against co-habitation. I'd have blamed the Broghen on the Ghen—that had been my first impulse when I gave birth—as though it were a deliberate act on their part.

Anarris wouldn't consider how such knowledge would terrify those already pregnant, or what it might mean to the future of our city if frightened young Bria refused to join. There weren't many who'd willingly bear a Broghen. No, if Anarris knew of Broghen, he'd use it to strike back at those who were calling him "selfish" and "immature" and "irresponsible" for not joining. I'd received such comments myself for my youthful opinions, and I knew.

I hated keeping such a terrible secret. Nevertheless, I wasn't prepared to see all my endeavors come to nothing in a few generations of frightened Bria. I wasn't prepared to watch my city die, or to have my younglings grow up terrified of their future. Nor would the Ghen stand by, unconcerned. Breath of Wind, I didn't want to think of what might happen if Bria refused to mate willingly…

Anarris was watching me intently. I realized my thoughts had disturbed me into stillness and resumed a courteous movement.

"I understand your position," I said carefully. "If you need the help of a councilor, come to me and I will listen. I want to represent your rights when I can."

He began to rise. He knew I was also saying, but I'm not one of you anymore. "Can I call on you if Single-By-Choice meets with opposition?" he asked.

"Call on me," I said, promising nothing. My moral compass had shifted and all my choices would be much harder now.

"I'm glad you're serving as Council Relations," he said as he turned to leave, "but not as glad as I was before."

༄

Ocallis grinned when he saw me coming, carrying my Bria babies while Igt'ur's youngster staggered behind. Although we lived only a few houses apart, I'd seldom had time for my sibling before the birth of our children. He'd been busy himself, becoming an accomplished glass-blower, but that wasn't the reason. We didn't talk about the beliefs that had separated us, or what we believed now. Our children and the two little Ghen played while we drank cappa tea, and I rested from my thoughts.

"Look at him," I said, amused as Mant'er's child, Heckt'er, crept through the swaying grasses after imaginary prey.

"Mant'er is pushing him too fast. He's just a baby," Ocallis said.

"You're not going to tell others how to raise their children, are you?" Ocallis's comment made me uncomfortable. He'd opted to take time off

28

while his infants nursed, only going into his studio occasionally to work on a special piece. I would have gone crazy taking care of babies all day. A little callan milk and the company of a watcher now and then wouldn't harm my children or Igt'ur's.

"No, but I worry. Mant'er says the forest has changed, and yet he takes Heckt'er into it so often."

"You think the Broghen…?" My throat closed over the rest of my question.

"Of course not," he assured me quickly, "they're too far south. But even a mangarr'h could harm a one-year-old."

I shuddered at the mention of the loathsome little creatures. They were too small to harm an adult, but they were predators. And like all predators, they bred in-species. It was obscene: you could look at a beast and not know from its appearance or behavior whether it was an infant-bearer or a fighter. Even worse, it might be both.

There are creatures where the differentiation between mating species is slight, such as the farmborra and the gock; both feathered avians whose wings we clip—but there the similarity ends. Gocks have clawed feet and knife-sharp beaks, which we file down for our protection. In size, in coloring, in behavior, there are other differences. As there should be, between a fighting species and a nurturing one. Predators, however, mate each other, disgusting as that is to contemplate.

"What does Mant'er think is wrong in the forest?" I asked. Mant'er was a good hunter—no, an exceptional one, according to Igt'ur. Ocallis's worries about him taking Heckt'er into the forest were probably groundless.

"He says the game is becoming scarce."

"Ghen might have to eat eggs and callan cheese." We laughed together.

I might have said more, but Ocallis puzzled me. He showed none of the anger and betrayal most Bria felt toward their mates after birthing a Broghen. Only the knowledge that our younglings would never have been born without Ghen growth fluid moderated the resentment of most Bria. No wonder my parent had been impatient with my complaints when Ruckt'an returned to the Ghen compound. He'd probably been relieved to see him go.

Mant'er arrived from his duty on the wall and took his child away from playing with Igt'ur's. Something had happened between them, but neither would speak of it. He turned away when Igt'ur came up to us.

I collected my two while Igt'ur tossed his squealing youngster onto his shoulders. I had never let him play with my children thus. I wanted them to find their own strength, right from the beginning.

Wasn't that what Anarris was trying to do?

Choices

Igt'ur

When I was four, my parent took me into the forest to track sadu'h. The first time I was able to find the trail of one and follow it without assistance, I thought I understood what it meant to be a hunter. I sighted the sadu'h in a sun-dappled shadow, stretching to eat the lower leaves of a cappa bush, unaware of my approach. I bit down hard on my tongue to release my muscles from the tension of my excitement.

Barely breathing, I pulled a stone from my pouch and positioned it in the thong of my slingshot. The sadu'h was at the edge of my range, but I dared not go closer for fear of startling it. It was right beside the opening to its burrow: a single bound and it would escape.

I swung the loaded slingshot and when the momentum was right, I let it fly. My aim was true, but the distance was too far; when I reached the sadu'h I could see it was only stunned. I knelt beside it, resisting the urge to grab it at once, and prayed as I had been taught: "Thank you for making me a guardian of Wind, servant of this creature that gives itself to sustain me, that I might guard the forests of Wind for all its progeny, as long as I live."

I sealed the promise quickly by drawing the flat side of my hunting knife across my forehead, while my parent watched approvingly. The sadu'h still lay on its side but it had twice kicked its hind legs convulsively as I whispered my obeisance. If it got away while I was praying, my parent would say that was the will of Wind, but I wanted to give Him as little time as possible to will it. The sadu'h's third kick propelled it into my hands as I lunged for it.

It struggled desperately. I had to drop my knife to hold it. I looked about for a rock or tree trunk to swing its head against, but there were none nearby. I could feel my heart panting for air like a Bria in stillseason as I strained to

31

hold the sadu'h. Finally I pulled it against my chest, pinning it against me with one arm, wincing as the claws on one of its hind feet dug into my chest. Then, all at once, it went still.

Surprised, I looked down. Its head was tilted upward so that I found myself gazing into its single eye, enlarged with terror. Against my breast I could hear its tiny heart, beating quick and high in eerie accordance with my own. I stared at it for a long moment, feeling… embarrassed? Guilty? Behind me, my parent coughed gently. I reached for my knife and drew it quickly and painlessly across the sadu'h's throat. As its blood spilled out across my chest, I understood what it was to be a hunter.

∾

Mant'er laughed when I allowed Rukt'an to take my place in helping Briarris to his house the day we joined. I grinned back, shrugging, and returned to the Ghen compound to collect my things, walking slowly to give Briarris plenty of time. I was in no hurry, myself.

"Igt'ur, have you changed your mind?" Saft'ir called as I passed the opening to the room where he slept. He was a year younger than I, a boisterous youth given to outbursts of righteous anger and teased for it, but he took it well. I liked him. I felt that he would always do what was right—as soon as he calmed down enough to see it.

"The deed is done," I said, trying to make light of the turmoil within me.

"You're joined already? You only left two removes ago!"

"So quickly one's life changes," I replied lightly, annoyed that he would make such a comment, as though my sense of time passing was less acute than his. Ghen count time as Bria do, in removes of the sun and moon. The sun shifts thirty-seven times its width across the sky, moving from its first rosy arrival to its final scarlet descent; the moon, starting higher in the sky, makes twenty-six shifts. They repeat their journey 583 times to complete a year, and the last sixty-three days are stillseason. Was he going to remind me of all this, as well? And of the wistful Sphere, Wind's mate, sitting beside Wind to watch the shifting display in the sky above them both, as though I did not know?

Should I remark to him that Bria use small glasses which trickle sand through a narrow middle from one side to the other, measuring the time of a single remove, but I, being a Ghen, have an instinctive feel for passing time. How could one hunt, alone or in a triad, without a keen awareness of every moment? A hunter must have good timing.

I shook my head. I was unsettled by the abruptness of my joining and by a sense of having over-reached myself. It was not fair to take this out on Saft'ir, who was doubtless unaware of the subtle insult his words implied. He would have been surprised if I'd pointed it out. "Think it: say it"—that was Saft'ir. He meant no slight.

He followed me into the adjoining room. We were alone there; all my roommates were at Festival Hall, still choosing their Bria mates. I knelt at the foot of my sleeping mat and placed my firearm across the end of it.

"Is he pretty? Are you pleased?"

"Yes, of course. All Bria are pretty." I wanted to say he was the most beautiful Bria on Wind, but my throat closed on the words. It would have sounded foolish, anyway.

"What's the house like?" He bent to hold the other end of the mat so I could pull it tight while I rolled it around and around my firearm.

"I don't know."

"You don't know?" He lifted the rolled mat and looked at me over it. I concentrated on wrapping my rope securely seven times around the middle then twice from end to end. Taking the bundle and placing it on the floor, I made the loop by which I could carry it, and knotted the end securely.

"Rukt'an took him to the house. He's Alannis's child, Rukt'an's first mate."

"You're supposed to help him home. Why did Rukt'an do it?"

I sighed and sat on one of the two sturdy benches I'd made to take with me, motioning Saft'ir onto the other.

"He's proud, Saft'ir—"

"They all are."

"—Proud and frightened." I ignored his interruption. "Imagine if you were he."

Saft'ir looked back at me silently. I waited. This was as good an excuse as any for prolonging my departure. Finally he spoke.

"Is that what you've got to do? Imagine you're a Bria for the next five years?"

"It's the way of the Ghen." I grinned to lighten my words.

"It's the way of the hunt, maybe."

"It's the way of a guardian." I rose, a little embarrassed, and reached for my backpack. Even to my own ears I sounded like Mick'al, our spiritual advisor.

Saft'ir reached for my polished iron-ore mug and held it while I packed the wooden platters. In Briarris's house I would use his pottery dishes; the platters and mug were my hunting gear.

"I still don't see why Rukt'an led him home."

"Briarris doesn't want me to see him helpless."

Saft'ir hooted with laughter. "Does he think you don't know he can't see in stillseason? Wind's breath, they're idiots."

"No, they're just different. It's a different culture."

"Just don't come back a Bria, five years from now," he said, still chuckling.

"I know who I am," I said, touchy because at the moment I was less sure than I wanted to admit. "I'm the servant of Wind. And the Bria are its heart." I said it because I believed it, though it must sound religious to him.

"It's pretty cold-hearted, then."

He wasn't alone in his criticism of Bria, but still I didn't like hearing it. I took the mug from him silently and placed it in the bottom of the backpack, beside the platters, then put my hunting knives on top. I knotted the sack closed and rested it on one of my benches. Turning, I stood with my back to Saft'ir, looking out the window. I tried to imagine living with only one room-mate, and that one a Bria.

Five years is a long time.

⁓

Leaving my cart of belongings in front of the house, I stopped at the door and coughed politely to enter. I had to cough four times before it was opened. Briarris stepped back quickly as I entered. He sat on one of his padded chairs at the table, watching me.

Awkwardly, I held out the traditional harrunt'h meat I had brought to him. Although it was properly dried and cured, he wrinkled his nose slightly, and made no move to take it. Of course I knew Bria abstained from eating meat, but most pretend to appreciate the symbolic offering. With it, I was promising to protect and provide for Briarris. Knowing him even as little as I did then, I was not surprised by his response. I bit my tongue lightly to keep from laughing as I walked across the room and placed it in the cold food box.

Returning, I caught in his widened eye the look of that first sadu'h I had hunted.

෴

I got through my first day living with Briarris without breaking anything. That was my initial concern. Then through the first week, the first month. Briarris ignored me. He would serve food onto my plate as I held it, standing beside him at his cookstove, then sit across from me at the table and eat—all without once looking into my face.

It was Bria food—leafy greens and callan cheese and farmborra eggs, tasteless like the poor, tame livestock it came from. Instead of frying their corn as we did when we found it growing wild along the river, they ground theirs up and baked it into loaves, which dulled its gritty flavor. At least the root vegetables were familiar to me, although they were boiled until they were too soft.

When I formed shapes with my hands and fingers, hoping we could learn to talk to one another, Briarris pretended not to notice. If I hadn't been so lonely, I would have given up. I watched him and tried to be patient.

My duty on the wall sustained me. It was a relief to be back among Ghen, where I was neither ignored nor resented. I appreciated my own kind more than I could have imagined. The guard on the wall was tightened as we neared stillseason. There were no more jokes about napping and even Mant'er ceased to grumble about wasting his time when he could be hunting. Not that we truly worried. The wall was a precaution for most of the year, a necessity only in stillseason, when all who were not mating guarded it.

෴

After our first mating, Briarris consented to learn to talk with me. We grew more comfortable together during our second year. Instead of lessening his attractiveness, Briarris's pregnancy drew me more and more to him. His vulnerable beauty, even his stubborn pride, moved me to a tenderness I wouldn't have imagined. I disliked deceiving him about the upcoming birth, but I told myself that I was merely sparing him needless fear.

When the Broghen was born, Briarris's shock and humiliation were terrible to see. I was bitterly ashamed of the role I had played in deceiving him. His horror was short-lived, nor did he slide into depression as I'd been warned. He breathed in courage like a hunter and reached to feed the newborn Broghen! I realized then that I loved him.

I held that image in my mind—Briarris's trembling hand stretching toward the monstrous infant—as I carried it to the Ghen compound. I tried not to imagine what it would have done to his defenseless hand had it not been caged.

I was one of the first to arrive at our meeting spot, a half day's walk from the City gate into the forest of the mainland. I had to listen to the infant Broghen's frenzied howls for two days, until all of the new Ghen parents had joined us. I gave it water and wild corn, but could not feed it more than that. Once it ate meat it would begin to produce the poison that made it such a lethal predator.

We headed west, carrying with us a hideous cacophony that silenced everything else within miles. I felt ashamed, as though I carried some vile disease and was about to release it upon Wind. I saw similar expressions on some of the Ghen faces around me.

We didn't speak—it would have been hard to make ourselves heard over the howling Broghen and we had nothing to say. We were doing what had to be done.

We walked quickly, the sound of our howling Broghen driving everything from our path. The ship was ready for us when we reached the Symamt'h River. A dozen older Ghen had gone out earlier to prepare and provision it. This was the first time I'd seen it. I stood back, allowing others to climb into the raft that would carry them to the middle of the river where the ship waited.

It sat high in the water, its wooden sides as taut as a young Bria's skin, flung with spray that sparkled in the sun. I could hear the slap, slap of the river against it as it moved in the water, eager to begin its trip. The front narrowed sharply almost to a point, but the middle was wider and the back cut straight across, so that it had the shape of an elongated half-circle. A tall staff rose from the middle of the deck. It was furled with bright cloth, which would soon be untied to form a wind-sail. I hadn't imagined it would be so large, or so beautiful.

Several Ghen bent over the back railing, hauling up the huge weights that moored the boat. Others leaned above the ladder, offering their hands to the Ghen climbing aboard. Two or three passed down lines to which the Broghen cages were being tied by those still on the raft.

"We won't even get wet."

I hadn't noticed Mant'er approaching. I was a little annoyed that he misinterpreted my silence for nervousness, even though his assumption was only natural.

"I was admiring it," I said, and left him staring after me, mystified.

Only Char'an, the steersman, stayed on the ship to accompany us. He soon saw that I was the most promising rivermate and had me maneuvering the boom, a long beam of wood to which the bottom of the sail was tied. He taught me to work the rudderpost, which was attached to a broad, flat piece of wood beneath the boat. When turned to left or right, it guided the vessel's direction. A most amazing thing, this ship! I questioned him extensively about its building and operation, and he was happy to talk about it. He was almost as disappointed as I, to learn that I was to be a councilor.

∽

"It's beautiful."

"Yes," Mant'er agreed.

We stood at the prow of the boat, looking out at the land. We'd been sailing south for several days under strong winds and were almost at the river's mouth. It would have taken us over a month, pushing ourselves hard, to travel this far by land. The river had widened considerably but was also much deeper, according to Char'an, so we'd been able to move in closer to the east bank.

The sun had just risen and the land was bathed in its glow. It had rained—it rained often here, light drizzles that cleared away quickly—and a rainbow arched over the riverbank. The vegetation was a brilliant green, lighter and brighter than any I'd seen in the north. There were only a few ugappas, scattered among orillias, a tree I'd heard about but never seen.

They had thick trunks, easily as wide around as three ugappas, which rose to about eight handspans in height. At that point a series of large fronds, each as big as a half-grown Bria, rose from short stems in a circle around the tree. Just at the point where one could begin to glimpse, through their narrowing tips, the diminished trunk, another circle of fronds began. This continued, with the size of the fronds and the circumference of the trunk shrinking at each level, until the treetop ended in a bright spray of tiny, new fronds. Many of the orillias reached as high as forty handspans into the air.

There were no cappa bushes, but such a mass of other shrub-like vegetation that it was almost impossible to distinguish individual plants. One type had long, thin leaves, about the length of a Bria's leg, but flat. The leaves were bright yellow and looked fuzzy, as though covered by tiny hairs. Another shrub completely surrounded itself with crimson spikes, each two handspans long, and as thick at the base as three of my fingers, narrowing into a vicious-looking point. As I watched, however, a strong wind came up and I saw the deceptive spikes bend in it.

Where the taller vegetation thinned near the riverbank, the ground was covered with a thick yellow-green plant that looked like a cross between groundherb and moss, and was dotted with tiny blue flowers. They glistened in the sun as though drops of the azure water had been flung up by the wind to crystallize on the shore.

Even more amazing were the birds. Their feathered wings and furry bellies sported all the colors of the rainbow, which appeared faded beside their brilliance. They flitted from tree to tree by the hundreds, pausing briefly now and then to open their throats in lilting melody. They were so numerous the entire forest was filled with their songs.

Now and again I saw, leaping between the trees, cousins of our mangarr'h. These were slightly larger, with yellow pelts more suited to the rich colors of the trees they lived in. No other creature came near them and so I surmised that here, as in the north, they were in-breeders.

What would it be like to breed within one's own species? I shuddered at the thought. Mangarr'h, liapt'h, courrant'h'h; the predators of Wind, large and small, were all in-breeders. Perhaps it was by necessity. They would have devoured any other species that let them come so close.

Along the shore I also saw an unfamiliar mammal, plump and unhurried, which divided its time between water and land. I knew by their gleaming blue-black scales that these must be wattel'hs. Every so often I caught a glimpse of their shy mates, more fish than mammal, the phora'hs.

It was thrilling to see species I'd only heard about. I found myself wishing Briarris was here to share these sights. Then I remembered the purpose of this journey and was ashamed of my pleasure.

I looked away from the land, down into the river. It teemed with fish of all sizes, as colorful as the birds overhead. They swarmed into our nets each morning in such profusion we had to let go as many as we kept to avoid breaking the nets. They were juicy and sweeter than any fish I had tasted.

I was enchanted; there was no other word for it. Never had I seen anything so lush and lovely, so full of life, as this southern land. Mant'er, admiring the view beside me, pointed along the bank where hundreds of anhad'hs nested in narrow inlets, their russet feathers blending in with the rich, dark earth. Stillseason was over and they would soon be flying north again.

They had molted during their flight south, and would molt again on their flight back. Although their back and wing coloring was only a little brighter now than when I had occasionally hunted them in the wetlands, the markings on their necks and under-wings were quite different. When they extended their graceful necks I could see bands of yellow, which continued to the underside of their wings. At dusk on the water, they tucked these markings away, but in the daytime, when they sunbathed on the land, they stretched their necks to lay their heads in the middle of their backs, between their wings, which they twisted outwards to reveal the dappled yellow markings. They were difficult to see against the sun-speckled, yellow-green groundcover.

Above them, the mossy bank was thick with their mating species, the terriad'hs, which apparently could not fly, but used their short wings to boost themselves in a series of hops onto the land or over the water.

I asked Mant'er if he thought we'd have a chance to stop and hunt, thinking he'd pointed them out for that reason. He expelled a noisy expletive of air. He didn't curse often, so his vehemence surprised me.

"Hunt?" he said, "There's no hunting here. Taking those would be more like gathering cappa fruit. But it's a good place to leave our Broghen offspring."

His comment struck me as somehow vile and before I could stop myself, I asked, "How can we do such a thing?"

He misunderstood me. "I know they've suffered. I don't like to see them so weakened, but Char'an tells me we're almost there. Tomorrow we'll feed them fresh fish. They'll have poison in their fangs only a few removes after we've left them on the shore, and be a match for all but each other. And there's enough easier game to distract them from killing one another."

"This is the most beautiful place on Wind!"

He grunted dismissively. "Too bright and busy. Too moist. I prefer our northern forest; the wind is less forceful here. Soft," he said, with disdain. "We'd grow soft here."

A thin and plaintive wail came from the center of the deck, where we'd lashed the wooden cages. Mant'er grinned.

"They won't grow soft," he said.

I turned away, sickened.

"Ocallis will be pleased to know our rejected offspring has a good place to live."

I looked back at him. He was watching me intently.

I remembered Briarris's words: *Let me feed him.* This was our offspring, regardless of its deformities and vicious nature. I was the unnatural one, not Mant'er.

When I looked back at the land, it appeared to have faded. The sky was overcast. Mant'er moved back, under the canopy, but I stood in the rain, heavy-hearted, looking out over the weeping land.

That night I held the boom while Char'an steered. In the night I heard the demonic screams of Broghen, as I had for two nights now. All the teeming and joyous daytime life lay trembling and silent under the savage dominion of those night-predators.

"Do you like this land?" I asked Char'an.

"I pilot this boat so that I can visit it," he replied.

I was silent a long time, while the shrieks of Broghen pierced the dark. Several of the caged infants cried out in weak emulation.

"What is the difference between hunter and predator?" I spoke softly, almost to myself.

"Conscience." Char'an had heard me and replied.

"I thought it was prayer," I said. But I knew that many Ghen did not pray when they hunted, including Mant'er. Yet they all cared about the land, loved the harshness and the sweetness of it, both.

"Conscience is prayer." Char'an's voice floated out of the darkness.

In the dark of night the shore was invisible, but I could see it in my mind, bursting with beauty and life. How many Broghen would it take to destroy it? I thought of Briarris, pictured him as I had last seen him, on his sleeping ledge, his face aglow as he nursed our three newborns and his hand reaching out to offer nourishment even to the one that would have ravaged him.

Char'an said nothing when I lashed the boom to hold the sail's position, although he must have heard me. I stepped carefully between the sleeping Ghen and reached for the wooden cage I had made. The Broghen inside whined in hunger as it felt itself lifted. At the railing I hesitated, wanting to pray, but none of the prayers I knew were suitable. Nevertheless, my hands were steady as I lifted the cage over the railing.

I heard a tiny splash as it hit the water, and then it was gone.

Hunt

Mant'er

"You went out in stillseason? In your first year of hunting?" Chair Ghen's tone was daunting, but I suppressed my discomfort and returned his gaze evenly.

"Everyone knows you're a fine hunter, Mant'er, despite your youth," he said, with an air of tried patience. Again I was silent. My triad had brought home four large harrunt'hs, during stillseason. They were being butchered and smoked by less capable hunters as we spoke.

"…but you owe it to your parent to sire a child before you take unnecessary risks."

"Because my parent died on a stillseason hunt doesn't mean I am at risk," I replied. He had aimed low with that barb and drawn my anger. I saw the sharp scales that rose over the ridge of his spine tremble slightly as he struggled with his own temper. When he looked up again he was calm.

"You will go to Festival Hall tomorrow and choose a Bria. You will not hunt in stillseason again until you have a youngling. I say this on behalf of all Ghen."

I bowed my head. When Chair Ghen invoked that phrase, his word was law. I had intended to go at any rate, but it irked me to be ordered about like a child. Even as I acquiesced, I murmured, "I hunted for all Ghen."

"You hunted for yourself!" he said, and turning sharply, left me.

❧

I noticed Ocallis and his sibling at once when they entered Festival Hall. Rukt'an led them in as pleased as though they were his younglings, not merely those of the Bria with whom he'd joined. They sat in the seats he led them to, catching their breath.

I turned back to my conversation with Igt'ur, for Bria must wait when Ghen discuss the hunt. Igt'ur is small and only a mediocre hunter, but Igt'ur notices things. Not only the track and spoor of the prey; Igt'ur notices tendencies, changes. The "hunting wind" he calls it, and "the wind is changing" is what he had to tell me. I realized as he talked that I'd noticed the same things myself: the harrunt'h herds drifting northwards, the flocks of plump terriad'hs that nested along the rivers diminishing, even the small sadu'hs, such prolific breeders, were becoming fewer. Not enough to be worrisome but something to keep an eye on, we agreed.

Igt'ur's gaze shifted slightly. When I turned, Ocallis was standing behind me. I saw him bite into his first taste of wild corn coated with liapt'h egg and I saw the taste of it please him. He was a hunter also, in his own way.

The thought amused me. I admired the tawny curls of his pelt, the long, slender legs and willowy body, the plump, soft belly and firm, enticing breasts. A heat rose in me as I watched the languorous movement of his body, the slow sway of his hips, the knowing laughter in his eye. He was the most beautiful Bria in the room and instinctively sensual.

I chose Ocallis not only because he was beautiful, but because he knew it, and knowing made him strong. I wanted my youngling to feel that strength while he was in Ocallis's womb.

☙

When my child was born I named him Heckt'er after the fabled Ghen who saved us from extinction by the Broghen. Why should my offspring not be as great as Heckt'er? He was strong and he had me to teach him.

Even as an infant Heckt'er was fearless. I had to pry his claws from the flesh of the Broghen infant at their birth, not the other way around. At one, he cried for meat and I gave it to him. He was already as big as a two-year-old. I would have had him weaned early but Ocallis said he needed milk as well as meat. Ocallis held him too often, but it pleased Ocallis to do so and didn't seem to weaken Heckt'er.

43

During the stillseason before he turned two, Heckt'er climbed the ugappa in front of Ocallis's house and leapt upon an unsuspecting bird. He missed his footing and fell to the ground. From treetop to ground he never lost his nerve, neither cried out nor loosened his hold on his prey. He was a worthy youngling for me!

When he was two I took him with me to the Ghen compound. He didn't cry to leave Ocallis and yet I know he felt affection for him. He asked me to tell Ocallis not to worry, that it was time for him to learn the forest. His words surprised me; of course Ocallis knew it was time. Ocallis had his Bria offspring to train and I had mine. What more was there to say? Nevertheless, I passed on his strange comment and Ocallis blinked in pleasure. As I turned to go, Ocallis signed, "Try to love him, Mant'er."

Love him? Hadn't I taken him along the wall and into the woods more often than any other Ghen parent, only returning when he was so tired he stumbled, though he tried to hide it from me? Didn't I praise him, perhaps overly, when he sniffed the wind and answered my questions well? Bria foolishness, I thought, and signed, "I will make him a great hunter," so that Ocallis would be reassured.

෴

Heckt'er understood the forests of Wind instinctively, as I did. I taught him the ways of the timid sadu'h, no taller than my knee, with their large eyes and soft, furred pelts, and showed him how to track them to their burrows. I pointed out the feathered terriad'hs flying back from their migration in the mountains to mate with the anhad'hs, waiting for them in the eastern wetlands. I described the majestic harrunt'hs, a third again as tall as I, fleet on their powerful legs and sharp-hoofed, formidable for all that they were herbivores.

I told him of the three large predators on Wind: the cold-blooded liapt'h with their long, fang-studded jaws, that swim in the rivers of the wetlands; the fierce courrant'h, silent, four-footed mountain killers that mass as much as an adult Ghen; and most dangerous of all, the Broghen that rage along the seashore on the mainland, far to the south of our peninsula.

I taught Heckt'er to read the messages brought by the wind and how to avoid letting it tell of him. I taught him to move in silence, to leave no trail and to follow any trail, including mine. When he found me, I praised him, and when he failed, I waited. Many times we stayed in the woods all night while he hunted for traces of my passage. He never cried or called out. He never rested. He never quit. When I no longer had to leave a sign, when he could find me no matter how I tried to escape his notice, then I was satisfied.

When Heckt'er was four I sent him to a farm for stillseason. The Bria had retreated into their houses, unable even to tend their tame callans and farmborra. Heckt'er accepted the extra duty as he accepted all my training, even though farm work is despised. The farms are, after all, an affront to Ghen hunters, a lack of confidence in our abilities. However, Bria are timid, superstitious creatures, who fancy droughts and famines and what-have-you in every change of weather. We indulge them.

The city itself had spread to the edge of the Symba River, which abutted the farms. In fact, some of the farmland to the west had been converted into additional housing areas, and every few years more houses had to be built. As the houses encroached on the farms, so the farms encroached on the woodlands, and we cut back the trees to increase the callans' pasturage. Someday we would occupy the entire peninsula.

I left Heckt'er on his own to care for the callans and farmborra on one of the large farms south of the city. I knew the callans would wander in their pastures, and a few would hide from him at sunset, some among the cappas, some in the river, evading the heat of stillseason. They would try to kick him every morning until he learned to milk them as though he were a calf himself.

The farmborra would hide their eggs from him and the cocks would wake him in the night until he came to understand their cries: the joke of false alarm or brief dreamstartle from the rare pitch of genuine terror when a mongarr'h had ventured from the southern woods in search of easy prey. I knew all this because in my youth I, too, had spent a stillseason on the farms.

"Become a callan," I told Heckt'er when I left him. "You will only find your prey when you can think as they think. You'll only draw close enough for the kill when you have learned to convince them that you are one of them." If Heckt'er could come to understand these pitiful, tame beasts, which give the Bria their milk and cheese and butter and the fibres they spin into wool, or twist into rope, or weave into their delicate, dyed fabrics, then he could understand their majestic mating species, the wild harrunt'h.

The morning that the wind returned, I went for Heckt'er. I didn't find him in the farmhouse or the barn or the roost-hut. He wasn't in the farmyard or the near pastures. At last I went to the far pastures where the callans grazed. I grinned to think that he had felt the wind on his face as he drove them from the barn and it had drawn him with them into the farthest meadows.

I searched the ugappas that lined the callan trail and saw here and there a bent branch or twisted leaf that remembered his foot as he climbed to feel the light, cooling breeze. I searched the groupings of callans but he wasn't among them, though I saw a disruption of pebbles where he had run with the young harrunt'hs. Soon they would be driven up onto the mainland to join a wild herd in the forest, leaving only a few to keep the callans productive.

I beat my way slowly through a dense copse of cappas, but Heckt'er was not resting in their leafy thickets. Along the bank of the Symba I thought I saw his imprint in the mud amidst the tracks of callans, who love to swim in the cool waters at midday.

Ghen don't swim. There is no buoyancy in our heavy bones and muscular bodies and the weight of our scales bears us down. I shuddered to see the callans gamboling in the current, remembering the worst part of my stillseason on the farm when I was Heckt'er's age: the evenings I had to wade into the swirling waters to drive the reluctant callans to their barn.

Three times I searched the meadows, the cappa copse, the ugappas; three times I returned to the farmhouse, barn, roosting-hut, before I stood again on the banks of the Symba. The sun was already sliding into the west. Bria, recovered with the returning breeze, were coming to round up their callans. I examined the gold-tinged waters anxiously.

And there I saw the tip of a slender, hollow reed moving as no reed moves, against the current. I could hardly credit what it must mean. Nevertheless, I plunged into the river and reached down. My hands closed over scales cold and slimy with the silt of the riverbed, sodden with long submergence. For just a moment, before I drew Heckt'er up to break the surface, I thought I had mistaken and held a fish.

໒ɔ

Heckt'er returned with me to the Ghen compound. There was nothing more I could teach him without taking him out on the trail, so I set him up to learn firearm production. Normally, he wouldn't have been studying this until he'd had his first hunt, but youths who showed interest were always welcome; the smithy needed apprentices. Not that Heckt'er would become one of those who made the firearms used by better hunters.

I had a new stock—one I'd carved during stillseason from the strong thigh bone of a harrunt'h I'd brought down that year. Heckt'er could observe the boring and rifling of the barrel, made from smelted bog ore; the insertion of the hammer and trigger; the placement of the crystal so the strike of the hammer would unfailingly draw a spark. A Ghen should see the construction of his weapon, and this would be Heckt'er's after he had had his first hunt.

"A youth firearm," I said to the smith, "and the youth to watch its making." I was warmed by the flush of surprise and pleasure on Heckt'er's face. He reached for the stock I'd placed on the smith's table and examined it.

I'd kept it hidden because its size would have given away the surprise. A youth firearm was smaller, lighter than an adult's. It had a shorter barrel and therefore a shorter range, but it was just as deadly. I'd outgrown my youth firearm quickly, as Heckt'er would, but I still had it. With that in mind, I'd taken great care in the carvings: liapt'h and courrant'h both on one side, and on the other, a Broghen.

"You'll be master over every beast on Wind," I promised him when he looked back up at me.

"Explosives?" the smith asked.

"Yes," I said without hesitation. Many Ghen wouldn't let their younglings observe the nitration of the fluffy seedballs produced by threadplants— so named because the Bria spun its fibers to make our woven bedmats. Occasionally, when a smith had failed to remove all traces of the nitric and sulfuric acids, the resulting nitrofiberballs could undergo spontaneous decomposition. This never happened to a master, and the smith accepted my compliment with a nod. Of course, I wasn't simply being polite; a Ghen who didn't know how to handle explosives didn't deserve a firearm. Heckt'er wouldn't be one such.

By mid-year the smith sent Heckt'er back to me, saying he'd learned all he could without apprenticing. Heckt'er couldn't practice shooting until he was a hunter, but I showed him how to hold his firearm braced between his chest and shoulder. I let him catch the trigger with his claw and bend his finger over it till he could pull it back, sliding his entire hand along the side of the stock. I loaded it and, pointing to a distant falling leaf, shot cleanly through it. A fine weapon.

လာ

"He's only four," Prakt'um said when I asked if we could go with them on the last youth hunt of the year. Prackt'um was twenty, the leader of the party. He was taking his second youngling, Dur'um, on his first hunt. The others were all fourteen, a year older than I, taking their firstborns out.

"He's ready," I said.

"He knows more than I do," Dur'um broke in. We hadn't noticed him approaching us on the training field and Prakt'um frowned slightly.

"That's beside the point, Dur'um."

"He's as tall as Dyit'er. They're friends already, and Dyit'er's coming with us."

"I'll ask the others," Prakt'um said to me.

I learned later that Cann'an, a large, sharp-eyed Ghen who liked to boss those smaller than he, had opposed our coming. Timb'il had also expressed doubts, mostly in deference to Cann'an, because their younglings were in the same hunting triad. I snorted when I heard that. I had no use for Cann'an and less for Timb'il; he always followed the prevailing wind.

My request was granted, however, because Dyit'er's parent, Piet'er, pointed out that another youth was needed to complete Dyit'er's hunting triad. Since Dyit'er and Heckt'er had often trained together, Heckt'er was an obvious choice. I was glad to team with Piet'er. He was a good one to have at your back, strong and unhesitating. From what I'd seen, Dyit'er was like his parent.

We passed through the gate onto the mainland and headed north into the forest, twelve hunters with their twelve younglings. Far to the south lay the seashore, where we left infant Broghen. East lay the wetlands, where terriad'hs nested. Succulent fare, but we were after bigger game.

The forest was dappled with shadows, its silence broken occasionally by the calls of birds. The wind carried near and distant scents to us: the dank smell

48

of moss and decomposing leaves on the forest floor, the sweet smell of ugappa sap, faint because it was no longer running but dried on the bark, the tangy scent of ripening cappa fruit.

At regular intervals one of the youths would climb a tall ugappa and sighting by the lean of the sun, confirm our direction. When it was Heckt'er's turn he altered our course slightly. Young Dam'an had climbed before him and frowned, about to protest, but the adults concurred. We knew this route well although we left no path to mark our frequent traverse.

When the sun lowered the youths made camp, rolling out our sleeping mats, collecting dry twigs and branches that would burn well, with little smoke. Dyit'er emptied two canteens from our store of water into the pot on the fire and made a warming brew for us to drink with our dried rations.

During one of our stops Heckt'er had taken aside Bab'in, the smallest youth, to pick ruberries, which they now shared around. Bab'in grinned with pleasure when we thanked him, glancing sideways at his approving parent, Mart'in. We appointed them the first watch. I was happy, sleeping in my forest, and proud to be taking Heckt'er on his first hunt.

It was several days before we came upon the tracks of sadu'hs and even then they were scarce, hiding in their burrows day and night. The birds had also quieted. Occasionally, branches rustled overhead as mongarr'hs leapt from tree to tree away from us. Their dark skin made them almost invisible in the treetops, but once or twice I caught the malevolent stare of a small, pinched face peering down at us, its muzzle drawn back in a silent snarl.

I thought it strange that they came so close. It almost seemed they were watching us. Sinewy and hairless, they were good for neither meat nor pelt, too vicious to be tamed, too small to be a threat. Nevertheless, their tiny teeth were sharp. The youths climbed noisily to sight our direction, not wanting to stumble onto a startled mongarr'h which, feeling cornered, might bite. On the sixth evening Heckt'er and Dam'an killed three sadu'hs with their slingshots and we ate well again.

At night each parent on watch kept his firearm close, more to teach his youngling vigilance than for any real need. Courrant'hs inhabited the mountains and Broghen roamed far to the south, while we had come north. But we were on the trail and the line between hunter and hunted can be as small as a single moment of unreadiness.

The increasing silence of the forest put us all on edge. When I saw the first sign of harrunt'hs—a disturbance of twigs, a single hair caught in the bark of a tree—I looked aside. This was our younglings' hunt. But I was relieved. I glanced over at Heckt'er and saw that he noticed as well, though he turned away at once. Why didn't he speak up?

Soon after, Dam'an and Sark'il called out, pointing with barely concealed excitement to the soft imprint of a harrunt'h hoof on the forest soil. It was several days old and faint; we were lucky there'd been no rain. Nearby, a few snapped branches and missing leaves indicated that a small herd had passed. The youths conferred together.

They were fortunate; the animals were heading northeast, into the wind. We could follow quickly without fear that our scent would reach them. Dam'an and Sark'il left their packs with their parents and ran silently ahead to scout. It should have been Heckt'er running ahead but I held my tongue, though it galled me. Heckt'er would have to learn to speak for himself.

We didn't see our scouts that night or the next, but the night after that we met them on the trail in late afternoon. The beasts were less than two removes away, moving slowly. We would rest for the night and fall upon them at dawn.

In the night the wind changed. I was awake at once, but Heckt'er was already going from blanket to blanket, quietly shaking the others awake. It was too late to move out of the path of the wind; we were too close. The youths would have to strike at once, before the harrunt'hs caught our scent and stampeded. We ran silent and intent between the trees, our eyes adjusting already to what little light filtered down from the starry sky above.

We heard the snorting and stamping before we saw them. The older ones were circling through the trees, nipping awake young adults and yearlings, gathering them close, heading east. The herd was small, two or three dozen at most. The youths split into their triads, racing silently toward the milling beasts. Holding their knives between their teeth they moved in circles as the beasts were doing, choosing their prey. Our nearness stirred the herd to greater fear, black shapes in the black night between tall, black trees.

Dyit'er led Heckt'er and Dur'um in their triad. He motioned them toward a young harrunt'h looking belligerently about as though deciding which way to run. Heckt'er and Dyit'er circled behind the beast while Dur'um pulled himself into the tree he had indicated and moved along its lower branches.

Suddenly an eerie whistle pierced the night and every beast took up the shrill cry until the forest rang with their alarm. The harrunt'hs stampeded, following the summons of their lead buck. The ground trembled under their hooves, branches lashing and snapping in the path of their flight.

The young harrunt'h whirled straight toward Heckt'er and Dyit'er. They leaped into its path, shouting and waving their arms. Its eyes widened, ringed in white terror, nostrils flared, as it pounded toward them. They stood their ground, faces pale in the night as they waved and shouted, knives ready and claws extended. We parents held our breath while the forest thundered with the rush of the huge beasts. At last the harrunt'h swerved, heading under the tree where Dur'um waited.

Dur'um dropped from the branches onto its back, sinking his claws into its neck. It bucked, rising and pawing the air with its hooves while it whirled in a frenzied circle. The side of its neck smashed into Dur'um's forehead. Caught off guard, nearly stunned, he let his knife fall.

Heckt'er and Dyit'er rushed forward with their knives but the flaying hooves kept them at a distance. Without warning, the buck threw itself sideways into the wide trunk of a ugappa and Dur'um leaped from its back barely in time to avoid being crushed. I watched him roll aside, then ahead I saw Heckt'er crouch to leap astride the buck when it raced by him. He was in a good position to do so, and it was bleeding, winded and running slowly enough that I knew he could mount it if his balance held. My youngling would bring it down alone on his first hunt!

It had almost reached him when Dur'um cried out. He lay on the ground between the trunks of two trees, holding his left leg. A large harrunt'h bore down on him, crazed with fear. Dur'um was too low to the ground to turn its path, it would trample him as it would a mound of dirt. Prakt'um was already racing toward his child, silent and desperate, but we were too far away. I looked back at Heckt'er in the moment that he made his choice.

Turning away from the buck, he raced to stand over Dur'um, waving his arms at the oncoming harrunt'h and yelling. It was too close to turn; the huge beast was almost upon them!

"Heckt'er!" His name caught in my throat, tore free, was lost in the screams of the beasts and their thundering hooves. I willed him to leap aside, to save himself.

He never flinched, not even in the last moment when the harrunt'h finally swerved, smashing against the tree beside him with such force it cracked, splitting in two as the harrunt'h swept around it.

A few moments later Prakt'um reached them. He lifted Dur'um in his arms, and then I was beside Heckt'er. He looked up at me. When I stood speechless before him, he hung his head.

"I lost the prey," he said.

I wanted to touch him, draw him against me. I wanted to fall to my knees and weep. I wanted to praise him for his courage and shake him and shake him for the risk he had taken.

"Two dead hunters will not feed our people," I said.

∽

Dawn was breaking as we returned to camp. Only one group of young hunters had brought down their prey. Another triad had wounded theirs. They'd started to follow its trail but their parents called them back.

"Let it try to keep up with the herd," a parent was explaining when we arrived, "until it falls from blood loss. If you pursue it now, it'll run for denser cover, and be that much harder to kill. In a few days we'll catch up with it."

We congratulated the successful triad, rolling up our sleeping mats while they skinned and butchered their kill to carry back to the city. We ate together the wild, juicy meat, cooking extra to take with us. The hot scent of harrunt'h blood and the savory odor of its flesh stayed with us long after we left the camp behind.

There were only twelve of us now, two triads of younglings with their parents. The triad that was tracking their wounded prey had followed the harrunt'h herd, but we continued traveling north. Better to find a new herd that wasn't spooked.

The next day I heard the Symamt'h River, which began in the distant mountains and ran southward through the grasslands. At the edge of the forest it curved east between the tree line and the grasses, then twisted back southward, skirted the edge of the eastern wetlands, and continued flowing south all the way down to the sea. By late afternoon, we were walking close to a section of it that veered in toward us. I was near the head of our group when I heard Timb'il cry out, pointing.

52

"There can't be liapt'hs here," Cann'an snapped in disgust as he climbed the slight knoll to where Timb'il stood staring at the Symamt'h through a break in the trees. The river ran fast and cold, five times as wide as its tributary, the Symba, which flowed into our peninsula. In the middle of the vast river, I was shocked to see the long, sinuous shape of a liapt'h, twisting through the water. Cann'an was silent as the rest of us gathered around. The mud-green lizard opened wide its long jaws to snap at a passing bird and the sun glinted off double rows of wicked, knife-sharp teeth.

"We should go back," Timb'il said. When no one answered, he continued, "There's something wrong and we all know it: the forest so silent, the game so scarce and now a liapt'h leaving the wetlands to swim in the Symamt'h!"

"So we won't go swimming," I said quickly, before his fear affected the others. I had never returned empty-handed from a hunt. I caught Heckt'er looking at me and I grinned to reassure him. He would have his hunt. "I've hunted the wetlands before. Liapt'hs don't frighten me."

Cann'an looked at me darkly and rose to the bait. "No one is frightened!" he snapped. "We'll continue."

"It isn't just the liapt'hs," Timb'il protested, "it's the whole forest. Listen!" he paused, looking around uneasily. "Not a single bird is singing."

For a moment my own scales tingled, then I laughed. It came out somewhat forced but broke the tension.

"You have too much imagination, Timb'il," I said. "We're on a youth hunt, don't forget. You can't expect youngsters to be as quiet as experienced trackers. Our noisy passage frightens the birds to silence and then their timid silence frightens you."

Timb'il flushed. The others looked away, turning to Prakt'um as leader of the expedition. He hesitated, looking at the liapt'h, then down at the hopeful youths.

"Timb'il is right, the birds are too quiet," he said, "but it may be because of us, as Mant'er says. We'll continue with caution."

He wants to leave, I realized, and felt again that ominous tingle down the long ridge of my spine. Something was wrong in the forest and in the river. I knew it. But I told myself, we are above it. We are outside the circle of prey and predator. We are Ghen. Prakt'um had deferred to my argument, for I was the better hunter, but he sensed that Timb'il was right.

There were no sadu'hs to be seen at all, now. It was good that we'd brought harrunt'h meat with us. Nor was there any birdsong to cheer us. The only sound was the rustle of mangarr'hs in the trees above. We'd grown accustomed to it and ignored them as we marched. Heckt'er walked beside Bab'in as though guarding the smaller youth. Dur'um walked with them, still limping from his fall. Bab'in's enthusiasm made him impulsive and Heckt'er saw that he stayed with the group.

Why would Heckt'er befriend such a scatterbrain? Despite his eagerness, Bab'in would never make a good hunter. His parent, Mart'in, was too good-natured to discipline him properly.

The sun was already setting when we stopped to make camp. Bab'in scampered up a tall ugappa for the evening look-out. We were stretching after our day's trek, laying out our sleeping mats. Several of the youths were gathering twigs and branches for our fire. Mart'in waited near the tree his youngling had ascended.

He had just bent down to open his pack when we heard a savage growling and Bab'in's scream, sudden and full of terror, and just as suddenly ended. We stood shock-still, unbreathing for one instant, listening to the snarl and whine of feeding mangarr'hs and the savage movement of branches high above us. With a cry, Mart'in sprang up the tree, climbing frantically, while the rest of us rushed over.

Prakt'um was already climbing after him. I ordered the youths to stay together at a distance and had Timb'il guard them. Already the sway and slap of branches in the treetops overhead was spreading out. I directed the other adults up into a wide circle of trees, wishing I could see through the thick covering of leaves, wishing that Bab'in would call out again. A shot rang out above me as I climbed and I saw a mangarr'h fall to the ground.

"Knives!" I screamed. We were all in the treetops now, hidden from each other, following the growls of feeding beasts. I could hardly believe we were fighting mangarr'hs! Even when I myself saw several tearing into Bab'in's severed hand, even as I swung my knife and watched them drop it and fall upon their wounded kin instead, even while I slashed at them again and again, I couldn't believe it was real.

We killed at least two dozen. If they had been less desperate in their feeding, most would have escaped. They were dark in the dark treetops and we were in the grip of a nightmare, slowed by disbelief. When we climbed down, the sight of Bab'in's small body torn apart, half-eaten, was unbearable. We wrapped him in his sleeping mat and built the fire high, cremating him at once.

No words were spoken. We were all in shock, shivering despite the mild evening and the blazing fire. When it burned down, we gathered his bones and ashes and presented them to Mart'in, bowing low with our claws retracted and our backs to the darkness beyond.

We did not bow long, baring our backs. Mangarr'h hunt in pairs, never in packs. Mangarr'h do not attack Ghen. Mangarr'h don't fight unless they are trapped. Their strange compulsion might be explained by the scarcity of birds and sadu'hs, but even so we were shaken as much by the manner of Bab'in's death as by its occurrence.

Death, from creatures no bigger than my arm! Creatures we considered pests, dangerous only to fish and birds and sadu'hs! The rhythm of the hunt was shattered, altered beyond recognition. The rules had shifted and all our acumen seemed suddenly uncertain.

❧

"I'm taking him back," Mart'in said as we lay unsleeping in the darkness. He hadn't spoken all evening and his voice was scarcely recognizable.

"Of course," Prakt'um said after a moment. "Dur'um and I will accompany you." Dur'um's blanket twitched in protest.

"We should all go," Timb'il's voice was high, nervous. I waited for Prakt'um to reply.

"We can't," I said finally.

"You're crazy!" Timb'il cried. "I don't care if we go back without a harrunt'h. You're going to get us all—" he broke off. Timb'il was a pathetic creature. I had to breathe deeply to keep the disgust from my voice when I answered him.

"We don't have enough provisions to get us all back home. We have to hunt."

"We could eat berries and cappa fruit."

I was speechless. Ghen travel hungry through the forest? Scrounging to keep from starving in our own forest? Why didn't Prakt'um speak up? I reminded myself that Timb'il was in shock, that we all were. I could hear the sound of muffled weeping from one of the youths.

"What happened to Bab'in is terrible." I paused at the inadequacy of the word, and took a breath. "But it won't happen again. We're not going home to say we're afraid of mangarr'hs!"

"Who's afraid of mangarr'hs?" Cann'an demanded.

"You are, if you go back before your youngling's a hunter."

"You're saying I'm a coward?"

"He's saying we all are," Timb'il cried. "I tell you, I'm not staying to satisfy his ego!"

"Timb'il, you take Sark'il and go with Mart'in," Prakt'um said, trying to calm us.

"No, Prakt'um," Piet'er's voice was firm. "You want to go because of Dur'um. And you're right."

"I'm okay. I want to stay," Dur'um mumbled.

"You've been limping ever since you fell from the harrunt'h's back. You can't hunt like that, it puts the rest of your triad in danger."

"Then we should all go," Timb'il repeated stubbornly.

"Only Prakt'um and Dur'um should go," I said. "The rest of us are needed for the hunt."

"Who made you the leader of this hunt?" Cann'an demanded.

"I do," said Prakt'um. "Mant'er's the leader when I go. We've argued enough. I've decided."

❧

Two days after they left, Dam'an found signs of a herd of harrunt'hs. Cann'an was mollified and Timb'il had no one left to grumble to. I suspected that once again Heckt'er had seen the trail first, for he stepped aside and let Dam'an go ahead just before Dam'an called out. But this time I was glad that Heckt'er had remained silent. Or I would have been, except that he was too quiet. We were all subdued, but Heckt'er most of all.

"I should have known what the mangarr'hs would do," he said when I questioned him.

"How could you have known? Mangarr'hs don't behave that way!" I replied.

"I should have been able to make myself think like a mangarr'h. Even like one of these."

56

I opened my mouth to tell him that that was impossible, and then I remembered finding him deep in the river on the Bria farm. It occurred to me that I'd never heard Heckt'er overstate his abilities.

"It wasn't your fault," I said at last, looking at my youngling as though for the first time.

༄

We spent seven days tracking the harrunt'hs, although their trail as we followed it was only a few days old. They were moving fast, almost as fast as we pursued.

What's making them hurry? I wondered uneasily, but for all my skill, I could detect nothing that would alarm a harrunt'h. Except for us, but we were downwind of them and too far behind. They were heading out of the forest toward the grasslands, long before stillseason was due. Already we were almost at the edge of the woods. I pushed us to greater speed, wanting to finish the hunt quickly and get home.

"No youth hunt has ever come this far," Piet'er said to me quietly, watching his youngling collect twigs for our evening fire. "And yet we've seen only one small herd of harrunt'hs."

"They've gone to the grasslands," I said, deliberately keeping my voice casual, "as the sadu'hs went early to their burrows. Stillseason will be early this year."

"No." Cann'an had come over in time to hear my reply. "Something is driving the game from our forests."

"I see no evidence of that."

"Something dangerous is hunting our forests," Timb'il broke in.

"That's absurd," I said coldly. "What signs have you found of this 'something'? What scent have you smelled? What sounds have you heard?" When they were silent I said, "Do you think if there were anything here, I wouldn't know of it?"

"Perhaps we haven't crossed its trail."

"An early stillseason doesn't leave a trail, except in the behavior of birds and beasts."

"Stillseason is no time for youth hunts," Piet'er said, seeking a compromise.

57

"You're right." I touched my breath in agreement. "We'll hunt the herd we're following, then return home at once."

"What if our younglings miss?" Timb'il asked.

"We should hunt also," Piet'er said. "We can carry two carcasses easily, and that way be sure of one to feed our trip home."

To calm them I agreed. "But let the youths make their move first," I suggested. The others nodded. We were, after all, all parents. We wanted to see our offspring become hunters.

The ugappas thinned to clusters of cappas and finally to grasses. The wide Symamt'h twisted back across our path and on its distant shore the grasslands stretched away to the horizon where we could just make out the peaks of the mountains, gray blue against sky blue.

The grasses were tall, reaching as high as our chests. They were golden in the sun, but something in their sinuous movement, in their sly rustle, struck me as threatening, malevolent. I shook off the feeling, angry with Timb'il for filling me with his phantoms. It was only the wind that moved these grasses, only the wind that shook a sound like moaning out of them.

The wind blew away from us, carrying our scent toward the distant mountains. Again I shivered, as though there were something out there that should not know of us. Dyit'er pointed westward across the curving Symamt'h and there was the herd we'd been tracking, feeding peacefully upon the grasses perhaps three days away. The sight calmed us all, and I was disgusted with my earlier misgivings. Too much imagination, distracting me from the hunt. A mere youth had sighted our game ahead of me.

The youngsters cut down a number of nearby cappas, lashing them together with the long grasses that grew beside the river. By evening they'd made three good-sized rafts and a number of limbs, widened at one end with their branches webbed by grass, to paddle us across. The youths went to fish while we made camp. It took them a long time to catch enough to feed us, but our meal that night was fresh and flavorful.

During my watch I heard the Symamt'h roiling with the sound of fish feeding on small night-fliers. The noise echoed in the dark over the water. I saw Heckt'er staring at the river.

"Stillseason's coming," I said. "The fish are beginning to hide from the sun. Already they only rise to feed at night."

Despite my explanation he looked uneasy. Most of the fish we had eaten had come from his line. Once again, I remembered his episode on the farm. Had he sensed something I'd missed?

The Symamt'h was quiet in the morning, with only the cool breeze rippling its surface. We lashed our packs to the rafts and set off. I had knotted all our ropes together and tied one end to the trunk of a cappa near the shore, playing it out as we crossed. The current was strong and the rope would speed our return.

We traveled three to a raft. Dyit'er came with Heckt'er and me while his parent, Piet'er, rode with Cann'an and Dam'an. Timb'il and Sark'il were on the final raft with two extra packs and the last of our provisions.

When we reached the middle of the river we paused to rest. I felt a bump against the bottom of my raft. A boulder or the upper branches of a fallen tree, I thought, though the river should have been too deep at this point for either to reach the surface. The bumping increased and, startled, I remembered the liapt'h. Could it possibly have come this far? I reached for my pack. Heckt'er was already scanning the water.

"There!" he cried.

A huge liapt'h broke the surface thrusting itself up onto the third raft. Its wide, elongated jaws reached for the packs of provisions, snapping eagerly while its short, clawed front legs scrambled for purchase. Green scales glistened as it pulled itself higher onto the raft.

Then another appeared beside it, and another!

Before we could reach our firearms the weight of their bodies had capsized the raft. Timb'il and Sark'il plunged screaming into the water, which was now alive with frenzied liapt'hs. I loaded my firearm while Heckt'er and Dyit'er beat at the shapes in the water around our own raft with their paddles. One monster tried to mount our raft but Heckt'er thrust his knife into its protruding eye and it lashed backward, almost pulling him with it, for he refused to surrender his weapon.

I shot one of the liapt'hs attacking Timb'il and Sark'il, but already several long jaws had clamped round their limbs and I could do nothing more as they were pulled under. Then I had all I could handle keeping the liapt'hs from toppling our own raft, as did those on the raft beside us.

Heckt'er and Dyit'er stabbed at one trying to reach us and I shot it. They pulled it aboard and crouched behind its lifeless form. The Symamt'h ran yellow with liapt'h blood before the others were satisfied to leave us and feast upon their own dead. We paddled in haste to the shore.

We dragged our rafts high into the grasslands, for the only way home lay once again over the river. I sank one of the paddles into the dirt and attached the end of the rope to it, so that it stretched across the water. We would want to cross back with all the speed we could manage. Then I leaned on the stick and closed my eyes. Breath of Wind, what was happening? Three dead on a youth hunt?

I heard the sound of sobbing and turned, sinking on wobbly knees to the grass. Piet'er and Cann'an tried to comfort their weeping younglings, while shivering with horror themselves. Heckt'er sat apart, pale but dry-eyed, staring at the river. Surely he didn't blame himself as he had when Bab'in died?

The thought made me wonder whether I had failed them. Timb'il had wanted to take Sark'il home, and I had stopped them. They would never go home now. Did Heckt'er blame me?

I couldn't indulge such thoughts. I was the leader, I had to keep them going. There would be time later for guilt and grief.

We had only four packs between us and two firearms; Piet'er's and Dyit'er's packs had been on the third raft, along with the last of our provisions. The herd of harrunt'hs was still two day's trek away. In the meantime, our only food was the dead liapt'h that Heckt'er had pulled onto our raft. I took out my knife and began to butcher it. Cann'an and Dam'an came to help me while Piet'er and Dyit'er silently built a fire of driftwood, encircled by rocks they had cautiously retrieved from the river shore. At night we burned the fire higher. I doubt anyone slept.

In the morning we found the harrunt'hs' trail and followed it through the grasses. They had cut a wide swath in their grazing, and we walked down it, keeping close together. In the bright sun, on the track of our game, I began to relax. We would soon reach our quarry. The wind blew our scent north to the mountains while the harrunt'hs drifted west and we followed them undetected.

Since we were now only a day behind the harrunt'hs, we slept without a fire. The night was dark and cool. The movement of the grasses increased with the rising night wind, as though with the passage of ghosts. Nobody spoke, but we were all thinking of our dead comrades.

I felt that I'd missed something: something I should have noticed, and it disturbed me. But tomorrow we would reach our game. We'd have fresh meat and our youngsters would be hunters. Then we could go home.

The wind howled, the grasses swayed, and the dark night became darker. I dreamed we were being stalked by the harrunt'hs. In my dream I gaped in confusion as a one-eyed harrunt'h closed its herbivore mouth over Heckt'er's arm, tearing into his flesh. I reached toward him but he faded, disappeared into the darkness. I could still hear his screams and I ran forward, gripped by the terror of nothing-as-it-should-be. He screamed again and the wall of nightmare that held me broke into reality. I awakened to hear Dam'an shrieking his parent's name.

The grasses waved furiously as Cann'an was pulled by some unseen force racing away from us. For a moment I hesitated, nightmare and night attack intertwined. Then I charged after him with Piet'er close behind. We couldn't shoot for fear of hitting Cann'an, and every step we took we fell behind while he and his assailant sped further and further ahead until, exhausted, defeated, we fell panting in the wake of his bloodied passage.

We returned to the youths. As we huddled together among the bruised grasses, I shivered in the cold night wind. It was then that I realized what I had over-looked.

The wind had been cool as it shook the forest treetops, cool as it chopped the broad Symamt'h into glittering wavelets. The wind was cool now as it raced in stealth between the concealing grasses. There was no hint of the heat of stillseason in the cool wind that shivered up our spines. I had convinced myself that an early stillseason was sending into premature hibernation birds and sadu'hs, fish and harrunt'hs. But Timb'il must have been right; something else hunted our forests.

"What was it?" Heckt'er asked me.

"We'll kill an extra harrunt'h," I said.

"It will be drawn to the scent of fresh blood." Piet'er understood at once.

Then Dam'an spoke: "and we will be waiting."

I saw that he knew his parent was dead, that all we could do was lay a trap for the thing that had taken him and kill it.

"You bring honor to your parent," I told him.

Walls of Wind

❧

We dropped our packs when we were close enough to hear the snorts and whistles of the herd, the tramping of their hooves and the swish of grasses when they lay and rose again. Piet'er wanted to rest until morning but I didn't trust the treacherous night to wait on us.

The herd wasn't large, a hundred beasts at most. We separated into two groups, Dyit'er and Dam'an with Piet'er, Heckt'er with me. Piet'er suggested we bring our firearms but I disagreed. Ghen do not hunt harrunt'hs with firearms. Besides, how could we shoot while our younglings were leaping onto the backs of harrunt'hs to kill them with knife and claws?

Heckt'er and I moved west, counting our steps as we circled the herd. Piet'er took Dyit'er and Dam'an to the east around the resting beasts. We hadn't finished walking when the lead buck's startled whistle rent the night and, lurching to their feet, the harrunt'hs stampeded.

I thought it must have been Dyit'er or Dam'an who alarmed them prematurely and I snorted under my breath. I had no time to think or I would have known my error, for the herd was thundering toward the east. I only had time to point to a young buck racing by us, to aim my knife at its throat as Heckt'er leaped onto it, sinking his claws into its neck. I raced after them, but I was unnecessary. By the time I arrived, Heckt'er was standing beside his first large kill. My youngling was a hunter.

I realized then that the herd had stampeded toward Piet'er and the youths, not away from them. They must have been caught in its path. But we could only step back and wait as the beasts surged past us. Then I began to wonder what had stampeded them.

I grabbed up my knife and yelled to Heckt'er to arm himself and so we were ready when the courrant'h swept down on us. It was in feeding frenzy, already bloodied with its slaughter yet seeking more. Predator, not hunter, killing beyond its need. I readied myself in its path, arms raised. Its eyes burned into mine as it crouched on its powerful legs and screamed defiance, exposing rows of reddened fangs.

It must have sensed my strength, for it swerved toward Heckt'er. He stood his ground while the beast leaped yowling toward him. It massed twice as much as he and only its face was vulnerable. The deep double thickness of matted hair that covered the rest of its body protected it not only from the mountain cold but also from the reach of knife and claw. Heckt'er's only chance was to sink his weapon into its open maw or one of its eyes, if he could do so before it tore him apart.

I've heard of grown Ghen, experienced hunters, turning and running before the charge of a courrant'h, but Heckt'er stood firm. He thrust his knife into the creature's right eye, his aim straight and deep, while the claws of his left hand raked across its sensitive nose. With a scream it twisted its face aside and its terrible fangs clamped onto his offending arm as it bore him down. I reached them then and slashed my knife across the monster's face, cursing myself for refusing to bring my firearm. It released Heckt'er's arm with a roar and turned to me.

I was full of a furious terror for my child and without hesitation I plunged my knife, fist and all, into the courrant'h's gaping jaws, and twisted. Retching and coughing, it reeled backward, dragging me over the bloodied ground, but I found my footing and thrust deeper until it groaned and fell, pulling me to my knees beside it.

∾

We found Dam'an first, trampled into the ground, almost unrecognizable, then Dyit'er, lying between the stiff legs of a yearling calf. He trembled and moaned but would not open his eyes. I carried him away where he wouldn't see the body of his parent. Piet'er must have thrown Dyit'er behind the dead calf and stood before them as long as he was able, frantically waving the charging harrunt'hs away from the path of his youngling.

Piet'er had been my friend, had trusted me. Cann'an, for all his belligerence, had followed me, and so had Timb'il. And their younglings. I should have led them home eating berries, as Timb'il wanted.

∾

Heckt'er's left arm was mangled but he was otherwise unhurt. I cleaned it and wrapped it tightly to stop the bleeding, then he helped me build a funeral pyre for Dam'an and Piet'er. I felt Dyit'er's eyes on me, almost as punishing as Heckt'er's refusal to look at me.

63

I dared not wonder what they might be thinking. I dared not think at all. Get them home, I told myself, and nothing else. Get them home, get them home… over and over, the words building a wall within my mind between the enormity of what I had done and the inadequacy of what I could now do.

For myself as well as them, I behaved with as much normalcy as I could manage. It is an insult to Wind to scorn the hunt we are given; therefore, I skinned the courrant'h while Heckt'er attended to the harrunt'h he had brought down. Together, we skinned two others the courant'h had killed. So much meat. I'd been too proud to lead my hunt home without meat. Now I had plenty of meat, and only two younglings to bring home.

We used the skins as sleds and packed the carcasses onto them, along with a fourth, half-eaten harrunt'h, which we dragged behind us. They slid over the taunting grasses with little resistance.

When we reached the Symamt'h we loaded everything onto one raft. I tied the half-eaten carcass around the edges of the other raft so that half the meat dangled into the water, and sent the baited raft down river. Using the rope I pulled us across as quickly as I could while the liapt'hs swarmed to our decoy.

ᘒ

As soon as we were in the woods I let Heckt'er and Dyit'er rest. We had a long trek ahead. I knew my forest and had no need to climb for direction, but now even the mangarr'hs had gone. A pall lay over the forest. We walked through the death-like stillness as though we were marked.

Every morning some of the meat was missing, no matter how we watched in the night. We found no footprints but our own, even when I brushed aside the leaves and twigs on the forest floor to leave damp soil exposed around us.

"It's only mangarr'hs sneaking down the trees to snatch pieces of meat and scurry up again," I reassured Heckt'er and Dyit'er. But it bothered me more than I let on. I showed them both how to use Cann'an's firearm.

Dyit'er believed the thing that hungered between the hushed trees was only a sly mongarr'h. Dyit'er trusted my judgment, as had every parent and youth who died on this hunt, may I some day be forgiven. During the night, on his watch, Dyit'er left the circle of our campfire to relieve himself behind a tree.

Even a great hunter can be broken by being awakened too often with death at his campfire. Even great pride can be shaken by too many losses, too many miscalculations. I grabbed my firearm and ran toward the sudden silence where Dyit'er's scream had broken off, pausing only to order Heckt'er to stay by the fire.

I found no trace of Dyit'er, not then, not in the morning. I saw signs of a struggle: snapped branches, blood spattered on leaves and soil. But I found only Dyit'er's footprints stamped into the bloody ground, round and round, as though he had attacked himself, then charged away into the woods. I followed the bloody prints till they were hidden by the fallen leaves, calling his name among the silent trees.

I was responsible for Dyit'er's disappearance. He was a youth in my care and I had failed him. I struggled again to push my thoughts aside, and yet they ate at me. Neither my pride nor my strength nor my skill nor my weapons had kept my companions alive. We were prey in our own forest. We were meat pretending to be carrying meat back to our people.

Heckt'er and I still had ten days' journey home through a forest I no longer knew. For the first time, I was afraid. I wanted to send my child to burrow, like the sadu'hs. I wanted to hide him, quiet and still in the treetops, like the birds. We were too far from our home, too far from safety.

We abandoned most of the meat, carrying only what we needed, and I pushed us to greater speed. Heckt'er was hurting badly, almost despairing. Dyit'er had been a close friend, had trained with him and accepted him despite the age difference, when most of the others hadn't. I told him that I would collect a party of armed hunters as soon as I got him home, and we would find Dyit'er; but he knew Dyit'er was already dead. I was too sick at heart to convince him otherwise. Sick with my failure, sick with fear for him.

We traveled for three days undisturbed. I began to hope that whatever prowled the spectral woods had been satisfied with poor Dyit'er and the harrunt'h meat we left behind.

Seven days from home. I barely slept. I was hallucinating with exhaustion when I finally lay on my mat. Heckt'er wakened me almost at once it seemed, but the night was half over and I felt a little better. I suspected he would have given me longer except that his own eyes were closing beyond his power to prevent. I rose and sat by the fire, making him sleep so close I could touch him.

I have never dozed on a watch before. I have never been so depleted, and I was lulled by four days without incident. Once, twice, my eyelids drooped and twice I startled into panicked wakefulness to find the night quiet around me. Against my will I dozed.

Sudden movement and Heckt'er's surprised cry awoke me in time to see the skins with the last of our harrunt'h meat disappearing behind a bushy cappa. Heckt'er leaped up to give chase and I lunged for him, grabbed his legs and pulled him down. I dragged him back to the fire and held him, though he did not struggle, held him tight against me with one arm while the other held my firearm, aimed into the darkness.

We were not disturbed again that night. At the first light of dawn we stamped out our fire and packed our mats, canteens and firearms. I spent a few minutes examining the trail of the skin, looking for clues to the fiend that shadowed us, but the skin had swept the ground clear except, here and there, for what appeared to be our own footprints.

We had not come from this direction. We hadn't stood in this spot, yet there were the partial imprints of our feet! I wondered in horror if something preternatural stalked us, leaving our own footprints behind. I was being mocked, my hunting skill exposed in all its sham!

It is my Pride, I thought, grown beyond control, taking on a malignant life of its own. My fears blew wild, toward madness. It only attacks when I sleep! It's after Heckt'er, because he's become the focus of my Pride. I was cold and trembling and I stopped looking for clues, more afraid of what I might learn than of being pursued. I returned to Heckt'er and we left.

Six days from home; five if Heckt'er could keep the pace I set. Even I could not make it in less. Five days with no provisions, only the water in our water skins and what we could find on the trail. Five days and four nights from safety.

It came again the next night. I sensed its baleful presence at the edge of our campfire, waiting for sleep to disarm me.

"There's something there," I said, willing now to strip my youngling of his confidence in me, if fear might save him.

"I've felt it," he said. "I've tried to become it, but it's not... I can't think like it."

A shiver of madness blew through me as his words confirmed my fears, but I also felt a thrill of pride. Under the shadow of death, Heckt'er still thought like a hunter. In the presence of demons, my youngling could not be made prey. And then I was more afraid than ever, because he fed my Pride even as I fought to subdue it.

"You can't think like the thing that pursues us," I said, bitterly. Heckt'er was not proud. Heckt'er had let the other youths go before him, had let them find the signs of harrunt'h, that they might learn what he already knew. Heckt'er used his skill to help his people.

I dared not sleep that night. The thing that prowled at the edge of our fire's light did not sleep either, but my watch held it at bay. In the daytime we traveled, pushing ourselves almost beyond endurance. Four days from home. Three nights away from safety.

We stumbled on until the gathering dark obscured our way and then I panicked, afraid my unwillingness to stop had made us wait too long to find enough firewood for a full night's fire. I slashed at living limbs with my knife, unwilling to let Heckt'er move out of my sight to gather dead branches on the ground. I needed a bright fire, but even a smoky one would do. Another hunting party might see it. We were almost near enough to meet with one and I was ready to accept any help that came to us.

It wasn't Ghen we saw that night, drawn to our fire. At first I thought the two eyes were embers, glowing through the smoke. Then they moved closer and I saw its body, pale in the darkness. The exact shape was obscured by wisps of smoke but it massed no more than I. That threw me off; that and my sleep-deprived deliriums, for I was half expecting to see myself, or some nightmare figure, the specter of my Pride. I suppose that, too, was pride, to think that only I could defeat myself.

Beside me, Heckt'er whispered softly, "Broghen."

Too small, I thought, too pale. But I recognized the crazed look in its eyes, the hideous deformity, the mix of fur and scales, the gaping jaw and vicious rows of teeth. It should have been taller but it was still fearsome, broader and more powerful than I, even at the same height. I felt, for an instant, limp with relief that I was not insane, then Heckt'er said, more firmly, "Broghen."

His voice broke the fire's spell and the monster lunged for him. I threw myself between them and felt its claws rake down my side sending lines of fire across my ribs and tearing my left leg open to the bone.

I fired sideways and knew the shot was poor but the Broghen howled and reared back. Heckt'er fired over me but he was inexperienced and only grazed the brute. It turned and fled into the woods. I reloaded and fired into the path of its retreat but it was too far away. I could hear in the distance the sound of slapping branches as it escaped. Worse, I had used the last of my ammunition. All we had left was a single shot in Cann'an's firearm, and our knives.

Heckt'er bound my leg and cut me a strong stick to lean upon and we traveled hard. At least I knew now why we had found only Ghen-like footprints. If it had been full-sized I might have guessed, for even half-obliterated as the prints had been, I would have seen they were too large to be ours.

Every step drove pain through the length of my leg, and every breath spread fire across my ribs. By afternoon I was feverish and the dressing on my leg was soaked with new blood, yet we hurried on. We had no respite but home.

At dusk we stopped. Heckt'er built a fire and watched while I slept until dark. When he wakened me, I sat against the wide trunk of a large ugappa with the firearm in one hand and my knife in the other. He fed the fire higher and placed several large pieces of wood where I could reach them easily, then I ordered him up into the ugappa to sleep wedged in its branches. Broghen cannot climb, but neither could I with my wounded leg. At first Heckt'er refused to leave me, but I insisted. He would be safe there even if I failed him.

Perhaps I dozed. Perhaps I was delirious with fever. But deep in the night I was abruptly awake and I was not alone.

I couldn't see it. It was beyond the light of the fire, waiting in the night, circling me, trying to gauge the extent of my weakness. I tensed, sweating in the cool wind, straining for the hushed sound of a footfall, the faint expel of breath, the barest movement of leaves.

To the left—behind me, but the ugappa shielded my back—to the right— pause—behind me again—pause. My hands gripped tightly the handles of my knife and firearm, my heart pounded and my leg throbbed in unison, but I was aware only of the threatening, soft sounds just beyond the perimeter of my sight. I dared not shoot blind.

To the right of me again. Pause.

There was a rustle in the tree overhead, very slight. I could tell by the weight that it was only a mongarr'h, maybe two. I didn't worry. Heckt'er would be a match for two mongarr'hs. It was the Broghen I must keep him safe from.

Why didn't it move? Had it circled around behind me again? I turned back to the left and in that moment it rushed from the shadows on my right.

As though in slow motion I swung my firearm, its muzzle drawing a large semi-circle in time, too much time, between the beast's spring and my aim. A single moment of unreadiness and I was its prey.

It was almost upon me when a small form dropped from the branches overhead. The blade of his knife reflected a gleam from the fire and I heard a snarl of surprise as the knife sank home. The Broghen pulled short its spring and reached for the fierce young hunter clinging to its back.

"No!" I screamed.

But already it had torn loose Heckt'er's hold and even with Heckt'er's knife buried to the hilt in its neck it pulled him around and sank its vicious fangs into his throat, bearing him down under it as it fell. I lurched over, afraid to shoot in case I hit Heckt'er. The Broghen was already dying as I clawed it aside frantically, but I fired my last shot into it, then dropped to my knees beside Heckt'er.

"Don't be a great hunter," I cried as I gathered his still form into my arms, "Be only my living child!"

℃

I couldn't burn Heckt'er's body. I carried him, as I had when he was a babe and I first took him into the woods. For a day and a night I walked, carrying my youngling home.

When my leg gave I rested on my knees, bent over his body, till I could rise again. I dropped the first canteen when it was empty, and then the second. When I fell at last and knew I could rise no more, I made a fire. I burned the green wood of the cappa I fell beside. Heckt'er's body was cold as I lay beside him, as cold as the forest shadows, as cold as the wind that would never wake him again. They found me that way, delirious, almost dead, beside the body of my child.

℃

I will no longer hunt but I teach every youth who comes to me to be a fine hunter, better than I.

Walls of Wind

I teach them that there are four large predators on Wind: the cold-blooded liapt'h that *winn* in the wetlands, the fierce courrant'h that prowls in the mountains, the *raging* Broghen that hungers to the south, and the hunter who feeds his *pride* instead of his people.

Council Relations

Briarris

I went with Ocallis to visit Mant'er after they'd carried him home. We entered the front door of the infirmary, a one-story building constructed, like Council Hall, around an inner courtyard. It was less imposing because it lacked the extra height, but was in fact as long and twice as wide, so that the courtyard was a square rather than a rectangle.

The external verandah was fully enclosed. Its many wide windows were framed by wooden shutters which could close as tightly as a house in still-season, to allow the Bria healers access to their patients' rooms. Illness and accidents do not wait on seasons.

Many of the doors along this front hall were open, indicating that the room was occupied. The rooms were small, housing a single patient, and windowless, since they backed on three sides onto other patients' rooms. Despite the open doors, which faced the wide windows of the verandah, and the fans that turned year-round, the place had a heavy, breathless feel to it that nauseated me.

We were directed through to the inner verandah which, being on the Ghen side of the infirmary, was open to the wind. Mant'er's room was on the far side of the courtyard. At Council Hall the courtyard was planted with grasses and flowers, with single ugappas here and there to add height, and trios of cappa bushes in each corner; a lovely place to walk in. This was the first time I'd seen the infirmary's courtyard and I was shocked to behold a shadowy forest of ugappas and cappas. I'd seen their tops above the building, of course, but had had no idea how densely wooded it was.

I was about to suggest we take the long way around, by the verandah, when Ocallis, anxious to see Mant'er, struck out into the trees. Reminding myself that we were still in the heart of the city, that there could be nothing other than birds and perhaps a few harmless sadu'hs among these dark trees, I followed him.

My heart was still panting from the oppressive courtyard when I stumbled into Mant'er's room behind Ocallis. Wind's breath, he was a mess: cut and bruised and blistered from dehydration, his left leg wound round with dressing from groin to foot, and raised to ease the swelling.

His eyes were open but he didn't notice us. He was looking at his hands, opening and closing them with a kind of desperate disbelief at finding them empty. It reminded me of an incident in my childhood when I'd been admiring my parent's favorite glass ornament and unintentionally dropped it. The suddenness with which it shattered beyond retrieval stunned me. Mant'er looked that way, now.

Ocallis sat on the floor beside his mat and signed to him something that temporarily lifted his despair, judging from the brief lightening of his countenance. I squatted beside Ocallis, dumb with pity. I had to stop myself from looking at Mant'er's hands when he began opening and closing them again.

Before he rose to leave, Ocallis blew into Mant'er's face. I looked aside, shocked and embarrassed, and rose quickly to leave. Ocallis soon followed. He stepped briskly out of the room, across the verandah and down into the trees—where he fell against me weeping. I held him there in the shadows where no one could see us until my arms ached and he had no more tears to shed but shuddered dry-eyed against my dampened fur. Then I helped him home and onto his sleeping ledge. As I turned to go, he said, "I'm going to have Mant'er's second youngling."

I stopped and stared at him. He sat with his legs hanging over the side of his ledge, weary with sorrow. Finally I managed to stammer, "But you already have your children."

"I can still carry his."

"Ocallis," I said, trying to hide my agitation, "You can't have more younglings. Let him mate someone else. Someone who would have Bria children also, to justify the horror of birthing a Broghen."

"He wouldn't. You saw how he is. Even if Chair Ghen ordered him, he wouldn't go to Festival Hall."

"You can't replace Heckt'er," I said, as gently as I could.

"I'm not trying to replace Heckt'er. I'm trying to save Mant'er."

72

Wind's breath, Ocallis loved him! Loved a Ghen, was going to put himself through unbelievable horror for two years for him. They were no longer joined, it was time Ocallis let go.

"Ocallis, he is Ghen." My parent's words came back to me. "Ghen leave, Ocallis. That's the way it is. Ghen leave us."

He turned to me with a fury I'd never seen on his face. "What does it matter if he sleeps in my house or in the compound? He hasn't left! He lives in my city, he guards the wall for me. Ghen don't leave us, Briarris. They're part of our lives. Forever." He slumped, exhausted from his outburst. "I need to sleep," he said, dismissing me.

e/&

The day after Heckt'er's funeral, Anarris asked to speak to me. When he wouldn't be put off, I agreed to see him in one of the meeting rooms reserved for councilors. This one was small, with only a single table and three or four chairs.

"May the wind give you sight," I said, not rising from my chair. Anarris paused mid-stride, then continued into the room. I didn't ordinarily speak so formally, but I was emotionally drained and had agreed to this meeting only at his insistence.

"Wind in your face." Anarris's curt half-statement of the appropriate response let me know that he wouldn't be put off by my formality. "I'm here because the Bria with Single-by-Choice are afraid there's going to be pressure put on them to mate."

"Parents want to be grandparents," I said wearily. "I can't stop that."

"I'm referring to the Ghen fiasco."

"The Ghen fiasco?" I spoke quietly: a bad sign, if he'd heeded it.

"Getting so many of themselves killed on a foolish hunt. They choose a life of danger, then act as though we owe them something when it backfires."

"Strange how they persist in wanting to eat every day."

"They don't have to hunt to eat. They choose to be flesh-eaters."

"There aren't enough milk callans and laying fowl to feed both the Ghen and the Bria." But my argument was half-hearted; however much I sympathized with Mant'er's suffering, eating flesh repelled me as much as it did any Bria.

"Let them cut down some of the forest for more farmland."

He really had no idea how the Ghen felt about their forest. Not that he would care. I looked at him coolly. This had gone far enough.

"Eleven Ghen died, and one is in the infirmary. He had to be carried to attend the funeral of his youngling."

"I consider them Lost-by-Choice."

His words revolted me, but they caught my attention. Had I been too immersed in my sibling's sorrow to recognize the building mood of the Bria? I'd never been overly sympathetic to Ghen who died on a hunting trip before. Rare as it was, it had seemed a sort of rough justice on flesh-eaters. Was the antipathy between Ghen and Bria becoming so strong that even the death of youths meant little to us? For the first time, I was afraid for my city. Fear made me harsh.

"You wanted something of me?" The coldness in my voice brought him up short. Good. Let him remember that I was not the one who ought to watch my tongue.

"I'm not here for myself," he muttered sulkily. I touched my breath perfunctorily.

"We thought, an announcement from Council. Something to the effect that…" he paused and I waited to hear how he would phrase it. "…that sad as this incident is, Bria shouldn't feel obligated to act against their beliefs."

"Maybe they should reconsider their obligations."

"Shouldn't be pressured to do so."

He was young and arrogant and foolish, but he was trying to work with me. And I was Council Relations. If I couldn't maintain the tenuous link I had formed between Council and him and his followers, they would blow free, and only the wind knew what measures they might resort to. For a moment I envied him his short-sightedness, his single-eyed view of our City. How clearly the eye can see from only one perspective.

Wait till he heard what Ocallis proposed to do!

I controlled my expression, hiding the dread that thought sent through me. Instead, I sighed, deliberately letting him hear the wind that bound us all.

"I can work with that," I told him.

He left without thanking me. I was just as glad; it wasn't a welcomed task, however necessary.

Sacrifices

Rennis

*I*am climbing Temple Hill at the southeast edge of the city. There is such lassitude in my muscles that I'm panting with the effort of merely moving forward. The air is almost motionless—I feel tiny puffs of heat that die out as they reach me. I struggle against nausea and dizziness. If I can make it to the top before the breeze stops altogether, I will be able to rest in the Temple winds.

Huge slabs of rock placed about the top of the hill stretch up into the sky just ahead of me. Within them are large, rotating blades that send stiff cross-currents all over Temple Hill. From deep in the heart of the hill comes the quiet hum of the pumps which maintain the year-round movement of those fans.

The effect is inexpressible: mesmerizing and inspiring. Wherever one stands on Temple Hill, one feels oneself to be at the very center of Wind, the focus point on which all winds converge. Pious Bria come here to pray and meditate, to remind ourselves that the Creator Wind has entrusted us to be the heart of Wind.

A Bria child is climbing beside me. I know him to be my youngling, although I have none as yet, in reality.

"Look, we're almost there," he pipes in his child's voice. I lift my head, but my eye is closed and I cannot open it. In my dream I do not wonder where his sibling is; I am concerned only about my eye.

"Open your eye, Matri," he says, puzzled.

"I can't." I force a small laugh, hiding my alarm. "It's very silly, sweetbreath. I'm not hurt, I just can't open my eye."

I've reassured him too well; he scrambles ahead, leaving me. I call out to him but perhaps he doesn't hear. The muscles of my throat are weakening as the air becomes more and more still. I must reach the top and feel the Creator's breath blowing into me.

The fur on my head ruffles slightly. My ears twitch; I'm almost there. With the last of my strength I stumble upwards, three, four, six steps, until I can feel the wind around me. I suck it into my lungs with a sob of relief.

The wind in the direction of my closed eye sputters and stops. I turn, gasping for breath, and the breeze from that direction also dies.

"Stop it! Stop it, Matri!" the child's voice cries, only now he is a Ghen child. What is a Ghen child doing on Temple Hill? Why does he call me 'Matri'? How is it that I even understand him? I know I should stand still, but I can't help turning, gasping in the effort to draw the motionless air into my lungs. Every fan my blind eye turns toward sputters to a stop until the very Temple of the Wind is as lifeless as stillseason...

I awoke from my dream drenched in sweat, sobbing for air even though the strong midseason wind blew in upon me through my open window. For a few moments I feared that my eye was still sealed shut but then I saw a scattering of stars outside my window and realized it was only the dark of night that blinded me.

Despite the cool wind coming through my window, I was still gripped by the desolate feeling that the Wind had withdrawn from me. Even in stillseason, I had never known such a sense of abandonment. I reminded myself that the Creator is not merely the wind, real or artificial. I know the Trinity of Life, which we all learn from childhood: Wind the Creator, Wind the world we live on, and wind the movement of air which is His breath. They are separate and yet they are all one. And in my dream, they had all deserted me. My feeling of personal loss was intense. It was almost a relief to hear Saft'ir's even breathing from his sleeping mat across the room.

༄

I remembered that dream now, nearly a year later, as I approached the Ghen funeral dais. Perhaps it's as wrong for me to participate in a Ghen religious service as I had believed the presence of the Ghen child on Temple Hill to be? But Wind has already abandoned me; what more have I to fear?

The Ghen funeral dais was a large, wooden structure that built along the side of the northernmost wall of the city. It was large enough to hold six to eight Ghen and Bria and was dyed blood-red, the symbol of death and of life.

Although I knew the bright yellow-red was made from a blend of ruberries and the centers of yellowhead flowers, it was so similar to blood color I had to force myself to climb up the three steps onto it, half expecting it to be wet and sticky under my feet. Holding my arms still at my sides, I mounted it without a word.

They positioned me behind Saft'ir's urn, between Council Chair and Chair Ghen. Savannis, the Voice of Wind, who teaches religious history to our children and gives us spiritual advice, stood beside Council Chair. On the other side of Chair Ghen stood the Ghen spiritual advisor, Mick'al.

I agreed to attend Saft'ir's funeral only at my parent's insistence. I stared rigidly above the heads of the huge crowd of Ghen and Bria gathered around the dais, waiting for the ceremony to be over.

Mick'al spoke first. The muscles in my face tightened as I imagined him referring to the Creator as the "Hunter", as I've heard they do. Mick'al was probably glorifying Saft'ir's death as a "noble sacrifice".

Because Saft'ir chose to die upon the wall—by his own hand, his heart torn on his own knife—because he waited out his watch then died, they call Saft'ir a hero.

Hero! A coward and a suicide and a murderer! Saft'ir's sacrifice! Saft'ir's revenge, more accurately.

The positions I took on Council infuriated him. I saw it in his measuring eyes, in his cool silences the morning after Council when he'd read Chair Ghen's translations. He presumed too much. I wanted to tell him so, to reach an understanding, but we didn't have enough language between us yet. The fact that we had joined, that he had stirred to life my infant seeds and I'd accepted his seed into my womb, the fact that we shared a house and would continue to do so for three more years—what right did any of this give him over my opinions? Or, for that matter, give me over his?

He had a right to expect courtesy, and so did I. I had a right to expect harmony of life-style, and so did he. He had a right to expect me to guard my health for the sake of all our infants. And so did I have that same right of him! Over my mind he had no claim at all—yet he persisted.

Naturally he disliked my issues. I am, after all, as committed to removing Ghen from Council as Briarris is. My reasons were different, however. I didn't dislike Ghen; I merely served the Creator. Having placed Bria upon

Wind to civilize it, He surely intended that Bria should guide that civilization. Ghen barely believe in the Creator, having turned their urge to worship Him into an adoration of the hunt. How could our city be the monument to the Creator that it was meant to be, if it was even partly ruled by those who held such false beliefs?

Mick'al's harsh Ghen voice, raised to carry across the listening crowd, grated in my ears. I flattened them against my head, knowing that my parent would later scold me for rudeness. My hands unconsciously cradled my swelling abdomen as Mick'al's voice reminded me of the day I heard of Saft'ir's death.

తా

It was the morning after Briarris and I won our motion, a Council seat for unjoined Bria. I rose at dawn and left my house. I walked through the city warm in my pleasure over our accomplishment, only turning back when I was sure that Saft'ir had had time to return from the wall, to eat his breakfast reading Chair Ghen's summary of Council as he always did; had had time to gnash his teeth and scowl in my absence, then get to bed to sleep away the exhaustion of night watch.

Returning from my walk, I was surprised to see motion through my front window. Opening the door I saw my parent, Maaris, with Naft'ur, the Ghen who was joined with him when I was born. I was even more surprised to see Chair Ghen and Council Chair waiting with them. Maaris had boiled a pot of water at my cookwall. He dropped dried ruberry leaves into it, waiting silently as they steeped.

Surely they weren't here to discuss my Council decision? The motion had already passed. I wondered where Saft'ir was, suspecting that he was behind this. Such silly thoughts annoying me.

At my parent's urging we sat around the table, wordlessly watching as he set steaming mugs of tea before us. The five of us filled every chair. Council Chair told me then. Even as I listened, I looked about for Saft'ir, unable to comprehend that he was dead. I felt a distant regret as for a friend whom I had known briefly, and then a thrill of revulsion at the news that he had died by his own hand; followed by guilt, as though my vote the night before to increase Bria seats on Council had somehow precipitated his violent death, although he couldn't have known of the motion before his watch had ended. Still I felt guilty that somehow my very opinions had done him harm.

Then I saw my parent's eye drop briefly to my abdomen and quickly turn away and I remembered the precious life quickening within me, waiting for future mating to mature and bring it forth.

"My babies," I whispered, falling backward against the chair. I caught the edge of the table to steady myself, my other hand resting over my abdomen. Feeling its swelling roundness, my hysteria grew.

"My babies!"

Naft'ur reached for me but I pushed him away, rising and screaming now, "My babies! Breath of Wind, my babies!"

I struggled even against Maaris as he tried to comfort me. His sobs, his anguished cries, "Rennis, Rennis!" his arms attempting to hold me, only ignited me further and I howled, over and over, "My babies! My babies! He has murdered my babies!"

∽

Upon the dais, I closed my eye.

Feeling Council Chair's hand grasp my arm, I straightened quickly and reopened my eye, inadvertently catching expressions of pity on the faces at the front of the crowd. I shifted my gaze to Savannis, who had stepped forward to speak.

"Death and birth are the same," he said. "They are a window, which is in itself nothing; a space cut out of something larger, through which the Creator's breath blows both ways. In our homes we, like Him, build parallel openings, for who can trap the wind? It will not enter without an exit. So life and death are both openings, through which Wind blows us into brief existence here, then back to Him again."

The hot endseason wind moved sluggishly around us, igniting the scorn within me. Savannis's losses were metaphoric; mine were real.

Savannis had come to speak to me the day after Saft'ir died. I had expected him to see Saft'ir's suicide as I did—a betrayal of his parental obligation in the very middle of procreation. When he spoke instead of "the will of Wind,"

I ordered him out of my house. As he left, he said he hoped I might come to understand some day.

"Understand! Understand a murderer? May the Wind give me Broghen before I understand Saft'ir!"

The very thought of it, as I stood upon the dais, made me ill with rage. That and the sight of every Ghen in the city standing at attention as Chair Ghen delivered the final eulogy. When he finished, Council Chair stepped forward.

It was hard to watch the sorrowing attention of the Ghen to Chair Ghen's unintelligible words, but it was worse to hear his praise of Saft'ir translated by Council Chair into my own language, the musical, lilting language of the Bria. I felt betrayed to see so many Bria weeping, and when I saw my parent was among them, I had to grit my teeth to keep from screaming out my rage.

Anger gave me strength. I rode my anger, rode it like a tempest in fear and trembling even while I lashed it higher; because, beneath the fury of my transport, grief waited for me. Such an agony of grief, waiting to entangle me and hold me still, as still as the dying infants within me, condemned by Saft'ir's death.

I had gone to the funeral house where Saft'ir's body lay waiting to be cremated. I was afraid of the Bria and Ghen I would meet there, afraid of the pity in their eyes, sharp enough to pierce my brittle anger. But I had to see his body, had to see and hold in my mind the physical image of our children's killer. I went, keeping my eye downcast, leaning on my parent—despite my anger, I could barely walk unsupported.

The door was open. Saft'ir lay stretched out on a long, low table in the center of the front room. Behind the table, the inside door, which led to the crematorium in the back, was closed. I stared down at his body. His left eye was swollen and bruised. I'd been told that a courrant'h had attacked him. The portion of the wall he guarded still bore the marks of its claws where it had tried to climb into our city before he killed it.

I could see the wounds he had sustained, vicious-looking bites and lacerations, but they need not have been fatal. I almost wished I could believe they were, looking at him so still and lost, even though it would have robbed me of my anger. But no, there was the cut, red and raw across his chest, where he had plunged his own dagger deep and ripped downward, not only through his own heart, no, through four!

I felt the three fetuses trapped within me twist as I looked at it, as I reached out with my finger and touched it, cold, repelling. I brought my finger to my mouth to taste death and it was even colder against my lips, so cold it burned. As cold as the ache within my womb.

He hadn't been mortally wounded. He did not need to die. Ah, but he understood the power of the martyr, and he was right. No more motions were being made to evict Ghen from Council now. He had defeated me. Was that worth our children's lives?

I was silent at his funeral, as I promised my parent. Only for a moment did I let down my anger. Not for sorrow, no, for a fierce joy when Saft'ir's ashes were thrown to ride the wind into the forest beyond the wall he guarded. It seemed to me, as I watched them scatter on the air, not an honor as the Ghen believed, but a disposal.

Then the Ghen in solemn unison raised their arms over their heads, claws fully retracted, and turned their backs to the wall to signify that even in death, Saft'ir's spirit guarded the wall so vigilantly that they may expose themselves defenseless behind it.

I walked to the steps and down from the dais, as though I believed the ceremony had ended, avoiding the ritual bow to the warrior's kin. Let Saft'ir's parent accept it. I was no kin of Saft'ir's and his child, dying within me, surely owed him no duty. I made my way through the crowd to Maaris, who helped me home without comment. Good. Silence was all I asked of anyone.

In silence I moved about my house and in silence I made my way to Council when I was stronger. I accepted the unjoined Bria seat I'd fought for, and for which I had lost so much.

In silence I voted. In silence I climbed Temple Hill, longing for answers, until the Wind's silence drove me away. For this, too, I blamed Saft'ir; it was he who weighted my prayers with such bitterness they could no longer ascend to the Creator Wind.

I moved slowly, my body bent over my abdomen as though protecting an open wound. My legs, too heavy to lift, shuffled along the ground, my ears drooped against my head, unresponsive to the sounds of the living around me. Was it just a week ago that I hurried down this same street buoyed up by the thought of all that I intended to accomplish, the years of my life blowing ahead of me like a joyous breeze? Now only the dust of the road rose to meet me, the ground pulled at me with every footfall, and my life loomed ahead as tedious, as repellant, as stillseason. I carried my unborn babies heavy within me. I would carry them in my womb until they died. Everything else was irrelevant.

☙

Approaching my house only two weeks after the funeral, I noticed two figures inside: heavy, solid shapes. Their silver-gray scales caught the setting sun as it fell through the window, reflecting flashes of light as they moved. Had they been still, I might not have noticed them. Already I was close enough to make out the glint of their long, sharp teeth as they spoke.

I drew back quickly. My hands fluttered involuntarily in fear and denial as their presence invoked the morning Saft'ir died. Then my rage rose up again. For the sake of my babies, I hated Saft'ir and for the sake of Saft'ir, I hated all Ghen.

"Get out!" I screamed, throwing open my door. "Get out of my house!" My words were Bria, but the meaning was clear. They stood transfixed. I glared at them, panting like one maddened. Maaris hurried over. "Rennis, they came to help," he said, "listen to them."

I shook his hand from my arm, still pointing to the open door. I didn't speak, afraid I might weep with anger, and it be mistaken for weakness.

"Rennis!" Maaris cried louder, "for the sake of your unborn children, listen to them!"

I almost struck him, for all that he was my matri. I might have, if I'd known how. Instead I fell to the floor, hating the frailty in me, hating the strength in Naft'ur as he rushed to my side. The other one hesitated, awkward, afraid to touch me.

I won't break, I thought. I'm not as fragile as you assume by this weakness in my legs. For two weeks I've carried death inside me. How could you, with your living bodies, harm me? The thought braced me. I allowed Naft'ur to help me to a chair while Maaris closed the door.

"This is Gant'i," Maaris said, seeing that I was looking at the Ghen beside Naft'ur. I recognized him then, Saft'ir's friend. I'd seen him when I joined with Saft'ir. At first I thought he was going to take my hand, until Saft'ir stepped ahead of him and reached for me.

82

Gant'i was looking at me intently, as though his gaze could draw understanding from me, or offer it. I turned coldly away.

Maaris and Naft'ur signed rapidly together, something I hadn't seen since his child was weaned and he left us to return to the Ghen compound. While they signed, I thought over Maaris's words: "…for the sake of your unborn children."

Ghen understand childbirth; they assist at every labor. Was it possible they knew a way to bring my infants to maturity and birth? I felt the cruel beginnings of hope weaken me. My parent cleared his throat and I looked up.

"Rennis, the Ghen have been talking," he began. "Saft'ir is a great hero to them…" He hesitated, and well he might. I flattened my ears and widened my eye to show my scorn.

"They feel it would be a great loss if Saft'ir's child and yours, also, were not given life. Gant'i has offered—Rennis, consider this carefully, before you decide—Gant'i is offering to take Saft'ir's place. To join with you. Chair Ghen has agreed to it. But Naft'ur says to warn you there may be risks, to you, and to the babies…"

I stared at her, the stirring hope bitter in my breast, but all I could say was, "Isn't Gant'i joined already?" I'd never heard of a Ghen who didn't join as soon as he reached adulthood.

"No. Naft'ur says the Bria he wished to join with chose another, and he was permitted to wait before choosing again. It was his decision to offer to help you." Maaris paused. "He seems to be a Ghen of much understanding."

Don't push me, Matri, I thought. But, may Wind forgive me, I was already considering it. Until I remembered: "What of his own seed?"

Maaris conferred with Naft'ur, who spoke to Gant'i. I watched Gant'i closely. This time it was I, trying to fathom him. Was he another Saft'ir? The very thought was surprising; weren't they all the same? But I wanted to hope. I wanted to break free of the anger that was suffocating me, even while it kept me from despair.

Naft'ur signed to Maaris, who turned to me. "Gant'i says to thank you for your concern, and to tell you there are things that can be done… potions, I think, to help his child-to-be mature more quickly. You'd have to mate again midseason, so that Gant'i can mate with you three times, even though you are ready for second mating. It's also possible to delay third mating a little, but you would be uncomfortable. Even with all that, there are no guaranties. His infant may still die. But it's very likely he'd survive, and the three you carry as well."

At that moment my anger, sitting like ice inside me, shattered. I wept as I have never wept before or since. I wept for my unborn children and Saft'ir's, and for Gant'i's unsuspecting child-to-be. I wept for the sacrifice of innocents and the silence of Wind, and for myself, that I must make a choice between one child and three. I wept to think that I could even consider going from Saft'ir, who had sacrificed his child, to Gant'i, who was willing to sacrifice his. And finally I wept because I feared that I would do it, because life was no more than a series of sacrifices and in the end I'd accept any terms that would give my own younglings life. Creator of Wind, forgive me. Forgive us all.

I didn't notice when the two Ghen left. I wept for several removes, while Maaris sat beside me. He didn't speak or touch me, for which I was grateful. He wouldn't lessen my grief with platitudes and did not try to hold me from it. He let me cry. When I was done, he set out bowls of stew, and bread, and fresh, hot tea on the table, and we took what nourishment we could.

"What are you going to do?" he finally asked, removing our bowls and bringing us each a second mug of tea.

"I'm going to find a way to have my babies," I said. I felt a small movement in my womb and smiled grimly. I would have touched my belly, cradled the tiny lives inside, but my pre-mating rash had come up and it hurt even to move, now that the pain was no longer blocked by anger. "First I'll visit Vixannis."

Maaris touched his breath in agreement. "All things conspire for good on the Creator's Wind."

I forgave him that because he hadn't once uttered a platitude during my despair.

⁊

It was terrible walking through the nearly airless streets alone. I had to force myself to take each step. Vixannis was surprised to see me at his door, so near to stillseason.

"Rennis," he said, pausing awkwardly. "…I'm sorry about…"

84

"Thank you," I said. When he didn't stand aside, I had to ask: "May I come in?"

He could see my breasts were weeping, even though my fur hid the dark rash on my belly. Didn't he want relief as much as I?

"Of course," he said, opening the door wider and stepping back. "I didn't expect you."

Now I was the one who didn't know what to say. Vixannis and Ragn'ar were our co-joining pair, after all. Ragn'ar had been my ritual second mate, at my and Saft'ir's first mating last stillseason. We wouldn't have co-mated again this year, but Vixannis and I should still be soothing each others' rashes.

As soon as I stepped inside I saw the reason for his awkwardness. I didn't know the name of the Bria sitting beside the shuttered window, but it was obvious that he and Vixannis had been in the process of administering to each others' rash.

"I didn't think you'd be coming," Vixannis repeated, sounding a little defensive.

"No, I'm late... I understand, but..." I gestured helplessly at my seeping breasts.

"Of course. I should have known, I should have come to you. I'm sorry."

He was right. He should have known, and he could have made it easier by coming to me. Then I remembered how unapproachable I'd been.

"It's my fault for waiting so long," I said. "Of course you didn't want to come and ask."

"Looks like I'm not needed here," the other Bria said, interrupting our insincere apologies. He stood up, revealing himself to be a year younger than I, about to have first mating, and motioned to his Ghen mate, who'd accompanied him.

"We could... we could all help each other," I suggested, embarrassed.

The strange Bria laughed. "That's not necessary. We," he gestured to include the Ghen, "already have a co-joined pair. I was just helping Vixannis." He glanced at my abdomen. "I hope you find a solution."

"I hope so, too," I murmured.

⁊

By the time Vixannis and I finished soothing our rashes with each others' breast fluid, our earlier awkwardness was forgotten. He offered me some ruberry tea before I left.

I accepted, adding that I wanted to talk to him and Ragn'ar.

When we sat down with our tea, Vixannis's expression was guarded.

"I think you can guess what I want to talk about," I began. "I need a Ghen to mate me…" I looked sideways at Ragn'ar.

"You need to join with another Ghen," Vixannis nodded. "Ragn'ar told me a Ghen named Gant'i has offered. I'm glad for you, Rennis. When you didn't come, I assumed you'd chosen a new co-joining pair."

"You don't understand."

"Yes, I do, really. I know it's hard. Seeing me must remind you… well, I'm glad you're staying with us. I'm sure Ragn'ar won't mind co-mating again, for Gant'i's child. I'll ask him."

"Vixannis! That's not what I want you to ask him. Let me talk."

Vixannis looked down at the table. He took a quick gulp of tea, not meeting my eye. His discomfort worried me, but I made my request anyway. I had to try.

"No," he said, when I was done.

"No? You won't even ask Ragn'ar?"

"You need a joined mate, Rennis. Gant'i has offered."

"I don't need a joined mate, I only need third mating. I told you, Saft'ir and I mated early, just before he died. Even though it wasn't in stillseason, I'm sure it'll do for a second mating. I only need Ragn'ar to mate me once, next stillseason."

"Who will deliver your babies?"

"Naft'ur can. He was joined to Maaris when I was born."

"You can't speak with him, you have no joined sign language. What if something goes wrong? Besides, hasn't he joined again to have his second child?"

"It's only their first year. It won't matter if he comes to stay with me for a week or so, until I give birth. Or any Ghen could do it, I don't care."

"You're not being rational, Rennis," Vixannis said quietly. "Someone will have to live with you for two years to raise Saft'ir's child while he breastfeeds. To teach him to speak Ghen, to be Ghen. You need a mate, not a mating. If you don't like Gant'i, maybe another unjoined Ghen…?"

"I don't want an unjoined Ghen! I don't want to carry an infant to be born prematurely. I don't want to risk another child's life! I can't accept such a sacrifice, don't you understand that? It isn't right!"

Vixannis completely stopped moving, an expression of shock on his face. Finally he turned and signed to Ragn'ar while I looked aside. I hoped he was putting forth my request, but I was disappointed when he spoke again.

"Ragn'ar says Gant'i's child has a good chance of surviving. He says both Mick'al and Chair Ghen believe it's the best solution. And Gant'i wasn't asked to do this, he offered."

"He's wrong to put his child-to-be at risk."

"How do you know? You can't see how things will turn out."

"Won't you even ask Ragn'ar?"

"It wouldn't be any use, Rennis. I told you, Chair Ghen and Mick'al agree with Gant'i's suggestion. Ragn'ar won't go against them. No Ghen will."

I rose and left without another word.

ↄ

It wasn't easy going to Savannis, but he was the only one who could help me convince the Ghen that my choice was better than Gant'i's.

"Rennis, I can't tell Mick'al he's wrong," he said when I was done. "How could I know that?"

"How can you not know that sacrificing a child is wrong?"

"Because I don't know that he's being sacrificed. Perhaps it's part of Wind's plan."

"What's happened to me is a violation, not a plan!"

"I know it seems that way now." His very mildness infuriated me. I glared at him.

"Rennis," he said sharply, "It is not your place to direct the Wind."

I turned to leave, but he touched my arm, stopping me. I pulled away from his frail touch.

"Rennis, listen. Imagine… imagine a fabric art. Here at this end," he fluttered the fingers of his left hand in a downward motion, to suggest a row of wind-blown streamers. "You have the green of ugappas and cappa bushes, and a single strip of red in their midst, to suggest the ripe cappa fruit. On this end," he made the same motion with his right hand, "you have the blue of the sea bordering our peninsula, and beyond it the lighter blue of the horizon.

87

"If the wind takes this red," he raised his left hand and closed his fingers around the middle of an imaginary fabric strip, "and blows it here," he moved his left hand to flutter beside his right, which was still raised, fingers extended and moving like strips of fabric in the wind, "it looks all wrong. Cappafruit red in the midst of sea blue and sky blue? Ridiculous, they can't both be right. They contradict each other."

He dropped both hands and looked straight at me. "But they both belong on Wind. The problem isn't in the pattern, Rennis; it's in us. We haven't got the perspective to see the whole picture. We're too small."

I was silent, thinking about his metaphor. Then the anguish of my situation reclaimed me. "You don't have babies dying in your womb," I told him bitterly.

When I got home I ripped out of my lifedance the gray strip of fabric I'd added when I joined with Saft'ir. I stood a moment, staring at it in my hands. Then I burned it in my cookwall and threw the ashes into the dung-pit.

ℰↃ

I accepted Gant'i. What choice did I have? The Ghen had taken all choice from me. Why should I resist, if they valued their offspring so little? Perhaps two Bria infants were worth the risk of a Ghen. Weren't we the heart of Wind? Didn't we follow the true religion, however Savannis clouded it with his "larger perspective"? My faith should have been sustained by this proof, not shaken. Yet it was, and still the Wind remained silent.

Gant'i came to my house and we mated that very night, although stillseason had barely begun. Ragn'ar came to co-join as it was Gant'i's first mating. I drank the potions Gant'i offered me, no matter how vile, swearing to myself that I would do everything within my power to bring all four infants safely into life. Despite my bitter choice I didn't want to be a Ghen, sacrificing children.

Daily I rose at dawn and prayed to Wind to spare Gant'i's child, but my prayers brought me no comfort. Who was I to pray for that infant, I who had knowingly put his life in danger? Nevertheless I prayed, I pleaded, I prostrated myself on Temple Hill and begged in tears, not for my sake but for his. I offered my life, and Gant'i's, if only the infants in my womb would all be spared.

I only asked for justice, nothing more; that the guilty be punished and the innocent go free.

❧

"You are still angry."

I stopped in the middle of my desperate bargaining. Who would dare speak to another on Temple Hill? I raised my head and opened my eye. As I'd suspected, Savannis stood above me. Pointedly, I closed my eye again.

"I'll wait for you at the base of the hill." His voice shook a little and for the first time I noticed how old he was becoming.

I heard him leave, not waiting for the acknowledgment I wouldn't have given. I thought of taking another route down, but that would be childish. After a while I abandoned my fruitless prayers and descended. Savannis met me.

"My anger doesn't matter," I said, to forestall another of his pointed stories.

"Of course it does. It's keeping you from seeing the Wind."

"The wind blows without my seeing it."

"The Wind blows to give you sight."

I made no response.

"Faith is like everything else," he persisted. "If you truly want it, you already have it. The hard part lies in not denying it."

"You make it sound easy." I turned and began walking away from him.

"Oh, no." He labored to keep in step with me, as though we had agreed to walk together. "Denial is much easier."

This angered me further and I ignored him. He was old and childless. How could he understand my anguish? He walked beside me until we reached my house. Before I left him, I asked, "Do you still think Saft'ir was right to kill himself?"

"That's not for me to say."

"I say it then! I say Ghen are all false. They don't even worship the Creator Wind. They think He's a hunter, a flesh-eater, like them. Their two eyes are so focused on this life they can't see Wind. We see more clearly with our one!"

"Wind made the forest as well as the hills. Perhaps we see distance, while they see detail. But we're both seeing the Wind's handiwork."

89

He had an answer for everything. The same answers he'd been giving for too many years.

"Why don't you ever say things outright? You hint at things, suggest! I want clear answers!"

"My task is to teach you Bria history and culture, to introduce you to the Wind, as Dayannis taught us. Not to tell you what He is, or what He wants of you, even if I knew. That's between you and Him."

"Well, He isn't talking."

I entered my house without a backward glance and shut the door.

* * *

Gant'i insisted that we learn to communicate as quickly as possible. At first I resisted. That hadn't been part of the bargain and I already knew as much about Ghen as I cared to. But Gant'i, patient and gentle in everything else, displayed such an urgency about this that it frightened me.

We began to develop a mixture of movements and gestures. Saft'ir and I had restricted ourselves to hand signs, but that was when I had had my eye on being Council Chair, and he saw himself as Chair Ghen. We were well-matched in that way; our goal was the same although our politics differed. Since Saft'ir's death, however, I'd come to view politics less as a skillful building than as a willful battle, in which our words were weapons, not tools.

I no longer wanted a method of communication that suited seated Council meetings. And Gant'i, although he was willing to sit with me on Council when his second year of guarding the wall was over, was now focused, like me, on the greater issue of our children's lives.

We used our whole bodies to communicate. Our language became a dance of nuances, the raising of an arm, slight lift of a knee, the tilting of a chin, nod of a head, blink of an eye, the sweep of hand over abdomen or touching of chest, all conveyed our thoughts and needs and understandings.

We used even stillness, as though by controlling our starts and stops, turning them into meaning, we could overcome the intrusion of Saft'ir's death that threatened the lives of our infants. The movements of our fingers defined more subtle words, the language of thoughts, not paramount as they had once been to me, but secondary. Gant'i used the extension and retraction of his long claws to mimic the supple flexing of my slender fingers, and I overlooked the discourtesy of his fighting claws being made visible to me. But they served as a reminder. Gant'i was Ghen. Ghen hands were weapons. Weapons demanded sacrifices.

I needed the reminder. There was a gentleness about Gant'i that I'd never seen in Saft'ir, nor thought to see in any Ghen. When I returned from my morning prayers on Temple Hill, he waited on me in his awkward way, seating me in the chair that got the most wind and bringing me tea and fresh bread that had baked overnight on the coals in my cookwall. He was equally solicitous when I came home tired after a Council meeting.

"Don't you care how I vote in Council?" I asked once, when we could finally communicate.

"Of course I'm interested," he signed back. "But what is that to this?" And he reached forward, lightly touching my swollen abdomen with his fingers. "This and your heart, which is strong enough to hold two Ghen." Then he said something I'd never heard any Ghen say to a Bria: "I want my youngling to have your courage."

I was ashamed and turned my head aside, for I knew how little I deserved such a tribute.

ça

In the height of midseason, Gant'i closed all the windows of our house. I lit the fire in my cookwall and let it burn until the room was as hot as stillseason and I gasped for air. My fingers ached to open the shutters and let in the wind that battered against them, but I did not. I lay on my sleeping ledge, with my back to the window. It was worse even than stillseason, for we left the fans off. At last Gant'i began to scent, and soon my breasts were weeping and my belly chaffed.

There was no relief for me—I was the only Bria on all of Wind suffering a pre-mating rash in midseason. Between the soreness, the itch and the lack of air, I thought I might go insane, but I remembered Gant'i's praise and was determined not to fail our children.

Gant'i rubbed oil over my belly, but it offered only a brief balm, not healing. On the second night of my rash, I dreamed I was comforted and woke in horror to find myself twisted almost double on my shelf, rubbing my weeping breasts against my own belly. I'd pulled off the cloth with which I'd bound my breasts and was self-soothing!

At once I ran to wash away the balm, berating my sleep-induced weakness and praying my younglings wouldn't suffer the ill-effects of such behavior. The rash remained for two more days. I made Gant'i tie my hands at night, embarrassed when he didn't ask me why.

As soon as it cleared, we mated. Then I rose from Gant'i's sleeping mat and threw open the windows. Oh, the joy of that first rush of wind over my face! It was only the cold wind of midseason, but I hoped Wind had seen my suffering and would turn His breath on me again.

In the following months I grew huge and awkward. I could feel the infants kicking more vigorously each day. Their movements brought me joy, to know they lived, they would be born. But sometimes in the night their struggles were so turbulent I wakened and was afraid. Were they maturing too quickly because of Gant'i's potions? I stroked my aching belly and tried not to worry. What was there to fear, now that they would live?

Stillseason came and went. My womb stretched taut beyond that of any pregnant Bria I'd ever seen, and still we waited. I cradled myself when I moved, immersed in the searing pains that convulsed my overburdened womb and reached into every part of my body. I prayed for strength, but it was my shame that sustained me. The day before I would have given in, as though Gant'i knew my limits, he came to me and we mated for the third time.

The next day the agony that lashed my body steadied into a rhythm; not lessened but directed, so that even though the pitch increased relentlessly, I felt a rightness to it, a driving need behind it that pointed to relief. I lay on my shelf while the contractions grew. Maaris bathed my face and body with sponges of cool water while Gant'i hovered nearby. When Maaris left me to start a fire in my cookwall, Gant'i bent and blew a single, soft breath into my face.

I was momentarily taken aback. I'd never expected such intimacy from a Ghen. I wasn't angry, as I once might have been; rather, it pleased me that Gant'i should wish to share his breath with me.

When had I stopped seeing him as a hunter? When had his hands, even with claws extended, begun to look like words instead of weapons?

He examined my abdomen gently, then his hand drew a quick arch in the air pausing at its highest point while his right foot rose and briefly held: "It is time to begin." He walked to his side of the room and returned with a final potion. I drank it at once. The pain receded though I could still observe the rigid furrows that clenched across my taut belly.

Gant'i bent toward me, his face solemn. "You must have great courage," he motioned. His body arched over mine. His hands, not quite touching me, met above my head and moved down the sides of my body to meet again below my feet: "I will not let harm reach any part of you."

My courage returned with the lessening of my pain. I raised my right hand, two fingers extended and curled like claws, while my left hand rapidly encircled my bulging abdomen: "I am two warriors' womb-parent."

Gant'i bowed his head. When he raised it, his face was damp, but he was composed. His left hand drew a circle around his eyes and moved to draw another around my eye: "You see things as I do." He drew a circle about my eye again: "See—"…and a straight line from that circle to touch my belly: "—into your womb."

I indicated my acceptance with a quick shrug, but I felt myself drawing back in fear. I wanted to look away, but didn't dare.

"You will bear a Broghen."

In the wake of his words I heard a strange sound, strong and rhythmic, pounding. I concentrated on the wild sound of my heart, until I could breathe again.

It never occurred to me to doubt him. The babies in my womb had been offered again and again in forfeiture; the first three by Saft'ir, the last one by Gant'i and by me. It was insanely fitting that the Wind should send a Broghen to accept our sacrifices.

"All second-year matings produce a Broghen," Gant'i signed, bending toward my body as though he sensed my retreat from him. "Always a Broghen is born. But I'll take care of it, it won't harm the others."

They think they understand each other. I heard my thoughts as if they were someone else's, referring to myself and Gant'i as though to strangers. *But the signs and movements can't mean the same thing to both of them.*

"Rennis, do you understand what I'm telling you?"

With a rush I returned to myself. I slashed my left hand downward, twisting my torso and face away from him as much as I could: "No! I reject what you offer!"

Knowledge. I was rejecting knowledge, if what he said was true. I looked at my belly as it shuddered with contractions I could barely feel through the haze of the drink he'd given me.

But I'd come to trust Gant'i. If he was telling me this, it was because I had to know, because my knowing might keep our infants alive. I didn't question why he hadn't told me before; I wished he hadn't had to tell me now. Reluctantly I cupped my ear with my hand: "Tell me."

"The Broghen will not hurt you. Pity it, rather than fearing it, at least in infancy. I'll capture it and take it far away where it can do us no harm."

"How...?"

"No one knows where it comes from, or why. It's created at second mating, we know that from our records."

Second mating. I felt the inaudible intake of air that was my breathing: so I was not dead. It was only the shadow of death, that had left me when I joined with Gant'i, and was returning now. It pressed down on me, stilled my heart within me, stilled even my breath. Into the weight of darkness pushing against me, into the stillness that froze my arms at my sides, I whispered, "Saft'ir and I had second mating."

I couldn't see Gant'i but I felt his hands on my shoulders. When my vision cleared, his face was almost against mine, as though he would understand my Bria words just by nearness. Slowly I signed to him what I had said.

"When?"

"The afternoon before he died. He scented early. We believed it wouldn't matter, stillseason was only a few weeks away. And then, when he died... Unborn is unborn at any stage. I didn't think it mattered."

Gant'i looked away from me. I wanted to ask him, but I couldn't. Sensing our distress, Maaris came from the cookwall where he'd set a large pot of water to boil, his last task before leaving us.

"Maaris must stay. He may be needed," Gant'i signed when he turned back. My throat closed over the words, I had to try twice before I could pass on his message. Maaris was a healer. When I told him Gant'i wanted him to stay, he touched his breath without asking questions, though I'd never heard of any but the Ghen father attending a birth.

Once more Gant'i's body arched over mine, his hands outlining my body. This time I took little comfort from his assurance. He would do all he could. Within my womb I imagined my Bria infants fighting for their lives against two Broghen.

I stiffened, almost resisted, as Gant'i moved to the end of the shelf and stroked my legs apart. I no longer wanted my questions answered. Better the slippery grasp of fear than the firm grip of grief. I had known both; I knew which one was better.

And so I was unprepared for the sight of my firstborn, unprepared for his delicate perfection or for the all-embracing joy that seized me when Gant'i laid him in my arms. His tiny, treble mewling, more lovely than the music of the wind, his fragile features, furless, almost translucent skin, skeletal little body wrapped in one of the warmed cloths Maaris had prepared, all so enraptured me that I forgot to be afraid.

"Look aside," Maaris said quickly, his Bria warble barely rising above the sudden, crazed shriek as Gant'i guided forth a writhing mass of fury from within me. My cry of horror added to the din before I could control it, but already Gant'i was deftly easing the infant Ghen from the Broghen's bestial grip, wincing as its claws pierced his fingers. Maaris reached for a small box I had not noticed before, lifted its lid with hands that trembled. Gant'i dropped the Broghen inside and closed the lid.

I tried to ignore its frenzied assault upon the walls that enclosed it, its demonic screeching, tried to concentrate only on nursing my child, and Saft'ir's, when Gant'i handed him to me. No sacrifices, I implored Wind, over and over, but my prayers brought no relief to the tightness in my throat, the pounding of my heart, the clench of fear as Gant'i reached once more into my heaving womb.

Again a struggling mass of Ghen and Broghen emerged, but smaller, more desperate. The Broghen, having had its full natural maturation, had the upper hand against the premature Ghen. I couldn't see how badly he was hurt but he bled from a multitude of wounds and when Gant'i eased the raging Broghen aside, his tiny youngling gave a sigh and lay limp. Maaris lifted the still body and laid it on the cloths he'd prepared. He bent over the tiny infant, massaging its chest, breathing into its mouth, counting softly as he worked on it.

Gant'i sat still.

"My second youngling," I urged him. He didn't need to understand Bria; the desperate edge to my voice was clear enough. He sat still, not looking at me.

"No!" I screamed, "Not my youngling!" I saw him close his eyes and bow his head. Weakly I flung my arms out against him until he looked at me again. "I did everything you said! I did everything right," I signed.

Maaris looked up from the table where he was now suturing the worst of the premature Ghen's wounds. Tears dampened his face, but his hand was steady. Gant'i sat as still as his child, staring at the little mound of bloodied flesh between my legs as though it had been he who'd failed to keep it safe.

"Rennis!" Maaris said, sharply, "There are two infants; three, I hope, who need you. There will be time for mourning later."

I stroked my infant's back as he suckled, trying not to think of the little sibling who should be lying against my breast beside him. Yes, I would grieve later. Grief always waited for me.

"Tell Gant'i to take the Broghen away while I attend his youngling," Maaris said. I touched Gant'i, unable to speak of the monsters I had birthed. He started, and glanced at the writhing beast still struggling in his hands. A look of rage crossed his face, so fierce I didn't know him. I gasped and shrank away. Perhaps he heard my breath, or felt a premonition of the sorrow that attends all sacrifices, even Broghen. He restrained himself.

I couldn't look at the Broghen. The thought of two of them coming from my womb nauseated me. I wanted to die for having brought such vicious, hideous things into the world. Long after Gant'i had taken them away I heard the echo of their insane shrieking. I would hear that sound as long as I lived.

Maaris kept up a continuous chatter, speculating on my youngling's future and offering stories from my own childhood. This, and the infants suckling at my breast, drew me slowly back from the abyss. Finally I slept.

Was it half a remove or half a day later when a feeble whimper wakened me? Maaris raised his head as I looked up, his mouth curving into a cautious smile.

"Gant'i's child will live," he said.

❧

Savannis came to see me soon after my delivery. I used to think he went to bless the babies and congratulate the Bria parents. That was when I thought they were recuperating, not hiding in shame and horror, unwilling to go outside and look on Wind with knowing eyes.

I refused to speak of the birth to Savannis. When he mentioned my lost infant, I stared him into silence. Then he spoke of Saft'ir, saying there was something I should know about his death. I lost all patience and ordered him to leave me in peace. I had all I could cope with, without reopening the past.

❧

I named my youngling Tyannis. Gant'i named his Yur'i, and the other Ghen infant Saft'ir, after its parent. It wasn't my place to comment on the naming of Ghen, but Gant'i saw my displeasure.

I had to force myself to put little Saft'ir to my breast. I couldn't help it; I felt that I was nursing a mangarr'h, born to betray any who trusted him. I resented his very health, his robustness. I had paid for my willingness to sacrifice an innocent: I'd lost a child. Gant'i had paid for his part also. His youngling was lame and had an illness that made him gasp for breath at times. Stillseason in the lungs, the Bria doctor called it. Often we sat up all night, massaging his little chest to keep him struggling for air, praying to Wind to spare him.

I prayed from force of habit, going through the motions of belief. Faith itself was too tenuous, too difficult—like walking on the wind. I'd lost the necessary balance long ago.

Yur'i was cheerful and uncomplaining, even in illness. He had his parent's gentle nature. I responded to him with an almost desperate care, partly guilt, because he was paying the price of Tyannis's life. Tyannis, too, had lost something, though he didn't yet miss the sibling-love most Bria grew up experiencing. Little Saft'ir alone emerged untouched by all our terrible choices. When fire rages, don't the victims always resent those who walk through it unscathed? Saft'ir was a hero, his youngling was strong and healthy. Where was the justice in that?

"Why do you avoid little Saft'ir?" Gant'i asked me at last.

"I don't," I lied. How could I say I wanted the child to suffer? Had I learned nothing at all? But I was as proud as Saft'ir had been, for in my deepest heart I still wanted to make the Wind's choices for Him: I wanted little Saft'ir to be ill instead of Yur'i. Or, if one must die, why hadn't it been him instead of my second youngling?

"It hurts him when you turn aside. You must be more kind," Gant'i persisted. His criticism stung me.

"Saft'ir!" I cried. "Always Saft'ir, adult and child both, forcing sacrifices on others while they sacrifice nothing!"

"Sacrifice nothing?" Gant'i looked at me closely. "Saft'ir sacrificed everything."

"For his pride!"

"Saft'ir was bitten by a Broghen. I thought Savannis told you."

"A Broghen?" I was shocked for a moment. But what difference did that make, really? "Even if he was, the wounds weren't fatal. I saw that for myself."

"Rennis," Gant'i took my hands in his, held them absolutely still, to say: "This is important." Gently he moved in our language of body and breath, as gently as a healer sews a wound.

"Saft'ir fought a Broghen, fought it alone. Perhaps the monster caught him unaware; Broghen haven't attacked our wall outside of stillseason in years. Saft'ir must have moved from his post for a moment to stretch his legs; his firearm was found leaning against the wall.

"He killed the Broghen with his knife and bare claws, before it broke into our city. Only when the wall was safe, the monster dead, did he drag himself over to his post and call for help. He took his life when he saw me coming to replace him."

I looked away, then back at Gant'i, "Saft'ir sacrificed my Bria children when he took his life," I signed. "Tyannis's sibling is dead because of him."

"No, Rennis. A Broghen's bite is poisonous from the moment it first eats meat. It isn't necessarily fatal to Ghen, but it is to Bria. Saft'ir couldn't mate with you again. He would have brought you death in his mating, you and your Bria infants."

"His dying almost killed them anyway. It did kill one."

"I killed your youngling. The Broghen of our mating caused his death. Saft'ir's youngling held back Saft'ir's Broghen. My Yur'i was too small."

"That's not Yur'i's fault!"

"No, it was mine. I wanted you too much. Saft'ir knew that, he knew I'd join with you. That's why he killed himself when he saw me coming."

"Why didn't he just tell me?"

"How could he explain to you? You didn't know about Broghen. And you would have refused to mate with another while he was alive. He must have thought he could only save you and your infants by dying."

"Why did you burn the Broghen's body? He could have shown me!"

Gant'i touched my cheek gently. He glanced at the mat where Tyannis lay sleeping beside the stockier Ghen infants.

"There's a story Mick'al tells of a time before the building of this city; a story of mated Bria destroying themselves for fear of the Broghen within them. We are sworn to secrecy because of this. Saft'ir might have given you more credit, tried to talk to you, but his motives were good. He was always impulsive."

Could I have lived for over a year knowing a monster grew inside me? Could I have slept at night, fearing that it was even then attacking my babies? Wouldn't I have started and trembled at every pain, imagining it to be the bite of a Broghen, devouring my insides? I could barely endure the knowledge now that it was over.

Would I have gone to another Ghen to breed my babies into life if my joined mate were still alive? To breed another Broghen? It was too much to think about. How could anyone tell right from wrong in such a world?

༄

Yur'i survived his infancy, though there were many nights I wakened to his labored breathing and carried him to the corner we'd set up with its steaming bricks and the single lounging board where I could rest holding him upright against me. Gant'i devoted himself to Tyannis and Saft'ir when I was busy with Yur'i. We cared for all three together, outside of custom, and therefore by necessity we taught all three the language of our joining.

We were criticized for doing so, but how else could Gant'i direct Tyannis to come in from play and settle for his nap, when I was in the steam corner with Yur'i? How else could I urge little Saft'ir to retract his claws around Tyannis, or entice him down from climbing the ugappa beside our house, while Gant'i went through the leg exercises he had to do daily with Yur'i?

In deference to tradition we at least taught them that our sign language was for us alone, and didn't sign to them away from our home. When I caught Tyannis using it with other Bria toddlers, I scolded him and took him home, so he'd remember.

Saft'ir was never a concern. By the time he was old enough to play games of hunt and fight with other nursing Ghen, he'd already sensed that our signing was not the talk of hunters. And Yur'i, Yur'i saw no children aside from Tyannis and Saft'ir. We worried about where he would fit in, Gant'i and I, but our first concern was keeping him alive.

In fact we worried about all three, their circumstances were so strange. There was a closeness between them that excluded other children, Ghen and Bria alike. They seemed to treat signing as the language of their hearts, and when Tyannis spoke Bria, or Saft'ir and Yur'i spoke Ghen, something was lost in translation: kinship.

Not even the same species, and yet they behaved as kin! How powerful is language, and we five shared one unique onto ourselves. I felt it myself. Yur'i, and even Saft'ir, began to seem not merely the offspring of my joined Ghen, but somehow related to me. I spoke to them—praised and reprimanded, guiding their growth as I did Tyannis's. Gant'i and I argued over their upbringing; gently, deferentially, with a sense of how ludicrous such discussions were. Yet, since all three must heed us both, we had to reach agreement.

We spent an inordinate amount of time together. When I took Tyannis to visit Bria grain mills and farms and factories, I dared not leave Yur'i. When Gant'i carried his child into the forests or along the walls, he didn't trust himself to also hold back Saft'ir, impulsive, fearless little Saft'ir. Occasionally he asked another Ghen parent and child to accompany him, but it was an imposition on their bonding time. And besides, I was so distraught when Yur'i was away from my sight, so worried that he might fall or lose his breath, I could not bear it.

"He's a hunter," Gant'i reminded me patiently.

"Not yet! He will be someday, but he's a baby now!" I'd protest, reaching for Yur'i, feeding him first to prove my point.

We agreed to take them places together. I had to address Council for a special dispensation. I pointed out that they had encouraged me to accept the risk in birthing their hero's youngling. This was part of the price. Briarris supported me at once, his loyalty surprising me. We had both once wanted to evict Ghen from our city, but much had happened since then. After some debate, Council agreed to my request.

We took all three younglings to Bria artisans and factories. Saft'ir ran circles of boredom around us while Yur'i watched wide-eyed from his parent's arms. Tyannis asked numerous questions, but with an air of resignation that puzzled me until I caught him later, at home, passing on the information to Yur'i, as if glad to do so and forget it.

The day we went to a farm… We only visited the farms once. Tyannis was interested, at least, which pleased me, until he stampeded the callans. "It wasn't me," he lisped, "It was the wind that did it!"

While we were apologizing, Saft'ir stalked a laying farmborra, leaped on it and tried to kill it. Its desperate squawking alerted one of the gocks, which flew at Saft'ir. Tyannis roared to his rescue ahead of us, forgetting that his furless skin was less tough than Saft'ir's. When we pulled them away, Tyannis emerged scratched, bleeding, and hiccuping in a cross between laughter and tears, while Yur'i gasped for air in my arms and Saft'ir struggled to return to the fray.

Gant'i spoke roughly to Saft'ir, furious, seeing for perhaps the first time the recklessness, the impulsiveness in him, that was bound to bring harm to others. So like his parent. And yet, I wanted to laugh.

I'd forgiven Saft'ir his suicide, mostly because of Gant'i, who shared more of my life than any other Ghen and Bria shared. I could accept the altruistic purpose behind Saft'ir's suicide, but I distrusted such impulsiveness. It was too showy, and in a way, too easy. I'd learned, from Gant'i's daily kindnesses, to see greater honor in smaller sacrifices.

Gant'i took Saft'ir alone to a Ghen construction site. What use in taking Yur'i? He was too frail for such an occupation and the dust would hurt his laboring lungs. I kept Tyannis home with us, despite his objections; Gant'i would have trouble enough keeping Saft'ir from rushing into danger. I'd hoped Saft'ir would find it interesting—perhaps he needn't be a hunter?—but I was disappointed in that.

We took all three on other Ghen outings. Yur'i could not walk on the sloping ground near to the wall but Saft'ir, holding Gant'i's finger, ran along it as though he owned it and Tyannis insisted, despite my reluctance, on racing with them.

The forest, even in the daytime, frightened Yur'i. I thought at first it was my shiver of dread in the wind-blocking shadows of the ugappas that made him cling so tightly, his small heart pounding against mine. But Gant'i admitted that Yur'i had trembled thus on every visit.

I ached for both of them. Here was Gant'i's life, in the wild forests of Wind, and this was the life expected of all Ghen, including Yur'i.

"Maybe later," I signed gently, "when he's older. He's no coward, Gant'i. I've seen him endure pain and make no sound. I've seen fear in his eyes when he can't breathe, and yet he only cries when he thinks Tyannis or Saft'ir are in danger. He has the heart of a warrior, Gant'i, never think otherwise."

Gant'i came to me and held me around his child, leaned his great head against mine and shuddered in the effort not to weep before the children. Yur'i reached out and touched his parent's shoulder as if to console, or perhaps apologize.

Tyannis and Saft'ir came to us then, twining between our legs. Feeling them, Gant'i straightened. Taking Yur'i from me, he held him in one arm and hoisted Saft'ir up onto the other while I lifted Tyannis. Gant'i reached to touch my hands and we danced together, a strange and joyous quintet, dipping and circling and laughing into each others' faces, alone and together in the silent forests of Wind.

I wanted us to dance this way forever.

☙

I didn't wean the children in their second stillseason. When Gant'i questioned me, I argued, "They were born late, they should wean late."

But it was I who wasn't ready. Saft'ir had stopped on his own, finding the meat Gant'i brought from the Ghen compound for him and Yur'i more filling, and Tyannis, running after him, had to be called back in order to nurse. Yur'i alone was content to cuddle in my arms, but it wasn't the milk he needed, it was the holding.

I could never hold him enough. Always he hung back, waiting for me to reach out for him, as though he thought himself undeserving. It hurt me, the look of acceptance in his eyes, expecting to be rejected. Something haunted him, and all my assurances couldn't erase it. How could I let Gant'i take him away? He would believe I didn't want him.

"They're old enough to be weaned," Gant'i signed to me finally. "Tyannis begins Bria school soon. Saft'ir and Yur'i must come with me, it's past time."

"No!" my hand slashed downward. "Yur'i isn't ready. You know he isn't. He'll cry in the night when you are on the wall. He'll stop breathing in the night, when you're on the wall! I'll wean him, but I won't let him go into the Ghen compound."

"He's my youngling."

"Then don't risk his life!"

"You want to raise my youngling here, among Bria?"

The question made me pause, until the immediate concerns reclaimed me. "We're only here for a day," I signed, before I remembered how frustrating that Bria expression is to Ghen.

"If he stays, I'll never see him." Gant'i looked at me, the question clear in his eyes. I wanted to answer it, to say: Mate with me again, I'll have your second youngling... but I couldn't, and how else could we live together?

"Wait a little longer," I signed at last.

∽

During the daytime Gant'i took Saft'ir and Yur'i to the Ghen compound to join the other two-year-olds learning to hunt and fight. Saft'ir ran ahead as though he were windborne but Yur'i dragged behind, miserable. One day Tyannis asked me why Yur'i couldn't come with him to school and storytime.

"Tyannis," I scolded, "you know that's impossible."

"But Yur'i hates fighting and hunting. Why must he do it?"

"Because he's Ghen," I said in Bria.

Tyannis looked surprised.

∽

When they had all gone off I began to sew into Tyannis's lifedance some strips of fabric he'd recently chosen. There were already five narrow strips sewn onto the long rod from which his lifedance hung. I lifted a brown one and fitted it into place beside the others.

"Is it the sand where Savannis draws at storytime?" I'd asked when he chose it, thinking of the brown my Matri had sewn into my lifedance when I began attending storytime.

"No, it's the training field, where Saft'ir fights," he'd replied. "I go there after school and sit with Yur'i. It's so exciting, Matri!" After a moment, he'd added, "But it makes Yur'i unhappy. Sometimes he has trouble breathing when he watches."

Why shouldn't Yur'i go to school with Tyannis? Wasn't he better suited to that than to Ghen training? I thought about it as I sewed the brown and beside it, the light gray Tyannis had chosen to represent Yur'i.

"Gray? Why do you want gray in your lifedance?" I had asked Tyannis.

"It's Yur'i, Matri. And this," he chose another, slightly darker gray, "is Saft'ir."

When we got home, he looked at my lifedance. "That's you," he said, pointing to the strip that was the color of my pelt. "And that looks like Tarris." He touched the piece that represented my sibling.

"You have a good eye," I said, smiling, but I felt my heart contract as it always did when I thought of all that Tyannis missed by having no sibling. Tyannis's attention was still on my lifedance. He was looking at the single strip of gray from my childhood, to represent Naft'ur, who quickened my seed before I was born.

"Didn't you have a Ghen womb-sibling, Matri?" he asked sadly, using the term he'd invented to refer to Saft'ir and Yur'i.

"I... didn't put him in. I didn't really get to know him."

"I'm sorry, Matri," he said, and blew into my face as though I needed comforting.

I reached for the darker gray Tyannis had chosen for Saft'ir. About to fit it into place, I paused. Tyannis was not lacking a sibling—he had two. That was the way he saw it, even if he was the only one in all our divided city who saw it so. And he was about to lose them.

I could prevent it by mating with Gant'i again, by offering to bear his second child.

But I still had nightmares of my pregnancy. Sometimes the babies in my womb were all dead. Sometimes they were alive, soundlessly screaming to be born, but I was unable to deliver them. Sometimes they were all Broghen, tearing their way out through my belly.

I couldn't go through it again.

✑

When Gant'i brought Saft'ir and Yur'i home for our evening meal together, Tyannis proudly showed them his lifedance.

"There's a lot of gray," Saft'ir signed, rolling back his lips in a grin.

"It's too bad you aren't... purple!" Tyannis replied, and the three of them giggled at the thought of a purple Saft'ir.

They came out of the room they slept in, into the front room, where my lifedance hung.

"There we are again." Saft'ir pointed to the two strips of gray I'd decided to put into mine, also, after Tyannis chose them for his.

"Matri doesn't know his Ghen womb-sibling," Tyannis signed to them solemnly.

"He had to, they lived together," Saft'ir responded. "Maybe he was another color?" They examined the strips of fabric from my childhood with interest.

"Maybe he was invisible?" Yur'i sometimes came out with strange ideas. "Maybe that's him?" He pointed to the empty space in my lifedance, to the ragged gray fibers left behind when I tore out the remnants of my first joining.

"Time to sleep." I waved them abruptly toward the back room.

"We're not invisible, are we, Matri?" Saft'ir signed. I thought of the fabric dyer, who had clearly not wanted to sell the gray pieces to me. Ocallis was the only other Bria I'd heard of whose lifedance included the child of his joined Ghen, and that was only added in memory, when Heckt'er died.

I patted Saft'ir's shoulder and reached over to stroke Yur'i's cheek. "No, you're both very real."

"Goodnight, Matri," Yur'i signed, rolling his lips back a little.

✑

I boiled a pot of water and made tea for Gant'i and me. We sat between the open windows sipping it, quiet and comfortable in the earlyseason wind. In the next room I heard Tyannis stir and whisper something in his baby lisp without awaking. On his sleeping mat, Yur'i slept deeply; he hadn't wakened breathless for awhile. Perhaps he was outgrowing the weakness in his lungs? Beside him, Saft'ir lay dreaming of childish hunts and unsuspecting farmborra.

"Rennis," Gant'i signed, "one could say I already have two younglings, Yur'i and Saft'ir. Why should I mate again? What if I went to the Ghen compound during stillseason? Councilors are joined for life. Why not live together in the seasons that we can?"

A gust of wind blew in and whirled about us, as cool and strong as the wind on Temple Hill. I turned and looked directly at it, but it kept blowing, blowing onto me.

I rose from my seat, touching Gant'i's hands. "Yes. Live with me here."

I drew him up beside me and slowly began to sway. We danced together, as we had danced among the trees. And as we danced he blew into my face, and I blew into his.

Council Relations

Briarris

"The Broghen that attacked Mant'er has been found. It wasn't one of ours."

Council Chair's statement was followed by a nervous stillness among the Bria councilors. I felt a turmoil in my stomach, and for a moment I was nauseous. Had the fans stopped? No, I could feel their forced breeze, yet still I felt ill. Not one of ours? I looked at Igt'ur, sitting beside me in the small room where closed-Council met.

In the eight years we'd been joined, I'd learned to recognize small indicators of his mood. He was sitting still, the muscles around his eyes drawn tight, his nostrils slightly flared. The rapidity of his breathing and the fingers of his left hand, claws slightly extended, drumming on the chair arm, gave him away. Chair Ghen's statement, which Council Chair had just translated for the Bria in the room, had also caught him by surprise.

Igt'ur and I had been admitted to closed-Council after we'd been on Council for six years. We were now among the senior councilors who met weekly in this small room adjacent to Council Chambers. Here, all the major decisions were made. Not that it came as a surprise. How could one not know, when five out of six times the senior councilors voted unanimously on a significant issue, and everyone knew closed-Council had met the day before? But no one objected. We'd all make closed-Council eventually. During our first six years we were gathering experience. Meanwhile, our ideas were listened to, even sometimes adopted.

Igt'ur hadn't lived with me since his youngling was weaned three years ago, but we were still considered joined; we shared a language and sat together on Council. Council Ghen knew they would mate only once. If Igt'ur had minded that, he would have refused to join with me. Only a child wastes time regretting a decision already made. The wind blows on and one must keep one's footing.

Chair Ghen was speaking again. I waited for Council Chair to translate.

"The Broghen was white, as Mant'er claimed, underneath all the black river mud crusted on its scales and fur. Not fair, like Briarris, there, is—" I jumped a little at the mention of my name "—but all white, skin and scale and fur. Also it was undersized, no bigger than a large Ghen."

He paused. I heard the tremble in his voice. It frightened me as much as the news he offered.

Igt'ur had arrived at my house only two removes ago, urging me to come with him at once to Council Chambers. I'd been astonished to see him, and even more shocked at the idea of a Council meeting being called during still-season. But when we arrived many of the senior councilors were already here. We'd waited, catching our breath, until everyone in closed-Council arrived.

Chair Ghen spoke again. Then Gant'i rose and addressed the Ghen councilors. I stared at Igt'ur, wishing I could hear through his ears. At least Chair Ghen kept his comments short, allowing Ghen and Bria councilors to learn the news more or less together. When Gant'i sat down, Council Chair stepped forward.

"The Broghen which attacked Saft'ir many years ago was also white, and not full-sized. Gant'i burned its remains before they could be seen by young Bria, and he confirms this. Moreover, a third was sighted by a hunting triad which just returned yesterday. It was on our side of the Symamt'h river." He paused to steady his voice.

I found myself still with fear. One white Broghen might be a natural, if unusual, occurrence. Not two, or worse, three. None of us Bria councilors had ever left our peninsula; many had not even visited the farms since childhood. The northern forest was enormous; the Symamt'h, with the grasslands and mountains beyond it, was no more than a story told by the Ghen, more distant to us even than the stars, which at least we could see. But something in the way he said, *"our side* of the Symamt'h" filled me with dread. I could see it had a similar effect on the others.

"Char'an, who sails our boat to the southern lands, has been questioned. He doesn't remember any white Broghen infants coming from our city." Council Chair paused again. I was acutely aware of the tightly-shuttered windows on either side of us, the slow rotating fan which barely moved the hot, sluggish air, the heavy stillness outside, and the tense stillness inside.

Drawing in a deep breath, Council Chair continued. "This suggests two possibilities. There may be some creature in the south, unknown to us, with which the Broghen we release are able to breed. We don't know if that's possible; we can't be sure that it's not."

Darillis, a year away from being Council Chair, slowly slid from his seat onto the floor, unconscious. It will be bad next year when he's in charge, I thought, but at the same time I was glad of the interruption, and more than a little relieved that it hadn't been me who caused it. A number of councilors were lowering their heads and taking deep breaths. The Ghen lifted Darillis onto the table, closer to the overhead fan, and his joined Ghen, Samm'ar, remained beside him, swishing his hands above Darillis's face to create more air movement.

Samm'ar and Igt'ur were about to carry Darillis to the infirmary when he regained consciousness. "Take me home," he whispered faintly.

We all had to wait while he was being carried to his home before the meeting could continue. The prolonged break was both a relief and a torment. How could Darillis bear not to hear the rest? But he'd always been one to look sideways at the wind.

It gave me time to think. Many had said that Mant'er was delusional, that he'd exaggerated the strangeness of the Broghen on his hunt. Given the state he was in, and the fact that he'd been attacked in the dark, their dismissal was understandable. But I'd believed him, mostly because Ocallis had; I just hadn't considered what that might mean. I'd been too concerned with the idea of Ocallis joining with him again. Why couldn't Ocallis be like Rennis, and simply let Mant'er live with him?

Not that it was that simple. Anarris, representing Single-by-Choice, had brought a complaint against Rennis and Gant'i to me as Council Relations. When I refused to move it in Council, Anarris took it to Triannis.

Triannis occupied the single Bria seat that Rennis left vacant when he moved back into his joined councilor's seat, once again representing the year after mine. Triannis was a member of Single-by-Choice. Most of the young Bria who chose not to be joined were members, and Triannis had graduated top of his class in City Admin. He was actually, therefore, more qualified than the joined Bria who represented his year. But Triannis would never make Council Chair, or even closed-Council, without a joined Ghen, and he'd never act as Council Relations; his focus was too narrow. Like it or not, that task remained mine.

Anarris and his group had stirred up the Bria in a number of the houses near Rennis's, to complain against the living conditions between Rennis and Gant'i and their three younglings. They filled the public gallery the day Triannis brought forward his motion to disallow Gant'i to live with Rennis. But Rennis and Gant'i were legally joined for life, as all councilors are, and there is no law requiring a Ghen to live in the Ghen compound.

Ghen are communal by nature, and choose to live together. But Gant'i and Yur'i and Saft'ir seemed to have redefined their community. I, personally, thought we were doing neither them nor Rennis and Tyannis any favor by letting them stay together, but no one on Council wanted to risk seeing Rennis return to the state he'd been in when Saft'ir died.

I looked across the closed Council room and caught Rennis watching me. When I blinked acknowledgment, he came and sat beside me.

"What do you think?"

"I hope it's not true."

He looked aside, then in a lower voice murmured, "I bore two of them."

"Rennis—" I began, then stopped. There was no consolation for any of us. Willingly or not, we nurtured the seeds that became destructive monsters, as well as those that became the builders of civilization. And unleashed them both on Wind. Much as we told ourselves we were responsible only for our small corner—this peninsula of civilization we'd created—we knew that all of Wind should matter to us.

"We all feel the same," I said, touching Rennis's hand gently. "But the wind blows on and we must keep our footing." It was a platitude, but it's also the way life is.

Igt'ur and Samm'ar returned then and the meeting continued.

"The other possibility," Council Chair said, after Chair Ghen had spoken, "is that we are not alone."

There was a brief hush while everyone took this in.

"There are other Bria on Wind!" Perallis spoke across the room, expressing all our awestruck thoughts.

"And other Ghen, perhaps," Council Chair agreed. "But we know nothing about them, if they even exist. We must proceed cautiously."

I breathed out sharply, making a low whistle of disgust. What had we to fear from any Bria? It was clear from the expressions around me that the other Bria councilors felt as I did. The Ghen among us shifted on their benches, uncomfortable. Had I become too complacent through my association with Igt'ur? My childhood memory of watching Ghen training came vaguely back to me. I'd been frightened then, maybe I should be now.

"There are strange Ghen involved, as well as Bria," I heard myself saying. "Ghen can be violent." I didn't mention the Broghen. We were frightened enough, we needed some time to come to grips with that news.

"What is proposed?" Perallis asked.

"A Ghen expedition to the south, as soon as stillseason ends. If that turns up nothing, another next year, heading north into the mountains."

"The trip south is more dangerous," Rennis objected. "Why not go north, first?"

"We have to know," Council Chair said gently.

If there were no white Broghen discovered in the South, they couldn't have come from our birthings. Rennis knew that as well as any of us. But if there were... if our Broghen offspring, presumed sterile, had found a way to multiply... Breath of Wind, it was unthinkable! No one was eager to have such a terrible thing confirmed.

"This will come forward at the first open Council meeting after stillseason," Council Chair continued. "It will be referred to as another Ghen exploration trip; nothing more. It should be passed with as little discussion as possible."

We all understood; we were part of the terrible secret, now.

"Agreed?"

I touched my breath with my hand and slowly raised it into the air, to show my consent. There were no dissents.

It wouldn't be difficult. The Ghen were frequently going on explorations. We Bria looked at their maps and their reports and shrugged, occasionally commenting that they learned about Wind to avoid learning about themselves. I understood from Igt'ur that Ghen, in turn, found Bria too self-reflective.

"While we're here," Rennis spoke up quickly, "I have a request to make."

"Rennis, can it wait? We're all a little overwhelmed, and it's stillseason…" Council Chair began.

"It's important," Rennis turned to face the councilors sitting around the room. "As you all know, Gant'i's child, Yur'i, is not strong. He can't participate in Ghen training. Even when he's watching, the dust kicked up by the others hurts his lungs."

"Rennis—"

"This has to be settled. He's being harmed!"

One would have thought he was fighting for his own child. The fact that it wasn't, that it was a Ghen child, made his concern shocking, and all the more compelling.

"I've spoken to Savannis," Rennis continued, "And he's agreed to let Yur'i attend storytime. I need permission to send him to Bria school, as well. He's bright and capable despite his physical weakness. He has a right to learn a useful trade."

I had to admire his timing. At any other meeting his request would have been scandalous, but after the news we'd just been given, it was greeted as but another quirk of Rennis's.

When Rennis paused Gant'i spoke, putting the request to the Ghen councilors himself instead of having Council Chair sign it to Chair Ghen. We Bria listened, further surprised by the implication that Rennis and Gant'i had discussed together the needs of Gant'i's youngling. The Ghen would be shocked. They'd think he had no pride, to be asking a Bria to help him raise his youngling.

Perallis rose to speak, the muscles in his face settling into a disagreeable tightness. Before he could begin, I jumped up and asked, "Is this what Yur'i wants also?"

Might as well shock them thoroughly, that even the child was consulted. But hadn't I always said I believed in freedom of choice?

"Yes," Rennis said without hesitation.

I turned to Council Chair. "I suggest, when making this decision, that councilors keep in mind we might soon be presenting our city with the existence of an entire community of strange Ghen and Bria. Their customs will be very different from ours. And yet, we'll be seeking peace and understanding. Isn't that what we all want?"

While Council Chair signed my words to Chair Ghen and he translated them, I looked around the room, meeting the eye of every councilor.

"If we cannot allow a Ghen child into our schools, to learn Bria stories and Bria skills, how will we open ourselves to complete strangers? Or do you intend to shun those others when we find them? To keep our distance, pretend they don't exist?

"Rennis and Gant'i's request isn't a problem: it's the beginning of a solution. We have to prepare our children for something we never thought to face—another civilization."

I chose my words with care. The councilors would do our city no good if they left this room with visions of chaos haunting them. Better to present a choice between making new friends or retaining the status quo. I only hoped we'd be so lucky as to have that choice. How ironic that I, so intolerant and prideful in my youth, should be the one now to encourage tolerance and calm.

Rennis looked at me in surprise and gratitude. I hadn't always been supportive to him. But he was given to such intense emotions and religious musings, I often didn't know what to say or do. This, at least, was a clear-cut, practical issue.

"You speak as though it was certain that there are other Ghen and Bria. We have no proof of that," Perallis said.

"Do you prefer the alternative?" I asked, subtly reminding them of the implications of the Southern expedition. My insinuation secured the vote of every Bria in the room.

There was, however, argument among the Ghen. But it was already clear that Council Chair and Chair Ghen agreed with me. Rennis was lucky Darillis, lying in denial at his home, was not already in that seat.

"There will be opposition," Council Chair said, "But we have a duty to think of the future, and try to prepare our people for it. The wind moves on and we must keep our footing. Whatever your personal feelings about this issue," he glanced at Parallis, "I urge you all to remember the good of our city demands that we face the coming wind."

∽

"What's this about a Ghen child attending Bria school?" Anarris paced before me, too upset to sit down for the interview he'd requested. "And I hear that Savannis has accepted him into storytime!"

"It's a change," I agreed, "as was the addition of an unjoined Bria seat. I'm for change, aren't you?"

This slowed him down. "What's Council's aim in this?" he demanded, hovering near the chair.

"Savannis makes his own decisions. As for attending Bria school, the child is weak, he can't participate in Ghen training. Perhaps he can become a useful citizen in other ways."

"You expect me to believe that?"

"That Ghen can be useful citizens? Consider it an experiment, then."

"You're a cunning politician, Briarris. I don't say you're dishonest, but nothing you do serves only one purpose." I was pleasantly surprised by his perceptiveness, but acknowledging the compliment at this time would serve no purpose. The fact that I wasn't insulted annoyed him.

"You've been completely converted, you know that? You used to want Ghen out of our Bria city!"

I wanted to tell him I'd learned something over the years, and it was a shame he hadn't. But he could make things very ugly. His voice might encourage others, even beyond Single-by-Choice, to speak up also. Not that that wasn't already happening; I'd had a stream of objectors through my office since the Council meeting. But they were, for the most part, more easily mollified than Anarris. I had to find a common ground with him, before the whole issue exploded.

"Perhaps I haven't changed as much as it seems," I said. "When I was young I questioned traditions, and I'm still doing so. You and I are alike in that." I paused. "You're making my neck ache."

He sat down. "Savannis is old. He's out of touch with young Bria. But he just tells stories. It's Bria school we're more concerned about."

"I'll tell you sincerely that I supported this motion because I want to encourage Bria to be less rigid, more open to change. That's the truth, Anarris. One small Ghen child in our schools won't make any difference to Bria who don't wish to join. But if Ghen, and older Bria, too, loosen their hold on traditions, it can only mean less pressure on your members."

"I don't believe you're doing it to lessen the pressure on single Bria."

"It will be a result anyway."

"Why are you supporting it?"

Why indeed? I was almost talking myself out of it. After all, I wanted young Bria to join. I was tempted to ask him if he truly wished to depopulate our city. However, I wasn't an individual having a discussion; I was Council Relations.

"There is one thing I have never believed in," I said at last, "and that is the use of force." It was true in my past, and true of my present views. I hoped that nothing in our future would change it. "If you believe that Bria should freely choose their lifestyle, show it by granting this young Ghen the same freedom. You'll gain respect for Single-by-Choice if you do."

He agreed, though he wasn't happy, and he left threatening to "watch me carefully" in future. Nothing new there.

When he had gone I rested my head against the back of my chair and closed my eye, weary beyond words. Were our traditions holding us back, or were they the only thing still holding us together?

Like most Bria these days, I found Savannis's stories of the past tedious and mostly irrelevant. But because of them, I was able to recognize our present in the past, and to imagine our future from the present, strange as that sounds. Because of the sense of time his stories had given me, I had learned to conceive the decisions that must shape that future.

The trouble was, every future I envisioned led to the destruction of our fragile civilization.

Sight

Savannis

I began to sway slightly as I slipped into the sing-song of the storyteller.

"...Then the Creator, looking down on Wind, on its rough, rugged mountains and bottomless seas, its windy tempests and sudden, lethal stillnesses, its dark, tumultuous forests where wild beasts prowled by day and monsters hungered in the night—then the One who made Wind sorrowed to see His world so bound in barbary. He placed the gentle Bria in its midst and whispered "tame my Wind" into our ears. And, so we would not perish before nightfall, He made the fierce and fearless Ghen to need us."

By the time I was half-way through, they were saying it word for word with me, the customary chant with which I began storytime settling them down. How many times had I repeated the creation story to fidgeting children? Would it be anything more to them than meaningless words most would forget before they were out of childhood? To their parents, I was the Bria Voice of Wind, their spiritual adviser, but to the children, I was the storyteller.

Leaning heavily on my walking stick, I rose to my feet, forcing my stiffening muscles to support me. It was time to draw the story of our city for them.

"Matri says I'm too old for your stories."

I stopped in the middle of explaining how Heckt'er, with the Creator Wind's help, built the wall above our peninsula. "Is that what you think, Pandarris?" I asked.

"Matri says I should be spending the time on my schoolwork."

Briarris would think so. As a child, he had had little use for tradition, even less interest in the past. Now his younglings, like him, were focused on the future, and only respected what could be proven. "How will you help our people, Pandarris, if you don't build upon the learning of history?"

116

"Matri says it isn't history, it's myth. Anyway, I'm going to discover something new, something no one else knows."

The other children looked at him admiringly, impressed with his boldness. A familiar weariness fell over me. Where among this generation would I find someone to take my place? There was a stridency about them all. Even the younger ones, downy curls barely covering their skinny limbs, were not immune. They wriggled restlessly as I told my stories, their feet twitching with impatience, ears pitched to the sounds of the busy city around us.

"Tell us something new," three-year-old Tyannis demanded and the others nodded eagerly.

At their age, I remember watching Larissis, the storyteller who taught me, with a hushed intensity, my little hands itching to grab onto his stick and draw the pictures with him. Only young Yur'i, the Ghen child, watched my stick that way as I drew pictures in the sand to illustrate my stories. But his interest was merely interpretation. Being Ghen, he could barely hear my Bria voice. I would have signed to him, but it was hard enough to persuade parents to send their children to storytime with him there; I didn't want to upset our customs further. Even the children were affected by the growing chasm between Bria and Ghen; for the most part, they ignored him.

By now I'd watched Tyannis translating my stories for Yur'i long enough to know their family language. I wondered how many of the children had begun to pick it up, while pretending not to watch. It was a beautiful sign language, full of liquid movements and gentle touches; almost a dance, although less so when lame little Yur'i was signing.

I glanced toward Yur'i now. He was urgently poking Tyannis, his womb-parent's child, who pretended not to notice. I eyed Tyannis sternly.

"Yur'i says we have to know the past in order to live together," he said, guiltily.

Pandarris gave a low whistle of disgust. The other children looked embarrassed. No wonder Tyannis hadn't wanted to pass on Yur'i's comment. Guilt by translation.

"There is no foresight without hindsight," I said, into their silent denial.

How could I teach them to be less dominated by the present moment? It was in our very nature. Daily I drew stories in the sand, telling them, as they watched the wind blowing away my drawings, that the past must continue to live in their minds even when it is gone. But they learn nothing from my stories. I sometimes imagine that we are all drawn in sand.

Did I remember to tell them the story of Riattis, who gave her life to save Ghen when night lightning struck the Ghen compound and burned almost a third of the city, 100 stillseasons ago? Of Garn'ar, who led twelve successful hunts, risking his own life to keep us alive the year callan disease killed most of our Bria livestock? For a brief while Bria, too, became flesh-eaters in order to survive. Surely I told them. Didn't I?

No matter, I told their parents, and what good has it done? Ghen and Bria grow more estranged each passing season. They have forgotten that the Creator bound them together, blending their mutual need into something greater than either species alone. Soon their estrangement will tear our city apart. I see it, but I am helpless to prevent it.

"Savannis?" I looked down at little Tibellis, tugging on my hand timidly. Caught daydreaming again.

"That's enough for today." I shooed them away. So weary, so overwhelmingly weary. No wonder I sometimes have trouble holding onto my train of thought. Does it matter? Every group of youngsters turns further from what I am trying to teach them. Wind over Wind, help me to teach them how to see beyond the present moment, before they lose their future with their past.

I looked up to see that Yur'i and Tyannis had stayed behind. Tyannis was gazing wistfully after the others scattering to play, but stayed because of Yur'i. Tyannis is a loyal one. Perhaps…? No, he hasn't the patience to be the Voice of Wind. He wants a life of action, not words.

Yur'i stood close to me, where I could lean on him to pull myself to my feet. I suppose being lame himself gives him some insight into the infirmities of age. I reached for him. My fur was thin with age and I had to be careful not to cut myself on the rigid scales across his shoulders and back. He motioned to Tyannis and the two of them helped me up the steps into my home.

"Thank you." Now that we were inside, I signed directly to him, without waiting for Tyannis to interpret as he did during storytime. The others teased Tyannis about it. Not in front of me, but I could see by his wariness toward them that they had done so. Perhaps I should sign to Yur'i in front of them? Such a break from tradition. Which traditions should I guard and which discard? How can I know?

I should break this one. I only maintain it because of the children's parents. They were upset enough when Yur'i joined their younglings at storytime, with Tyannis translating. Such a furor about sharing Bria stories, you'd think they cared about them!

Rather, they didn't want their children to see womb-siblings signing to each other, an unheard-of practice. Even the word "womb-siblings" shocked them. Tyannis invented it, implying a whole new relationship between Ghen and Bria. Unfortunately, none but Tyannis saw that relationship.

Hypocrites! They didn't really care about the intimacy of sharing a language only with their joined mate. That tradition, meant to keep a joined pair together, is unnecessary now that we live in a civilized manner. What was intended as a bridge, they now use as a barrier. But if I push them too far...

Tyannis brought me a cup of tea and some bread from my cupboard. He fidgeted as I took a sip of the sweet, hot liquid. Such an active child, trying so hard to pretend he didn't long to run outside. His parent is very religious. Perhaps too intense at times, but that's understandable. And it has had good effect upon these two. Who do they remind me of? Let me see, which story was that...?

"Yes, child? Ah, my tea." I lifted it to my lips. It was cool, but I drank it anyway. I wish they had brought it to me when it was still hot.

"Would you like to go?"

Tyannis hesitated, too polite to say "yes" outright.

"Run along."

Yur'i looked up as Tyannis moved toward the door. He'd been examining the paintings on my walls. How did they look, from his two-eyed perspective? Could he have done better if he had the long, jointed fingers to hold my paintbrushes?

To me the paintings were exquisite with meaning, but now, viewing them objectively, they appeared flat, motionless. You cannot paint the wind into a picture. It didn't bother me that other Bria would never look at them; they weren't like the moving, three-dimensional sculptures or the flowing fabric art of our artists. They were memories, nothing else. Yet I relied upon them more and more.

"Do you want to stay?" I signed to Yur'i as he shifted to follow Tyannis. He nodded, his eyes downcast, only glancing sideways briefly at me.

There is something about this child that worries me. Why won't he meet my eye? It's more than the shyness of being forced into a strange culture; that much I would expect. The little Ghen bears a heavy stillness, but he is secretive about it, as though ashamed of something. Ah, the burdens of childhood. I must talk to Mick'al about him. I keep forgetting.

I waved Yur'i over to a large stack of papers: my pictures, rough drafts mainly, for the few that I turned into paintings.

"Look at them. What do you see?"

He examined the first one. "The Ghen-Bria Council."

"Do you like it?"

"I like paintings."

"But?"

"They're... flat. Everyone is sitting all in a row."

"Of course they look that way." Was I hoping for praise?

He lifted the top one, looked quickly at me for permission, set it aside at my shrug and examined the second picture. He was silent a long time, looking at it.

"Well?" I asked finally. At the sound of my voice he turned, his jaws open in a wide, fang-studded grin.

"Ah, you like this one?" I signed.

"It makes me feel sick," he signed back happily.

"Yes." I leaned back. The painting was of stillseason. "That's how we feel, without the wind." He touched his breath and returned to his examination of the pictures. I closed my eye.

My pictures were all like stillseason; they are pauses in the wind of time, a single moment flattened onto paper, a little death. Any yet, without them, all that I have struggled to remember and teach the children would be lost...

∽

I woke in alarm. Who was that in my house? A gray-scaled Ghen! Going through my things while I slept!

"What are you doing?"

He looked up quickly. I peered more closely at him. He returned my pictures to the table and took a limping step toward me. Ah, Yur'i. I repeated my question in signs, my motions sharp, agitated.

"Looking at your pictures," he signed back. On the top of the pile I could see my map to the cave.

"Who told you you could look at those?" Could I not even take a nap without being invaded in my home, my secrets disturbed?

"You did," he signed, the surprise so clear on his face I could not doubt him.

"I did no such thing," I signed back, anyway. "Go home now."

My irritation was not with him but with myself, at my forgetfulness. Fear rose in me, a bitter taste on my breath. Parts of my life were disappearing. The faces of the children I have taught, the stories of my life, even as I paint them, blink on and off like sputtering oil lamps, beyond my control. Yesterday, halfway through a story, I lost the thread of it. The children sat waiting, whispering, finally giggling.

I looked down into my lap, hiding my panic, thinking of the cave. Desperately I ran through it in my mind, seeking the lost story, clutching to me what little I could salvage, always less and less, my people's stories, my very self, like water falling through my fingers. Blind! The eye of my people is going blind!

I wept for my failure, wept for my people. I wept all the more because they didn't know enough to weep for themselves. They don't see the gathering blindness that is descending upon them.

The whispering, the giggling hushed. Small bodies pressed forward, small hands patted me, tender little lips blew on my withered cheeks. "Don't cry, Savannis, don't cry." "I love you, Savannis," and a chorus of "I love you's" rose timidly around me.

Then a small voice piped up, "Jan'ar went out to fight the terrible courrant'h that had killed so many hunters…"

Jan'ar, of course. Jan'ar. But who had spoken? Tyannis. She faltered as I looked at her, but I nodded eagerly. And then she looked at Yur'i, who signed to her.

"Jan'ar took five triads of hunters with him, but it was Jan'ar who…"

☙

That night, the wind paused.

It is possible that for a moment in my sleep I held my breath and thought the whole world stopped. But I am the Voice of Wind, attuned to stillness even more than other Bria. In that momentary interval I woke, knowing.

How long had I known, not admitting it? Like layers of gauze, forgetfulness has settled on me, slowly, irritating at first, then a growing distraction, gathering weight and darkness until it bears me down, a shroud, leaving me blind, breathless, gasping in the vacuum of a mind that was once rich and wise and powerful.

I am the storyteller, the memory of the Bria! Where will they find their past when I have lost it, misplaced it in the relentless twilight, creeping like poison over my mind? Ignorance will reclaim them, all the more terrible for their veneer of civilization.

Whether the world trembled or only I, that tremble wakened me. I lay in my bed motionless with fear. I was intensely aware of the cold midseason wind raging in through every open window to soothe my ruffled fur. My house shook in the night storm, but that single second of breathless hesitation now made the wind's jubilant boisterousness seem mere bluster. Will I be the last storyteller?

The cave! I must go to the cave. All of my stories are there. I will see my stories in the cave where past and present meet, see and remember and take them back to the children who will not giggle and whisper, but will listen. And one of them will rise and take my stick in his small hands and draw with me, when I have remembered the stories, when I have told them so well that they call out to the next Bria storyteller to draw our past in the sands of our city, to trace it in the hearts of Bria children, the children of Wind.

I rose and hurried into the night. I didn't need the map. Even now, old and frail and pursued by shadows inside and out, still I know my way to the cave. I could feel my feet growing younger, smaller, the feet of a small child hurrying after Larissis, who is leading me for the first time to his cave. My cave now.

The tempest raged through the forest. Trees shook in its path as if to jar the darkness from me as I stumbled forward, clutching branches for support, relishing the wild wind, the strong living breath of Wind.

Lightning illuminated the night, surprising me. How many years had passed since the last lightning storm? I should have been afraid, but instead I was reassured. I took it as a sign from the Creator that there would still be time for memory to light the black recesses of my mind and shake our history into a child's cupped hands.

Bolts of lightning hit the earth, like the outstretched fingers of the Creator Wind, touching the heart of His creation and lighting my way. Ahead of me I had a long walk through the woods, then a slow crossing over the slippery rocks barely rising above the swollen Sorran river, and a wearying climb up the steep, rocky slope of the escarpment, before I could rest at last.

I was halfway over the Sorron, balanced precariously erect between two mossy boulders amid the rampaging current, when the lightning struck. Brilliance and beauty and pain flamed through me in a single instant, intense, excruciating.

With a flick of His finger, Wind tossed me into the cold and savage current. I gasped in air, and water, and air; I was battered against rock, swept into eddies and tiny, frantic whirlpools until at last I was caught in a net of branches reaching out from a fallen tree lying half-submerged across the river. The cold water had quickly put out the fire that burned through me, but I was bleeding and raw under my scorched fur, and breathless from my wild ride. More dead than alive, I crawled through the jagged branches and pulled myself onto the rough bark of the horizontal tree trunk. I was grateful when oblivion closed over my agony.

I don't know how long I lay there, darkness and light washing over me in alternating rhythms, a slow tempo to the counterpoint of pain flowing and ebbing with the tide of my heart. The tree rested in the water, higher toward its base, still rooted in the riverbank. I lay on my back along the top of it, so that from the chest down I was almost submerged in the cool water. Occasionally the wind would fling a spray of liquid into my face to slack my thirst. A number of the leaf-stripped branches which had rescued me stood like the spokes of a crib to guard my sleep. Feverish and delirious with pain I drifted in and out of consciousness while Wind itself held me and bathed me and healed me.

Even so, I would have died. Held in a crucible of agony I retreated, back through the stories of my life and the stories of my people, back and back and back to the dawn of consciousness. Slower and slower flowed the stories in my mind until, like a setting sun, I hung balanced in the moment between day and night…

The grunting of an animal intruded into that trembling moment before my final descent. Its guttural sounds came closer, tipping me at first toward night then, as recognition slowly dawned, inching me back up to consciousness. Guttural noises, repetitive, pitched in the keening cry of a child's sorrow. Not a Bria sound, not Bria to Bria like the passing of a lamp from hand to similar hand. Not what I wanted, but what I was given. The hard, furless touch of a Ghen. Wrong, all wrong.

And then, his small, dissimilar hands in mine, shortened Ghen fingers gently moved my fingers. Up and down in a strange rhythm, over and over until the repetition reached me. Patient and urgent, both, he moved my fingers: Savannis, Savannis, come back. Come back, Savannis! Come back and teach me, Savannis!

Yes, I tried to whisper. A cooling spray of water touched my face. I licked my parched and silent lips. Cupping his little hands and dipping them into the river, Yur'i lifted the clear water and tipped it into my mouth. I swallowed, fluttering my hands. He reached for them.

"Yes," I signed. And gently, carefully, I cupped his small Ghen hands together inside mine; the hands that would next hold the memories of the Bria.

Council Relations

Briarris

"Savannis makes his own decisions," I repeated. "The storyteller has always chosen his successor, without interference from Council."

I might as well have been talking in stillseason. I'd already argued the issue in closed-Council; I had little hope of changing their minds now, in open session. Not with a crowd of Bria sitting in the public gallery, making their opposition clear. Anarris was there, but his group was only a fraction of the protesters. Yur'i would not be recognized as Savannis's apprentice while Darillis was Council Chair.

Darillis was afraid. The increasing menace of the white Broghen unnerved him. The questioning look in every Bria eye left him breathless. The crowds that came to Council demanding that customs be upheld and those that came demanding they be set aside, equally frightened him. Like a plague, I'd watched his hysteria infect the other councilors.

I felt it myself. And we councilors weren't the only ones affected. Now this: a Ghen as the spiritual advisor of the Bria? What was Savannis thinking? If ever we needed to hear from Wind, it was now. But He would have to speak to us through Bria lips. A part of me wondered, could one set conditions upon one's Creator?

But that was not why I spoke up. I spoke up because it was I who had insisted Yur'i be allowed to attend story time. How could I not defend what I had set in motion?

At any rate, there were more urgent issues before us. Last year, seven Ghen had died on the expedition to the south. Childless Bria had responded with indifference or scorn at the inexplicable and dangerous activities of Ghen. Those who had given birth and knew what the Ghen had met up with in the south resented the reminder of something they'd rather forget.

125

The Ghen, in turn, were embittered by these reactions, frustrated at being unable to exonerate their dead. We'd discussed the growing tensions in closed-Council, but what could we do? We were the only Bria who knew the real reason behind the excursion to the south, and we couldn't tell what we knew.

At least no white Broghen had been discovered. It wasn't our own striking back at us. Our relief was immense, if short-lived. Ten days after the Ghen returned, a white Broghen attacked our walls, severely wounding a young, unjoined Ghen. He lived, but now could never mate. Then, in stillseason, two more attacks occurred. With the sadu'hs hibernating in their burrows and the anhad'hs migrated to the south, game was scarce in the forest and wetlands. The night guards had been tripled, and only Ghen who had already parented were allowed to take night duty.

When stillseason ended, Igt'ur told me that some of the Ghen were suggesting infant Broghen be destroyed. We were in the habit of meeting two or three removes before Council began, and were walking along the banks of the Symba. His comment shocked me. I stopped in my tracks. He waited, his face impassive. I realized I wasn't as shocked as I wished I was.

"I can hardly bear to know I birthed one of those things," I confessed to him. "To think that it may be out there, waiting to devour us…" I bent my head.

After a long moment, Igt'ur signed to me, "Would you be happier knowing otherwise?"

I looked up from his hands into his face. He held his calm expression, but we'd been joined for eight years, now; I'd learned to read his face. In that moment I wondered if I knew him at all.

"I don't think I'd like to know that, either," I signed, my hands shaking.

 батько

Officially, courrant'hs were blamed for the attacks on our wall. Young Bria began treating Ghen with more respect. A courant'h at one's doorstep is intimidating.

But every Bria who'd given birth knew, or suspected, that it wasn't courrant'hs stalking us. Few spoke of it, but in almost every eye I saw a mixture of horror and guilt: is it mine? Is it my own flesh that has come hungering for us?

126

No one said it out loud. Even so, young Bria were affected by the tension in their parents. The secret was bound to come out. One could explain away deaths on a distant expedition, but even young Bria began to question these recurring attacks upon our walls. A sense of approaching disaster hovered over the city.

"We have to tell Bria about the white Broghen," I argued over and over in closed-Council. "We don't have to admit the truth of our own birthings; we can say these Broghen come down from the mountains. At least that's not another lie." I spoke too bitingly. The strain was telling on me, too.

"We don't know that for sure," Perallis argued; just the opening I was looking for.

"We must send a second expedition to the mountains, as we planned."

"No!" Darillis's voice was shrill. "We need the Ghen here, defending us. If one of those… those things… gets in—" he rushed from the room, unable to continue. This was the third time closed-Council ended thus.

Then a young Bria killed himself the day after giving birth. And on the morning the new Ghen parents left to take their hideous burden south, a crowd of Bria grandparents spontaneously assembled before dawn at the gate in the wall to watch them leave, even though stillseason was not yet fully over.

The silence was heavier than the air in stillseason; so oppressive that even the hungry infant Broghen were hushed. Darillis was called, but he refused to come. Only after the last Ghen had passed through the gate and disappeared into the forest, did the silent throng disburse.

Is there anything more corrosive than shame?

Secrets

Yur'i

"I'm too young to die!"

One of my earliest memories is crying that out to my parent. Something had brought on one of my attacks of breathlessness and as I struggled to draw air into my aching lungs, I somehow found the strength to protest.

"Don't be silly," my parent replied. To him it was obvious that I wasn't suffocating, but the episode had come up so quickly it overwhelmed me. I was seized with a panic so profound that even now I feel it and cannot bear to recall the incident too closely.

I remember thinking then, with absolute certainty, that life was fragile, capricious beyond our control. And that I had already failed.

∽

I wasn't yet four when Savannis was lost in the lightning storm. I'd been attending storytime for a year and a half and knew most of the stories by heart. At night I lay on my mat repeating them to myself before I fell asleep. I hadn't yet seen the storyteller's cave, although I knew about it. Savannis had a map leading to it among his drawings.

On the third day after his disappearance I followed it, telling no one. He was secretive about that map, angry when I'd accidentally come upon it. But I was desperate.

He was air to me. The illness in my lungs released its hold when I slipped into his tales or lost myself in the colors of his paintings. I would have torn the dark and deadly world apart to find him.

When they carried Savannis home from the river, he had me move in with him at once. Because Savannis was so sick and so insistent, the healer put aside the protests of the Bria present.

I don't know how my parent felt about it. I waited while Matri talked to him, both terrified and hopeful that he'd refuse. Afterwards he merely asked, "Is this what you want, Yur'i?" and somehow I found the courage to touch my breath.

Matri helped me pack and carry my things to Savannis's house: my sleeping mat and headroll, the medicinal herbs he boiled into a soothing tea when I had trouble breathing—although it rarely happened any more—my slingshot and a handful of smooth pebbles, the hunting knife my parent had given me. Gant'i had already carried my Ghen chair over, before his duty on the wall. At Savannis's door Matri set down my things and bent to sign to me.

"Listen to me, Yur'i." He waited. I had to look into his eye, something I rarely did. Eyes are too honest; I didn't want to know what they might tell me.

"The way we are—Gant'i and me and you and Tyannis and Saft'ir—I wouldn't have it any other way. I want you to know that."

I cringed a little inside. What did he mean? Did I want to know?

"'All things conspire for good on the Creator's Wind.' That saying used to annoy me, but I believe it now. The Creator Wind doesn't make mistakes, Yur'i. Do you understand?"

I touched my breath, a little uncertainly.

He leaned forward and gently blew into my face. I blew back, trembling a little, beginning to regret my decision, but before I could speak he rose and coughed at Savannis's door.

ের

At any moment of the day or night Savannis would call to me, remembering a story he might not have told me yet. Most of the stories I heard a dozen times and had already heard at storytime, yet not a word was changed between the tellings. Even when memory failed, Savannis wouldn't change a tale, but stop signing completely, looking bewildered. Then he'd notice me and I'd continue the story until he nodded, comforted.

All this time I was wild with impatience. When would he teach me to draw? When would I make paper shout and dance with image and color? At least now I could look freely at his drawings, thinking to myself how I might render similar scenes. Now and then, I examined the map to the mysterious cave, wondering what treasure it concealed. But I said nothing of any of this to Savannis, afraid he might change his mind and I might never learn to draw at all.

It was almost stillseason when he was well enough to resume storytime. He showed me how to move his drawing stick through the sand to illustrate the stories.

"You'll get the feel of it," he assured me. "It's only to hold their attention. The stories are what matter, and you know them." I felt deceptive, but how could I tell him now that it was the drawing I hungered for, even more than the stories?

The Bria children trooped up while I was still practicing with the stick.

"You saved Savannis's life," little Tibellis said through my womb-sibling Tyannis, just before Savannis began the first story.

"No, of course not, how could I?" I signed for Tyannis to translate. "The healers saved him. I only found him."

"He found me because Wind led him to me," Savannis said, signing as he spoke. He was reclining in the lounge from which he now told the stories. "And Wind led him to me because I was too blind to recognize the next storyteller without His intervention."

The Bria children sat perfectly still, staring at Savannis. If I had been surprised by Tibellis's praise, it was nothing to their shock at seeing Savannis sign to them, and call me the next storyteller. He did not acknowledge their reaction in any way, but simply began the morning's story.

I drew the story as Savannis spoke and signed it, tracing the illustrations in the sand as he had taught me. They were not well done. Wind and sand together resisted the stick, which was too tall for me and shook in my unaccustomed hands. But Savannis nodded his approval. I was glad at least that Pandarris and his peers, all a year older than I, hadn't come back to storytime after Savannis's illness. These puzzled, younger faces watching me were difficult enough, without those scornful, older ones.

Savannis insisted that I would be the next storyteller; insisted not only to the children but to the entire Bria-Ghen Council, who came to him in ones and twos when the parents began to complain. Finally, Council Chair and Chair Ghen visited. I waited outside the house to hear my fate, embarrassed that they might think I had presumed to be the Bria storyteller, but even more terrified they would disallow it. If they did, Savannis would never teach me to paint.

After they left, Savannis called me inside. "They'll debate it in Council," he answered my anxious signs. "Don't concern yourself about that. You are my apprentice, with or without their approval. As if they have any say when Wind has made His choice."

When storytime ended for stillseason, Savannis continued coaching me. By the time the wind returned I knew every story as well as he did, and I had begun to paint.

The hardest part had been learning to hold the sharpened chalks and paintbrushes in my short straight fingers, then to move them deftly across paper or cloth with just the right pressure to blush a cheek or darken an eye. Savannis taught me patiently what he knew. The rest I taught myself; shadows and spacing and depth, foreground and background, the difference between stillness and arrested movement, between calm and passion.

Everywhere I looked, pictures jumped out at me. I painted in a fever, as though the integrity of each moment in time was threatened, and only I could hold it safe upon my paper. I saw all of us—but perhaps it was only I—balanced on the edge of chaos.

⁊

"They are not all sitting in a row." Savannis smiled at me before glancing back at my painting of a Council meeting. "But why are they so angry?"

I looked at my painting again. My womb-parent's mouth was open as though in protest, while councilor Briarris sat stiffly beside him, frowning. Council Chair's hands were balled into fists in his lap and Chair Ghen gripped the arms of his seat, his extended claws piercing the wood. Extended claws? What had I drawn?

"It's not good," I signed, crumpling it into a ball.

"It's good, Yur'i." Savannis took the paper from me, smoothed it out, looking at it thoughtfully. "Perhaps it's time I took you to the cave. You'll be the storyteller then, whatever Council decides."

Origins

Savannis

"Mind the rocks. They give sometimes here," I signed to Yur'i as he scrambled up the slope after me.

"We need to rest, Savannis. Listen to your breath."

His breath was as loud as mine, I considered telling him; then I reconsidered, and stopped and leaned upon my walking stick. Yur'i squatted on a large boulder staring at the ground, then shifted and looked backward down the steep incline we'd just ascended. Avoiding my eye.

His eagerness when I proposed this trip has been replaced by nervousness. I have been too silent; he's caught my mood. What should I say? Nothing will prepare him for what he will soon know.

"I have a story to tell you," I signed, sitting beside him on the wide, flat rock. He looked up, grinning a little.

"It is a frightening story," I cautioned. "I've never told it." I looked past Yur'i, down the incline to where the dense ugappa forest began. I won't come here again. Even in daytime when the forest is safe, the walk is too long, the climb too steep, the memories too bitter. I do not want to die here, in our past.

"…A terrible story. But it has a good ending." I forced myself to smile at him.

He did not grin, but he met my gaze. I was proud of him then; I felt it like a cool wind racing through me.

Where should I start? I began to sway slightly, and slipped into the sing-song of the storyteller, signing as I spoke.

"Bria are not made to withstand violence. Born into a brutal world we are fragile, helpless. We would not survive without the Ghen—"

He knew every word I said, but hearing the familiar calmed him. My hands itched for the drawing stick with which I illustrated all my stories, but I had

132

only my heavy walking stick. The ground was rocky here at any rate, and soon enough there would be pictures for him.

"...So goes the story of creation as I taught it to you."

He blinked at the abrupt change in my voice as I began to peel the sweet story away from the truth lying underneath, as hard and unpalatable as a fruit-stone.

"What I didn't tell you then is that Dayannis made the story; painted it on the wall of a distant, secret cave. He made it out of the nightmare of his youth, so hideous it nearly destroyed them all..." I paused. "Forgive me, Yur'i, for what I am about to show you." I rose stiffly to my feet.

"Dayannis made the story of creation?" Yuri signed.

"While he painted, Wind moved his fingers, his charcoal, deep in the cave where there is no wind," I replied. "As I have felt Wind moving my brush inside that cave. The Creator speaks through us."

"Will He speak through me?"

Could the Wind speak to Bria through a Ghen? I chided myself for my doubt. Had He not chosen this child? "If you let Him," I signed.

I resumed the climb. Yur'i followed silently.

Before long I could see the stark angle of rock ahead. "We'll need wood for a fire," I told Yur'i, gesturing at the scrub brush around us. He gathered an armful of branches and dry twigs while I rested, leaning over my stick. Then I led him around the protruding rock, stopping before a wide cappa bush.

"No one knows of this cave. Heckt'er himself rolled those stones to block the entrance, leaving only one small opening behind this bush." I turned to him, feeling a guilty joy at the prospect of surrendering my burden.

"Do you remember the time I used the end of a fire-log to draw a picture on the stone beside my house? Yes? I thought you would. You cried when the rain washed it away. I should have known then you were the one." I paused. But self-recrimination serves no use, and I continued. "Inside this cave, where neither the wind nor the rain can erase them, Dayannis drew pictures of our people's past.

"Whatever is not in these paintings is lost, vanished into dreams and fears and prejudices. Just as our unmoving Bria eye requires motion to see the present, our shifting memories require stillness—the stillness of these paintings—to see the past.

"Bring the wood you've gathered and come inside."

ᴇ⁊

I swayed in the small, dark cave, waiting to become accustomed to the stillness. The other caves, where the Bria had once lived, had wider entrances facing into the wind. This one was narrow and its opening blocked. But I had learned to endure its stillness.

I took the wood from Yur'i and began to arrange it within the small circle of stones in the center of the cave. I found my way easily in the darkness, as familiar with this cave as with my own home. Reaching into the pouch at my side, I lifted from its clay nest a glowing, moss-wrapped coal and set it among the smallest twigs. Yur'i bent and blew upon it gently.

"I've seen you watch me drawing stories in the sand," I signed to him as we waited for the fire to catch. "I've seen you smile as the pictures flow like voices from my stick and move in the breeze, sand sifting over earth as the wind blows over Wind. I've also seen you frown, watching the lines of meaning shift away. No other child frowns into the wind. Do not protest, child. I'm not accusing you of anything. These are the signs of a storyteller." Again I felt my guilt, and shook it off. The wind blows on.

A tiny spark leaped up at the edge of a twig. Yur'i fanned it and it grew, spreading along the fragile twig, seeking sustenance.

I stared into the dark recess of the cave. "They watched their parents dying while they ate."

Yur'i looked up, aware that I had spoken but unable to understand my words. I beckoned and he rose, following me to the paintings nearer the cave entrance. I didn't show him the one that I'd begun. We would discuss that later, since he would have to finish it for me. I showed him the paintings of the stories he already knew, of Garn'ar and Riattis and Jan'ar and all the others, painted when they occurred, by generations of storytellers.

"They were real!" he signed excitedly.

The fire was brighter now. I motioned him to add more branches and led him further down the wall, to the earlier pictures.

"This is our walled city, before it was built. Dayannis painted this to show Heckt'er his vision; a place of beauty and safety, where Bria and

134

Ghen could live together. It came to him in a dream as clearly as you see it on this wall."

He stared at the painting in reverence, as though he could see Dayannis's hand stroking lines onto the bleak rock wall. I waited, giving him time to savor this moment. But I had much to tell him, and we still had a long journey home before dusk made the way too dangerous.

"I must tell you about Dayannis's paintings as they were told to me," I signed. "As they have been told to every storyteller through the ages, back to the time when Dayannis himself spoke to the first storyteller." I waited until he touched his breath. Then I began in a voice no longer my own, but Dayannis's, signing as I spoke.

"In my dream I was running, fleeing through the forest, alone, lost, terrified. It was stillseason and night. I was blind in the motionless woods, nauseous and breathless and dizzy. I ran desperately, breaking branches, stumbling over rocks, falling on tree roots and leaping up again, blood on my hands, my legs, my arms… Will I ever be free of blood?

"Behind me, closer and closer, I heard the hot, insane shriek of the predator frenzied for its prey. I felt it, like a devouring darkness at my back and I ran, blind and sick and hopeless.

"Then, as I threw myself between two tall ugappas, they moved together, tightening against each other. They reached out their branches and drew other trees to them, until the sense of safety at my back stopped me.

"I turned and watched with amazement as tree after tree tilted and bowed and shifted into line until I was surrounded by a circle of ugappas, their leaves tossing and rustling with laughter despite stillseason. Outside their strange protection monsters raged in confusion. I walked around the circle touching my garrison of ugappas and I felt invincible. I knew then what Bria were meant to be: the soft and treasured heart of a wild, young world that had only begun to dream of civilization."

I paused. Yur'i looked intently at the picture Dayannis had painted of his dream, the walls of ugappa rising from the forest to shield our homes, where children, Bria and Ghen, played safely in the open wind. At length he looked up, fascinated to be hearing a new story.

"At that time our ancestors lived near here, in two large caves further up the escarpment, one for Bria and one for Ghen. Heckt'er told the Ghen about Dayannis's wall and they began to build it."

I slipped back into Dayannis's voice: *"All the Bria, except for me and the younger children, were dying. Dying from the sight of too much death, from the callousness of a barbarous world, from the horror that filled their souls in place of hope. I thought they were dying; I did not understand that they were already dead, that they were waiting only until their infants were old enough to be weaned. I painted this picture for them. But it was already too late; they never saw safety."*

"What happened to them?" Yur'i signed, his nervousness returning. He turned, looking toward the front of the cave as though he contemplated leaving. I resisted the urge to apologize again. He had to know. I touched his arm.

"Are you ready to know the truth about our past?"

I waited for him to touch his breath. Finally he did, a small movement, made without looking at me.

I remembered my earlier concerns about him. He carried a secret burden already. I had questioned him about it but gotten nowhere. I suspected that the experience occurred so early in his childhood he'd forgotten it, and remembered only some sense of loss, or failure. Was I right to place another burden on him? But it was too late for misgivings, we were already here.

"You must guard this truth and never speak of it. Hide it beneath the gentler stories that you will tell the children when I am gone." I waited till he glanced at my face; waited still, until he touched his breath once again.

"You will see the truth in Dayannis's paintings."

The flame of our fire was dying down. I went over and put more branches on it. Then I led him to the very back of the cave, to the first painting of all. It was smaller than the others, its lines more hesitant, as though drawn by a child's hand. The detail was missing, but it was clearly the work of a budding artist.

"Dayannis is young in this first painting, four years old," I signed. "His sibling died at birth, as many did then."

Yur'i started and backed away, turning from me. I remembered that Tyannis's sibling—Yur'i's womb-sibling, in their family language—had also died. I waited. He didn't turn back for me to continue until I touched his shoulder.

"Do you want to be the storyteller, Yur'i?"

He understood my meaning but he hesitated. For a moment I was afraid he would change his mind. I noticed then how he trembled and panted for air, and I hesitated myself. Then I thought, Wind has chosen him.

At last he touched his breath.

136

"It all began with the drought and the terrible famine that followed. Bria ate meat in those days; the Ghen hunted and brought it to them." I glanced at Yur'i. He was not as shocked to learn that as I had been. I turned back to the painting.

"This is Dayannis's playmate, Sharris. He is three here, too little to understand what is beginning. He's reaching eagerly for his small piece of meat. The Bria tending the fire are young, too, pregnant or nursing parents. They were permitted to eat to nourish their infants. So young themselves, in such a terrible time." My breath caught. They had not looked so young when I first saw this painting, still emerging from childhood myself. I wanted to touch the painting, to stroke these lost children, as though my pity could reach through time and comfort them.

"*We were not allowed to give our parents food.*" I resumed in Dayannis's voice, reciting the story as it had been told to me, and signing as I spoke. "*We seldom spoke, even after the meat was eaten and the Ghen had left, and when we did it was mostly in tearful whispers to our matris who came to console us, as long as they could.*"

"*This is my matri, sitting with the others behind the row of Ghen. Not that the Ghen were needed to hold them back from the cooking meat. None of the parents would have taken food from their children. The Ghen gave us something to blame while we ate what little food they could bring us.*

"*I am looking at my matri in this picture, and holding my piece of meat in my hands. 'Eat it, Dayannis,' he said.*

"*'Eat it, Dayannis.' The sound of his voice and the taste of that meat are one to me, beautiful and terrible, the sound and the taste of living and dying interwoven; that which nurtures and that which kills. My mouth was so dry that I choked but I wanted food so badly my hands shook. I accepted the flesh that died to sustain me, meat and matri both.*

"*I wept as I ate. We all did. The parents wept with hunger and the fear of dying, and with pity for their children; the children wept with guilt. Even the Ghen were weeping, because the drought had driven the game away, or killed and rotted it; because they thought they'd failed themselves and us.*

"*We ate because we could not stop ourselves when the Ghen put meat into our hands; because our bellies cried out louder than our tears; and finally, because we needed the strength to bury our parents.*

"We wept until we had no more tears to shed, until our eyes and our hearts were as dry and lifeless as the drought-ridden land. More terrible than all our tears were the days when we no longer wept."

I took a deep breath, trying to control the shaking of my hands as I signed, to stop the tears rolling silently down my face. Yur'i stood very still, panting for breath. The air on the escarpment was thin; I was panting myself, caught up in the horror of those children. But I remembered that Yur'i was Ghen.

"Later Dayannis learned that the older Ghen refused to eat, also," I told him. "They hunted for as long as they had strength and gave it all to the younger Ghen to share with the Bria. Only the best of the older hunters ate, and only because their skills were needed."

Yur'i watched my signing but would not look at my face. I had no choice but to trust the Creator Wind, and continue.

"Heckt'er was born with me from the womb of my parent. There was never a time I did not know him. We played together as infants until we were weaned and he was old enough to leave my parent. I hadn't been separated from him for more than a month when the drought began and he crept back in secret. My parent held us both against the gathering dark."

"Many Ghen were killed fighting Broghen at that time. See this shadow at the entrance to our cave? The Broghen also suffered from the drought. They also hungered and found the forest hunting poor. The Broghen returned from their wild wandering, and we were their prey.

"We huddled, still with terror, in our cave, caught between the sighs of our dying parents and the shadows of Ghen and Broghen battling over us; one for our flesh, the other for our wombs. Deeper and deeper into the cave we moved, and further from the wind of clarity, into distortion.

"When the drought ended, when the game returned and the grasses and the birds, the wild roots, the berries and the nuts, when it all returned, we were alone. We were a band of orphans with only three seasons of young adults nursing infants, too traumatized themselves to deal with us.

"Often we slept on the graves of our parents."

I paused, almost able to feel the bone-chilling cold of that unnatural bed. I found myself shivering and motioned to Yur'i to add more branches to the fire. I saw that he was shaking as he did so.

"Heckt'er consoled Dayannis when his matri died," I signed to Yur'i. "Here he is in this next picture sitting beside Dayannis, his hand on Dayannis's shoulder. Look at him first, before you look at the next painting. I can only look at it after I have looked at them finding some comfort together. Perhaps they started signing then. There must have been a time when it began, but Dayannis did not paint it."

I gave him time to look at it before slipping back into Dayannis's voice. *"We were all children, weak from a year and a half of near-starvation, sick to our souls from burying our parents, Ghen and Bria alike, and terrified that the Broghen, having finally withdrawn into the forests, might at any moment return. And so they did, from time to time, in the dark of the night. One seeks one's own. We understood that. We, like the Broghen, no longer knew the difference between loving and feeding.*

"But we wanted to. We gathered berries and nuts, we cooked the wild roots and legumes, and sprinkled in the tender fronds of silis for flavor. We would no longer eat the meat Ghen brought us; we wanted to forget the taste of death.

"At night, when the Broghen hunted, we huddled at the back of our cave behind our fires, far from the friendly wind, and tried to sleep while Ghen walked the entrance guarding us. We tried to heal, and we might have done so…

"But then the pregnant Bria gave birth."

"There is a little wind in this picture." I motioned Yur'i closer to see it more clearly. "It moves across a full season. Here, in the corner, Heckt'er and Dayannis are squatting with the other children, waiting to eat. Such a small puff of wind, like a moment of sleep between night terrors. A single green season between the drought and the time of that birthing.

"Ghen didn't attend births in those days. Bria parents took their pregnant children to the birthing cave and assisted them there. But all the parents and grandparents who would have led the young Bria, at the breaking of womb-water, into the birthing cave, lay dead in their graves."

Yur'i was panting for air again. I remembered how I had felt, hearing all this for the first time. Should I take him outside? But we still had a long trip home. "Shall I continue, Yur'i?" I signed. He gasped beside me, but did not answer. Nor did he turn away. I took that as assent.

"The pregnant Bria probably knew they should go to the birthing cave. Most certainly their parents told them to, before they died; warned them of what to expect, how to prepare. They must have been too terrified to believe it, or else remembered only the word 'Broghen' and could not bring themselves to go alone and helpless and in pain into the birthing cave. And so they just lay down on the floor among the other children. Here, in the middle of this second painting, you can see them."

I meant to explain the painting to Yur'i myself, but could not bear to continue that way. I had to slip back into Dayannis's narrative, as I had learned it. I had to tell it as a story.

"This one is dead. See the two infant Broghen sitting on his corpse? The first has bitten through its own umbilical cord and attacked the second, which does not know whether to chew its cord and breathe, or kill its sibling. There another, having no one to birth it, is emerging through the gaping wound it tore out of the Bria's flesh for its escape.

"Here is a Bria crazed at the sight of his Broghen newborn tearing the fragile body of his Bria infant. Here a nursing Bria holds his youngling above the hungry jaws of a two-day-old Broghen, while his still-nursing Ghen turns to attack, his mouth still wet with milk. Not so the Broghen infant: its mouth is wet with blood.

"This Bria has left his own infants to attend the fearful birthings. See how his arms are bitten and scratched from pulling the infant Broghen aside, how his eye turns to seek his own unguarded younglings huddled at the back of the cave with the rest of us, wide-eyed and screaming, screaming, screaming!

"We screamed for days, screamed and whimpered and huddled in tearful, exhausted sleep and woke to the hot breath and the fierce pain of tearing infant Broghen teeth and screamed again!

"Between our screams, we heard those who had birthed the monstrous Broghen crying out to their dead parents, begging their forgiveness, believing in their delirium that this was their retribution.

"And yet, hideous as they were, these were their babies. The conflict of emotions tore them apart as much as the sharp little teeth of their terrifying offspring.

"Heckt'er and the nursing Ghen children struggled to defend us, but they were no match for the demented Broghen erupting into predatory life straight from the womb. The older Bria by now were throwing themselves in the path of the Broghen, crying their remorse, as though the Broghen could tear their guilt from them along with their flesh."

"At last the Ghen in their distant cave, coming to deliver the food they had gathered for us, beheld us in our bloody and terrible chaos.

"They killed the Broghen. Before our eyes they killed them, savage and merciless in their unschooled youth, the oldest of them no older than any of us. They pushed aside the Bria who tried to stop them, not knowing that they were shedding their own blood, not understanding why we shrank from them, why killing adult Broghen was different from destroying these small savages still wet from our wombs, blind and desperate and hungry but even so, our offspring: ours and theirs.

"We watched as they were murdered in front of us, and we moved into a place beyond screaming.

"We lived in that silent place for a long time. We almost stopped moving, except when it was necessary. One by one, the pregnant Bria killed themselves.

"We understood. We were even grateful. Death was more real to us than life. Silent and still, we all felt the pull of death. It called to us in the voices of our starved parents, our dead or dying friends, our slaughtered, monstrous infants.

"Here at the end of this picture you can see us as we were then. No more tears, no more screams. Just silence. Only a single flicker lights the campfire on this side of the picture. A single ember aglow. One more drop of blood would have licked it out.

"See the Ghen standing here in the corner while all the Bria of mating age huddle in the back of the cave? See the sharpened rock in this one's hand? It is stillseason again, after two years of dying. Had even one Ghen approached that group of Bria, they would have killed themselves.

"Even the infant Ghen were shunned. Unweaned, they stumbled to the cave entrance where they were gathered in by the Ghen and taken to their caves. The youngest ones surely died, not yet able to chew and swallow meat.

"I tried to stop it but the nursing Bria shrank in revulsion from their infant Ghen, whimpering in my arms, as though they were Broghen. I could not reach them, they were so filled with nightmares.

"The ashes of too much death lay heaped about us, smothering us. How still we sit, waiting for the wind to blow away the ashes of our desecrated childhood, to relieve us of the guilt of living."

Beside me, I heard Yur'i gasping for breath. But the past held me too tightly; he was less real to me than Dayannis, now.

"Of all the older children, only I healed," I continued in Dayannis's absent voice, signing automatically, as though the movements were part of the

story. *"It was not that I grieved less for my parent, or that I had feared less giving birth to Broghen. No, but I painted some of the horror out of my soul. And I had Heckt'er. I learned, through his signing, of his own sorrow and the sorrow of all the young Ghen.*

"They had never seen infant Broghen before. They had arrived to see a horde of vicious predators attacking Bria in a cave of blood and death and they reacted. I trusted Heckt'er and I understood him. You cannot hate what you understand.

"Here in this painting I am surrounded by the children. Those who were too young to remember the horrors of the past two years came to me happily; those who remembered, came to me desperately. They left their parent's breasts as soon as they were full and came to blow on my face with their milky lips. Each breath blew more of the ashes from my heart.

"I told them stories of hope, of Bria children whose parents were not troubled. Stories of Bria who did not fear to roam, who even played with Ghen, as Heckt'er and I had played. As we played still, for we were barely leaving childhood ourselves, though it seemed we had lost it long ago. I tried to prevent another generation of Bria from hating Ghen.

"But there I failed. For now and then, their parents also talked. They talked about Ghen with tremors in their voices, shrank from Ghen with horror on their faces, whispered of Ghen in their sleep: Ghen who had starved their parents in front of them, Ghen who had killed their infants in front of them, Ghen who were all murderers!

"I had my drawings to tell me the truth; they had their fear and their guilt to tell them otherwise. The children came to me for love, but they believed their parents."

I turned and looked into the fire, as though it could burn away the bitter past. Yet it was I who guarded it, maintained it. I had become Dayannis, just as Larissis did when he brought me here. It is the weakness and the strength of a storyteller, to enter his stories so fully that they are more real to him than he is himself.

"And I had my own nightmares to deal with. I dreamed of all of us old and dying childless, our unborn infants dead within our wombs, for lack of mating.

"I dreamed of Heckt'er and the young Ghen in their distant cave, who had done their best to save us; dreamed them old and despairing, not knowing the reason for their rejection.

"I dreamed of Broghen waiting in the forests, howling their victory in dissonant shrieks above the music of the endless wind. And I dreamed of Wind, its woods and mountains and waters.

"I dreamed of restless young Wind and of its failure to nurture thought. Perhaps it was the Creator, bending over Wind, who sent my dreams, who whispered into my nights for love of Wind."

I stared at the painting, gripped by the past, as always. After a few moments I continued signing.

"At first Dayannis denied his dreams. He couldn't overcome his fear. No Bria, knowing the truth of childbirth, would willingly face it. Furthermore, there were no parents or grandparents to help him; he would be utterly alone in his birthing. No, he refused!

"And then he dreamed his answer. He saw himself leaving the Bria cave to go with Heckt'er into the birthing cave. He saw Heckt'er leave the Ghen to live with him there until he bore his Bria younglings and Heckt'er's Ghen child.

"He saw the Bria children who loved him creeping from their parents' cave to hear his stories and to see how Ghen and Bria could live together. He saw them playing with his and Heckt'er's younglings and forgetting all they had heard of the birth of Broghen. It was in the birthing cave, where Dayannis lived with Heckt'er after their first mating, that Dayannis dreamed the dream of the walled city and Heckt'er began to build it.

"He dreamed his dreams of hope in the night while by day he buried every Bria old enough to remember their terrible past.

"Sharris died last. Bria are not made to withstand violence."

I shivered in the fire-warmed cave, looking at the paintings of our primitive past.

"Heckt'er attended Dayannis's birthing. Heckt'er spared the fearsome infant Broghen of their mating, releasing it into the forest far away. That is our atonement and our salvation; that we forbear to shed the unhappy blood of Bria and Ghen."

I took a deep breath and began the final chant, back in Dayannis's voice. I swayed with weariness as I signed.

"This is the story of our people, the story of our city, recorded in the paintings in this cave. It must not be forgotten. How easily it could be destroyed! Three swipes of a sadu'h pelt across the walls and a portion of our past would be erased as though it

never happened, and Bria would walk once more through the days of our lifetimes blind to all but our immediate sensations. We would move from birth to death as a bird lying on the wind moves, knowing nothing but nest and food and the demands of our young, one life lived by all, over and over; the life of the body, the life of beings without thought. These pictures lift us above the current of our blood that moves us at its whim. Many Bria fear the gift these pictures give us, the gift of decision, of choices, the gift of the knowledge of time. So I have hidden them for you to guard.

"Always remember the faces of the young Bria, pregnant with their brood, after they had seen Broghen. Always remember the extremity such knowledge drove them to. So we must wait, telling our younglings only that the Broghen live beyond the wall, but never how they come there.

"You will guard this cave when I am gone. You will remember our past and paint our present and dream new dreams of our future. Step by step, like the small puffs of a summer breeze, we will give an answer to the Creator. We will tame His wild Wind."

I stood, staring silently for the last time at the gruesome drawings of our past. I was both saddened and relieved now that I had discharged my final duty. Would Yur'i understand why it was so important to remember? Even I longed to forget.

I turned, becoming aware at last of his desperate breathing. He took a step toward me before his legs crumpled. I caught him as he fell and staggered out of the cave, ignoring the lacerations his scales made across my arms as I carried him.

"Forgive me," I begged, as I lay him on the ground. I put my mouth against his, forcing into his body the air from my own lungs. He was too young. I should have waited. "Wind over Wind, save him!" I prayed. I breathed into him and each breath was a prayer: "Save him!"

At last he gave a strangled breath on his own.

Secrets

Yur'i

With every step I took deeper into the cave, my breathing grew more labored. The paintings of past storytellers leered at me from the dark walls, caught in the light of Savannis's flickering fire. His motions, signing the tale behind each picture, floated before me, now reassuring, now threatening to reveal some dreadful secret I dared not know. We were almost at the back of the cave.

"Here are Dayannis's paintings," Savannis signed. "Now you will know the truth about our past."

&

I opened my eyes to find Savannis leaning over me. Where was I? How had I got from the back of the storyteller's cave into the open wind? The sun was a black circle in the sky, sloughing off darkness instead of illumination, the Sphere lying in its shadow, a mocking ghost. I closed my eyes. At least I could breathe again.

"Are you all right?" Savannis signed into my hand.

I shrugged weakly, not wanting to remember the growing stillness in my chest, the rush of panic, shallow gasping after air, the dancing lights like falling stars as I plunged into the darkness behind them.

"You are too young. I should have waited. But there's so little time and so much to teach you."

"I'm all right." My fingers stumbled over the signs. I tried to sit up, but swayed as the dizziness returned. Gently he pushed me down and I lay back. "It's just my illness. Not your fault," I signed when it had receded again.

"The paintings are too frightening for a child. I should have remembered my own reaction, and I was a parent then."

What was he talking about? I struggled to remember what I'd seen inside the cave. Pictures of the stories that he'd taught us, Riattis, Jan'ar and then... ominous, dark images filled my mind, veiled by a sense of horror which rose to panic as I tried to break through it. I gasped for breath.

"I thought that Ghen were told. I thought you knew about Bro..."

My lungs were closing, I was drowning in the sunny air! Savannis continued signing, but I could make no sense of his motions, my eyes going in and out of focus as I tried to breathe.

"There's always... at birth... But it's not... Yur'i. The infant Ghen... holds it back... no harm to..."

"No!" I screamed it as I signed it, using the last of my air, but Savannis had already stopped, had realized the moment before I screamed.

His face dissolved in flashing lights, and blackness closed in on me again.

એન્ડ

I should never have visited that cave. Those paintings weren't meant for me to see. That's why I have so little memory of them. Ridiculous to imagine that a Ghen, who couldn't even speak to Bria children, should be the next Bria storyteller!

Savannis was silent on the trip back to the city, and his fingers were still as he sat at his table watching me pack my belongings. Finally I sat back on my heels, looking at the neat, small pile of my things. Should I take the pictures I'd drawn? No, better to leave all that behind. I wanted to forget living with Bria entirely. I'd go to the Ghen compound, not back to Rennis's house. I could learn to be a recorder for their expeditions, or run their printing machines. Even a lame Ghen could do that.

"I'm leaving," I signed unnecessarily, looking at Savannis at last.

"You'll be back. You are the storyteller now."

"I can't speak to Bria children, Savannis. I can't even... Choose someone else."

"You'll be back."

"Goodbye, Savannis."

∾

It wasn't hard to learn the printing press. It was useful work, though they didn't really need me. There already were two printers, and a youth a year younger than I came every day after his hunter training. But they let me help.

There wasn't much to print—only what was significant to all Ghen—records of explorations and joinings, Chair Ghen's reports on Council, a small bulletin that Mant'er had begun for hunters.

Mant'er intrigued me, with his scars and his limp. He seldom spoke and never laughed. His translucent inner eyelid, which enables Ghen to see even in the most severe winds, drooped permanently, so that he looked weary and remote. I didn't really want to know his story but the young apprentice told me anyway. From him I learned what other Ghen already knew: Broghen exist. I didn't ask why I had not been told. The only possible reason made me ill with shame.

Mant'er's story haunted me. The dangers of the forest that pressed in on us, the brightness of young Heckt'er's courage, the depth of Mant'er's despair. It was an important story; it should be recorded.

I found myself tracing Mant'er's brooding face on scraps of paper. His expression fascinated and repelled me. A certain downward twist to the lips and at the edges of the eyes. The weary angle of the eyebrows, of the shoulders. An empty look about his hands, as though something vital had slipped through them and been lost. Chaos had found him.

Over and over I drew that expression, until I began to see it on other faces. Savannis's—yes, it had been there often although I'd never recognized it, looking at him only as a child looks at a teacher. My parent's face—when had I seen it there?—but yes, it was a true picture, I knew it. He looked at me that way sometimes, when he didn't think I noticed. I drew myself as a child, looking back at him, and on my face—No! I ripped the paper into pieces. What reason would I have to look that way?

"Why wasn't I told about Broghen?" I finally demanded of Gant'i when we were alone together. Then, before he could speak, I turned and limped away. I wasn't ready to hear it, after all.

"Yur'i!"

I walked faster.

"It wasn't your fault!"

"Shut up!" I screamed, breaking into a lop-sided run.

ℰᴖ

My dorm-mates had to waken me that night. I was shaking and feverish, uttering whimpering cries into the darkness. That was the first. Night after night the dreams returned. I would wake in the dark remembering only vague terrors and lie for the rest of the night on my sweat-chilled mat, waiting for sunrise.

I began to be afraid to go outside. I avoided looking into the faces of other Ghen, for fear of seeing the scorn and disgust I knew would be in their eyes. The very thought of the forest so near smothered me—I imagined ...specters... lurking between the black trees.

I stopped going to the printing press. Mick'al came to see me then, but I refused to speak to him. He told me other Ghen had sometimes felt as I did, Ghen who had lost friends on a hunt, or who had been born with a Bria that died.

"What have they to do with me?" I screamed at him. "Go away!"

After that it got worse.

I only left my sleeping quarters to eat. Carefully I picked my way to the eating hall, turning aside from any who passed by me, detouring around shadows, circling entire buildings to avoid seeing the wall and the forest beyond. When I finally reached the hall, more often than not I couldn't eat.

Everything smelled of death. If I forced myself to bite into a piece of meat, it tasted fetid, making me gag until I spit it out and ran to rinse my mouth. Soon I couldn't even look at food.

Gant'i came to see me, then Saft'ir, but I would speak to neither of them. They even sent Tyannis, who begged me to go to a healer. I did not want to be healed. I didn't deserve to be.

When Rennis came I ran into the washing room and locked the door. I sat huddled in a corner, holding my ears and banging my head against the wall behind me to block the sound of his weeping on the other side of the door. I could still hear him long after Gant'i came and half-carried him away.

Several Ghen broke down the door and took me to the infirmary. I lay on a mat there, waiting to die.

At least they stopped my parent and Rennis from visiting. I allowed the Ghen healer to entice me into drinking something, but the next day I was more alert and I could feel the liquid, like putrid water, lying in my stomach. I scratched my throat with an extended claw to purge myself again and again until I vomited blood and collapsed on the floor.

When I awoke they had wrapped my hands in leather pouches. My throat was on fire. I was groggy and had been drifting in and out of consciousness for a long time. Beside my mat, Savannis half-lay in a reclining chair.

I blinked.

He was still there. He leaned forward when he saw that my eyes were open. "Yes, I'm here, Yur'i," he signed.

I watched him carefully.

"I brought some pictures." Savannis held up a piece of paper. My hands itched at the sight of it. With an effort I closed my eyes. When I opened them cautiously a minute later, the paper was back in his lap.

"It's only one of the stories I tell the children. I need pictures to help me remember. I won't show it to you again, but I'll tell you a story if you'd like?"

He waited while I thought. It took a while to realize that I'd been asked a question, and then consider what was needed by way of an answer. Finally I looked up again.

"The one about Dimet'ir, I thought," Savannis signed in answer to my unspoken question. Again he waited, until at last I raised a bound hand to my lips.

Savannis signed the humorous story of a young Ghen who couldn't keep silent in the forest. Every time he went hunting he frightened the game away until no one would hunt with him. He was a good recorder, but expeditions go into unknown territory and even in the most tense moments Dimet'ir couldn't resist whispering to the Ghen beside him or whistling to a passing bird.

Finally, forced to stay in the city, Dimet'ir eventually transposed Ghen language into symbols, carved the symbols onto blocks of wood and created the first Ghen printing press. It's said that only Dimet'er could have invented a way of talking even when he was finally being quiet.

"Would you like to see the picture?" Savannis waited until I motioned to touch my breath, then held the paper up. I looked at it closely, frowning a little. He bent and leaned it against the wall so his hands were free, but I could still see it.

"Would you do it differently?" he signed.

I thought about that for a long time. Too long. Savannis was old and the effort of telling a story, even a short one, had tired him. He was asleep when the infirmary assistant came, grasped the back of the wheeled chair on which he sat and gently pushed him out of the room I lay in. That was when I noticed the blanket that covered him, and realized that he was also a patient.

When the Ghen healer came to see me, I asked him if I could visit Savannis. I had to whisper, but that was my only concession to the burning ache in my throat.

"Will you eat?" he asked.

I thought of the taste of meat and shuddered.

"Why won't you eat?"

"It's not good."

"It doesn't taste good?"

"Rotten." Even saying it made me want to gag.

"It isn't, you know," he said.

I looked away.

"Will you try?"

"Will you drink, then?" he asked when I was silent.

After a moment I raised my bound hand to my breath in agreement.

It took me the entire evening to get down one glass of ruberry juice. I closed my eyes because the red color... well, I closed my eyes. But they unbound my hands and I drank it, and kept it down. When I choked down another the next morning I was allowed to visit Savannis.

He was asleep when I entered his room. I sat on the chair beside his sleeping ledge and watched him. It was a Bria chair, and at first I perched nervously on the edge, but it was solidly built and besides, I wasn't much heavier than a Bria, now. After a while I closed my eyes.

I wakened to the sound of a strangled cry, but it wasn't my nightmare this time. Savannis moaned and twisted on his ledge, calling out. I hurried over and shook him gently. He looked at me without recognition, speaking urgently in Bria. I signed to him but he stared back, uncomprehending. Then he began to weep, great, despairing sobs that shook his frail body.

I couldn't bear that sound. I ran to the door and shouted, banging the door frame, shouting even when I saw two attendants running toward me and a Bria healer coming from the other direction. I cried for help, my breath ragged, shallow, not enough air, I couldn't breathe, and all the while the sound of Savannis's despair was at my back and all because of me!

"I killed him!" I screamed, the words barely rising through the vacuum in my lungs as I pitched forward into the arms of a terrified attendant.

When I awoke on my mat I saw a glass of ruberry juice on the floor beside me. I picked it up and poured the blood-red liquid over my head for everyone to see. Then I began to claw my chest, my arms, my legs, tearing desperate wounds into myself.

But not fatal ones. As soon as a cut went deep enough for the pain to penetrate my mental anguish, my claws retracted. Again and again I tried. Finally, reaching for the cup, I smashed its rim against the floor, leaving a jagged edge. As I lifted it to my throat, an attendant raced through the door and threw himself upon me, and another behind him. They tore the cup from my hands and held me down until I passed out again.

❧

"Do you remember what you said in Savannis's room?" the Ghen healer asked when he came to see me. His voice was calm. He knew I was listening although my eyes were closed, my face turned away. "They tell me you said, 'I killed him.' Is that right, Yur'i?"

I'm asleep, I thought fiercely, I can't hear you. But my chest was already tightening, my breath coming faster.

"You didn't hurt Savannis. In fact, you helped him. You called an attendant when he needed one. He's better now."

Wrong. Stupid. I concentrated on breathing. In and out, carefully.

"Savannis would like to see you. Would you like to see him?"

In and out. In and out. I half-raised my bound hand to my lips, dropped it again. In and out.

"Do you understand why you have these attacks of breathlessness?"

I began to pant. "My lungs," I gasped. Inandout.

"That was true when you were an infant, but you've outgrown that. It isn't your lungs now, is it, Yur'i?"

Inandout, inandout, inandout. "Yes!"

He said nothing for a while. I didn't look at him. Finally he sighed. "I'll tell Savannis he can visit, shall I?"

In and out. "Yes."

⁊

It wasn't Savannis who visited that afternoon, it was Tibellis. I barely recognized him. He'd gone from a lisping child to a youth in the two years since I'd seen him.

"Hello, Yur'i," he signed. The attendant, crouching beside my bed, unwrapped my hands so I could answer him.

"How did you learn my signing?"

"Savannis taught us at storytime."

"Why?" I was unreasonably angry and Tibellis's answer, "Because you're the next storyteller," threw me into a rage.

"Do I look like a Bria storyteller? Do I act like one?" I half rose on my mat, incensed. The attendant shifted nervously.

"My matri says you do."

"What does that mean?"

"He saw one of your drawings. He told me to wait and see."

"Stupid! Stupid!" I screamed it as I signed, causing Tibellis to shrink back into the chair, but I was unable to stop. I raised my hands, extending my claws with a snap and shook them in his face. "Do these look like storyteller hands?"

The attendant leaped forward and grabbed my hands, forcing them down.

"You don't know me!" I screamed. "Leave me alone!" My words were in Ghen, but I could see by his shocked little face that Tibellis understood.

When I had been subdued, my hands rebound, Tibellis was still there. Too frightened to move. Drowsy with medication, the thought brought me only slight regret.

Tibellis rose from his chair and stood shaking beside my mat. "The children miss the stories," he signed, as though he hadn't seen my madness. "You don't have to be the storyteller. Just come and tell us the stories until there is one."

There was something about his face, in the droop of his shoulders, in the way his hands hung, empty…

I closed my eyes.

❧

Savannis was wheeled in the next day. He pointed to my hands and spoke imperiously to his Bria attendant. They argued briefly. Savannis turned to me and signed, "If he undoes your hands, you won't hurt yourself." I hesitated.

"You'll keep your claws retracted while I'm here, child!"

I touched my breath quickly. Savannis glared triumphantly at the attendant. The young Bria, as intimidated as I was, untied me.

"I taught that child every story he knows!" Savannis signed, his eye flashing as the attendant hurried out. I glanced sideways at my hands, not even tempted.

Savannis sighed and leaned back into his chair. "I'm tired, Yur'i. Old and tired. I told the story last time, now it's your turn."

I stared at him.

"Any story. It doesn't matter. You know them all."

"…I don't remember…" I signed slowly.

"That's my excuse, not yours. You remember. Take your time, I'm not going anywhere."

I pulled myself up till I was sitting against the wall. Slowly, with long pauses, I signed the story of Riattis, a lazy and quarrelsome Bria who died saving Ghen when lightning struck their compound and caused the Great Fire.

"Word perfect," Savannis signed when I was finished. "Now draw it." He leaned down and placed paper and chalks beside me. I stared at them, lying on the edge of my mat.

"Sit up, child, you're not dead yet!"

I pulled myself up straighter out of habit; Savannis often said that to inattentive children during storytime. He pointed to the paper: "Draw on that."

It took me six removes. I forgot my stinging cuts, my aching stomach and raw throat, forgot the obtuse healer, the impersonal room in which I waited to die, forgot even Savannis dozing beside me. I sketched reluctantly at first, then willingly, then in a fever, as though I were drawing my redemption, not Riattis's.

I drew him standing in the center of an apocalypse of flames, peaceful at last with nothing more asked of him. Those he had rescued stood to one side and those he had failed were with him in the pyre. When I was done I lay back. The familiar tightness in my chest had eased.

The attendant came for Savannis and wheeled him away still sleeping in his chair. Then I, too, slept through the evening and the night without a single dream.

Savannis did not come the next day, nor would they take me to him. "He needs his rest," was all the explanation I was given.

I asked for water and drank it slowly, staring hard at Riattis's peaceful, dying face in my picture. With the tightness in my chest eased somewhat I felt more alert. I turned the picture over and looked at the clean, white back.

First I drew the tree near Rennis's house, which Saft'ir and Tyannis used to climb. I drew them high in its branches, only their faces peering out. As I drew, their faces turned angry, scornful and accusing. Under my chalk, Tyannis's hand appeared, raised, drawn back to fling something: a large nut, hard and hurtful. His hands were full of nuts; he and Saft'ir had gathered them from the branches to throw down at a shadowy figure crouching on the ground.

Who is he? Why are they so furious at him?

Instead of houses, trees appeared; they were in the forest. I hate the forest, I've always hated the forest. Dark and tight and dangerous, its massive trees constricting the flow of air. Things lurk behind those trees, terrible things... The forest is an attack on Wind, an illness.

I sweated as I drew, breathing quickly and reaching repeatedly for the glasses of water and juice the attendants replenished without disturbing me. Even the Ghen healer, seeing my frown of concentration as I took a sip of juice without looking up from my drawing, sat down without saying a word: a miracle almost as great as paper.

I drew the dark, silent forest and stretching from behind every tree I drew ominous shadows: the fierce, nearly-forgotten shadows I'd seen in Dayannis's painting. Broghen. I felt my chest tightening. My chalk moved of its own volition back to the figure huddled beneath the central tree.

I wanted to make him leap up and run, but where could he run, surrounded by the menacing specters of Broghen? I wanted to make him climb to safety, but the accusing faces above would not allow it. Why was he staring at the ground? Reaching down as though something had fallen from his hands? What was that, lying tiny and still and broken at his feet?

Suddenly I was drawing a hail of nuts pounding down on him. "Kill him,"

I muttered, "Kill him!" I threw down my chalk and snapped out my claws.

Just as quickly other hands grabbed my wrists and held them still.

"No!" my parent cried. "Hate me, Yur'i, despise me! It's my fault, not yours."

I looked at Gant'i, holding my wrists so hard my fingers were growing numb, as though if he held me tightly enough he could pull me back to sanity.

"You never told me!" I cried. "Everyone knew why Tyannis had no sibling, everyone but me."

The healer, still sitting beside my mat, spoke now: "Didn't you know, Yur'i?"

I looked at him, and the pain burst over me. I gasped for breath, snapped open my claws again to tear at my closed throat, but my parent still held me. "I knew!" I screamed, "I knew! But no one would talk about it!"

"I was afraid!" Gant'i's anguished cry broke through to me. I looked at him, shocked. My parent, afraid?

He sank back on his heels still holding my wrists, but more gently now. "Afraid you'd hate me for putting your life at risk. You were born a year premature, Yur'i, struggling to hold back a fully-developed Broghen. The miracle is that you prevented it from tearing apart Rennis's insides and hurting Tyannis, as well. You saved Rennis and tried to save your womb-siblings. It's not your fault the Broghen killed Tyannis's sibling. It's mine! I put you all at risk." He released my hands, helpless now.

"I don't ask you to forgive me." His voice was so low I could barely hear him. His eyes, staring at me, were as dry as death. "I ask you to blame me. Blame *me*, and live."

I swayed backwards, exhausted. Gant'i slumped before me, his head bent.

"Leave us," the healer spoke gently to my parent. "Yur'i needs to rest. Perhaps he can begin to heal now."

I slept for a long time. When I awoke, the picture of my guilt was still beside me. There was Riattis, standing between those he had failed and those he had saved. Riattis at peace.

I turned the paper over again and began to draw. In one corner I drew my parent's face as he watched me trying to die. In another I drew Mant'er's face with its terrible lines of loss. In the third corner I drew Savannis, the way he looked at the children when he forgot a story in the middle of its telling. And in the last corner I drew my own face.

I'd already drawn myself in this picture, crouching under the tree looking down at the tiny womb-sibling I'd failed to protect. This time I drew myself looking up at the three faces in the corners. At Mant'er, who needed me to tell his story. At Savannis who needed me to pass on the stories and paintings of the Bria. And at Gant'i, who needed me to forgive us both.

I drew my face at peace, like Riattis's. I drew my hands not open and empty but cupped, as Savannis had cupped them when I was a child and found him wounded on the river. He had agreed then to come back to life for me. I could do no less for him.

I drew what I hoped to become, not what I was.

❧

Before Savannis died I went to his room and told him that I would tell the children's stories if Council allowed it.

He reached for my hands. "Whether or not," he signed into my palm.

"Whether or not," I agreed, "but only until I find a Bria storyteller."

Council Relations

Briarris

"Excuse me. Sorry. Forgive me." I navigated my way as carefully as I could between the crowded Bria, flushing at the need to brush against them, infringe upon the personal space I'd been taught to honor all my life. I tried to ignore the fact that I was deliberately and repeatedly stepping between Bria and the breath of Wind. But how else could I reach the steps that led to Council Chambers?

I was shocked that they didn't move aside, that they forced this vulgar behavior upon me. Looking up, I caught sight of Anarris standing on the top step of the verandah. His face was wreathed in a triumphant grin. I lost some of my hesitancy then and pushed my way forward without apologies.

Ahead of me I saw Rennis, his eye cast down, still murmuring his regrets as he reluctantly advanced. I caught up to him and clasped his arm. He looked up at me, startled. I tilted my head significantly. He followed my gaze and I felt him stiffen when he saw Anarris watching us.

"A friend is more than breath to me," I said, giving him permission to break the short space between us. Never had I uttered those words with more sincerity and I could see the relief on his face also, as he braced himself against me. Together we made our way through the crowd and up the stairs.

When we reached the verandah I turned and surveyed the crowd. I had dreamed of serving these Bria, of being lifted up by their gratitude and support as I fulfilled my Council duties.

I have done everything for you, I wanted to cry out to them. How can you deny me your approval? But I said only, "Forgive me for coming, even for a moment, between you and the breath of Wind." Let them reflect on the fact that they had forced it on me. The shame was theirs.

We waited a full remove, Rennis and I and a handful of other senior councilors, sitting in the closed-Council room. One of the Ghen offered to clear a path through the throng of Bria, with the help of the other Ghen councilors present. The Bria with me sat silent, stunned by the suggestion. Finally I managed to murmur, with Igt'ur translating, that relations between Ghen and Bria were strained enough without a show of force on the part of Ghen councilors.

At least Darillis was no longer on Council. He'd canceled the last session of closed-Council at the end of his term, when a crowd half this size had come to object to our meeting. I suspected that Triannis had set this up with Anarris, letting him know whenever closed-Council met and what the issues might be.

Triannis hadn't been invited onto closed-Council after his sixth year as a councilor, and knew now that he'd never be admitted. I could understand his resentment, but it was his choice not to join and bear children. Closed-Council members had to know of Broghen, and how could we entrust that secret to a Bria who didn't carry the shame of birthing one? Who didn't go home and look into the soft eyes of his younglings and realize what such knowledge would do to them?

I was glad to leave that train of thought when Council Chair and the last of the councilors arrived. There were only two proposals before us: Yur'i's offer to be acting storyteller until he could find and train a Bria storyteller, and Chair Ghen's request that an expedition to the mountains be dispatched at once. Our discussion lasted for five removes, even though there was no real dissension. None of us was in a hurry to face the crowd outside again. Both proposals were accepted.

When we left the building we saw two lines of young Ghen forming a walkway for us between the waiting Bria. Shock and outrage were clear on the delicate faces of the Bria where they stood, swaying slightly, behind the heavy presence of the Ghen. Council Ghen ordered the Ghen back to their compound as soon as we Bria councilors had passed through the crowd.

My legs trembled under me as I walked home. It was clear from Chair Ghen's reaction that the young Ghen had acted spontaneously, giving us their assistance.

But a line had been crossed. Ghen had stood against Bria. Ghen had stood between Bria and Bria, throwing their weight into the fragile balance of a

Bria dispute. Were we still Bria councilors, now that the Ghen had made our position theirs? They had broken a trust between Ghen and Bria with their display of force, and made it appear that we councilors had broken faith also with those we had promised to serve.

Could the trust that made it possible for us to live together ever be restored?

Shadows

Tyannis

Curse the street lamps! I crept between the houses, hugging shadows. Why do Bria so dislike the dark? As if in answer I stumbled over a large rock. I stopped, hardly breathing.

The night was silent (another reason to dislike it) with all the reassuring sounds of birds and insects and small creatures quieted in sleep. Their stillness made me nervous. The night is as much a part of Wind as daylight is, I reminded myself sternly, and no more fearful for my inadequate sight.

"Wind is full of shadows," I once told my matri, after a trip to the woods with Gant'i and Saft'ir.

"Wind would be dark without us," he replied. "The Ghen are like the oil in a lamp, protecting the Bria at their center, its slender wick. Together, we create light."

"We create shadows, too," I argued, annoyed by his habit of turning everything into a moral lesson. I looked down at my own shadow, hiding behind me from the evening lamplight. I hopped a little to see it dance.

"Light and shadow, both," Matri murmured.

A silly conversation and sillier still the nickname that came of it: Shadow. The Ghen call me that because my fur is black and because I can move in the forest as silently as they, and stand as still, without ever letting on how dizzy it makes me. They say it with amusement. The Bria call me Shadow because I follow the Ghen into the woods. They say it with derision.

I don't let on that I care either way. At least, I prefer "Shadow" to "Tyannis." When I was little I once asked Saft'ir and Yur'i to call me "Tyn'is." Saft'ir just laughed, but Yur'i looked at me sadly. He knows what it is to want to be what you're not. It was he who first called me "Shadow." He says it with understanding.

160

I needed to be a shadow now. Just a shadow, creeping through the city to the northern wall behind the Ghen compound. If I were to be seen, my bedroll and bundle of food would give me away at once. As though I were doing something wrong! I'm not a captive in my own city. Ah, but I feel that way, as I navigate the narrow walls of convention, wishing I were neither Ghen nor Bria, just myself.

Passing the Ghen compound, I moved even more cautiously. Ghen see well in the night. I was glad of that, even if it made my escape more difficult. I would be following the trail of the Ghen exploration party. I could take comfort in the knowledge that the darkness of the forest had already been pierced by their sight. They would leave safety in their wake for me to walk through.

I approached the wall carefully. Stillseason was over, but it was still well-guarded. On the other side I heard heavy Ghen footsteps retreating to my left. I must get over before he returned. I unwound the narrow rope I carried, tied a loop in one end and tossed it over a flapping pennant on the wall. It slipped down around the raised post that held the pennant. I pulled myself up, balancing precariously at the top to pull the rope free, then jumped down on the other side. Saft'ir had thought it amusing to show me how young Ghen sometimes sneaked into the forest at night, and was surprised when I mastered the trick. Even he misjudged me.

I paused a moment at the edge of the forest. So dark! No, not darkness, just shadows: black shadows, like me. Shadows that would hide, not harm me. I ran into their cold embrace before the guard walking this corner of the wall could come upon me.

℘

The Ghen trail was difficult to follow, even though they weren't being particularly careful this close to our city. I walked until the darkness turned to gray, until the sun had climbed above the trees and pierced their leafy canopy. I walked, and rested, and walked, following the trail of the Ghen.

Although at night I feared the forest, in the daytime I loved walking through it as I always had, with its dappled pools of sun and shade, its soprano of birdsong and rhythmic rustle of wind-shimmering leaves. Early one morning, still shaking off the tremors of the night, I came upon a small sadu'h, nibbling on the branches of a cappa bush. He froze when he saw me and I stopped, too, regarding his wide-eyed terror with compassion. His mating species were diggers, not hunters.

What if my ancestors had had no Ghen to protect them? What if today we had no farms producing food, behind the wall that kept our peninsula safe from the predators on Wind? What if we had to leave our city daily to feed ourselves within the capricious forest? I meant to prove that I, too, could live here, but I had more understanding of what such a life might cost after three days and nights alone in the woods.

"Go in peace, little sadu'h," I murmured. "May the Creator Wind guard you and all the small and helpless children of Wind."

I would have to be careful not to say such things when I finally joined the group of Ghen. They ate wild sadu'h. As though he heard my thoughts, the little thing leaped in fear and dashed away. But I felt safer after that, because I had dispensed life on a creature even more timid than I.

It is our culture as much as our inherent nature that makes Bria weak and dependent. We should be taught to fight and to use Ghen weapons and to walk unafraid in the forests. Such opinions did not make me popular among my Bria classmates who had not been raised with Ghen, but I didn't care. I'm right, and this adventure would prove it.

After that, I found it exhilarating to walk alone through the forest. I knew I would join the Ghen in another day or two, when they'd gone too far to send me home. In the meantime, the sense of omnipresent danger made me feel intensely alive. The leaves were greener, sun and shadows sharper, the ruberries more crimson and sweeter than any I had tasted. The noises and the scents of the forest were as clear and vivid to me as Savannis's stories were to Yur'i, and I walked, haloed in the great excitement of simply being alive and young and on an adventure.

I finished my water on the fourth day. I'd hoped to make it last five, but my throat was dry with nervousness each night no matter how I reassured myself, and during the days I had to travel hard to keep up with the Ghen. The more I tried to ration myself, the stronger my thirst grew. I dared not leave the trail to find a stream, though I knew there must be one near enough for the Ghen to send some of their number to fill their water skins. Even knowing their general direction and walking less than a day behind, I had trouble tracking them.

Although they weren't being particularly careful, they left almost no sign of their passage: leaves brushed aside on the forest floor, ruberries plucked neatly instead of eaten off the vine as an animal would have, a trail of discarded stems leading away from the patch. If Saft'ir hadn't taught me to track, I would have lost them. The thought terrified me. Rather I suffered a little thirst than find myself completely adrift in the forest, so far from home.

I conceived a daring plan. I would sneak that night into the Ghen encampment and steal some of their water! I increased my pace in order to catch up to them, but they were also moving quickly and at dusk I knew by their trail that I'd only gained a little. I'd have to walk all night and enter their camp when dawn was beginning to lighten the dark woods. The advantage of my black fur in the night would be lessened, and I'd be tired.

Perhaps it was my exhilaration at having already accomplished what no Bria ever had—living alone in the forest for nearly five days—or else the knowledge that even the juicy ruberries wouldn't slack my thirst another day. Whatever the reason, I decided to do it. After all, they were Ghen. Saft'ir was among them. Even if my plan failed and I was caught, I had nothing to fear from these hunters. But if I succeeded, they would be forced to accept me as an equal.

How could I have imagined that I, a Bria on my first journey through the forest, could steal past an experienced Ghen watch into their camp? Even considering myself more Ghen than Bria, it was sheer youth and arrogance to believe I might succeed. But that youthful arrogance saved my life.

If I hadn't been so intent on the meager trail I followed, and half-blind in the dark and the lack of birdsong, which was more than sight to me; if I hadn't been hurrying to reach them before dawn, I might have felt that other presence. I might have noticed some scent or sound or sudden silence behind me, closing the distance between us faster than I was homing in on my Ghen.

I thought it was the silence of sleep that stilled the forest birds and creatures. I thought it was the darkness of the night, setting my fur on end. I scorned the inherent timidity of my species, which urged me to hurry faster between the tall and somber trees, but still I felt compelled to greater and greater speed.

I glanced behind. A ghostly, white body flickered between the black trees. In a shock of terror I broke into a run. The thing pursued me! I ran full out, imagining I could already feel the heat of its hunger. No matter how fast I ran, it drew nearer! I began to scream.

The forest echoed with the sound of my screaming and the responding roar behind me as the monster broke from its stealthy pursuit into an all-out charge. Fear gave me strength and I fled, gasping for breath. The desperate sound of my terror mingled with the ravenous howls of the demon and ricocheted from tree to tree until the woods were alive with our frantic contest.

At first I thought I imagined the movement of gray bodies between the trees up ahead. They were too distant to be part of this nightmare. Racing closer, they came within my sight. My screams subsided into sobs and I wavered between despair and hope as the breath at my back grew hotter. The entire situation began to seem unreal. I ran in slow motion while the horror at my back reached out to overwhelm me.

I felt the rake of claws against my back even as the first knife whistled past my head and the howls of hunger behind me changed to pain and rage. Like a supernatural thing the monster tore into the flesh of Ghen who were forced to come within its reach in order to cut between it and me. Choking on tears I ran until I stumbled against the wide trunk of a ugappa and sank, on legs that suddenly buckled, to the ground. When it was over, they carried me unconscious to their camp.

I'd like to think I saved their lives as well. That, but for my alarm, they might have been caught unprepared. Perhaps not only Kant'on would have died, without my warning.

I'd like not to wonder if it was I who drew the danger to them.

I woke to the smell of Kant'on's funeral pyre. I rose slowly and stood, trembling and silent, as the Ghen completed their ceremony. It was not the reunion I had planned. For all my bravado, I hadn't expected to come face to face with death—mine or anyone else's.

When the ceremony was over, Saft'ir turned to me. "What are you doing here?" he signed, his movements stiff, furious.

"I followed you."

Koon'an, the leader of the expedition, motioned to Saft'ir to interpret for him. "You followed us? You've learned a lot from watching Ghen training sessions. What do they call you? Shadow?"

I touched my breath, then signed through Saft'ir, "Why shouldn't I watch? Why shouldn't I learn? The forest belongs to Wind, not the Ghen. I have as much right to be here as you do."

"You put our lives at risk as well as your own. Koon'an paid the price for your 'rights'."

I couldn't help myself, I began to cry.

After a moment, Koon'an bent down, touching my shoulder, and spoke more gently. "Enough," Saft'ir signed his words. "Tell me why you have come after us?"

"I want to explore the mountains with you."

Koon'an looked hard at Saft'ir, who shook his head quickly.

"This trip was discussed in Council." I paused to wipe away my tears. "My matri, Rennis, sits on Council. It wasn't a secret."

"No, it wasn't a secret," Koon'an replied, "nor was it open to uninvited Bria."

"You should include Bria on your explorations. Wind is our world, too. We include Ghen in our city."

"It's our city, also."

"Then you see things as I do."

For a moment Koon'an looked annoyed, then he grimaced in laughter. "You have courage for a Bria child."

"I'm not a child. Saft'ir became a hunter last season, and I'm his womb-sibling. This is my specialization year." I paused, then signed boldly, "I choose to specialize in exploration."

Again Koon'an grinned briefly, but he said, "You will slow us down in the day, and alarm us with your night fears when we need rest."

"I've been in the forest for five days, following your trail. You had a head start, yet I caught up with you. I've slept in the forest alone. I'm not afraid. And I'm not going back."

He looked at me silently for a long moment, then he said, "No, you can't go back." He glanced at the smoldering logs from Kant'on's cremation. "The... animal that chased you escaped us. I've had to send several Ghen to track and kill it. Three others will leave us to scout out our route when we reach the Symamt'h. I can't reduce my party even more by assigning a third group to take you back to the city. You're getting your wish, small Shadow, but you've made a very dangerous wish. I don't guarantee your safety, you understand?"

I touched my breath, but his warning startled me. Was he trying to frighten me? His next words confirmed my suspicion.

"You'll stay within the camp at all times. Do whatever anyone tells you at once, without question. You won't engage in hunting or in fighting, if that becomes necessary."

Of course I wouldn't hunt! As for the rest, when I had proved that I wasn't an ordinary Bria he'd see his restrictions weren't needed. In the meantime, I agreed to do as he said. Satisfied with my promised obedience, he left.

Saft'ir left also. My appearance had embarrassed him. Despite my protest to Koon'an, Saft'ir knew his excitement over the expedition had made me want to join it. He'd been honored by being chosen to accompany them as recorder, despite his youth, but if my appearance were traced to him, he'd be held accountable. There was something more than anger in Saft'ir's expression, however.

Later, I asked what kind of animal had chased me, but Saft'ir refused to speak to me, except to translate the orders of Koon'an or the other Ghen. They were a group of sixteen, all mature hunters who'd already had their younglings, except for Saft'ir.

"Why are there so many?" I asked Saft'ir. For once he deigned to answer.

"There are courrant'hs in the mountains. It's dangerous."

"Is that what chased me?" I asked, shivering.

He looked away, silent once more.

❧

At every evening's campfire we shared a meal of dried meat and fried corn, with cappa tea. I couldn't bring myself to share their meat, but supplemented my corn with ruberries and dried cappa fruit which I'd brought with me.

Afterwards, Saft'ir recited the progressive events of the trip. The older Ghen corrected or added parts until they were satisfied. I'd been surprised initially when Saft'ir told me he'd been chosen as trip recorder. He wasn't one of the better recorders of his birth-year, being by nature too impatient to respect details. He was better at tracking, but even so, not one of the best.

What Saft'ir was good at, what he was really exceptional at, was fighting. No one said so, especially not in front of me or Rennis, but I often watched the fight practices and I knew. Saft'ir was strong and resilient and he fought to win. He never got angry, never lost his head, never inflicted more hurt than he had to, but he never quit. He simply refused to lose a fight.

What did that have to do with being the trip recorder? In the end, I decided they wanted to honor him because of his dead parent. Which was unfair, because he had Gant'i and Rennis, the same as Yur'i and I.

On the third evening after I joined the Ghen, I rose to speak when Saft'ir had finished. "Tell me also," I signed, looking at Koon'an while Saft'ir translated. "I can be a recorder as well, for the Bria."

A circle of breathy grimaces greeted my request. Unlike the Ghen, Bria rely on writing. Only the storyteller's memory is word-perfect and reliable—and he's recalling myths. But when I pulled a stylo and several sheets of paper from my pack to show them, they quieted. My supple fingers could write quickly and legibly without the awkward typesetter they used to print for them. I smiled triumphantly, but not a single face turned toward mine was grinning now.

"You don't intend to keep this trip secret from Bria, do you?" My question was rhetorical. I only paused a moment. "Then why not have a Bria record for Bria?"

After a moment, Koon'an touched his breath and Saft'ir signed his record for me. I noticed a few pauses, and a brief discussion among the Ghen before he signed the account of my attacker, but I made no comment and wrote what he signed. When I finished writing, Koon'an spoke and Saft'ir made me sign back to him what I had written.

"There's only one record of a trip," Koon'an said, though I already knew this. "The group record. You'll write nothing that isn't agreed to by the group."

I touched my breath at once. It was part of my plan, to show that I could be a reliable trip recorder. I'd already proved that I could travel as fast as they could and sleep soundly at night. Now they would also see that I could be useful to an expedition; that even a Bria had a role on Ghen explorations.

☙

When we came upon the Symamt'h and I saw the flat lands across it, with the outline of the mountains beyond, I laughed aloud with delight. The wide river sparkled as though fragments of the sun had splintered and fallen onto its wavelets, shining there so brightly they hurt the eye. The tall, golden grasses gleamed on the other side, continuous breezes moving over and through them so that they whispered a merry song and danced to it, twisting and dipping as the wind changed course, incessantly. I felt I was watching Wind itself at play.

And how far I could see! The magnificence of the view stunned me. I felt a deep reverence build in me as I looked across this hallowed land. When I finally turned from the beautiful sight, the Ghen were already stripping saplings and lashing them together into rafts. As soon as the first was finished, Koon'an sent Kur'ad, a friend of Gant'i's, and two other Ghen I didn't know, across the Symamt'h on it to scout out our path into the mountains. A dozen Ghen lined the bank, their rifles pointed at the river as the scouts crossed.

It was a disappointment when Koon'an made the rest of us camp for the night on this side of the Symamt'h. I was eager to cross the brilliant river, impatient to run into the grassy arms of Wind. But I was rewarded for the delay by the sight of the sun setting over that wide and endless land.

Never had I seen such bands of crimson, rose and lavender, stretching from horizon to horizon. I tried to fix it in my mind, wishing I could write it into my record to capture the sense of awe and splendor, and the magnificent play of colors. Bria knew nothing of this. Closeted within the perimeters of our city, hemmed in by the brooding forest, what did we know of Wind? I wanted to describe it so well that others, too, would be enticed to venture into danger to see the Creator Wind's handwork.

&

We crossed the Symamt'h the next morning. Ghen stood watch, firearms ready, on every raft, but the trip was uneventful. I would have liked to trail my hands in the bejeweled waters but I was placed in the center of the raft and ordered not to move. Later I asked Saft'ir why we had been so guarded.

"Liapt'hs," he signed.

I'd heard of them. "Aren't they in the wetlands?"

"They've been known to venture north. It's better to be prepared."

They were equally vigilant all the way across the grasslands. Koon'an pushed us, as he had in the forest, and we traveled the entire distance, about 200 miles as the Ghen recorded it, in fourteen days. We would have made better time but the scouts had taken most of the dried provisions, so the Ghen detoured to hunt. I was relieved to wait with Saft'ir and a group of five others. I didn't want to watch any creature die.

I'd forced myself to eat some of the fish they caught in the river, since my dried provisions were almost done, but among the grasses I discovered a type of wild stringer, which produced long, slender pods. The Ghen assured me they were edible. I found them chewy and slightly sweet, filled with soft, fleshy seeds.

When we reached the foothills I saw my first courrant'hs. Two of them were lying across an enormous boulder, dozing in the warm sun. They were no more than 150 armlengths from us, huge, powerful beasts, their shaggy, thick fur in alternating bands of beige and brown. I froze at the sight. These were the creatures attacking our city.

I was afraid to move, to take my eye off them. One of them raised its head and blinked at us, lazily, as though the effort of moving was too great; in its dark eyes I saw a flicker that set me trembling. Saft'ir pushed me forward, breaking my locked gaze.

"Don't look directly at them," he signed. "It's a challenge."

"Will they attack?"

"Not in the daytime. They only kill at night, but you don't want them to remember you."

I shivered.

"Don't worry." he signed, "You're safe with us. They hunt singly or in pairs; we're more than a match for them."

Although I didn't look back, I could feel the courrant'hs eyes following me. I had to force myself not to tremble. The feeling of having a predator at my back returned to me. Something was wrong about these creatures, though.

"Do all courrant'hs look like that?" I signed.

"Yes, they all look the same," Saft'ir replied.

"Are there no white courrant'hs?"

"Saft'ir, are there any white courrant'hs?" I repeated.

"No."

"What was it that chased me, Saft'ir?"

But he said nothing more.

I remembered Koon'an's words, then: "I don't guarantee your safety." Perhaps he hadn't simply been trying to frighten me into obedience. In fact, the more I considered it, the less I believed that. A leader of Ghen would not make such a statement to a Bria unless he had to; it went against the basic understanding between our species. What was he warning me of, if not courrant'hs?

∾

Three days later, the quiet night was broken by shouts from the guards. My bedroll was in the center of the encampment alongside Saft'ir's. All about me Ghen were leaping awake to the cries of the watch, grabbing firearms and knives and racing to form a circle around our camp, gray scaled bodies between us and the dark. I half rose, reaching for my own knife, but Saft'ir held my arm.

"Recorders don't fight," he signed to me.

I might have protested but Saft'ir also sat passively as the others fought around us and I knew he wanted to join the fray much more than I did. Nevertheless, we held our knives ready to defend ourselves, if necessary.

Bloodcurdling screams from the things attacking us tore through the blackness. Our warriors roared in response. The struggle was too close and the night too dark for firearms. I strained my eyes, wishing my night sight was better, but all I saw were shades of darkness: the wide, black shapes of huge boulders, the grunting, grayer shadows of the Ghen and beyond them, now and then, a blur of white.

"What is it? What are they?" I signed to Saft'ir but he ignored me, holding his knife tightly and trying to look in every direction at once.

Suddenly, in front of me, a Ghen went down. Beside him another, and the circle was broken. Raging toward me I saw the ghostly shape of a monster!

It stood on two massive legs, like a Ghen or a Bria, and yet it was neither. It was nothing I'd ever seen or heard of, yet it was familiar, like a half-forgotten nightmare from one's childhood. Reaching its arms toward us it rushed forward, coming into focus nearer to the fire's light.

The white scales that covered its body were dotted with tufts of thin fur,

170

matted with gore. Long, blood-drenched claws extended from its hairy paws and equally bloody were the rows of fangs in its gaping maw. The heat and smoke of our fire distracted it, and it hesitated. The intimate sound of its half-suspended breathing was more terrifying than its earlier crazed shrieking had been.

I shrank back until the campfire behind me singed my fur. My mouth opened to scream but my throat was frozen and I watched as from a distance while three of our fighters sank their knives into it. The monster fell on the ground before me.

I stared, holding my breath, half-expecting it to rise up again more hideous in death than when alive. I didn't notice that the battle had ended until its carcass was pulled away by two weary Ghen and flung onto the rocks beneath our trail.

With its removal the spell of horror was shattered. "What was that?" I screamed over and over, pounding on Saft'ir's chest until my voice broke and my head sank to my knees. As Saft'ir bent down, I whispered to myself the answer: "Broghen."

Saying it, I began to shudder. Soon I was shivering uncontrollably. I wanted to go home. Creator of Wind, I wanted to go home! Only the greatest effort of will kept me from sobbing it out loud. Saft'ir breeched the wind's space between us and built up the fire near me.

I couldn't feel its heat. Ice-winds reached into my heart and I shook as though I'd been born in a warmer climate and suddenly been transported to a cold and alien world.

Koon'an came and stood frowning over me, but I was barely aware of him. He ordered hot tea brewed. I drank mug after mug of it, hardly noticing the scalding liquid as it disappeared into the coldness inside me. I stared blankly at the Ghen as they prepared for the cremation of their two comrades who'd died in the skirmish.

Koon'an was wrong not to tell me about Broghen when we were sure to meet them. I nearly died of fear, unprepared for such a sight. I sat by the blazing fire, cold and shaking, watching the funeral pyre for our dead.

I went to Koon'an the next morning. "Tell me the truth about this expedition," I signed. When Saft'ir translated, Koon'an looked at me as though deciding what to say.

"What are you really looking for in the mountains?"

"The source of the white Broghen," Koon'an replied.

"Broghen come from Ghen and Bria mating." I wanted him to deny it.

"Yes."

"Are these Broghen from our city?"

"No."

I was so relieved I had to lean back against a boulder to support myself. So we, ourselves, did not give birth to Broghen! Dayannis had stopped it, as Savannis taught us. Who, then, had created them? I signed my question to Saft'ir.

"We don't know," Koon'an said when Saft'ir had translated.

"You think there are other Bria and Ghen in the mountains? Savages who still bear Broghen?"

"It's possible."

At that, I became so excited I nearly forgot about the Broghen. The Ghen would fight them off. I was focused on the thought of another community of Bria and Ghen. We weren't alone on Wind! I would be an emissary from my people, the only one able to speak to these wild Bria. I could teach them so much. Why, they'd think of me as we thought of Dayannis! My ears twitched with delight, despite Koon'an's frown.

Saft'ir caught my arm. "You will obey Koon'an," he signed. "This is a very dangerous expedition."

"Of course," I responded, but I was no longer thinking of the danger.

❦

A week later, a solitary Broghen attacked us. The Ghen killed it but the sound of its battle roar alerted others in the vicinity and two more attacked, each from a different direction. They didn't interact, not even showing as much teamwork as a pair of mongarr'hs raiding a farmborra roost. They struck at the same time only because both of them were close enough to hear and scent our struggle with the first Broghen. Several Ghen were wounded, two quite badly. For the first time it occurred to me that I might not make it home, even in the company of Ghen.

I wondered at the strange sense of relief among many of the fighters afterwards despite their wounds, until Saft'ir explained to me that the Broghen they'd killed had had their fangs removed.

172

"Removed?" I signed, shuddering at the memory of white jaws full of sharp and bloody teeth, leering at me in the night.

"Their poison fangs," Saft'ir clarified. He explained that on each side of the Broghens' front molars was a longer tooth filled with poison. Holding out his arm he showed me a ragged wound, bleeding but not deep. "If they still had their fangs, this would be infected. It might not kill me, but I'd never be able to mate. Others feared this, too. But every Broghen we've met has had its poison fangs removed."

"If none of them have them, how do you know they exist?"

He hesitated. "Koon'an knows."

"Koon'an's run into Broghen before?"

He made no reply, but I had my answer.

One third of our group was gone. We were well into the mountains now, following the trail left by our scouts. They'd passed here several weeks ahead of us, travelling light and fast, marking our way.

One morning a small footprint was found which Koon'an believed to be the track of a mountain Ghen. The print was no bigger than my own foot and looked to me like one from a four- or five-year-old, but Saft'ir told me that, given the size of the Broghen, the Ghen themselves would be small.

"How do you know that?" I signed, but he turned to speak to the Ghen beside him as though he hadn't seen my question.

When we stopped for the evening I asked him to come with me to speak to Koon'an. "You believe these Ghen are smaller than you?" I asked. I didn't wait for his answer. "If so, they'll be afraid of you. I should approach them first. They won't fear a Bria."

"Too dangerous. Their customs might be different from ours."

I was taken aback for a moment at the thought of a Bria having to fear a Ghen. Then I pulled my knife from its pouch and threw it into the ground an inch from Koon'an's foot, before he could move. "I'm not without resources," I said.

My words were sheer bravado. Despite my excellent aim, I had never sunk my blade into a living thing and doubted that I could. But Koon'an laughed in approval and said he would consider my suggestion.

❧

We had climbed high into the mountains by now and had reached the mist line. The thought of walking into clouds had thrilled me when I'd seen them above us, but the reality wasn't pleasant. I'd expected something soft and warm, like a veil of white sunshine. Instead, they were cold and damp. They surrounded us until we could barely see our own hands, like nighttime painted white.

The trail markings left by our three scouts stopped. We found no bodies, no signs of a struggle. The ground was swept clear by wind and rain. Like everything else, they had simply disappeared into the fog.

Koon'an had us tie ourselves together with lengths of rope, something we hadn't even had to do in the dark of the forest at night. Despite the rope, I felt cut off from the others. I kept touching it to feel its tautness, to feel the pull of living bodies before and behind me. I needed to reassure myself that I wasn't alone in the fog, following an imaginary trail that led nowhere.

Anything might be hiding in this white darkness which even Ghen sight couldn't pierce. The dampness washed the wind clean before it could bring any warning scents to us, and the birds and mountain creatures were either frightened into silence or their movements and voices were muffled, as were ours. I could hardly tell whether the few sounds that came to me were near or far.

I might have succumbed to my fears except that the wind blew the mists aside every so often. When that happened, I could see that I climbed a real trail in real mountains surrounded by living companions. Then the clouds closed in again, swallowing everything, even the silent shadow of our passage.

ᘓ

Our tension increased daily. At night the watch was doubled. There'd been no sign from our scouts for several days. I dreaded walking into the cloying fog and even the Ghen packed up their bedrolls slowly, glancing over their shoulders now and then, lingering near the sallow illumination of the fire. Finally Koon'an spoke.

I approached Saft'ir for translation and he told me that we would travel in a tight group, close enough to touch one another whenever the clouds moved in. It would be slow but safer if anything tried to attack us.

So the Ghen felt it too. I was torn between relief that I was not imagining things and panic, to think that even the Ghen were frightened.

Saft'ir and I, along with the two Ghen who'd been wounded by Broghen, were placed in the middle of the group. We carried double loads to free the arms of Koon'an and the other seven who might have to defend us.

I no longer minded being given a protected position among them. I'd never known fear until I learned of Broghen, and had never been free of it since.

After three more days of walking through thick clouds, I became certain that we were not alone. But the wind, which occasionally blew the clouds aside, seemed to blow those other presences away also, for each time the clouds cleared I could see only the towering boulders glistening with sweat around us. The sight did not relieve me. I felt hidden eyes watching us from behind them, and the nervous glances of the Ghen proved they were worried, too.

I signed to Saft'ir, grateful for our silent language. I imagined that the slightest sound might bring some awful terror down upon us, like lighting a candle under Ghen firearms. Saft'ir signed that he felt it also, but that we were guarded by the best fighters in the city.

"Including you," I answered.

Day after day we walked as noiselessly as possible, our every sense tingling yet at the same time all—sight, hearing and smell—dampened by the heavy clouds. Touch alone sustained us, or so we hoped. We believed that the bodies we felt in the mist and occasionally bumped against, were our comrades.

But we also sensed, with increasing certitude, that the mist was populated by more than our small band. A muffled clatter of pebbles too far ahead, a soft grunt off to our left, the small sounds of swift movement from boulder to boulder, suddenly ceasing when we stopped to listen, all had us on constant edge. At every step the trail closed in on us, huge rocks rising steeply at our sides, hemming us in.

I caught myself murmuring prayers to Wind, something I hadn't done for a while. Perhaps He heard me because the clouds thinned and drifted away. One hundred armlengths ahead the route narrowed. On the left, the mountain rose at a sharp incline and on the right it fell away almost sheer, into a deep crevice. Between the two was a treacherous path no wider than two Ghen walking abreast.

In front of this passageway stood perhaps two dozen figures, guarding the entrance. They stood so still I didn't see them until, noticing the tension around me, I looked again, harder. I yelped in fear when I made out white bodies, nearly twice as many as our own party.

Saft'ir, guessing my impression, signed, "Ghen, not Broghen."

I was only slightly relieved. The strangers were obviously on the defensive, ready for battle. Subtly our group shifted into similar lines, gently nudging Saft'ir and me and the two wounded Ghen to the back. Koon'an led us forward cautiously until we'd covered half the distance to them. Some of the strangers held what looked like slingshots, into which they had placed stones, while others raised against us stone-head axes and shafts sharpened into knife-like points.

Koon'an had us wait while he walked slowly forward, holding his hands empty before him. He was within fifteen armlengths of the white Ghen when his foot slipped on a spray of gravel and he lunged forward. One of the savages yelled and let loose his short spear. It caught Koon'an in the upper thigh just as he was straightening from his stumble. He cried out, falling onto the dirt. With howls of outrage our Ghen surged forward but Koon'an struggled to his knees and raised his hand, stopping us.

Before I could lose my nerve I pushed my way to the front and walked forward alone as Koon'an had, holding my hands out in front of me. Koon'an saw me coming but didn't stop me although he still held his arm up, warning the others back.

I passed Koon'an and kept walking, slowly, toward the strange, white Ghen. Although they were no taller than I, they were mature adults so their mass was greater. My legs trembled. I willed them to hold, afraid that if I stumbled or fell now, the Ghen behind me would think I'd been attacked and would rush to my rescue. I could see the alien Ghen glancing at one another, the arms that held their weapons slackening, relaxed though not lowered. A few shifted on their feet as though embarrassed.

I looked for the one the others looked to and directed my attention toward him, stooping slightly to make myself appear smaller than I actually was. When I was only a few armlengths away he stepped forward, motioning impatiently to the others who returned their attention to Koon'an and the Ghen behind me.

I stopped and spoke out loud for all the white Ghen to hear, "We come in peace, hoping to be friends."

I didn't expect them to understand my words, but my treble voice would confirm that I was Bria, even though I might appear as different from their Bria as they were from my Ghen. Watching me closely, the white Ghen leader lowered his slingshot and axe to the ground beside him. To my immense surprise, he began to sign.

His signs were as indecipherable as my words had been to him and I was shocked by the implied intimacy, but I signed back as I would have signed to Saft'ir or Yur'i or Gant'i, to let him know that I understood he was trying to communicate. Then I stepped forward carefully. He let me take his hand and lead him to Koon'an, still kneeling in the dirt.

Koon'an had not moved, not even to remove the stone spear. I bent and pulled it out as gently as I could, then turned and offered it to the white Ghen leader. He accepted it gravely and reached out his hand to help Koon'an to his feet. Koon'an called to our Ghen to put down their weapons and when they had, the white leader motioned his followers to do the same. Cautiously the two groups approached.

When they stood within arm's length on either side of us, Koon'an blew into the palm of his hand and extended it to the white Ghen. A moment's hesitation while I held my breath, then the white Ghen blew into his own palm, and reached out. Koon'an grasped his hand, palm to palm, and raised their joined hands in the air for all to see. They turned, facing first one and then the other group of Ghen, motioning their followers closer as the clouds once again moved in. Slowly gray and white hands reached for each other, until every Ghen was standing, hand clasped in a stranger's hand, and raised into the descending cloud.

Just before it enclosed us all, the white leader signed quickly to his troops. Still clasping our hands, the white Ghen began to lead us forward across the perilous mountain pass.

I marveled at Koon'an's foresight. He'd seen the clouds returning and cemented our fragile trust with the assurance of joined hands. And we needed those hands. Without their guidance few of us would have survived that unfamiliar, treacherous path through the clouds.

I found it easier to follow my guide when I didn't have even partial visibility—when the mist blew away, the gaping ravine on my left and the wall of rock towering over me to the right intimidated me until I could barely move forward.

The trail inclined steeply upward for most of our trip, then slightly downward. Our hosts drew us to a stop just as the wind once again blew the clouds aside. Spread below us was a wide valley. At the far end, the mountains rose steeply again. I could make out a number of black spaces in the sheer rock, which I took to be the entrances of caves, as a number of white Ghen and equally-pale Bria moved in and out of their shadows. There were at least a hundred Ghen and Bria of varying ages, including infants in arms, moving about the valley.

They live in caves, I thought, like Dayannis! I imagined myself going back in time to meet my own ancestors, rugged, primitive people like these.

Our guides led us down into the valley. Hundreds more Ghen and Bria emerged from the caves and came to look at us, gaping openly at my black fur and keeping a nervous distance from our Ghen, who stood two heads taller than any of them. Their reticence was fortunate. They crowded one another closely, without respect for personal space. That would take getting used to. Nevertheless, I smiled benignly. How much I had to teach them!

The crowd parted to admit a strong, middle-aged Ghen. He wore a stone amulet tied with leather about his neck. The leader of the party that had discovered us made a brief obeisance to him and began to sign, pausing each time the larger Ghen raised his hands to insert a question or comment into the narrative. I stared in amazement. Ghen signing to one another? It looked obscene, a public intimacy. The Ghen from my city looked away, embarrassed.

When he was done he bowed slightly once more. At this point Koon'an stepped forward, dipping his head to the dominant Ghen then, pointing to his own chest, said, "Koon'an." The leader of the valley Ghen stared, as though affronted. After a moment he nodded slightly and murmured, in a hoarse voice that sounded unused to speech, something which Saft'ir later translated for me as "Teralish". There were grimaces on many faces in the crowd as he did so, and he himself turned quickly away, gesturing to Koon'an to follow him. We were led across the valley to the caves.

The caves lay at varying levels in the rock face. When we got closer I noticed rough steps dug into the rock leading up to the higher ones. Teralish led Koon'an to one of the highest caves, which I assumed to be his own until I saw several Bria sitting with their youngsters and two other white Ghen at the entrance. The rest of us were taken to a small, mid-level cave. We climbed a narrow set of steps single-file to enter it, past an armed Ghen standing at the base of the steps and another at the top, just at the cave entrance.

Inside, on a pallet of woven grasses lay Kur'ad, one of our three missing scouts. He moaned and twisted in a semi-conscious state as a young Bria bent over him, carefully placing across his chest the long, broad leaves of some mountain plant. I caught sight of a terrible, bloody gash reaching from his right shoulder down across his right breast.

In fact, he was covered with the leafy bandages. Remembering our own battles with the white Broghen, I shuddered. Kur'ad appeared to have fought them off with his bare claws. We had no way of asking about the other missing scouts, but we were grateful for the gentle care the strange Bria was giving Kur'ad. Before leaving, he carefully spooned into Kur'ad's mouth a thin gruel in which I could see a number of tiny seeds I didn't recognize. Shortly after swallowing them, Kur'ad fell into a deep, untroubled sleep.

Two more Bria entered carrying a clay bowl of water and a woven basket full of the same unfamiliar, broad leaves. Gently they removed the strips of cloth with which we'd bound the wounds of our two comrades. They washed the deep cuts and applied to them the pungent sap from several of the leaves. Then, using a stone knife, they cut shallow slits in one side of the remaining leaves and wound them, cut side down, around the wounded arm or leg. As the sap entered their wounds, the facial muscles of both Ghen visibly relaxed.

I tried to speak to the Bria but they were intent on their task. They kept their gaze averted, but patted my arm now and then, as one would do to a prattling child one wished to calm. They didn't speak to each other, either, so I wasn't sure whether they were intimidated by our strangeness or were unable to speak. Perhaps they had not yet developed a full spoken language?

At dusk we were led outside. At least two thousand Ghen and Bria had gathered. They parted to let us through. Teralish, with Koon'an beside him, stood near an assortment of steaming pots of meat and root vegetables, and baskets heaped with fruit. He gestured grandly toward the spread of food. We bowed our heads briefly. He accepted our homage as his due with a quick motion of his left hand, which we'd witnessed when his own people bent their heads to him.

I hadn't eaten all day. My mouth watered at the tempting smells, until I saw that every pot contained meat as well as vegetables. I was nearly sickened by the sight of Bria hands scooping up meat from their bowls and eating it with obvious pleasure. I tried to select only vegetables. When I accidentally placed a piece of meat in my mouth, it was all I could do not to vomit in the midst of their feast.

Afterwards there was music made by clacking stones and sticks and thin reeds with holes that produced a whistling sound, but I was exhausted and returned to our cave. There would be plenty of opportunities to observe their customs, and I had had enough strangeness for now. Being an emissary was more difficult than I thought.

In the morning the guard was gone from the entrance of our cave. We wandered into the valley and found left-overs from the previous night's banquet. Many of the cave-dwellers were already breakfasting on them. I was careful to choose only from the baskets of fruit. While eating, I wandered over to a Bria who I judged to be about my own age despite his smaller stature. Swallowing my mouthful, I said: "My name is Tyannis."

I meant to show my willingness to learn to speak with him, but I wasn't prepared for the look of surprise that crossed his face and his grimace as he covered his mouth with his palms, as though trying not to laugh aloud.

"Tyannis," I repeated, patting myself on the chest, then pointing to him I asked, "What's your name?"

This time he doubled over, unable to control his laughter. I looked around and those nearby were grinning also. Didn't they understand? Perhaps they had no language at all. I'd seen them gesture to one another, but the Bria who cared for our wounded had ignored my attempts to communicate. How would I teach these people anything if they didn't even have a language?

Just then, a Bria toddler bounced in his parent's arms and, reaching toward me, burst into a high-pitched lisp of meaningless baby-talk. At once the entire group burst into loud laughter. When it subsided, the parent turned to me, his face a mixture of embarrassment and mirth, and with exaggerated slowness signed to me what was obviously an apology.

An apology to the poor primitive who spoke baby-talk.

My ears twitched with embarrassment and I turned to leave. The Bria I'd first approached touched my arm. Composing his face as best he could, he signed to me. I stared at him, neither speaking nor moving for fear of becoming the butt of their humor again. He patted his chest as I had done and signed again.

Did he expect me to share a sign language with him, as though we were joined? Would those around us be shocked to see me presuming to do so? But he was watching me, waiting for a response. Hesitantly, I pointed to him then mimicked the movements his fingers had made.

He grinned with what looked like approval and signed again, slowly, letting me see a slight correction in the placement of first and third fingers. This time I signed his name correctly. Glancing around nervously, I was rewarded with a wide circle of smiles.

I signed my own name, "Tyannis," as I would have signed it to Saft'ir. The young Bria signed it back directly and looking up I saw others signing my name also, Ghen and Bria alike, nodding encouragement.

They're teaching the savage to speak, I thought incredulously.

༄

Shebabeth, the young Bria I had befriended on my first day here, climbed with me out of the valley. We followed the mountain trail up around towering boulders, then downward again. Rounding another boulder, I saw a stone wall in the valley below us. I led the way toward it.

There was a small tower at the corner, which I climbed in order to look into the walled enclosure. At first I thought the ground inside was covered with snow; it was as white as the distant mountain peaks I could see from my cave. Then something moved and I leaped back in shock. The ground was a mass of sleeping Broghen!

After a moment I calmed myself and edged forward on the tower platform to look again. Some of the Broghen inside were quite small, probably born during the past stillseason. The eldest appeared no more than three years old. According to Saft'ir, even from birth these creatures were vicious killers. I imagined the carnage among them when they awoke.

"Broghen are killing Broghen," I signed. Shebabeth looked in surprise at the young Broghen.

"No," he signed.

181

"Broghen are awake. Broghen are fighting."

"No." Now he regarded me with surprise, but I was too frustrated to care. I understood their sparse signing now, after only a few weeks among them, but it was impossible to ask a question in their language, which had neither past nor future tenses, let alone the conditional. If there was some subtle sign of the interrogative, I'd seen no indication of it. Nor any other indication of curiosity. They lived entirely in the visible present.

Would Shebabeth have shown me these Broghen if I hadn't led us this way? He hadn't led our walk, but he'd also made no attempt to guide me in another direction, which he could easily have done. Would I have to stumble blindly onto everything I learned about these people?

My mind teemed with questions I couldn't ask. Why were these young Broghen here, being fed and raised in a stone pen? They were obviously drugged by the same poro seeds given to help Kur'ad rest, but they must wake from time to time to eat and defecate. I looked around for more pens.

"Adult Broghen are here."

"No."

Did that mean that they didn't keep adult Broghen, or that there were none in this pen? Probably the former. Whenever possible, these people preferred the evidence of their senses to the subtleties of language. If there had been adult Broghen, Shebabeth would have shown me their pen.

"Broghen are freed."

"True," Shebabeth confirmed, "Teralish frees Broghen."

I marveled at the compassion of these rough people, who took such care of even their monstrous progeny, ensuring that they at least reached adulthood safely.

"Teralish takes out Broghen poison fangs," I signed.

"Ghen take out Broghen poison fangs in ceremony."

"Tyannis sees this ceremony."

He shrugged, which I'd learned to take as denial.

I was disappointed. I had come to believe this community was an example of complete equality. Except for the biological requirements of Bria pregnancy and Ghen hunting eyes and claws, they appeared to cooperate in all aspects of their lives. They spoke one language and shared their caves according to family bonds, not species bonds as we did. They farmed and cooked and reared their children jointly. I'd even seen Bria and Ghen journey together into the mountains to collect the leaves, seeds and roots they used as herbs and medicine. Perhaps that was why they'd shown little surprise to see me in the party of foreign Ghen.

For my part, I felt accepted here as I never had in my own city. My upbringing with Yur'i and Saft'ir, which created such a rift between me and my city peers, had helped me to accept their sign language and their intermingled lives more easily than Koon'an and his Ghen warriors could. They were a primitive model of my own family.

I told myself to stop making assumptions. No doubt there would be many surprises before I knew everything about their customs. Perhaps Saft'ir and the others would be invited to the Broghen ceremony and could tell me about it. I didn't like the thought of being once more denied something merely because I was Bria, but it seldom happened here and besides, I was a guest. I accepted Shebabeth's response without argument.

❧

I meant to tell Koon'an about the young Broghen, but when I got back to our cave after my walk with Shebabeth, Koon'an was in a heated discussion with the rest of our group.

"We're leaving," Saft'ir signed when he saw me.

"No!"

"Yes, Koon'an has decided."

"I won't go!" There was still so much to do! I was just earning their trust, learning their ways. I hadn't begun to teach them. If we left now, would they even remember me when I managed to return? They lived so much in the present. And I might not be allowed to return at all.

"Tyannis, if we don't go now, we won't make it home before stillseason. The journey's dangerous enough, without traveling in stillseason. Koon'an's right. We have to leave now."

"We could stay, and leave when stillseason's over."

"And let everyone at home believe we're dead? Besides, Koon'an was ordered by Council to return before stillseason. There are Broghen in our forests and these are our best fighters. They're needed on the wall."

"Koon'an already knew about the Broghen! He must have guessed at what we'd find here. Surely you were supposed to do more than greet these people and leave?"

"We were to try to convince them, if we found them, to release their Broghen on the other side of the mountains. Koon'an tried. Their leader, Teralish, wouldn't listen. He won't talk at all to Koon'an. Perhaps he doesn't understand. Council will have to decide what to do next."

"If we stay, if we get to know them and show them a better way to live, we can teach them how to avoid having Broghen. We don't have Broghen."

Saft'ir hesitated. Then he signed, "Koon'an has orders from Council. We will obey them."

From the back of the cave I heard a deep moan. Kur'ad's bandages were being changed by Meliath, the same young Bria who'd been attending him since we arrived. Shebabeth had told me that Meliath would mate with Kur'ad when he was well. I heard another groan, followed by garbled shouts, as though Kur'ad was still fighting the Broghen that had wounded him. In the weeks we'd been here, Kur'ad had not regained lucidity, except for these periodic screams, calmed only by more of the small poro seeds. I tried not to wonder what nightmare he'd endured before the white Ghen found him and brought him here.

"I need to talk to Koon'an," I signed, when Kur'ad's cries subsided. Koon'an and some of the other Ghen had learned a bit of the native sign language, but they refused to sign to me, so I was still forced to use Saft'ir as a translator.

I tried to draw Koon'an aside for such encounters, to avoid the derisive amusement of the mountain people when they saw our Ghen communicating with sounds. I'd discussed it with Saft'ir in our own sign language, and he'd tried to tell Koon'an. Koon'an understood, but knowing and feeling are different. Koon'an couldn't feel embarrassed about speaking, any more than he could feel comfortable signing to any but a mate.

"What will you do about Kur'ad?" I asked Koon'an, through Saft'ir, "and Brod'ar and Sim'en? They can't go on such a long trip."

Brod'ar and Sim'en, who'd been wounded in our last battle with the Broghen, had healed well in the time we'd been here. They'd be able to accompany us, but they'd slow us down. If Koon'an was worried about stillseason, he wouldn't want that.

"They'll stay here," Koon'an replied. "Teralish has indicated that they will be welcome. When Council has decided what to do, I'll lead another expedition up here. They can return with us then."

"I'm staying here with them."

"Less likely than wind in stillseason."

"I've already made a Bria friend. I could get to know their ways, teach them ours."

"No."

"You don't have Council orders for me. If you did, they'd be to let me stay and learn more about these people, to increase our chance of reaching a peaceful agreement. We have to consider what's best for our city. You're needed back there, but I'm more useful here."

Koon'an turned away sharply. I didn't press him. By his silence he was admitting I was right, although he didn't like it. When they left a few days later, they carried my written record with them.

The part I had feared, had dreaded, was losing Saft'ir. But when I went to him the morning they were preparing to leave, he told me he wasn't going.

"But you're the recorder."

"Rennis can read your written record and sign it to Yur'i, so he can typeset it and print it for the Ghen."

"Koon'an agreed to that?"

"I told him we were joined." He held his hand out to me. "We would have joined anyway, this stillseason, wouldn't we?"

When I was silent, he added, "I couldn't go to Festival Hall without you."

At once I reached for his hand. Of course no one else could have him. "I want to be joined the way these Ghen and Bria are: for life," I told him.

"The way your parent and mine are."

"More than that. I'll be the one who bears your second youngling."

Now it was Saft'ir's turn to be surprised, to hesitate.

"You don't know what's involved." The look in his eyes even more than his words, unnerved me. But then I imagined him going to the home of another Bria, living with him for five years… Unthinkable!

"Ocallis is carrying Mant'er's second son. Am I less steadfast than he is?"

He looked at me for a long moment. "I'd like that, Tyannis, but I won't hold you to it. Remember that."

Walls of Wind

◈

Shebabeth was pleased that I stayed. He taught me the chores that made up his life: how to cultivate the communal garden and which section belonged to each cave; how to dry and use the spices and medicinal plants that grew along the mountain slopes; how to wrap meat and vegetables together in broad cappa leaves and bury them under the cooking fire to roast slowly. By now I was accustomed to their eating habits, but I wondered how Bria from our city would respond to these flesh-eating Bria.

One day Shebabeth took Saft'ir and me to collect poro seeds and the healing leaves applied to wounds. A strong wind came up, and with it a small whirlwind, blowing twigs, leaves and stones in a circular frenzy. It swayed and darted in a ring about us and then continued on its way. Shebabeth grinned broadly.

"Wind accepts strangers," he proclaimed.

I was familiar with the way these people personified wind and water and rock, revering them as deities, and knew enough to answer, "Strangers thank wind." I intended to teach them about the Creator Wind, and how He was more than the wind, but I had to know them better first.

When Shebabeth was busy in his family's cave, Saft'ir and I explored the surrounding area together. Saft'ir had his firearm in the cave we slept in, and we both had our knives. Even so, we always went out in the brightest part of the day, when Broghen slept. I took him to see the enclosure of young Broghen and told him what little I'd learned from Shebabeth.

One day we went further than usual. Cresting a rock-strewn incline we stood looking down into a deep, hidden valley. Here, too, there were high stone walls, but these were loosely covered with thorn brambles and long, dried grasses, so that we couldn't see inside. We could make out that a large area in the center had been left uncovered, but it was far away and the angle was wrong to look down into it. We descended to look at it more closely.

A thick wooden door was built solidly in the middle of this end of the enclosure. It was bolted with three broad external beams, as though secured against an assault from the inside rather than from the outside. We tried to walk around the perimeter but it filled half the valley and the afternoon was lengthening. We had to return.

That night I woke in the dark. I wandered to the cave entrance. The moon was almost full and I shivered in its cold light. I had dreamed of Saft'ir on the training grounds, engaged in mock combat as I had seen him what seemed like years ago, but was in fact only a few months before this trip. Two of his comrades had already left the field, leaving Saft'ir and one other against all four of the opposing team. The result was a foregone conclusion to all but Saft'ir, who circled and charged, kicking, grasping, butting, leaping aside and returning again and again.

When his last teammate left the field it was three to one and Saft'ir had already taken the worst of it. He was barely standing and his opponents, who stumbled with exhaustion themselves, wept as they knocked him back.

"Saft'ir, give in!" someone called from the edge of the meadow. But he fought on, perhaps not even aware of the terrible beating he was taking, until at last he alone remained on the field. He turned slowly around, looking through swollen eyes as though surprised, before he pitched face first to the ground, only then feeling his injuries.

The memory filled me with a strange foreboding. I returned to the cave and pulled my pallet closer to Saft'ir's.

In the morning, Teralish came to our cave. "Ceremony," he signed. "Come now." I stepped forward with the others, but Teralish motioned me back.

"Ghen go alone," he signed in the native language.

The words sent a chill down my spine, but when Saft'ir and Sim'en and Brod'ar were instructed to leave their knives behind, Saft'ir grinned at me as if to say, you see? It's a peaceful ceremony. There's no danger, no need for knives. I was still jealous at being left behind, and gave him a cool good-bye.

Evening came and the Ghen had not returned. I went to Shebabeth's cave to pose to him another series of frustrating, inaccurate statements.

"Ghen are returning."

"No."

I closed my eyes, leaning my head sideways across folded hands. "Sleep." I opened my eyes, raising my head. "Awake. Ghen are returning."

He surprised me then. Perhaps he'd begun to imagine the meanings behind my strange comments. Taking my hand, he led me to the edge of the cave and pointed up at the night sky.

"Moon is large," I observed, gazing at the full moon.

"Moon is small." He cupped his hands in a semi-circle, looking embarrassed and confused, as though he barely grasped himself the concept he was trying to express in his inadequate language. "Moon is small. Ghen are returning."

Half a month. He expected well over half the adult Ghen to be gone for half a month?

"Ghen are far away."

"Ghen are close." Shebabeth pointed in the direction Saft'ir and I had walked a few days before.

"Ghen are in valley, stone walls."

"Yes."

Knowing that they weren't far reassured me and I slept more soundly. I woke refreshed and went with Meliath to work in our portion of the garden. The village seemed strange, too quiet. I began to worry, until I realized I was just missing the absent Ghen. How quickly I'd become used to living in such close harmony with them. I'd almost begun to think of the mountain Ghen and Bria as one species.

Perhaps I would live all my life here, among these congenial people, as they seemed to assume we would when Koon'an left without us. I doubted they'd have been as easily accepted by our city Ghen and Bria, if they had come to us.

That afternoon, Kur'ad awoke. His eyes were clear for the first time and I thought he recognized me as I hurried toward him. He looked around as though searching for the others, but not seeing them he cried out in despair and the nightmare he lived with returned until Meliath's poro seeds helped him to sleep again.

The next morning I woke to find Kur'ad staring intently at me. I smiled at him but he didn't return my smile. He spoke in a hoarse, urgent voice, his Ghen sounds meaningless to me. If only Saft'ir were here, I thought. Then, if only our city had a common sign language like these mountain Ghen and Bria have.

Kur'ad half raised his hands as though to make some gesture, but the effort was too much. Letting them drop again, he closed his eyes and drifted back into sleep.

I was heartened, however, and when Meliath returned from his early morning trip to collect fresh healing leaves I signed to him, "Kur'ad is healing." He grinned and signed his agreement.

In the afternoon Kur'ad woke again. Meliath and I raised him into a semi-reclining position to eat the vegetables and sadu'h meat Meliath had cooked and cut into tiny pieces for him. He accepted Meliath's administrations in a way that appeared almost guarded, looking away when Meliath tried to sign to him. For some reason, Meliath seemed disappointed. Had he expected Kur'ad to learn his sign language while drifting in and out of sleep and nightmare these past weeks?

Kur'ad stared at me repeatedly. I wondered if my presence upset him, reminded him of our journey together and of its painful ending for him. He might have been wondering where the others were. My smiles and reassuring pats gave him little comfort but they were the best I could do until Saft'ir returned.

When I signed to Meliath, Kur'ad looked startled but made no attempt to learn to sign himself. Meliath and I settled him down to rest. I was about to follow Meliath outside to work in our section of the garden, when Kur'ad grabbed my hand. Was he afraid to be left alone? I paused to stay with him, but the poro seeds Meliath had put into his food took hold quickly and I was able to join Meliath before he'd even reached the garden.

❧

In the middle of the night, something small landed on my chest. I was awake at once, thinking that a rock spider had dropped onto me. Reaching quickly to swipe it aside I touched only a pebble. A minute later another one hit my shoulder.

It was pitch black. I could barely make out the pale mound of Meliath's body between me and the cave entrance. A third pebble plinked against the ground, falling just short of me on the other side. Pulling myself up I peered into the darkness, frightened, until I heard a hushed whisper from the place where Kur'ad slept. I dimly made out his half-raised form and crawled over to him. He was staring at me with an urgency that frightened me.

When he touched my hands, I felt his fingers moving. It took a moment to realize that he was signing, using the stilted, primitive language of our hosts. How had he learned it? But I needed all my concentration to make out by touch what he was trying to tell me.

"Ghen are here."

I hesitated.

"Ghen are here!" Did he mean our Ghen? How would he react to hearing that they'd left without him?

"Saft'ir and Brod'ar and Sim'en are here. Koon'an and many go city. Stillseason. Windseason. Koon'an and many return."

He peered about in the darkness of the cave. "Three are here." He didn't know the natives' signs for our names; we'd come here after him.

"Three here, not here," I signed, "three with Teralish."

"With Teralish in cave." His fingers trembled so I could barely make out the words. His hands were tight on mine, hurting me. I tried to wriggle my fingers. His grip loosened enough to let me sign.

"Three with Teralish in valley. Walls valley."

He gasped. I felt his sudden terror, so palpable my own heart panted for air. I gripped his hands, not noticing this time that his grasp had tightened again. I signed desperately, "What? What is it?"

"Danger!" he signed, "Broghen! Walls! Danger! Broghen! Walls!" He punctuated each word by pulling sharply on my hands. I thought of the young Broghen sleeping soundly in their walled pen. Had he seen and been frightened by them?

"Small Broghen sleeping," I signed.

"Adult Broghen, walls valley," I could hear him panting, at the edge of his strength. "Ceremony. Broghen fighting Ghen." Pulling my left hand forward, he pounded it against his healing scars. "Adult Broghen fighting Ghen! Three Broghen fighting three!"

I leaped to my feet as he sank back exhausted. I could hardly believe what he'd said. A ceremony in which Broghen and Ghen were pitted against one another? Why would they do such a thing? I wanted to disbelieve him, but his terrible wounds and nightmares were undeniable. And how had he learned these people's sign language, unless he'd lived among them *before* he was wounded, not after, as we'd assumed?

Teralish had ordered Saft'ir and Brod'ar and Sim'en to leave their knives behind. Breath of Wind! They were defenseless against three adult Broghen! I fell to my knees, barely able to turn the scream that rose in my throat into a smothered whimper. Nearby, Meliath murmured in his sleep.

I held my breath, waiting for him to relax, then crawled on hands and knees across the floor, not trusting my legs to support me. Reaching under Saft'ir's empty pallet, I pulled out his knife. The strong, cold steel gave me strength and by the time I had gathered up all three knives plus my own, I was braced by the knowledge of what I must do.

Glancing at Meliath to make sure he was still sleeping soundly, I dug into the stony earth at the back of the cave, where Saft'ir had hidden the firearm. Saft'ir had shown me how they worked, had let me hold his, but I had never used one. I doubted I'd be able to.

But Saft'ir needed it. I lifted the leather bag containing the firearm and swept the dirt back into the hole, smoothing the ground flat. Dropping the knives into the firearm bag, I pulled the leather strap over my shoulder and across my chest. Wind's breath, it was heavy! I was lucky it held only a youth firearm.

By the light of the full moon I could see several white Ghen moving about the edges of the valley, guarding it while the Bria slept. Once again I was a black shadow, slipping down the steps from the cave, running silently through the deeper shadow of the rock cliff and up, away from these deceitful creatures.

Nearing the place where I had seen one of the watches, I slowed and dropped to my knees. If I were caught carrying the weapons of my comrades, they would surely guess my intent. More was at stake this time than a young Bria longing for adventure.

On hands and knees I crawled over the south ridge of the valley, flattening myself against the ground just in time as two white Ghen crossed below my path on the other side of the rise, just twenty armlengths downhill. But they were watching for white shapes, not black, and they moved on, not noticing me.

When they were gone I scrambled down and across the next slope, keeping low to the ground. With no shrubs or boulders for cover I felt completely exposed even in the dark night. Although I tried to move carefully, I couldn't help dislodging a few pebbles in the stony ground. I was certain I'd be caught before I crossed the slope and rejoined the mountain trail beyond sight of the valley guards. When I finally crossed the hill and descended out of sight of the watch I slumped with relief.

How far was the valley? Saft'ir and I had walked since early morning the day we discovered it. I ran, banging my feet and ankles against rocks in the darkness, walking when my legs shook and my sides ached for breath, then running again when the image of Saft'ir in hand-to-hand combat with an insane Broghen rose up greater than my pain and weariness. I began to stumble. I twisted my ankle and forced myself to rest, afraid I might injure myself so badly I wouldn't be able to continue at all.

Half a month, Shebabeth had said. Perhaps the fighting began later? Yes, for they'd brought Kur'ad back to the caves to care for his wounds. The fighting must be near the end of the ceremony. Perhaps Saft'ir and Brod'ar and Sim'en still didn't know what was in store for them? I'd have to find a way to talk to them in secret. The thought of having time to do so calmed me. I felt my ankle. It was sore and beginning to swell, but it would hold me. When my breathing was even again I rose and continued, limping only a little.

I passed the enclosure which held the infant Broghen. I considered climbing the tower to see whether they were still there, but Kur'ad had insisted the battle was against adult Broghen, and I couldn't be sure the fighting hadn't already begun. The thought sent me running again. The ache in my side was intense and my throat was raw from gasping after air. My legs were beyond pain, numb with exhaustion. The leather strap of the firearm bag bit into my shoulder; I'd switched it from side to side until both shoulders ached.

Now I could see well enough to avoid the larger rocks, which both helped and terrified me. The creeping dawn was my enemy.

Teralish and the white Ghen were still sleeping when I crawled over the crest of the last hill and peered down on them. The day was just breaking and in the half-light I might have mistaken them for a drift of snow lingering at the far end of the valley. I focused on them despite their stillness, searching for a patch of gray in the blanket of white.

The valley was white and green, rich with vegetation near the end of a full growing season. Saft'ir and Brod'ar and Sim'en were not there. All was white or green, except the high, gray walls of stone that cut into the peaceful scene.

I was surprised not to see a watch patrolling the perimeters, but half a dozen armed and vigilant Ghen stood at the far end of the stone enclosure, a few hundred armlengths from where the others slept. What were they watching for?

Two more guards stood in front of the wooden door, down slope from me. It hadn't been guarded when Saft'ir and I walked here, but they guarded it now. Something was already imprisoned inside, something desperate and deadly.

Walls. Broghen fighting Ghen. Three Broghen fighting three. In walls.

I examined the stones as though the intensity of my stare might penetrate them. Whatever horror waited there, Saft'ir and Sim'en and Brod'ar faced it unarmed. Eight days had passed since they left with Tyrannish. Perhaps they were dead already, like the other two scouts who had been with Kur'ad? I almost embraced the idea; I wanted badly not to go inside those walls.

But no, Saft'ir wasn't dead. I would know if Saft'ir died. I would feel it as an emptiness inside me. No, Saft'ir was alive on the other side of two white guards and a bolted wooden door.

To my left, halfway down to the valley, a small group of cappa bushes clung to the side of a narrow creek. Slowly I inched my way across and down toward them as sunlight broke over the mountain.

From the protection of the bushes I watched the guards. How would I get past them? Even if it were possible, could I make myself kill them? What if I tried and failed?

Ridiculous. Of course I couldn't do such a thing. Only desperation made me think it. I would have to sneak by them somehow.

The morning lengthened. The distant Ghen were awake and the two below me showed signs of impatience. From their position at the door, they couldn't see the others. I watched them gesturing in wide, forceful signs, but I wasn't close enough to read the words. Finally one of them turned and stomped away along the wall. He reached the corner and turned toward the Ghen camp, out of sight.

This might be the best chance I got. I rose to a crouch, taking my knife from the pouch. I was about to burst from my cover when movement at the corner of the wall caught my eye. Two fresh guards approached. Whatever chance I might have had, I'd lost.

I watched two more changes of guards as I waited impatiently for night. Each set was more lax than the one before, as though the likelihood of an attempted escape from within grew less and less with each passing remove. The more their attentiveness decreased, the more desperate I was to get inside.

"Hold on, Saft'ir," I began to whisper into the wind, willing it to carry knowledge of my nearness to him.

The night was as cloudy as the day had been clear. I crept from the cappas and down the hill, certain that between the night and the low clouds I was invisible, even to Ghen eyes. When the land flattened out I hesitated, knowing I was very near. A single wind blowing the fog away might leave me revealed despite my black fur. Where were the guards?

I heard the rustle of a heavy body not five handspans from me as one of the guards rose from a squatting position against the door. Silence. They must be leaning close, signing to one another. An angry grunt, followed by retreating steps. I'd guessed right; it was close to the time of a changeover and they'd grown impatient. Soon the other rose and followed the first, his white body briefly visible through the fog as he passed by me.

I ran forward. My hands, stretched out ahead, slapped against cold stone. So little time! Was the door to my left or right? I felt to the left. No, the guards had walked that way, I wasn't thinking. I moved to the right, running my hand along the wall. Here!

The wall ended and I felt rough wood under my fingers. I ran my hands rapidly up and down to find the first bolt. The beam was heavy. I struggled to raise it. Push, and again, push! How long did I have before the new guards arrived? At last the beam rose clear of the latch. I lowered it as quietly as possible to the ground. I was panting and had to stop to let my arms rest.

The second was even harder to raise, then almost impossible to lower slowly, silently. My arms trembled with fatigue. In the distance I heard footsteps. I paused, listening. They were steady, growing louder.

I lunged at the final beam of wood, struggling to raise it. It stuck, wedged too tight against the latch. I leaned under it, pushing upward with all my strength. Again and again I bent my knees and heaved as the footsteps in the fog drew nearer.

"Saft'ir, Saft'ir!" I sobbed under my breath. Leaning my head against the beam of wood I pounded it with my fists.

The whack of a hand against stone reached me as the guards groped their way through the dense fog. I pulled myself up. Leaning into the beam I heaved with one last tremendous effort. It moved.

Slowly, resisting every inch, it rose out of its bracket until with a final gasp, I freed it. I had no strength to lower it carefully. It fell to the ground against the others with a dull clatter. One of the approaching guards cried out and they broke into a run.

I bent, my hands sweeping the ground. Where was the pouch with the weapons? There, my foot knocked against it. I caught it up and pulled the door open, throwing myself through it into only Wind knew what horror.

It was pitch black, blacker even than the foggy night. I hurried forward, arms outstretched, blind in the darkness. Three steps and I banged into the opposite wall. What was this place?

I slid my hands to the right along the wall ahead of me. A sharp corner, three steps, another corner. Three more steps and my hands felt the wooden door again. I pulled it shut. I must be in a narrow hall that ended just beyond the door, so that I could only go left. I moved away from the door quickly, before the guards could open it again and reach in, grabbing me.

They didn't even try to open the door. I heard them groping cautiously against it as I hurried down the corridor, and then stifled grunts and a low scraping as the first of the beams rose and sank back into its bracket.

I stumbled, mid-step. They were locking me in! I was trapped in this dark, disorienting tunnel of stone where monsters lurked! I ran back, on the verge of crying out that I'd changed my mind, when I heard ahead of me a low, wild snarl. I froze.

It came again, no louder, no softer. It wasn't as close as I'd feared; it wasn't as fierce. Outside, the last bolt rasped home. Saft'ir was somewhere ahead, wounded perhaps, or dying. Unarmed. I reached into the pouch and drew out my knife. Hefting it like a single claw in my soft hands, I cautiously moved forward.

I almost stepped on him. Already he smelled just a little, the smell of the body when Wind has claimed its breath. He must have died the first day they entered, only a short distance from the door. I pulled back sharply as my foot touched his, only after a moment making out the gray mound of his body on the fog-covered ground. I would have screamed but I was too afraid to make any sound. Bending down I touched him. The rigidity of death and the sticky residue of his wounds repelled me.

My breath caught in sobs which I could hardly smother. Now that I was closer I could tell, even in the dark, that it was too big to be Saft'ir. Then I saw the scab of a nearly-healed wound along his left shoulder and part-way down his arm.

It was Brod'ar. Brave Brod'ar, always grinning. Brod'ar had come here already wounded. "Leave me, I'd only slow you down. They'll take care of us," he'd told Koon'an. What chance had he, unarmed, against a Broghen? What chance had any creature on Wind, against a Broghen?

I rose and walked for countless removes as the corridor twisted and turned. Each step terrified me. Again and again the passage split, forcing impossible choices upon me. Sometimes I took one fork only to find myself in a dead end, having to retrace my steps and take the other.

I walked to the hair-raising accompaniment of a Broghen's death cries, sometimes behind me, sometimes ahead, sometimes almost beside me, on the other side of a wall. Already I might have taken the wrong passage and be irrevocably walking away from Saft'ir. At any corner, I might come face-to-face with a Broghen. I wanted to call out to Saft'ir but was terrified of calling the wounded Broghen to me.

Every step became harder, every turn more fearsome. Finally I could go no further. I sank to the floor, my back against the cold, relentless stone, staring wide-eyed into the dark.

∾

Sunlight wakened me, falling in a narrow, warm stroke across my brow like a light brush of the Creator's fingertips. I looked up. The roof was thinly thatched with a crisscross of long grasses and thorny brambles. Sunlight filtered through to fall like slivers of glass upon the ground. But it was daylight, however filtered. I could see where I was going, at least as far as the next corner.

I picked up my knife, which had fallen in the dirt beside me, checked that the pouch was still firmly strapped around my chest, and rose. The dying Broghen was silent at last. A death for a death. But neither it nor Brod'ar had come here willingly. When, nearly a full remove later, I came upon it stretched dead across the ground, I felt pity as well as horror.

I had drunk from the mountain stream and eaten several handfuls of cappa fruit as I waited the day before, but by now my stomach ached and my mouth was raw with thirst. My left shoulder was matted with dried blood where I had scraped it lifting the wooden beams and I had had little more than a few removes of sleep.

As I walked, I heard now and then the scream of a Broghen, its predatory hunger bouncing from wall to wall until it seemed to come at me from all directions, louder and still louder. I fell back against the wall holding my ears and closing my eye as though to prevent the insanity from entering my very heart.

On the evening of my second day inside the walls I heard the sounds of a battle: the savage howls of a Broghen and the throaty yells of a Ghen. Saft'ir! I thought, and then another voice: Sim'en!

I broke into a run, pounding down the corridor only to be blocked by a sudden twist in the wall. If only the walls weren't so high—but even two or three Ghen standing on each other's shoulders could not have scaled them. I took the turn, trying to find a route back in the direction of the cries I'd heard, but their echoes were all around me now and every twist confused me more until I no longer even knew which way I wanted to turn.

Finally the noises of the battle subsided. Into the heavy silence I began to scream, "Saft'ir!" I ran forward, blinded by tears, falling against one wall and then the other, all the while screaming, "Saft'ir! Saft'ir! Saft'ir!"

I no longer cared if the Ghen waiting outside learned there was a Bria in their hideous ceremony, didn't even care if a Broghen lurked around the next corner, drawn by my screams. I only cared that somewhere in this hell Saft'ir was fighting monsters with his bare claws, and I might be only a corridor away with knifes and a firearm when he died in its jaws.

My screams soon died in my parched throat. Still I stumbled on until the narrow corridor twisted once more and spewed me forth. A sudden sense of space stopped me.

Wiping the tears from my eye, I stared in amazement. I stood at the edge of a courtyard perhaps as big as an unjoined Bria's house. The sky was clear overhead and the last of the evening light poured in unhindered by any kind of covering. Half a dozen cappa shrubs grew about the clearing and in the middle was a huge fountain.

I was almost afraid of such open space after being constrained by walls for so long, and was at first convinced I was hallucinating. Saft'ir was dead and

I wished I were, also. Even so, the fountain drew me. I went to it and submerged my burning head beneath its cool waters.

When I emerged, I heard a low moaning from behind the fountain. There, beneath a cappa bush, lay Sim'en. He was feverish, barely conscious. I brought him water and he swallowed, weakly at first, then greedily. I fed him cappa fruit and ate some myself.

While picking them, I came across a patch of bannot roots. Yanking on their leafy tops I tore a half-dozen from the ground and washed them in the fountain. They would be hard to chew uncooked, but I was glad to find them. I cut small pieces with my knife and gave the smallest ones to Sim'en, who swallowed them whole. When he had drunk and eaten, he raised shaking hands.

"Brod'ar dead," he signed slowly in the mountain language. "One Broghen dead."

"Yes, Tyannis sees Brod'ar and Broghen."

"Broghen wounds Sim'en. Broghen is hurt, runs away. Saft'ir little wounded, carries Sim'en here."

I waited, almost unable to breathe. Afraid to ask.

"Saft'ir goes into walls," Sim'en pointed to an opening on the opposite side of the courtyard. I barely stopped myself from rushing toward it.

"Saft'ir hears Tyannis screaming. Tyannis is outside. Saft'ir finishes labyrinth to find Tyannis outside."

"Labyrinth," I signed. It was a symbol I hadn't seen before.

Sim'en gestured around us. "Walls narrow, turn. Pathway difficult. Labyrinth."

The enclosure, he meant the entire enclosure. And Saft'ir meant to finish it. Was there a way out of these walls, then? A way not barred and guarded?

"Ghen not let Saft'ir leave labyrinth," I signed.

Sim'en waved his hand in the negative. "Saft'ir finds path out. Ghen happy. Saft'ir brings help Sim'en. Saft'ir, Sim'en join Ghen."

"Saft'ir, Brod'ar, Sim'en come in labyrinth happy." I couldn't believe it.

"No. Must come in labyrinth." He paused then grimaced painfully. "Leave happy."

I touched my breath.

"Tyannis follows Saft'ir." I pointed to the opening he had shown me.

"Saft'ir marks trail."

Now I grinned in earnest. No more guessing at every crossroad, no more retracing dead ends or searching the ground for footprints that went both ways, footprints that could be Broghen as easily as Ghen. "Tell Tyannis."

"Stone." Sim'en picked up a pebble, rubbed it against the palm of his other hand. "Stone marks trail on wall."

"Tyannis brings weapons." I opened the pouch and handed him his knife, and then the firearm. He took the knife in his hands, almost lovingly. Briefly he held the firearm, stroked it longingly before he gave it back to me.

"Saft'ir, Tyannis die: Sim'en die. Saft'ir, Tyannis live: kill Broghen, bring help Sim'en."

Tears came to my eye, but Sim'en was right. If there was a way out and we could find it, we might all live. Otherwise, we would surely all three die. I returned the firearm to its pouch.

Sim'en showed me the small water-skin he'd been given on entering the labyrinth. I refilled it from the fountain for him and drank again myself. After taking one last look at him, I turned and left.

At the first turn in the corridor I found Saft'ir's mark—a rough > scratched into the wall at eye level. I ran to the next corner, which was a fork leading off in two directions, and searched until I found his > again. I didn't care whether he'd chosen correctly or not; I was glad I no longer had to choose for myself.

The evening had lengthened while I was in the courtyard and soon I was unable to see Saft'ir's marks and was forced to stop. I almost cried in frustration to finally know my direction and be unable to follow it. Saft'ir was still weaponless against two Broghen. What if he died tonight, with help so close? I banged my feet and hands against the wall like a child in a temper, but I couldn't risk going on blind and losing his trail.

I heard the roar of Broghen in the night, sometimes far away, sometimes coming nearer; twice so near I expected to see one turn the corner and fall upon me. Always, the walls came between us, like the hands of Wind, keeping me safe. Like the walls around our distant city, that protected us against our own Broghen.

In the long, dark night I faced the fact that we, too, must birth Broghen. I had recognized it in the sleeping, white infants, heard of their existence in

Saft'ir's silences, in the way he turned away from me when I denied it. In the long, dark night I sat with a wall at my back, protection and prison both; as solid as the wall of ignorance I'd lived behind all my life.

Walls were not the Wind's work. We built them and it was up to us to tear them down. All through the long, cold night, monsters raged; and they, like the walls we built against them, were all our doing.

I sat out the night with my knife in one hand and Saft'ir's firearm in the other. I had cocked it in the dark, bracing it in the sharp corner of two walls and using both hands to pull the trigger back until I heard it lock with a "click!" as Saft'ir had shown me. The Broghen howled continuously. They were crazed with hunger now, as desperate to feed as we were to escape.

At the first light of dawn I rose and ran through the corridors, pausing only to locate Saft'ir's marks on the walls. I stumbled when the screams of a battle erupted suddenly behind me, and fell against the wall, my every instinct urging me to turn and run toward the sounds, even though I knew I'd never reach them that way. None of my senses served me here. All I had were a few marks scratched on the wall before I arrived. Scratches made by someone as lost as I was. I ran, clutching the knives and the firearm, as fast as I could away from Saft'ir's screams.

The corridor twisted at last and I was able to race back toward the sounds of battle until it turned again, and once again I had to follow. At the next turn I almost ran over the white body.

My sudden appearance stirred it from its death throes and it half raised a gory arm against me. I leaped away, slamming against the wall behind me. Even dying, it terrified me. I would birth one of these? And unleash it on Wind to destroy everything it came across? I gagged, nauseous with horror and disgust. The dying monster fell back, the last of its life spent. Only my ragged panting filled the corridor.

My panting and the distant shrieks of the third Broghen. I leaped over the still, white form and ran on. There were no more marks on the walls. I didn't need them; the trail I followed now was marked in blood.

Why wasn't Saft'ir screaming?

"Hold on," I whispered as I ran.

"Hold on," I sobbed, still hearing only the Broghen up ahead.

"Hold on!" I screamed, "Saft'ir, hold on! I'm coming!"

～

One last turn and I saw them. Saft'ir lay bleeding upon the ground, backed against the wall with his arms raised before him, claws extended. His breath was ragged, as though he were drowning in the blood that covered him. Over him leaned the Broghen, sensing that Saft'ir's wounds would soon weaken him beyond resistance.

At my approach it shrieked anew, raising its massive arms to claim its prey before I could intrude. And in that moment I raised Saft'ir's firearm and pulled the trigger.

The recoil threw me to the wall, knocking the breath from my body. The thunder of its eruption echoed from wall to wall throughout the labyrinth. Blinded by spots of blackness and flashing lights, and deafened by the noise, I staggered back up. The Broghen lay dead on the ground, its lifeless arms stretching toward Saft'ir still.

It was repulsive even in death, a thing capable only of destruction. I looked at the firearm in my bruised hands, and threw it from me in revulsion. A thing capable only of destruction.

When I looked up, Saft'ir was staring at me. "Are you all right?" His hands shook as he formed the words.

I closed my eyes for a moment, forcing down hysterical laughter. Was *I* all right? I knelt beside him. There was so much blood I couldn't find his wounds. "Where are you hurt?" I signed.

He grimaced. "Everywhere." Then he reached up, touching my lips to feel my breath on his fingers.

Before Saft'ir would let me help him through the final turns of the labyrinth, he made me bury the knives and the firearm. The mountain Ghen knew nothing about firearms, but if they saw us with one they would guess it to be a weapon. Without visible evidence, however, they could make what they would of the noise they'd heard.

I dug in the soft earth to make a hiding place. I felt I was stabbing my knife into Wind itself, opening a wound into which I would insert, like poison, the weapons which made me a killer.

"We'll have to come back for them later," Saft'ir signed as I stamped down the earth, trying to make it look like the rest of the ground, which was torn up anyway from the fight between Saft'ir and the Broghen.

The dead Broghen stank in the close walls. I began to shake with reaction and weariness. The worst of it was, I wasn't sorry. In fact, I half wanted that firearm in my hands when we met Teralish at the end of the labyrinth. The thought shocked me so much I began to cry.

I hated the mountain people with a rage I hadn't known I could feel. Hated them for what they'd put us through, and even more for what they made me into. I wasn't the heart of Wind. It was only a matter of degree that separated me from the vicious beast I'd shot.

I heard Saft'ir's gutteral voice and saw through my tears that he was signing, but I was too ashamed to tell him the reason for my grief.

"For Brod'ar," I signed. I cried harder. "And I was afraid." I remembered racing through the corridors after Saft'ir's screams had stopped.

I slid to my knees, rocking in the dirt, my arms tight around my abdomen. Saft'ir crawled forward slowly, until he reached me. I lay my forehead against his arm and howled, a sound as hideous as any made by a Broghen.

When the worst of my grief was spent, he touched my shoulder gently.

"We have to go," he signed when I lifted my head. "Sim'en is waiting for help. Can you face them?"

I touched my breath.

"You make too much of them," he signed, when I had risen.

"Not anymore."

"Now as much as ever."

I helped him stand and eased myself under his arm to support the wounded leg. Together we made our way through the last twisting corridors of the labyrinth.

ℰↃ

When we emerged, we were greeted with smiles and signs of welcome.

"Rock accepts Saft'ir!" Teralish signed for all to see, the pleasure and relief clear on his face. He gestured to the assembled mountain Ghen: "Welcome Saft'ir."

They cheered again. Then, "Rock accepts Tyannis!" he signed, and turned once more to the Ghen: "Welcome Tyannis."

I was shocked at being included in the ceremony until I saw Shebabeth standing among the Ghen.

"I told him that our Bria don't fight Broghen," Saft'ir signed to me. "Otherwise you would have been included from the start."

"You knew about this?"

"I began to guess some of it when I saw the sleeping Broghen. Their children are all taught to fight."

"They put their own children in the labyrinth?"

"At three years of age both Bria and Ghen, together with the Broghen of their birth year, run the labyrinth. The children have been trained to fight together and the Broghen are outnumbered three to one. Not many Broghen survive, but those that do are freed. And the children, apparently, are never again afraid of Broghen."

"Those who survive."

"Those who survive," he agreed.

Because they know they are more deadly than the Broghen, I thought bitterly.

The Ghen approached us and gently lifted Saft'ir onto a courrant'h pelt stretched between two poles.

"Sim'en waits beside fountain," Saft'ir signed to them. "No Broghen lives." Several of the Ghen hurried into the labyrinth with another of the crude stretchers.

Shebabeth came up to me. "Tyannis strong. Rock accepts Tyannis." He grinned happily.

"Brod'ar dead. Saft'ir, Sim'en hurt," I signed.

"Rock accepts, not accepts." Shebabeth touched his throat in a gesture I'd come to recognize as resignation.

I raised my hands to sign that I didn't accept rock, or any of their gods and ceremonies, or them. He saw my face and grabbed my hands to quiet me.

White and black his hands and mine were, together.

Light and shadow, shadow and light, intertwined.

We bear Broghen, too.

Council Relations

Briarris

When I approached the sandy field beside Savannis's—no, Yur'i's—house, I was surprised at the number of adult Bria already there. I'd been told Yur'i put out benches, encouraging parents to visit storytime, but I had no idea so many attended.

"I'm glad you came," Tibellis greeted me.

"I'm glad you suggested it." I looked around. There were so many young-sters I had trouble picking out my grandchildren, Kayjais and Zipporis. They must have been watching for me, however, because in a moment they came racing over.

"This means so much to them..." Tibellis stopped, embarrassed. I touched my breath, fluttering my hand. Pandarris wouldn't consider interrupting his work to attend storytime, even when his children were involved. I could im-agine the look he must have given Tibellis when he suggested it. But I'd been just as preoccupied with my work when Pandarris was a child.

"One has more time for grandchildren," I said as Kayjais and Zipporis threw themselves into my arms. Nodding over their heads at the Bria parents and the crowd of Ghen and Bria children, I added, "This appears to be some-thing a councilor should know about."

When Yur'i called all the children to him, I moved with Tibellis to the benches. "Sit here," I said, "and translate everything."

He sat beside me. I said once again, "Translate everything. Every sign the children make, even to each other. And everything that Yur'i signs to them."

He touched his breath and I saw in his expression that he had intended to invite a councilor as well as a grandparent.

დ

"The Story of Riattis." A solemn little Bria stood beside Yur'i, translating his occasional narrative comments for the parents.

Kayjais leaped as far as his small legs could carry him. He landed on his tiptoes, arms outstretched, his long fingers extended, pointing to the ground. He stood poised a moment, then leaped again. The two- and three-year-olds, Ghen and Bria alike, followed him and everywhere he landed several of them stayed, twirling, bending, shooting up and twirling again.

"You are fire," Yur'i reminded a little, grinning Ghen, and immediately a more solemn expression crossed his face. "Good."

Kayjais reached the first of the four-year-old Ghen lying together on the ground in pretended sleep. Just as he reached them his sibling, Zipporis, followed by a line of four-year-old Bria, came racing between the twirling little flames toward the sleeping Ghen. Zipporis bent over the first one, urgently shaking his shoulder.

The Ghen child rose, looking about. Kayjais leaped toward him and he drew back. Then Zipporis pushed him in the direction of the line of Bria. They pushed and pulled him down the line until he was safe, away from the twirling sparks.

Now it was a race between the two, Kayjais and his attendant flames against Zipporis and his Bria rescuers. If Kayjais touched a sleeping Ghen first he curled on the ground, allowing the sparks to dance around him; if Zipporis reached him first, he was handed down the line to safety. The sparks tried to surround Zipporis, too, but he dodged between them before they could clasp hands around him, until the last Ghen was either rescued or encircled in sparks.

"I was a good Riattis," Zipporis signed, counting the standing Ghen when the play was over.

"I was a better lightning!" Kayjais signed back, pointing to the Ghen now sitting up among the giggling sparks.

"No," Yur'i signed, sweeping his arm to include both the standing and the sitting Ghen. "Every one of those Ghen would have been yours, Lightning, except for the courage of Riattis and his Bria rescuers."

"Can I be Riattis next year?" one of the three-year-olds signed.

"Would you risk your life to rescue Ghen?"

"Oh yes," he signed, still caught up in the story.

"Then you must do something nice for a Ghen child this year, and he must tell me about it. All right, children. Tomorrow we'll start on the story of Garn'or. Who knows it?"

A few hands rose tentatively in the air.

"I'll draw it in the sand. That may help the rest of you remember."

⁊

I congratulated my grandchildren on their play, enjoying their excited chatter until the young Bria guarder who watched them in the afternoons arrived. For the first time in—how long? Too many seasons—I felt that the problems in our city were not insurmountable. Why hadn't it occurred to me to give the children a common language and have them play together?

Because I was focused on adults, not children. And between every adult Bria and Ghen lies the accusing face of an infant Broghen neither can forget. They don't really want to speak together. They don't want their children to play together, don't allow it outside of storytime. The change Yur'i had begun could not have come from Council; Council can't outlaw shame.

The silence between Ghen and Bria cripples us, but do we dare break that silence? Ghen must know of Broghen in order to waken and face them in the night; Bria must not know of them in order to sleep in the night with infants in their wombs. Yur'i was following an unpredictable wind in teaching our children to talk together.

As I walked, the problems that faced our city returned to me. The crisis that was developing could not be put off until these children grew up. Nor would it leave them unchanged. Without a solution to the white Broghen outside our walls—and the gray ones born within—all of Yur'i's work in bringing the children together might be lost.

⁊

I was nearly at Council Hall when I saw Anarris. He saw me at the same time and approached, grinning broadly.

"Our numbers are growing," he said. "One third of the Bria graduating from their specialization year have joined us!"

"Do you want to depopulate our city?"

"It's the Ghen compound we'll be depopulating." He laughed aloud in triumph. "Even if we get half the young Bria next year, Bria will hold their numbers. The city's becoming crowded, anyway. But we'll prevent older Ghen from having a second child. In a single generation, we could half their numbers!"

halve

"Can you imagine the Ghen will allow that?"

His expression changed. His lips actually curled back so I could see his teeth!

He spoke in a low voice, almost a hiss: "It's stupid of you, dangerously naïve, to think they'd never turn their violent nature against us. At least if we outnumber them, we may have a fighting chance!"

I pulled away from him in horror and almost ran up the stairs into Council Chambers.

Secrets

Yur'i

"All right, children. Tomorrow we'll start on the story of Garn'or. Who knows it?"

A few hands rose tentatively in the air.

"I'll draw it in the sand. That may help the rest of you remember." I picked up Savannis's stick.

Even two years after Savannis's death I still thought of it as *his* drawing stick. When I left the infirmary and moved into Savannis's house, Darillis's year as Council Chair was over. A number of Bria objected when I began telling the stories, but Council supported me—or at least declined to forbid me.

Savannis had already taught the children my signing in preparation for my return, of which he had been so certain. Some parents refused to send their younglings to me, especially when I invited Ghen children, too—but there was no one else to teach the Bria stories, and they wanted their younglings to hear them.

"That was wonderful," Tibellis signed, approaching me from the bench where he'd been watching. Councilor Briarris, with Kayjais and Zipporis dancing at his sides, came up to us.

"He says to tell you he's very pleased with what you're doing." Tibellis's eye shone as he translated Councilor Briarris's words. I felt a tension I hadn't been aware of ease out of me.

"When he has time, he wants to learn your signing!"

I grinned and touched my breath.

☙

Tibellis stayed after the others had all left. "How is your work coming?" I asked.

I'd hoped to pass Savannis's storytelling stick to Tibellis, but he chose to specialize in sculpture. He was building his journey-piece now, a large work: five children listening to a storyteller. He'd almost completed the hollow forms of the children, ready to put inside the delicate springs that would make them fidget, tilt their heads and stamp their feet as they watched the storyteller drawing in the sand.

He'd captured the expressions of childhood in their features, in the way they held themselves—wonder and delight and that intense involvement in every moment. But he would be judged mainly on the realism and artistry of their movements.

"I might not have been so impatient during storytime if ours had been like this."

"It was like this for me." But I grinned to take the sting away. Tibellis was only trying to praise me, not criticize Savannis. "Necessity is the wind behind creativity. I can't use my voice to stir them, so I have to use actions. And they have so much more energy than I do."

Tibellis smiled. It wasn't the full-hearted, lips-rolled-back grin of a Ghen— Bria didn't smile that way. Saft'ir told me that other Ghen thought Bria smiles were too controlled, too slight. They found Bria cold. Tyannis told me that Bria were often afraid of the wide, fang-exposing grimace of the Ghen. They saw something predatory in it. Are Saft'ir and Tyannis and I the only ones who simply see a smile on Ghen and Bria faces?

Tibellis didn't leave. I waited, wondering what was on his mind. At last he signed, "Have you thought of joining, Yur'i?"

"No." Surprise made me abrupt.

"Why not?"

"Because of what I would pass on." I shrugged a goodbye and went into my house.

☙

His question disturbed me and made my sleep restless. In the morning I awoke with the image of Broghen in my mind and a brooding sense of failure and despair. It was difficult to concentrate on the children's story.

Halfway through, out of the corner of my eye, I thought I saw a Broghen stealing toward us. I leaped up with a fearful cry, but it was only a shadow and my imagination. By the time I'd calmed the children down, the thread of the story was lost, so I sent them home.

I had been through this before, fleeing from ghosts of the past and terrors of the future; I couldn't risk letting them overwhelm me again. I decided to go to the cave of paintings. I hadn't been back since Savannis took me there as a child; it was time I faced up to them.

ↀ

Inside the cave, I lit a fire and walked from one end to the other, looking at the vivid paintings. As I neared Dayannis's, at the back of the cave, I slowed down. They had revealed a terrible truth, which had almost destroyed me.

Nevertheless, I forced myself to look at them: the drought, the famine, the orphaning of the children, the uncontrolled birth of the Broghen, the terrified violence of the young Ghen.

I had expected to face an onslaught of panic. Instead, the paintings aroused in me a profound pity. Why hadn't I noticed before how young they all were? Of course, I was a child myself when Savannis brought me here, and these paintings depicted the worst nightmares of childhood.

I pictured the faces of the children who came to me for stories. Do they fear courrant'hs? Liapt'hs? No, they spoke of them sometimes with shivers of delight: dangerous things, but under the control of adults.

I looked again at the painting of the children who had survived the drought: our ancestors, left alone in a cave, with no adults to dispel the monsters for them. They were too young to face Broghen, as I had been. Too young to understand the fault wasn't theirs.

"Parents stand between their children and disaster." What story was that from? Ah, Narv'al, speaking to his youngling. In the story he'd been wounded defending the walls of our new city. "As the Creator Wind stands between our civilization and chaos," the story ended. But it was not the Creator who built walls.

I examined the first painting, the one of the drought. There were the Bria parents, standing at the back of the cave, refusing food. Standing like a wall

210

between their children and starvation. I imagined Heckt'er and the other young Ghen later building our wall to stand between them and the insanity of Broghen. A wall of stone, in place of caring adults.

"I didn't do it," Tyannis had said when, as a small child visiting a farm, he'd stampeded the callans. "The wind did it."

I didn't do it, Dayannis's response was the same. *I didn't have a Broghen.*

Wind did it, Heckt'er said. And Dayannis told the children: *They're out there, beyond the wall. Not our fault. Not our responsibility.*

They built a city of secrets: secret monsters, secret languages, secret paintings of a secret past. What was the storyteller but the guardian of all those secrets?

I was well-suited for my role. Hadn't I buried my own secret deep in my heart to fester all my childhood? What power there was in secrets! It had nearly killed me, all that secret power I gave to the infant Broghen that killed Tyannis's twin.

But I was an adult now; we were a city of adults, as well as children, now. Yet we were still denying the Broghen, hiding their birth in our secret hearts and laying the blame elsewhere.

Madness lay in that direction. I knew it, I had been there. And wasn't that madness slowly creeping over our city?

I returned to the front of the cave, to the painting Savannis had been working on. "You'll finish this when you're the storyteller," he told me years ago.

It was a painting of our city from the northeast wall. It showed the first trees of the forest and all the way down into the center of the city. There were Bria and Ghen in the streets, and in the foreground Savannis was drawing a story while Bria children listened.

Savannis's paintbrushes lay on the floor of the cave in front of the painting, cleaned and ready for use. I brought water and mixed the powder dyes in the clay bowels beside the brushes. I began painting Broghen, as I'd been seeing them at the corners of my mind ever since I left the infirmary.

Caught up in my painting, I lost all track of time. I painted Broghen on the wall; monstrous adults climbing into the city, small ones climbing out, into the forest. I placed a Broghen at the back of every Ghen and every Bria. Behind the children, I drew small Broghen. Even behind Savannis I drew one, and he as blithely ignoring it as every person in the painted city.

I'd been painting for two days and nights, leaving the cave only to drink from the stream and pick wild berries and roots to eat, or cut more firewood to light my work. On the third evening I cleaned my paintbrushes for the last time and studied what I had done.

I had painted an end to the secrets. Only I knew how it had all begun. Only the Storyteller, guardian of the past, could see our civilization from the distance of time, and imagine another way.

But how could I take us there safely?

Exhausted, I lay down in the cave to sleep.

When I woke it was mid-day. The sun filtered through the cappa leaves at the cave entrance and there in its dappled pool stood Tibellis, staring at my picture.

"Do you really think they'll get into our city?" he signed, his hands shaking slightly as he formed the words.

"How did you find me?"

"I followed this." He held out Savannis's old map. I was reminded of how I'd found Savannis with it. I didn't want Tibellis to care that much for me.

"Do you think the Broghen will get into our city?" he asked again.

I looked back at him, indecisive. What would the knowledge do to him? But it was time storytellers stopped keeping Dayannis's secrets.

"They already are."

I could see him trembling as he stood looking at the painting. Had he understood my meaning? Finally, still not looking at me, he signed, "Don't they see them?"

"They're secret Broghen."

He shuddered. "That's even worse."

"Yes," I agreed. "That's much worse." After a few minutes I signed, "Will you help me expose them?"

He turned quickly and left the cave. I followed him into the daylight. The pupil of his eye was still large from its adjustment to the dim cave and he trembled as he walked so that now and again he stumbled, almost falling. I wanted to reassure him, but I didn't. I would no longer stand between Bria and the truth.

We were almost home when he signed, "That is why you won't join."

Caught off guard, I hesitated, then touched my breath.

"Yes, I'll help," he signed.

I was ashamed of my fear in the face of his courage.

Council Relations

Briarris

"**I**s there any further new business to report?"

I held my breath as Koon'an rose from the Ghen section of the public gallery and slowly approached the Chair. He passed between my seat and Rennis's, and I had to hold myself from shrinking away, as though he carried disease. There was a pounding in my ears and I panted after air, but these things I also hid. I was acutely aware of Rennis, rigid in his chair, and was tempted to touch his hand or shoot him a pacifying look. Instead I put an expression of cheerful curiosity upon my face and looked only at Koon'an, who stood a few armlengths from Council Chair, in the center of the U-shaped oval of the Council.

Of course I knew what he was about to say. We had rehearsed it all in closed-Council, and agreed to have it unfold at the last Council before still-season: the meeting when we honored Ghen and Bria accomplishments over the past year—artists, musicians, builders, athletes—those foremost in every category. We wanted as many as possible to hear the news as Koon'an presented it, not as others repeated it.

Fortunately the Ghen, and some of the Bria, were aware that Koon'an had only just returned from his expedition north, so it was believable that we were hearing his report for the first time, along with them.

"I have returned from leading an expedition far into the northern mountains," Koon'an began.

As he spoke, Chair Ghen translated his words into signs for Council Chair, who repeated it sentence for sentence in a loud voice for all to hear. What an act he would have to put on as he pretended to hear this for the first time, while the gallery of Bria hung on his every word. Thank Wind I was not yet Council Chair!

"In the mountains we discovered..." he let Council Chair translate so far before he loosed his first shock over them. I stared almost desperately at Council Chair, willing him to carry it off.

"...another civilization of Bria and Ghen."

Council Chair's artificial gasp of surprise was swallowed by the response of the audience. Good. We hoped they would expend their shock on the positive news.

I risked a glance at Rennis. He was not even trying to act, but stared tensely down at the table before him. I was grateful for his silence, at least. I could not imagine how I would feel if Koon'an had left my only youngling in the mountains with savages, despite his reassurances of Tyannis' safety.

"They live together in peace, as we do. They met us in friendship. They helped us safely across a dangerous mountain pass, and even now, in their village, they are caring for three of our expedition who were wounded and couldn't return with us."

The breathless excitement in Council Chair's voice as he translated affected the crowd just as we had intended. Many looked stunned, others laughed aloud in delight, a few were even hugging one another. There had been speculation on this possibility from time to time, but to actually find others, to know for certain that we were not alone... I found, after all, that very little acting was needed; the news had an unreal quality no matter how often one heard it.

Anarris, sitting with a group of Single-by-Choice, was frowning. Could he sense the conflict that he was trying to build in our city slipping away? I would have preferred to see him caught up in the news. As it was, he might be looking for an opportunity to spread division, and he was sure to find it in what was to come. With a crowd this large... I firmly put an end to such speculations.

Sandarris, at the edge of their group, was clearly unaware of the mood of their leader. He clapped his hands in delight and grinned when I smiled at him. My naïve, idealistic youngling.

I rose to speak. "What do they look like?"

Koon'an waited for the translation as though he hadn't known the question was coming.

"The Ghen are smaller than us, and their scales are white, not gray," he replied. "The Bria also are smaller than city Bria, and their fur is paler than

Briarris's, white-blond. Aside from their coloring and child-like size, they look like us."

So far our plan was going smoothly. Koon'an's deliberate emphasis on our advantage in size reassured those who had appeared nervous at first.

I rose again. "Do they live like us?"

As I sat down, I noticed Pandarris looking at me intently. He was here because he'd been honored for his work earlier. My performance wasn't fooling my cool-headed youngling, so different from his sibling. Well, I could talk to him later; it was the rest of the city I had to worry about now.

"They are much more primitive. They live in caves, like our ancestors. We have much to teach them. And, in fact, we have already begun. There was a Bria in our expedition." He paused for the gasps of shock that greeted this revelation, first from the Ghen in the audience then, when it had been translated, even louder gasps and cries of surprise from the Bria.

"Councilor Rennis's offspring, Tyannis," He bowed to Rennis casually, as though Tyannis's going with them had been planned and agreed to all along. "He is well and chose to remain among our mountain neighbors until we return next season for him and for the Ghen, who presumably will be healed by the time we next see them, thanks to the excellent care they are receiving. Tyannis has already learned their language and made friends among them."

Rennis, to his credit, forced out a smile and nodded to Koon'an, as though delighted by the accomplishments of his youngling.

The silence in Council Chambers was profound as Bria and Ghen alike grappled with so many shocking disclosures. We gave them a few moments to take it all in, and then the youngest councilor in closed-Council cried out in apparent delight, "So we are not alone on Wind! The Creator Wind has given us a sibling civilization!"

By now I was breathing easier. We had the crowd with us, if only we could keep them. As if on cue, Triannis, the Single-by-Choice councilor, leaped to his feet.

"What is it that wounded three Ghen in the mountains?" he demanded. "What is attacking our walls?"

We had intended to come to this next revelation more slowly. At least we had had time to introduce the premises on which we would spin our half-lie.

"Our mountain neighbors share one more misfortune with our ancestors: they bear Broghen. A few of these have begun to find their way into our forest."

I watched the parents in the gallery absorbing this; the relief of knowing it wasn't their deformed offspring returning to attack us, mixed with horror at our formal acknowledgement that Broghen were real.

As though we could still keep that secret, with the increasing attacks upon our walls! At least we had pointed the blame away from us. The innocence of our young was only partially compromised.

The second-year councilor, eyes wide with shock, touched his growing belly and cried out involuntarily, "Oh the poor mountain Bria! We must help them learn better ways!"

Despite our deliberate attempt to mislead young Bria, it continually surprised me how easily they were fooled. I suppose we believe what we want to believe, for as long as we can. Nevertheless, his involuntary response was just what we had hoped for. It sent an immediate message to the Bria parents as to what our stand must be, and I saw them touching their breath across the gallery, especially those who had younglings sitting with them.

Anarris wasn't about to accept our performance as the other Bria did. Breaking all precedent he leaped to his feet and demanded, "And how did the mountain Broghen find our city? Isn't that the Ghen's fault? With their hunting forays, didn't they lead the Broghen to us?"

The question couldn't be left hanging, the last thing Bria heard before Council ended. Chair Ghen was compelled to respond.

"The white Broghen are no threat to you," he said, looking across the wide gallery of Bria, as Council Chair translated his words. "We are more than a match for the few who come this far."

"Because you are just as violent as they!" Anarris screamed. "Today the Broghen attack us; tomorrow the Ghen!"

Several of his followers stamped their feet in agreement, although others looked uncomfortable, even shocked that he would say such a thing here. Sandarris was one of those, I noticed. I hoped Anarris had gone too far and would begin losing followers instead of gaining them.

Meanwhile, Ghen in the audience who had had Anarris's comments translated by Bria partners, began calling objections. The entire gallery was becoming involved, ignoring Council Chair's calls for order. I sat frozen in my seat, unable to think what to do.

Suddenly, Anarris ran over and threw himself on the nearest Ghen, hitting and kicking and even biting him! What could have possessed him? I could hardly believe my own eye.

The attack was so sudden, the Ghen nearly retaliated. His arms rose, claws snapping out in reflex. I expected to see Anarris cut to ribbons before us.

Chair Ghen's voice thundered across the room.

The Ghen came to his senses and lowered his arms, retracting his claws. He stood there, letting Anarris abuse him, until Anarris's own followers pulled him away. Voices silenced under Chair Ghen's stare. Slowly, order was restored.

"In the night while you sleep, in stillseason while you are blind, we risk our lives to protect you." Chair Ghen's voice rumbled throughout the chamber, followed by Council Chair's voice, shaken but still strong, as he translated. There was no pretense to his shocked reaction now.

"It has always been so. It *will* always be so. We are your protectors, never your enemy!"

An uneasy silence hung over Council Chambers. Before it could be broken again, Council Chair stamped his feet twice.

"Council adjourned."

Distortions

Pandarris

"Look through this, Pandarris. Careful, it's sharp."

Gingerly I lifted the small bubble of glass, a bubble that had fallen from Ocallis's blowpipe and hardened.

"Here, look at this through it," he said, placing on the table before me a paper design for the delicately patterned vase he was currently staining.

I raised the slightly curved glass and stared down at a cloudy blur of white paper. I'd seen opaque glass before, so I put it aside, murmuring something polite, but he was frowning thoughtfully over his vase again. I looked around the large studio my parent's sibling shared with a dozen or more other glass blowers. The room sparkled with their compelling nonsense.

When I was younger, I remember staring for countless removes at the slender limbs and glittering leaves of the little glass ugappa Ocallis had made for my parent. It moved slowly on its rotating platform, each tiny leaf barely a third the size of my smallest fingernail, jiggling in the breeze and tossing rainbow circles back and forth from branch to fragile branch. We had only that piece, given as a gift. How could a councilor afford one of Ocallis's priceless glassworks?

Like everyone else, I admired the beauty of his creations, but what practical use were they, really? I tried to hide my boredom. In order to avoid the public embarrassment of his demonstrative affection, I'd feigned illness the day our class visited the glass-blowing studio. As a result, my parent had ordered me to make it up today, on my free time.

"What did you see?"

His voice startled me out of my musings. I looked back at the discarded glass bubble. What did he expect me to say? "It looks like a cloud," I guessed, trying to be creative. How soon could I leave?

Ocallis laughed, a sound I always associated with sunlight shimmering on glass. Ordinarily I do not care to be laughed at, but there was too much warmth in Ocallis's laughter for anyone to take offense at it.

"Bring it closer to your eye. Now move it around a bit. Not like that, Pandarris. Angle it."

I pasted a smile on my face and did as he suggested, trying not to... suddenly the paper on the table leaped into focus, the central lines of the design on it clear but wildly out of proportion. I leaned forward.

"No, pull it back, Pandarris. Bring the glass closer to your eye, not your eye to the glass."

There it was again, in perfect detail, but six, twelve times as large as it should be. Was my eye playing tricks on me? I blinked. The design on the paper was once again an opaque blur. I turned the glass slightly. Again the design appeared, enlarged beyond belief.

Raising my head, I held the bubble of glass in front of me and looked about the room. Ocallis's face sprang toward me. Startled, I pulled back from the glass. No, he hadn't moved. I looked through the bubble again. He was huge, almost on top of me; so close, I took an involuntary step backward even though I knew the image was false.

"What is it?" I examined the bubble, unable to believe I held in my hand merely a piece of glass, no different from the cups we brewed our tea in. Ocallis smiled, pleased by my interest at last.

"Look at its shape. See how it curves so it's thicker in the center than at the sides?"

"What difference does that make? It's still just glass."

"I don't know. But only leftover bubbles curved in that way cause that effect."

"Could you make a bigger one curved like this?" I looked around eagerly, hoping he'd already done so.

"Why would I do that?"

"To see things, to look at things through it." I raised the bubble again and looked around the room.

"Put it down, sweetbreath. It doesn't show you anything real. It's all a distortion. I only thought it would amuse you." Reluctantly I handed it to him, watched as he placed it in a pile of scraps for remolding.

ᴇʍ

I couldn't get that bubble of glass out of my mind. I'd look at cappa leaves, the petals of flowers, the delicate wings of an insect or the aerial threads of its web and wonder what each of them would look like seen through such a piece of glass.

When I graduated from general school, Ocallis gave me a glass fish suspended from a golden rod so that it swam in lazy circles on its turning dais. I bent down and tried to look through it, hoping its curved body would magically enlarge my world. Swallowing my disappointment, I straightened up to thank him. Instead of thanks, I heard myself saying, "I'm going to specialize in glass-making."

"Glass-blowing, Pandarris?" my parent asked, setting a bowl on the table and taking the chair beside mine. "You've never…" He paused, glancing at his beaming sibling. "Are you sure you have the patience for that?"

Before I could formulate an answer, my grandparent's voice rose petulantly further down the table. "What's that?"

"Jellied ruberry sauce, Gramatri," my sibling, Sandarris, said.

"Ruberry sauce?" He peered into the bowl. "I don't see any ruberries. We used to put whole ruberries in when I was making jellied sauce."

"They're there, Gramatri." I had a sudden urge to laugh out loud. "Only as large as life!"

My journey piece was a great disappointment to Ocallis. Gramatri, however, saw ruberries again.

ᴇʍ

That single invention, the enlarging glass, was so successful I could put aside all pretense of making dishes and ornaments. I spent each morning forming the large, convex circles of glass, or placing the cooled spheres on my curved metal plate and grinding them to the necessary contour with sand, then polishing them smooth with a dab of paste on a leather cloth.

It left me free to spend the rest of my day as I wished. I sat at a small table directly under a window, looking through my own enlarging glass at all sorts of things; or else I wandered through the city collecting new objects to examine.

I wrote extensive notes about everything I saw. The more I used my glass, however, the more frustrated I became with its shortcomings. No matter the slant or distance, only the center of an object was clear to my view, and when I shifted sideways the movement of my hand, however slight, threw everything out of focus once again. Around that central focus, all was blurred and often further obscured by rings of color. This was at its best. Depending on the angle of the sun, I frequently had trouble positioning my glass so that the entire object wasn't overlaid by shimmering rainbows or by a glare of light.

Struggling one morning to bring into focus a blade of grass, I lifted a small sheet of metal one of the glass-blowers had left on my table and held it in front of the glass to cut the sun's glare. At once the dancing colors disappeared and I could see my magnified blade of grass clearly. I looked at the metal more closely. What if I used a permanent metal plate to block the sun? But I'd have to keep rotating it, as the angle of the sun shifted… A metal tube, then, with one of my glass circles inside it?

It was easy enough to fashion one, but when I lowered my eye against the top of the tube I cut off almost all light to the object on the table below.

Every time I solved one problem, I created another.

"The wind blows against you," my sibling, Sandarris, declared smugly, when I vented my frustration over dinner.

"Contrary winds make us strong," Matri said.

Even a year before, Sandarris and I would both have groaned at the platitude, but our parent looked worried now, burdened by things he wouldn't discuss. Perhaps he had taken more pains to hide it while Igt'ur and his youngling, Bruck'ur, lived with us; or else we'd been too young to notice. It was clear to me now that his comment was meant to bolster his spirits as much as mine.

"I'm glad you feel that way, Matri," Sandarris said, "because I've decided to join Single-by-Choice."

Matri stared at him. I could tell Sandarris was hoping for an argument, to prove his resolution, but Matri said nothing.

"Eventually, we're going to wipe out the Ghen entirely."

"Has it occurred to you that that will eliminate us, as well?" I demanded, rising to the bait our parent declined.

"If we must sacrifice ourselves to rid Wind of the violent Ghen, it's a noble sacrifice."

"What have you got against Ghen?"

He looked at me, speechless, more surprised than angry at first. Oh, yes, I remembered now, he'd been spouting some nonsense lately about Ghen being killers, flesh-eaters. As though that was new information. I hadn't paid much attention.

"At least you listen," he said to Matri.

"At your age I felt the same way," Matri replied.

Sandarris glared at me triumphantly and stalked out the door.

"You agree with him?" I asked our parent.

"I understand him. He's an idealist."

"Rubbish! He's a coward. Afraid of the Ghen, and even more afraid of thinking for himself. If he did, he'd have to do something himself, not just spout someone else's nonsense."

Matri grinned. "He'll get to that. He's taking the long route."

I shrugged impatiently and rose, collected our dishes and carried them to the wash-bowl. As I washed them, I looked out the window. It was getting dark. Sandarris would return soon. He would be able to see us, in the lighted room, before we could see him in the darkness.

He would see us because the light was behind us...

"What if there was light coming from under the objects?" I cried. "If I put them on a raised piece of glass?"

I could hardly wait to get back to my studio.

☙

Over the next few weeks, I devised a raised glass platform to lay my objects on, suspended nearly an inch above a second flat piece of glass, the back of which I silvered, like a looking glass, to reflect light back up at the object lying directly beneath my enlarging tube. I also built in levers to move the platform in tiny increments without losing the focus of my glass.

On the whole, this worked quite well. Then I tried using two glasses together, hoping to double the magnification. The effect was disappointing. The brief, blurry images I saw were indeed much larger, but the distortion was so great and so consistent that the double-glassed tube was useless. Nevertheless, the single-glass tube was better than ever, now.

At the end of my specialization year, I joined with a Ghen named Brock'an, even though my work was too important to interrupt for a pregnancy. But what use were my achievements if there was no one to remember who had made them?

Sandarris should have been the one having children, not me. His life was otherwise useless. I was so annoyed I deliberately chose a Ghen wanting second mating. Not only to spite Sandarris, of course; I hoped an older Ghen would take up less of my time. My days and evenings were spent in the studio. I would have slept and eaten there as well if I could have, absorbed in my enlarging tube and in writing up my observations.

Brock'an was amused by my preoccupation with work. My enlarging glass intrigued him, and he frequently used one to look at the things I'd observed through my tube. He found it a strain looking down into the tube through only one eye and had to close the other. When I saw him doing so I grinned to myself, pleased that our single Bria eye was superior in this, at least.

I made no attempt to start a sign language, so Brock'an taught me the one he'd used in his first joining. I learned it quickly—much faster, I'm sure, than he could have learned another. At first I only wanted the obligatory task out of the way, but as I noticed his interest in my discoveries, I thought, why not let the Ghen admire my work, also? After that, I was more willing to sign to him about it.

My search for objects to examine widened. On one of the farms, I built a large pen to hold a dozen farmborra which had each laid a clutch of eggs on the same day. I retrieved one egg every day, staring down my tube in fascination at the yolks as, day by day, they matured into living chicks. I wondered how similar this was to what would happen inside me soon.

The growth of the farmborra eggs interested Brock'an, also, and every few days he brought his enlarging glass to see the changes in their development. His interest flattered me without making any real demands on my time.

☙

I'd been making enlarging glasses for almost three years before I thought of filing a glass circle the opposite way, narrower in the middle. I had half-guessed the result, but I was still amazed when it made objects appear smaller.

When used with an enlarging glass, I expected the shrinking glass, as I called it, would bring an object back to normal size. Instead, when I held it to my eye above the enlarging tube, the distortions I'd come to accept disappeared! There lay the object, still magnified, but clear and focused. I designed a new tube at once, using both types of lenses.

Through my new tube, I discovered an entire species of infinitely small living things, which had been completely invisible until now. They squirmed about on nearly every substance I examined—water, plants, dirt, the skin of animals. Even on my own skin, within my spit and skimming on a drop of my own blood, a host of tiny creatures crept and swam.

I was both elated and horrified. I'd discovered a new world of life, was seeing what no one had ever seen before. Moreover, these creatures moved continuously. There was a thrill in knowing that even in the appearance of stillness, life swayed and danced in constant motion beneath our awareness. The wind of life was infinite!

"The Creator Wind creates motion," I murmured, "even where it cannot be seen." Luckily, no one was near to hear me turn religious in the thrill of my discovery.

But what had I discovered? What were these tiny creatures that crept invisibly over my skin, through my fur, even submerged themselves in my sweat, my saliva, my blood and tears? Unconsciously I began to imagine the tickle of their movements, until one of the other glass-blowers wondered aloud whether perhaps an increase of bathing might mitigate my constant itch.

At that, I shared my findings with them. They weren't easily convinced and returned to look through my tube again and again. Eventually, however, I had them all scratching.

☙

The councilors received the report of my findings with the same initial skepticism. One by one, they trooped into my studio during the following week to stare through my enlarging tube. It wasn't as easy to show them as it had been with my glass-blower colleagues who were already familiar with my tube. Some of the councilors had never used an enlarging glass. They were confused, half-disbelieving even when they finally located the bit of skin or drop of blood upon the raised glass platform. Many returned several times before I was called back to address them at Council once again.

"Write up your findings," Council Chair Perallis eyed my enlarged belly, "before you are too busy. They'll be printed for all to read. And translated," he signed to Chair Ghen, who touched his breath.

"Thank you." I bowed my head slightly. My work to be printed! And I was not yet ten!

I glanced at my parent, whose expression of pride almost caused me to forget my dignity and grin at him. Too busy? Let lesser Bria fuss over their younglings; my life's work was in my studio. Bad enough the portion of my energy they'd stolen, growing in my womb. Once they were born, Brock'an could take over, bringing them to me when they needed suckling. He'd know how to care for them better than I, anyway; this was his second time.

"I want you to show your findings to Tibellis." Council Chair was speaking to me again.

"Tibellis?" I barely remembered him from my last year at storytime. He was three years younger than I, nothing special when I knew him.

"Tibellis is a sculptor. Very gifted. I want him to do a moving model of what your enlarging tube shows."

A sculptor? An artist? He wouldn't even understand what he was seeing. I would have to waste precious time explaining everything to him. I frowned slightly.

"I don't know what exactly you've discovered, Pandarris, but it should be shared. Not everyone can use your enlarging tube." Council Chair smiled slightly. He'd visited my studio four times trying to fathom my enlarging tube before he could see what it revealed. "But everyone will be able to see Tibellis's model."

I felt my parent's eye intent upon me so once again I bowed my head.

"You may go," Chair Perallis said. "You have a lot to do before stillseason. And Pandarris—" I looked up. "Well done, child."

⁙

I found Tibellis easier to work with than I'd anticipated. He had a quick mind as well as a creative one. Despite myself, I liked the tiny reproductions he made after looking repeatedly into my enlarging tube, especially the one of an outstretched Bria finger, sporting a tiny cut from which a drop of blood had fallen (suspended by a near-invisible thread), while another drop was yet emerging. The blood drops were made of red glass and inside each one, a dozen or so clear, glass replicas of the opaque creatures I'd seen in my tube trembled in tiny movements so that the blood itself seemed to throb with life.

Tibellis brought it to me for approval before he showed it to Council. It was completed only a few days before the stillseason of my third mating.

∽

I didn't spare a thought for my delivery until the first pains came. "Tell me about childbirth," I signed to Brock'an, easing my bloated body back onto the bed.

"You're going to find out for yourself." He grinned reassuringly.

"Tell me now. I don't like surprises."

"Don't worry, Pandarris, I'll take care of—"

"Do I look worried?"

Brock'an laughed. "You look annoyed."

"Of course I'm annoyed! I was planning to cut open and examine the mongarr'h they caught last night on one of the farms."

"Not today."

"Obviously not today! All right. At least I can make the best of this interruption." I grimaced as a particularly assertive cramp gripped my abdomen. When it had eased, I continued, "See that large looking-glass in the corner? Set it up against the end of my sleeping ledge."

"Why?"

"So I can watch, of course!"

"I don't think that's a good idea."

"Not a good idea? My ideas are in print. Are yours? Bring the looking glass! …No? If that's the case—" I heaved myself up, swung my legs over the edge of the ledge, steadfastly ignoring the increasing pains. "I'll lie on the floor in front of it, then."

"Stay put. There's a reason you shouldn't look."

I waited.

"You're going to bear a Broghen."

I would have hit him for the insult if he'd been nearer. I didn't believe him until the thing emerged as I was watching in the looking glass.

Then I knew anger such as I'd never imagined.

"Let me see it," I signed, when Brock'an had separated the howling beast from his Ghen infant. He paused, about to drop it into the open box beside the bed. I reached out for it.

"Its bite is vicious."

I stared him down.

Reluctantly, he handed me the monster that had usurped my body for its nest. I grasped the back of its head in one hand to avoid its snapping jaws and held its struggling body with the other. Raising it to eye level, I examined it coldly. It had roughly the same body shape as Brock'an, though it was a little larger than his youngling. It was covered with Brock'an's dark gray scales, but between them were tufts of my tawny fur. Like a change-lizard trying to camouflage itself, it had even stolen some of my appearance while hiding in my womb! How dare it use my body thus! I gave a sharp twist. Brock'an lunged forward, but I heard the crisp, satisfying snap before he could stop me.

Later I regretted my act of rage. I would have liked to have examined it along with the mongarr'h.

♋

The next day, Sandarris and our parent came to see my children. Sandarris's expression as he watched Brock'an's youngling suckling on my third breast made me itch to slap him. Brock'an, who barely trusted me with his infant after my reaction to the Broghen, quickly moved up beside my ledge. As though my righteous wrath could be compared to my sibling's still-sighted zeal!

"Matri named you well, Sandarris," I said, furious at the look on his face. "Without children, your name will be written in sand."

"I've sacrificed myself to make my people strong when the confrontation comes," Sandarris replied. "I'll live on in Bria hearts. It's you who'll be forgotten."

"My name is already in print, and will be again. I'll live in Bria minds. But it's good you've chosen their hearts; the members of Single-by-Choice have no minds!"

Sandarris turned his angry face toward our parent. Briarris's expression of sympathy disgusted me. Before he could think of something conciliatory to say, Sandarris rushed out the door.

"How did I produce such stubborn, ill-tempered offspring?" Matri cried, vexed with us both. But I was angrier than he.

"Why wasn't I told about Broghen?" I demanded.

"It is our custom not to tell young Bria," he replied officiously.

"Should I take my question to Council?" I briefly considered it, but Matri was only one seat away from Council Chair and wouldn't appreciate public embarrassment.

"I hear you killed it."

"Yes, I killed it." Brock'an must have told Igt'ur, who of course would tell Briarris.

"Perhaps you would have mated, then, even if you knew. Few Bria are as strong-willed."

"I had a right to know."

"I thought so, once, myself. But what would you have done about it?"

"Prevented it!"

"Then why didn't you?" He was angry, too, now. "If you paid any attention to what's happening around you, you could have guessed the truth; you're bright enough when you aren't buried in your glass tube!"

∽

Instead of abating as the days passed, my anger increased. Brock'an had known full-well about the Broghen—had made me a co-conspirator in its birth—and then been horrified at my response! The fact that I'd destroyed it kept me from the despair I saw in the eyes of other Bria parents.

I hadn't noticed that before. Perhaps I should spend a little less time looking through my enlarging glass and a little more looking through my own eye, as Matri suggested. My proud words to him stayed with me. Could I have prevented the Broghen from stealing its way into my womb? Despite its tufts of

228

fur and raised ears, it was mainly gray-scaled and fierce in nature: Ghen-like. It must have come from Brock'an, along with his infant.

I began to wonder about Ghen mating fluid.

⁓

I didn't discuss my new objective with anyone, but I continued to include Brock'an in my observations. It was important that he remain involved. Together we compared the breast milk I was producing to feed our younglings, with that of a callan. The similarity was deflating, and it was annoying to have Brock'an aware of it, but at least I was keeping him interested in my discoveries. When stillseason approached at last, I asked him, casually, if he could provide a sample of his mating fluid for us to examine. He agreed without questions.

I really didn't expect to see anything. After all, Brock'an had had his second mating. I wanted to see what Ghen fluid looked like on its own, so that I would recognize the difference when I did find the seed of life.

But there it was, looking up at me like the round, dark pupil of an eye, with the trail of a tear falling from it. In fact there were several of the tiny creatures, their slender tails wriggling in the fluid to propel their movement. They were larger in size and more determined in their movements than the unmotivated creatures around them, which I was used to.

Broghen.

Brock'an fidgeted beside me. I was half afraid to show him. Surely he'd want to suppress my discovery. At the same time I relished the moment when he would be confronted with his guilt. I moved aside and let him look.

He gazed down through the enlarging tube.

"Younglings," he signed at last.

"How can they be? You've had your second child."

"Ghen can have many children, not just two."

So like a Ghen. Even when shown proof, he denies it. Brock'an must have seen my disgusted disbelief, for he began signing again.

"At the time of the second famine—you know the story of Garn'ar?—and again when lightning burned the Ghen compound—the Ghen were nearly decimated. Both times they were permitted to mate with many Bria."

"How many Broghen were born?"

"The same as now, one Broghen at each birth."

"There must have been more Broghen if there were more Ghen." I was so determined to condemn him, I risked letting him discover that there was more than curiosity behind my interest.

"How did you get around the custom of joining? Don't tell me they allowed mass matings?" I tried to imagine Council passing that one—or any Bria agreeing to it—just to repopulate the Ghen compound. He must be lying.

"Of course not." He grinned. Was he amused again? "Joining was strictly adhered to by the Bria. Only each Ghen joined with several Bria, instead of one. That was to the Bria's advantage, too. Think how many would have gone unjoined and never had offspring if they weren't willing to share a mate."

"How do you know all this?"

"We keep records. It's important that Ghen who are related don't co-join. That produces a weak child."

I touched my breath. We didn't exchange breast fluid with siblings, for the same reason.

"I'd like to see those records."

Brock'an hesitated. "They cannot be moved, but I don't know why you can't look at them. There are two sets, one in the Ghen compound and a copy in the Council building. What, right away?" I'd already started for the door. He rose to escort me.

It was nearly stillseason. The air was like warm soup, barely moving. I was panting by the time we reached Council Hall, though I hid it. Council had ended for the year and it was strange to walk through the silent chambers. Our footsteps echoed in the huge room. Since Council didn't meet in stillseason, there were no overhead fans—they would have been too high to be of help, anyway. I felt as though I were suffocating.

We crossed the room as quickly as I could manage, and passed through the back door onto the inside verandah. Brock'an led me down the steps and directly across the courtyard to a small room on the opposite side of the building, where the Ghen records were kept.

Here, again, there were no fans. Ghen had little need of them. "Will you be alright?" he signed, as I sank onto a Ghen bench, gasping for air.

I raised my hand toward my lips; I had no breath to touch my fingers to. I closed my eye to concentrate on breathing.

When I felt a little better, I looked around. One wall of the room was lined with shelves, on which the Ghen records sat, a solid wall of thick, leather-bound volumes. Brock'an was looking through them for the one we wanted. I sat on a bench with my back to the door, facing a table large enough for ten Ghen to comfortably sit around. There were benches along all four sides.

Brock'an found the volume he was looking for and brought it over to the table. The records came from the Ghen printing press, and Brock'an had to translate them for me. They consisted simply of a delineage of names, parent to child, with the co-joined Ghen noted beside, and every Ghen's year of birth. During the two eras we were looking at, several Ghen infants were born to each Ghen, as Brock'an had claimed.

"How far do these go?" I signed, gesturing to the shelf of books.

"As far back as Heckt'er."

"You're saying he was real?"

"Of course."

If one can believe Ghen records, I thought, remembering that he'd lied to me about Broghen. "Is this how you learned that Bria and Ghen seeds enter Bria wombs in the first mating and Broghen in the second?" I masked my scorn as I signed it. Of course they maintained that Ghen and Broghen arrived separately; how else could they absolve themselves?

"Yes." Brock'an failed to detect my sarcasm. "Those early years were difficult. Before we began taking them far to the south, Broghen attacked the new city often, sometimes getting over the wall and killing Bria as well as Ghen. When a pregnant Bria died, his womb was opened so that we could record the death of the infants, also."

The idea impressed me; I'd give a lot to have been at one of those examinations. Too bad it wouldn't be tolerated today. Brock'an closed the book we'd been examining and returned it, selecting the first volume on the same shelf and setting it on the table in front of me.

"That's what this means," he pointed to a page in the middle of the first volume and signed a listing of a Bria with three partially-formed infants—two Bria and one Ghen, all dead. A mark beside his name indicated that there hadn't been a Broghen.

"He must have had second-year mating, too. You said they only cut open those who were obviously pregnant."

Brock'an lifted his hand dismissively. "There may have been a Broghen seed, after all. Without your enlarging glass they wouldn't have known till it had had a chance to grow."

Perhaps it was the flattery, but I began to believe him. Nevertheless, the fact that Broghen were conceived later didn't change the fact that they came from Ghen.

"Are there any records of two Broghen being born?"

He leafed through several pages, moving backward toward the beginning of the first book. Closer to the myth of Heckt'er and Dayannis, I thought, wondering if it would tell me anything I could rely on. At that time the records must have been part of their oral history, typeset by later generations.

"Here," he signed, stubbing the top of a page with his finger. "And here, again." He touched a name lower down.

"Where does the birth of multiple Broghen begin? Where does it end? Look for anything different they did then," I signed, excited despite my reservations.

☙

"BAM!"

I leaped in my seat, as the door slammed open behind me. Brock'an's head jerked up. Mick'al shouted at him, his voice so low I could only hear the vibration of the air around him.

Mick'al repeated his question, his face twisted in outrage so that he appeared to me more like a snarling animal than the Ghen religious adviser. In age his gray scales had lightened. Looking at him, I understood for the first time the nervousness other Bria had expressed about the Ghen.

Brock'an's voice was defensive when he answered, but after a few exchanges he, too, became angry. I shrank into my seat. At last Brock'an snapped the book shut and returned it to its shelf. Without a word he came over, took my arm and escorted me out. As we passed Mick'al at the door the tension between them was so thick I dared not even breathe.

☙

"I don't know why Bria shouldn't see Ghen records," I signed, when we were safely back in my house and I had stopped shaking enough to boil some ruberry tea.

"Mick'al is concerned about the growing division in our city. He doesn't trust you," Brock'an replied, growling as he signed.

"I am not my sibling."

"So I told him. But you can be… impulsive, when angered."

I took a sip from my mug. "The records support your belief that we saw a Ghen seed." As though it were merely a passing thought, I added, "If only there were some other samples to examine."

"You want a Ghen to sacrifice his youngling for you?" The ridge of scales along Brock'an's back still trembled from his encounter with Mick'al. It was intimidating to have the residue of that anger focused on me. "Be thankful for what you've seen from me. At least my seed would not have been born anyway."

This was the second time today Ghen anger blocked my work. Were they too stupid to understand its significance? Or were they being very clever at hiding something?

"What are you really looking for?" Before I could formulate a response, he answered his own question: "A Broghen."

"I need the growth fluid of a second-year-mating Ghen to learn what makes a Broghen," I signed after a moment's hesitation.

I couldn't read his expression as he looked at me. I tried not to hold my breath. Should I have denied it?

Brock'an touched his breath. "That may be possible. Who would mourn the lack of a Broghen, if that's what it costs?"

His reaction surprised me. Didn't he realize that if I found what I sought, it would prove their guilt?

And why did he say he wouldn't mourn a Broghen? He'd been upset enough when I'd killed the monstrous little thing, although we'd never discussed it. But that was a year ago. There'd been more sightings of white Broghen recently, with stillseason almost on us. Whether they were ours or not, violence blows back on the wind that quickens it.

"I'll go to Festival Hall and see what I can do."

I kept my surprise to myself. He often humored me, being so much older.

And what did I care about his reasons, as long as I got what I needed?

❧

When I heard the cough at my door I was annoyed. It was a Bria's high-pitched cough and I was only interested in hearing Brock'an's when he returned with samples for my enlarging tube. Nevertheless, I opened the door. Tibellis stood outside, leaning on Yuri's arm and panting. I greeted Tibellis, ignoring the crippled storyteller. At least it wasn't my parent or my foolish sibling, come to vex me again.

A breath of heat, barely enough to stir my fur, entered with them. It was time to turn on my house fans. I always put off succumbing to that need.

"I haven't spoken to you for a while," Tibellis said. "I wanted to come before stillseason. I think I waited too long."

What did he expect me to say to that? I could hardly put the fans on now, as though he'd caught me in an oversight. Anyway, I didn't need them yet. Ahh.

"Do *you* need me to put the fans on?"

"Yes, thank you."

It's hard to believe he's such a good artist, I thought, as I turned the handle near the door, winding up the large, overhead fan. He has no pride at all. Yur'i limped across the room and took over the task for me.

"What are you working on now?" Tibellis walked over to my sleeping ledge on which I'd set the enlarging tube I kept at home. My sleeping mat was bundled on the floor beneath.

"It's in progress."

"May I look?"

I realized I wanted to talk about my project. I had learned, working with Tibellis on his models of my discoveries, that I could trust his discretion. However, although I didn't think Tibellis sympathized with Single-by-Choice, he hadn't mated, either; he didn't know about our birthing Broghen. I couldn't tell him what I was looking for, but I could show him what I'd found. What would he make of it?

He stared down the tube for a long time. The overhead fan began its slow circles. I heard Yur'i sit on one of Brock'an's stools at the table behind us.

Finally, Tibellis straightened. "What are they?"

"Ghen seed."

Almost as soon as I said it, I wished I hadn't. But it was out, and the look on Tibellis's face was all I could wish for. He didn't doubt me for a moment.

"Taken from Ghen growth fluid," he said, more statement than question. I touched my breath, appreciating his quick mind once again.

He bent down, looking into the tube. "How would I catch that movement?" he murmured to himself.

"Not yet," I interrupted. "Not until I'm sure."

He looked at me. "You're sure. What are you waiting for?"

"I need more samples. Brock'an's bringing them."

"This is only one? Why are there so many seeds?"

I waved my hand to show I had no answer.

While we were talking, my infants and Brock'an's woke up from their nap and came into the room. I began pouring mugs of juice for all of us.

When stillseason passed, my younglings would be one-year-olds, old enough to attend storytime if I chose to send them. I didn't care if they mingled with Ghen, and it would keep them occupied while I did my work. And then, Sandarris was so opposed to storytime being taught by a Ghen, it was worth it to send them for that reason alone. Except that our parent supported storytime. I regretted not being able to frustrate them both.

Yur'i signed to my children.

"He says hello," Tibellis told them. Their eyes widened. "Everyone signs at storytime," Tibellis said, "so you can understand one another." While Yur'i solemnly took their hands and showed them how to sign their names, Tibellis straightened and looked at me. I made no comment.

※

Brock'an returned soon after Tibellis and Yur'i had left. When he handed me six vials, each from a different second-year-mating Ghen, I almost forgave him for getting me with a Broghen. I carried the samples to my tube at once.

And there they were, in every sample I examined, their dark center staring up at me like a glaring eye—the seed that would become a Broghen! They were darker than the Ghen seeds, as night creatures should be, and instead of a tail, each was surrounded by an opaque, oval-shaped rim which appeared to bend inward and push out again in an effort to propel itself forward. They were larger, also, as Broghen are larger than Ghen.

The surprising thing, once again, was that each vial held so many. Perhaps they destroyed each other in the womb, till only one was left? I shuddered at the thought. But if so, did that apply to the multiple Ghen seed, also?

"Did you find anything?"

"Look for yourself."

He bent over my enlarging tube, closing one eye as he had learned to do, and looked down at the samples for a long time. At last he looked up.

"You think these are Broghen seed," he signed.

I didn't even bother to reply, but stared back at him coolly.

"Second-year Ghen co-join at the first mating. Yet Broghen don't appear in the womb till after second mating."

I stayed quite calm while he did his best to stir up dusty doubts. When he had done, I signed, "All of that is beside the point. There are two kinds of seeds, and they both come from Ghen. Whichever way you look at it, one must be Ghen, and the other Broghen."

"There's something more that you aren't seeing."

"I see what you don't want to see."

"You see what you want to see. But whichever way you look at it, there must be Ghen in order for there to be Bria."

I held my temper, but my arms trembled with the effort it cost me. He hadn't been invaded by a monster, hadn't been unwittingly used to create something vile. The thought of it was so humiliating and so infuriating I could hardly contain it. I wanted to destroy the Broghen, utterly destroy them, and I didn't care what it took to do it. But I was sane enough not to let Brock'an see this.

"I need more samples."

"What will more samples tell you?"

I turned on him a look of desperate urgency, but I didn't reply. He assumed it was merely the same intensity with which I had always approached my work and, grumbling to himself, headed back to the Ghen compound.

☙

I was waiting impatiently when he finally returned, empty-handed. "Why—"

I began to sign, but he looked away. Ignoring me, he called to his youngling.

"I'm taking Jon'an to visit the Ghen compound," he signed as Jon'an ran to him. He still wouldn't look at me.

I reached out to touch his arm, but drew my hand back again. Instead I stepped in front of the door. "Where are the samples?" I signed.

"You won't get any more, Pandarris,"

"Why? What's happened?"

"Mick'al was there. He spoke to us—to all the Ghen."

"About me?"

"About your work."

I was flattered, but also annoyed that I hadn't been asked to be there. "What did he say?"

"In short, that what you're doing is wrong. You're tampering with life itself. Who knows where it will end?"

I waited for him to tell me what Mick'al's concern was. When I realized he thought he already had, I asked, "It's wrong not to know where a thing will lead? You mean, we should only learn what we already know?"

"Not knowing isn't wrong. Not caring is."

"You think I don't care?"

"I know you don't." Then he reached out and lifted me—lifted me!—aside, and left.

I care! I fumed to myself. You can't imagine how much I care! But not in the way he meant it. He was right: I didn't care for a windless moment about the consequences, if I could find a way to destroy the Broghen seed.

I thought of my sibling then, and didn't like the comparison.

⁂

It was a full six days before I remembered Tibellis's offer to help me. By then, I'd been staring down my tube, examining the now-motionless seeds in the second-year-mating samples and comparing them to Brock'an's, until I thought I would go blind.

We were well into stillseason. I was weary and cross from the interminable heat. My fan was working continuously, yet still I labored to breathe. Surely it couldn't be much worse outside. I checked to see that my younglings were still napping and plunged through the door before I could change my mind.

How still and silent the streets were. I found myself treading as softly as I could and trying to quiet my breathing. It was foolish; there was no danger within our city. But still I couldn't help myself. At first I tried to look about, but visual disorientation caused me such nausea I settled for staring at the ground in front of my feet. That, too, was frightening, for I felt lost and unsure of my direction. Would I walk forever, one foot in front of the other, in these deathly-still streets?

I bumped into a lamppost then and the pain, combined with the ridiculousness of my situation, humiliated me. I became annoyed rather than afraid. Looking up to get my bearings, I took a deep breath and struck out more firmly.

One... two... three... I counted each footstep under my breath, glancing up after every sixth one. Finally I saw Tibellis's house and staggered toward it. Yur'i opened the door. His look of amazement gave me great satisfaction.

"I can't stay long," I told Tibellis, as he handed me a mug of ruberry juice. "The children are sleeping."

Actually, I wasn't concerned about them; I was afraid that if I delayed too long I wouldn't be able to make myself go outside again.

"Where is Brock'an?" Tibellis translated Yur'i's signing.

I waved my hand dismissively.

"Did he bring you the samples you were waiting for?"

I realized he was referring to the last time he saw me. "Yes, but my findings aren't conclusive. I need more samples, and Brock'an won't help."

"Why not?"

I hesitated. He'd find out soon enough, though. "Mick'al opposes it."

Tibellis looked me straight in the eye. "Because he knows you're looking for the Broghen seed."

While I stood there, speechless, a cough came at the door. Tibellis and I turned as Yur'i opened it. Tyannis stood outside, leaning on Saft'ir's arm.

Tibellis knew them through Yur'i, and introduced me when they came in. They'd read my past work and asked some thoughtful questions about it, which showed their intelligence. There we were, five of us talking and drinking juice as though it were a party—in the middle of stillseason!

I'd read Tyannis's account of the mountain Ghen and Bria he'd lived among for nearly a year. I'd thought of going to talk to him about it, but I was always too busy. It seemed to me there were gaps in the story. After all, what was so terrifying about being lost in a maze of walls for five days? I asked him.

"There were Broghen in there with us."

"You saw one?"

"I killed one."

I looked at him with respect. "Is that why you left? They made you go?"

"That's why we returned, but not because they rejected us. We were expected to kill the Broghen. It was a test they put us through right after Koon'an and the others left." Tyannis said this bitterly.

In the tone of someone making a confession, he continued. "All my life, I have believed that killing is wrong. And yet I killed a Broghen. I don't know who I am anymore. I had to come home to find myself."

"Have you found yourself?" I only asked to be polite. My initial respect was waning.

"No, of course not." He glanced at Saft'ir. "Because I'm glad I killed the Broghen, regardless of whether it was right or wrong. Sometimes I dream about it, though…"

"Pandarris is studying Ghen growth fluid," Tibellis said into the awkward silence, "through his enlarging tube." He signed for Saft'ir and Yur'i as he spoke.

"What are you looking for?" Saft'ir signed.

"Broghen seed," I said coolly, when Tibillis translated Saft'ir's question.

Tyannis looked up. "Have you found it?"

"I've found that Ghen won't give me any samples."

"You've spoken to your parent?"

He meant, of course, had I talked to Briarris as the next-in-line Council Chair.

"He's barely spoken to me since I killed the infant Broghen I bore." I watched Tyannis carefully as I said this and was not surprised to see his momentary shock. He recovered quickly, however, and said he understood.

"Me or my parent?"

"Both." He looked gloomy again. I found this tiresome.

To Tibellis, I said, "I thought Yur'i might have some influence. Could he get me some samples? Particularly from first- and second-year mating Ghen."

While Tibellis signed to Yur'i and Saft'ir, I held my breath, hoping they wouldn't realize the possible consequences. I wasn't dealing with stupid Ghen, however.

"You know you're asking us to go against our spiritual advisor?" Saft'ir demanded, through Tyannis.

"Yur'i is also a spiritual advisor," I replied, "What does he say?" I didn't wait for his answer but pressed on, watching Yur'i, trying to persuade him. "Unless we're prepared to take risks, we'll never know much more than those mountain savages you stayed with. Is that Wind's will?"

"Are you interested in the Wind's will?" Yur'i asked.

His question surprised me. Without thinking, I told the truth. "Not really. But I believe what I'm doing is right."

"Everyone does," Yur'i said.

"What if I could find a way to stop Bria from bearing Broghen?"

"Without stopping them from bearing Ghen?" Saft'ir demanded.

"I'm not Single-by-Choice," I said, insulted.

Tibellis and Tyannis were so busy signing translations they had no time to speak, but I saw their expressions. I had won them over. Yur'i saw it, too, and he was their advisor.

"We'll talk about it," he said.

"Stillseason has already begun. If I don't get samples soon, there won't be any for another year!"

"You're only eleven, Pandarris. You have plenty of years to make amazing discoveries."

Saft'ir's words stung. There was some truth in what he implied about my motives. Tyannis interrupted and the two of them signed back and forth for a few minutes while I fumed silently. Then Tibellis signed. He seemed to be agreeing with Tyannis. I wished I could understand their signs. I would learn when I had time, I promised myself, watching their faces intently.

Yur'i stepped in and signed then. His movements had a quiet finality about them. When he was finished the others touched their breath. Saft'ir did so last, somewhat reluctantly.

"Saft'ir and Yur'i will try to get you some samples," Tyannis told me.

"What did Yur'i say to them?"

"That when we're in a labyrinth, we need to pursue every path."

"What's that supposed to mean?"

"We can't all kill our babies, Pandarris."

"You prefer to shoot them when they're older?" I retorted.

He shut his eye for a moment and I wished I'd held my breath. Then he said, "Yur'i thinks you're going to find us a better solution."

Not the way it's going, I thought. But his confidence in me was gratifying and he had talked them into helping me. I began to smile, until he added, "Yur'i also believes that Wind is working through you, despite your arrogance and impiety."

⁊

Several days later Saft'ir and Yur'i came to my door. Between them they carried five small vials, each neatly labeled with the donor's name and year of mating. Three were first-year matings and two were second-year. I barely saw Saft'ir and Yur'i out, I was so eager to get the samples under my tube.

When I looked down at the first sample of second-year mating fluid, I cried aloud with satisfaction. By its purposeful movements, I knew it—no, them, there were several—to be the seed-creatures of Broghen, with their large, dark centers each surrounded by an opaque, oval-shaped rim.

I was almost sorry that Brock'an spent so little time here, now. I would have liked to show him this. Grinning to myself, I began examining the first-year mating samples Saft'ir and Yur'i had brought me. In each I saw the same creature, or creatures: the small Ghen seed, propelled by its little tail.

The last sample was marked, "Cammis, second mating".

There were the same small organisms I'd seen in all the first-year samples. Not two or three, but half a dozen. Whoever Cammis was, he must have labeled his joined Ghen's sample under his own name, misunderstanding Saft'ir's instructions. In fact, there might be a number of samples all in the one vial. And why had he called it "second mating"? It was filled with the creatures of first-year matings.

Although I was annoyed at the contamination of samples, I recorded my findings and decided to follow all of these joined pairs. To do so, I needed to learn whom Cammis's samples were really from.

Stillseason or not, I made my way to Tyannis's house, so I could speak to Saft'ir.

⁊

"Tell me about these samples," I said, through Tyannis. That mutual sign language would be useful. I decided to send my younglings to storytime.

"What do you want to know?"

"Are the donors all adults, all joined Ghen?"

"Of course," Saft'ir signed, but he double-checked the names on the vials to satisfy me. "All joined adults. But this one isn't Ghen." He held up the vial in which I'd found so many Ghen seeds.

"Not Ghen? That's impossible!"

Saft'ir insisted that it was a single sample from Cammis himself, not his mate. Cammis told Saft'ir it was the secretion from his breasts, prior to his second mating. Of course it wasn't, but I'd have to get the truth from Cammis, himself.

Saft'ir helped me home. I tried not to lean on him, but the unnatural stillness nauseated me. I closed my eye, willing myself not to be ill in the street. That he should see me so! After I eliminated Broghen, I'd work on this problem.

თ

I said nothing to Brock'an about any of this. We had little to say to each other anymore. His child would be weaned in another year, and they would leave.

As soon as stillseason was over, I went to Cammis's house. Despite my disbelief, Cammis insisted that the fluid was his.

"I wanted to help," he said, reaching for my hands. I resisted the urge to pull them away from his clasp. "And Tann'an—my joined Ghen—refused. We were late mating. I didn't want to go at all, but Tann'an made me!" He was openly weeping now. "I'm going to have a Broghen, aren't I? Just like the ones outside our walls!"

Now I did attempt to disengage my hands. I tried to back away, but he held tight.

"My matri says your work is evil." I stood still with surprise. "He says you're trying to usurp Wind. That we birth at His will, and must accept whatever He sends us, with humility. But I don't want a Broghen inside of me!" His voice rose into a wail.

"No, no, don't upset yourself," I murmured, trying to calm him. His display of emotion embarrassed me; I really only wanted to escape. "And …thank you for your sample." I pulled my hands free at last and hurried toward the door. "It's very helpful. Yes, it showed a lot."

I thought that would please him, but instead his wailing increased. I left so quickly I was nearly running.

When I'd put some distance between myself and his house, I slowed down to think. Ghen embryos in Bria breast secretions? Impossible! Ghen were Ghen and Bria were Bria. But I had no doubt now that the fluid was Cammis's, just prior to his second mating.

Could they be Bria embryos? No, I'd smeared my breast fluid on my co-joining Bria's rash. If those were my embryos, I'd have no children.

Was I entirely mistaken that these moving things were embryos? Perhaps they were like the other tiny creatures I'd found? But they were larger, distinct, more like the embryos I'd watched develop in the farmborra eggs. I felt certain I was right, even though I couldn't imagine why they should be in pre-mating Bria breast fluid, not to mention in such numbers.

Had I got it all wrong? For a brief moment I wondered if Bria could be responsible for the creation of Broghen.

Ridiculous! The idea was preposterous! Bria had nothing in common with Broghen. It was the Ghen who were so aggressive.

All my assumptions must be completely wrong. I had simply discovered a second type of organism, which had nothing at all to do with procreation. I'd have to examine more samples, but it was too late for this season.

It was galling to know I'd have to wait a whole year. I wrote up what I'd seen, but didn't approach Council. What did I have to show them? Hints and guesses.

I wanted to scream with frustration at the way the Broghen eluded me, hiding the mystery of their creation from my searching mind just as the one had hidden itself in my womb.

I'm sure I'm the only Bria who ever looked forward to the return of stillseason.

Council Relations

Briarris

I stood at the northern edge of the city, just outside Pandarris's house, the last one on the street. Ahead, the road became a narrow path running into a meadow. The silver grasses sang their lisping melodies as the wind moved through them.

One hundred armlengths away, the wall stood tall and ominous even in the bright, mid-day sun. Its pennants snapped in the fresh breeze, as though issuing sharp warnings: danger, danger, danger!

Even knowing that I was perfectly safe—as long as the sun was shining—didn't prevent me from shivering at the sight. Did I once call that wall "antiquated"? My ears twitched at the memory of my own ignorance.

There was an uninhabited feel about the area even before the houses stopped. Most of the Bria living here had left, taken new houses closer to the city center or, if necessary, moved in with their parent. Only my own stubborn offspring had remained. At least Brock'an was still there with him. When Brock'an's youngling was weaned and they returned to the Ghen compound, I hoped Pandarris would have the sense to move away from the wall.

I reached Pandarris's house and coughed at his door. Almost at once it was thrown open.

"Matri," Pandarris said, clearly disappointed. "I was expecting the child-guarder. I must get back to work."

"It's only the first day of newseason, Pandarris. He'll take a day or two to acclimatize before resuming his duties. Most Bria do, you know."

"Two days? He's had all stillseason to—" he took a breath. "Would you like to spend some time with your grandchildren, Matri? You haven't seen them in a while…"

244

"Where's Brock'an?"

"He's taken his youngling to the Ghen compound for the day."

"And left you here alone?"

"No! He refused to take my children! Isn't that unfair? His youngling still suckles at morning and at night, and I don't refuse my duty."

At that point the children came running to greet me. Pandarris made ruberry tea while Zipporis and Kayjais told me about their stillseason adventures and complaints.

"Run outside and play," Pandarris said, carrying two mugs of tea to the table.

"Certainly not!" I said, over the delighted cries of my grandchildren. "Our walls are under attack, Pandarris."

"Oh well," he said, "We'll take our tea outside and watch them play, then. If I can't work, at least I can sit out in the wind."

We sat in the soft grasses and enjoyed the mild breeze as the children ran about, tumbling and somersaulting. I hated to spoil the peaceful scene with my news.

"I haven't told anyone that you already knew what Koon'an would report," Pandarris said mildly after several moments of silence. "You can trust me with whatever you've come to tell me."

"I didn't expect you would tell."

He grinned. "When did you realize I knew?"

"The minute you realized it."

"It's almost as though we're getting to be friends."

"Almost." We both grinned then, as though we'd been joking.

"So what is it?" he asked.

"There was an incident in Festival Hall this stillseason." I took a long sip of tea to soothe the emotion out of my voice. "A Bria became hysterical."

"Who was it?"

"You wouldn't know him. His name was Cammis."

"I know him."

I hesitated. "I'm sorry."

"What happened?"

"He stood up in the middle of the Hall and screamed, "We're all carrying Broghen!" I took another drink to calm myself. "Then he grabbed

Tann'an's—his joined Ghen's—hunting knife, and plunged it into his belly, before he could be stopped."

"Breath of Wind!" Pandarris whispered.

His hand trembled as he lifted his mug to his lips. It wasn't much, but I took it as maturity, this first sign of empathy.

"There must have been chaos."

"Very nearly," I said. "Luckily Ocallis was also there, with Mant'er. He stood up on a chair and called for silence over the screams and moans and weeping of the terrified Bria, while Tann'an and two others rushed Cammis out to the infirmary, pretending he was only wounded.

"Ocallis reminded them that he'd already given birth once, which quieted them down to listen. 'Would I be here a second time if Cammis had anything to be afraid of?' he demanded of them. 'It was the fear in his heart, not a Broghen in his belly, that brought him to harm, may Wind restore his sanity. Your own imaginings are all you have to fear.'"

Pandarris shook his head as though to deny my story. "They'll all despise him when they've given birth," he said, his voice quiet, shaken. "Those who have pieces of his work will break them."

I closed my eye and shuddered. The wall of anger that would rise against Ocallis would hurt my gentle sibling more than the broken glasswork, but it was no use trying to explain this to Pandarris.

"We'll stand by him," he said with grim resolve, and I felt a cool wind of pride rise in me. "Did it work? Did he stop the panic?"

"Most of them had already mated, and their joined Ghen led them home. Two Bria, who had just arrived for their first mating, refused. They, too, were escorted home, and the joining was dissolved.

"Only one Bria, coming for his second-season mating refused. "You'll kill our offspring," his joined Ghen told him, but he was panicked and wouldn't listen. When he couldn't be convinced by reason, the Ghen cried, "I cannot let my youngling die!" and forced himself upon his terrified mate."

"Wind's breath!" Pandarris cried. "It can't be true."

I touched my breath.

"They let him?"

"Everyone was too stunned to react. By the time they pulled him away, the deed was done."

"But he'll be punished?"

"He's to be banished after they mate next stillseason."

"They're going to let him force the Bria again?"

"What else can they do? He's had second mating; it's too late to turn back. If birth isn't stimulated next stillseason, the Broghen will tear its own way out!"

Pandarris looked ill. At last he said, "What about the other Bria? Will their resolve hold?"

"Ghen who are joined to pregnant Bria have been released from their duty on the wall to guard their Bria."

"Guard them from what? Themselves?"

When I made no reply he jumped to his feet, pacing in agitation. "You have to stop it! They're…" he searched for words to express his outrage, "they're treating us like callan!"

"I can't stop them. Besides, what would you prefer? Mass panic? Suicides?"

"This will only convince them that Cammis was right."

"Not if we all deny it," I said firmly, but there was desperation behind my words and I knew he heard it. "Igt'ur tells me you're looking for the Broghen seed."

He looked surprised at the change in topic.

"Do you really think there is such a thing?" I asked.

"I know there is."

"And you think you can find it?"

He saw where I was going. "Perhaps, if Mick'al allows Ghen to support my research," he answered cautiously.

"Mick'al will allow it. I'll see to that. And you're going to have help."

"I don't need help."

"You don't need this kind of help," I agreed. "But you're getting it anyway. A young Bria named Kirabbis has declared his intent to specialize in 'enlarging tube research'."

"He can't just walk in and take over my invention!"

"Your invention is published now, it belongs to all Bria."

"Then let him make his own."

"He will if he must. But it would be better if you welcomed him. Let him apprentice under you. Frankly, I'd rather he do his research under your direction."

"It sounds like you don't trust him. Or is it me you don't trust?"

"He's a member of Single-by-Choice."

There was a long silence between us.

"Does he know what I'm working on?"

"I don't think so," I said. "All I know is that he's decided to specialize in your field. And if there is a Broghen seed, you'd better be the one to find it."

Distortions

Pandarris

Icouldn't get a child-guarder to come out to my house. I had to escort my younglings to Yur'i's house for storytime myself, and arrange to have them met there after storytime and brought to my studio to suckle, after which they were taken to school. I was forced to stop work when their school ended, no matter what I might be in the middle of, to take them home. The constant interruptions to my work were aggravating, but they would be weaned in another year and then I would be free.

Kirabbis was another interruption. However, after I taught him how to make an enlarging glass, I realized I could leave that repetitive task to him. This somewhat mollified me.

His enthusiasm when I began showing him objects through my enlarging tube revived for me the thrill of my early discoveries, and I began to thaw to him. He was clever and likable, but very timid. I suspected his decision to join Single-by-Choice was more the result of a fear of Ghen than of ideology, but we did not discuss it. I'd heard enough of that group's beliefs from Sandarris.

I helped him build his own enlarging tube, and was rewarded by his excitement and delight when he saw for himself the tiny creatures I had discovered two and a half years ago. I left him happily slicing his own finger to examine pieces of skin and drops of blood, and returned to my own research. Not that much could be done until stillseason arrived again, but I repeated the experiment with farmborra eggs, to see if I had missed anything.

Kirabbis was interested in the eggs, but not as much as he was in the blood organisms. Perhaps it was because he would never have children himself. I was relieved—it would save me lying about the existence of Broghen, and sidestepping questions about what I was searching for—but also a little disappointed. I'd begun to enjoy being a mentor, and here he was already striking out on his own.

He was too intelligent to remain a disciple; he leapt ahead. Despite his quick mind, he was very thorough. He examined blood samples from dozens of Bria, and from every creature on the farms, and then he screwed up his courage to ask the Ghen.

"Why are they all the same?" he asked me one day. "Why should the blood of Bria and callan and farmborra and Ghen all host the same organisms?" I had no answer. I hadn't even thought to ask the question. But I was his teacher, I had to say something.

"Perhaps the organisms serve some purpose? Perhaps they are needed in all blood, not just ours."

Kirabbis looked at me, surprised. "Serve a purpose," he murmured. "What purpose?"

He was talking to himself but I answered anyway. "Maybe a better question is, what happens when they're missing?"

He blinked twice. When his eye lost focus I returned to my own work. I know how to let someone think.

Stillseason was approaching when he made his great discovery. He went to the infirmary for blood samples. Those who had been wounded in some way showed nothing unusual in their blood, but those who were suffering from the burning sickness had an entirely new group of creatures, even smaller than the ones I had discovered, swarming through their blood. Four days later, he examined a fresh blood sample from one of his donors who had now recovered, and the creatures were gone! Only the now-familiar, slightly larger ones remained.

"Write up your findings," I said, with a mixture of respect and envy. He was even younger than I had been, but I knew this should be published.

"Both our names will go on it," he declared.

"This is your work."

"I wouldn't have found it without your guidance. You asked the questions that led to it."

How could I not like him?

⚸

My parent was as good as his word. When stillseason approached, Brock'an began bringing samples from Ghen into my studio. Now that my work was approved, our relationship had also improved, but I didn't trust him as I once had.

I examined sample after sample, until my findings were conclusive: in first-year mating Ghen, the tear-drop seed, in second-year mating Ghen, the oval seed. But did I dare announce what I had found? What if I was wrong? Brock'an was still convinced I was missing something. He had me second-guessing myself now.

I couldn't prevent Kirabbis from looking at the samples without appearing to be concealing something, but he was more interested in his own work. One day, however, easing himself back from his enlarging tube, he noticed my frustration.

"What if you put the two together?"

"What?"

"Put them together on one slide. See what happens."

"Why should anything happen?"

"Well, my two organisms—or rather, the one you discovered in healthy blood, and the one I found in the blood of those with the burning sickness—they attack each other."

"Attack each other?"

"Maybe not attack. It's more like a game of stones and sticks. One sort surrounds the other, caging it in. Whichever side has the most, wins, I guess. At least the blood ends up with mostly that kind of creature."

"Let me see," I demanded, and then, looking down his tube, "Why didn't you tell me about this?"

"I was about to," he replied. "But you're engrossed with your own research. I know how to let someone work."

I tried it at once. The tear-drop and the oval seeds swam about on my glass until two of them—one of each kind—collided. Then, under my disbelieving eye, they joined. Completely joined: became one creature, larger and darker than either had been separately. The others, instead of joining as well, began to slow their movements until they were perfectly still, and only the single, joined seed continued moving on the glass. Again and again we watched this, in sample after sample. Some signal was given or released when one pair joined, that stilled the others.

"That's why they have to co-join with a second-year Ghen," Kirabbis said, in one sentence destroying all my previous conclusions.

Still the Broghen eluded me! Walking home with my younglings, I thought of how I had been kept ignorant until I birthed. Was it Bria or Ghen who thought of that lie? Regardless, it was the storyteller who continued it. And it had made a fool of me! If I couldn't stop the Broghen, I could at least guard Zipporis and Kayjais from those lies. I decided to keep them home from storytime.

"We can't stay home, we can't!" Zipporis wailed. "Tomorrow we're perform-ing the story of Dayannis and Heckt'er!"

"It isn't important," I said, "It's just a myth." A lie, I thought, and only the first of many. But I didn't say this; I hadn't decided yet how to tell them.

"We're going, Matri," Zipporis said. "They're counting on us to play our parts."

His eye was the same clear green as mine—a rarity among us—and his face bore the stubborn determination that I was often accused of. Beside him, Kayjais trembled, his wide blue eye blinking back the urge to cry. Without shifting his gaze from me, Zipporis reached sideways to clasp his sibling's hand, thinking I wouldn't notice.

Had I never looked at my children before?

I remembered the seed-creatures in Cammis's breast fluid. Where had these children come from?

I was being ridiculous. Zipporis was the exact image of me; he could be no one else's. Kayjais, on the other hand, resembled me only in fleeting expres-sions when I looked beyond his dark fur.

Both of them, however, had inherited my persistence. I stood firm at first, but they gave me no peace. Finally I relented, but I decided to go with them and confront Yur'i with his lies.

∾

I was not surprised to see Tibellis in the storytelling grounds when I arrived. Everyone knew he and Yur'i spent more time together than most joined pairs. But why was Tyannis here? Had he nothing to do, now that his work with the mountain people was over? For a moment I pitied him. My work was slow, but I still had work to do. I would be in print again, perhaps after the coming stillseason.

Tyannis approached me. "I'm glad you came after all, Pandarris. Your younglings didn't think you would."

I looked at him in surprise.

"Sit with me," he suggested. "I'll translate for you." He pointed to the end of a long bench placed at one side of the area. Tibellis and a number of other adult Bria and Ghen were already seated along it. The three- to five-year-olds kneeled or sat on the ground in front of them.

On one of the benches, Sulannis and Jar'od were sitting together. What were they doing here? I hadn't seen them since they had co-joined with Brock'an and me. I stared at Sulannis's face, shocked. Why hadn't I noticed before? He caught my eye and smiled. I should probably greet him. And then what? Ask him why my Kayjais's fur is dark, like his? Why Kayjais has his blue eye? Children often had the look of their parent's co-joining Bria. There was nothing new in that. Why should it so disturb me now?

"They're about to begin," Tyannis whispered beside me. I followed him to the bench. The one- and two-year-olds stood in the center of the storyteller's area, fidgeting with excitement.

"This is a very important story," Tyannis translated Yur'i's signing.

Yur'i appeared to be addressing the older children seated on the ground facing him, but he made sure the younger ones, waiting to perform, could see what he was signing. I was embarrassed to notice that even the adults seated on the bench understood him. I was the only one who needed a translator.

How long had he been teaching? No, wait, Savannis had taught the sign language first, hadn't he? That was the year I'd convinced Matri to allow Sandarris and me to quit storytime. Savannis's last year as storyteller. That's why no one had stopped him. He was so old, our parents had all been his pupils. Everyone my age and younger must know it. I glanced along the bench. Sulannis and Jar'od watched Yur'i's signing without embarrassment, as did all the others. In fact, I saw Sulannis use the same signs to make a comment to Jar'od. Joined couples no longer created their own language! What a release of time. Tyannis's voice brought me back.

"The reason the one- and two-year-olds are performing," Tyannis whispered as Yur'i signed, "is because I want you all to remember that the Ghen and Bria in this story were children. This is a very frightening story—you won't be afraid, will you?" He had turned, addressing this last remark to the little actors who giggled self-consciously. Frightened? Hadn't they been practicing it for weeks?

"No? But you must pretend to be afraid, because Dayannis and Heckt'er and the other children this happened to were frightened at the time."

The one-year-olds, including my Zipporis and Kayjais, stared at him solemnly, while the two-year-olds shrugged happily, proud that he took their roles so seriously. I'd been wondering why he'd chosen the youngest children to perform his story and was caught short when he referred to Dayannis and Heckt'er as children. That wasn't the way I'd heard it.

The next remove was almost a surreal experience. Familiar parts of the story blended with outrageous additions that I could hardly credit, and yet they explained so many of the questions I'd had about that ancient tale. The three-year-olds appeared as the children's dying parents—Breath of Wind, why would he have the children portray such a horrible thing?—and yet they seemed undisturbed by it. It was just a story to them. The blend of the new and the old was what made it shocking to me.

Later, the three-year-olds appeared again as raging Broghen, screaming outside the cave where Dayannis and his peers huddled in fear. I wasn't the only parent who panted for breath, stunned into disbelief. The bench was so still with motionless Bria it could have been one of Tibellis's models, before the springs were added.

The most shocking part, however, came at the end when Dayannis, alone with Heckt'er in their separate cave, gave birth to a Broghen! What a distortion…

…or not, I thought. My little Kayjais played the Broghen, his dark fur lying on the pale gray arm of the small Ghen playing Heckt'er. He half-carried, half-led Kayjais away while Kayjais dramatically rolled his blue eye and stuck out his tongue in a parody of madness. It made him strange to me, so that I found myself wondering again where he had come from, even while part of my mind recognized the question as foolishness.

"Don't tell anyone!" Tyannis whispered beside me. I looked at him in surprise, but he was just translating little Dayannis's signs to the pretend Heckt'er as he led my youngling, the Broghen, away into the forest. His role finished, Kayjais skipped around behind the others and ran to climb onto my lap. I held him stiffly.

The child playing Dayannis had risen to deliver his final soliloquy. "I gave birth to a Broghen as well as two Bria and a Ghen," he lisped it as he signed so that there was no need for Tyannis to translate. "I thought it was bad and I kept it a secret. But it was just the way things are. We all have a Broghen. But it's just a baby. It didn't hurt me and it won't hurt you."

The children took this calmly but I heard gasps along the bench. Not from Tyannis or Tibellis—they must have been in league with Yur'i in plotting this.

Sulannis rose from the bench, his blue eye fierce with anger. "How can you tell the children such lies?" he cried.

Kayjais twisted in my lap, looking up at me. Over among the now-seated one-year-olds I could feel Zipporis, who had played Dayannis's young friend, gazing at me as well.

Tyannis stood up. "I gave birth to a Broghen," he said, signing as he spoke. "Every parent with children in this city has borne a Broghen, and every parent to be will bear one." He looked along the bench, challenging us all.

I looked down at Kayjais who had played the infant Broghen. What had I done? It was an infant!

Would Kayjais and Zipporis be driven to do the same one day?

"You're wrong," I said, rising. The eyes of every child turned to me but I saw only two: one blue eye and one green. "You won't bear Broghen," I promised them. My arms rose in the wind as though to take a vow, but then I clasped them behind my back, hiding my guilty hands from the children. "You won't birth a Broghen because I will put an end to it!"

✌

Yur'i was able to have that story performed by three sets of children before Council stopped him. All the children had seen the practices and heard his version of the story, however. Those whose parents had kept them home because the storyteller was Ghen heard about it from their playmates. Every child in the city learned about Broghen.

Most of their parents denied it but some appeared relieved by the end of the deception. And it was completely ended, despite any attempts to retain the old lies.

Not only by Yur'i's story: Tibellis had made a life-sized statue of a birthing. They kept it at Yur'i's house, where the children could see it, and anyone else who wanted to. Also, I believe, to keep it from being destroyed. I went to see it. Tibellis, after all, had worked with me to display my findings.

It wasn't life-sized; that would have been too much, but it was so realistic it fascinated me. The subject was repelling and yet I found the statue as a whole reassuring; it was so much less horrible than my memory of the event. I hoped, for Tibellis's sake, that others who saw it would feel the same.

The Bria was sculpted lying upon a sleeping ledge, with a Ghen and two Bria newborns suckling at his breasts. The Broghen was no larger than the infant Ghen, and the look on its face was pathetic rather than fierce as it struggled helplessly in the attending Ghen parent's large hands. Its scales were the dark gray most common among our Ghen and the tufts of Bria fur which poked out at intervals were the same light brown as its Bria womb-parent.

For parent he clearly was, staring at it in a mixture of pity and regret which only heightened my discomfort. The adult Ghen stood calmly beside the birthing ledge, holding the infant Broghen. The entire sculpture swayed slightly, as though cupped in the hands of Wind.

A peaceful scene for children to look upon. More peaceful than the reality. Well, secrets must be revealed with care.

Later, I asked my parent why Council hadn't banned it.

"We've been asked to," he admitted, "but the harm is done. It would be worse if we tried to hide it now, and let memory exaggerate it. We have to learn to live with the knowledge of Broghen. Personally, I hate it. I'd rather forget. But it may assuage the pregnant Bria's fears. Right now, that's more important."

"Single-by-Choice are teaching their members to fight. Sandarris told me."

"That's not what we were born for."

"What were we born for, Matri? For deceit?"

Instead of reacting to my sarcasm, he asked, "Have you ever spoken to Brock'an about hunting?"

"Hunting?"

"Once, when I was weary of responsibility," he smiled dismissively, "I asked Igt'ur why Ghen always returned home from their hunts. They love the wild forest, they love the hunt. What brings them back?" He paused to give me time to think about it.

I thought of the young Bria who were coming to my studio daily begging me for answers, as desperate as Cammis had been. My impulsive promise at storytime to stop the birth of Broghen had been repeated until I heartily regretted it. How peaceful my days had been before. Oh yes, I understood my parent's question.

"Igt'ur mistook me," he continued. "He replied that Ghen always know where home is. One of those instinctive things, like a wild bird finding its way back to the same tree to nest in every stillseason. I was too embarrassed to tell him that I'd been wondering about will rather than bearings. I'm glad I didn't try. He wouldn't have known what I was talking about. For Ghen, home is an orientation; intent and direction both."

"You're implying that they're more moral than Bria? More responsible? They kept the secret, too."

"Not from each other."

"They kept it from us."

"We kept it from ourselves." He held my gaze until I looked aside.

"A subtle difference," I murmured.

"An important one."

"Look where subtlety got us."

He touched his breath. "Off-track, I agree."

"'Off-track'? You think we simply lost our path?" I asked. "What path were we supposed to follow in birthing monsters?"

"'The Creator put us here to civilize Wind'," he quoted.

"I don't believe those stories."

"It enlarges us, doesn't it? Larger than life, perhaps." He smiled, using my terms. "But you know how to correct for that, don't you? What's the word you use for that other glass?"

"The shrinking glass."

"Shrinking, yes. Personally, I think learning to kill is too great a correction. Something between the two distortions is needed. Do you think you can find it for us, Pandarris?"

☙

My parent wasn't the only one on Council putting pressure on me to bring my work to a conclusion. I, who had longed for acclaim, now regretted the loss of anonymity. Everyone wanted to know about my work, and I had nothing certain to report.

Young adult Bria were angry, resentful, terrified. The children might receive Yur'i's revelation about Broghen as easily as the other stories he taught them, and accept their parents' promise that they need not fear it; but those of mating age had been raised with lies and gave no credit to anyone's reassurances now. How could they feel otherwise?

Everything didn't rest on me, fortunately. Ocallis, carrying Mant'er's second child, was a visible symbol of Bria courage. He was often called on to speak before groups of young Bria, trying to give them strength.

Ocallis did what he could to reach the young, but it was the older Bria, those who'd had their children already, who most admired him. He stood for parenthood, and they were parents.

Which made them the adversaries of their young, who were beginning to openly rebel. Many who had joined but not yet mated dissolved their union, and those who weren't joined were very unlikely to do so. Some who had mated once declared they would not mate again, preferring to let their younglings die in their wombs. They considered my promise just another lie.

Kirabbis looked at me with that same suspicion. Although I'd never lied to him about Broghen, I hadn't disclosed the truth, either. Another subtle difference.

Finally I said, "Kirabbis, I'm not your matri. And even as your friend, what can you accuse me of? That I didn't warn you? You were never joined, there was nothing to warn you about."

"My understanding of our relationship was wrong," he said with the righteous dignity of the young. "I thought we were both bound to the truth." After that he was silent.

He didn't come into the studio the next day.

Stillseason was almost on us. The mood in the city was tense. I felt the tension as I fruitlessly sought a third organism, one I could clearly identify as Broghen. Finally I put my samples aside to work on a new enlarging tube I had agreed to make. Another young Bria wanted to study with us after stillseason.

Ocallis and the other glass blowers were working in the studio as well, mostly ignoring me. It seemed that everyone who knew me felt betrayed because I had not shared discoveries they hadn't cared to ask about, and now

I was not making the ones they wanted. I sat alone, the object of their hope, the subject of their resentment and distrust.

I don't know when I first became aware of the commotion outside. The glass blowers must have heard the distant voices coming nearer, settling into a steady chanting, because most of them were already at the windows when I finally looked up.

I was on the point of inserting a lens into the still hot tube which I held in my gloved left hand. I'd removed the glove from my right hand to hold the long tweezers with which I was trying to wedge the lens between the narrow grooves half-way down the tube before the metal cooled and tightened around it, enough to keep it from falling but not so much that the tiny screws on either side couldn't make minute adjustments to its distance when I turned them. Not an activity conducive to interruptions. I frowned, trying to tune out the chanting crowd. Some idiot had opened the studio doors. Had none of the glass blowers anything better to do than satisfy idle—

Suddenly my light was blocked off. I looked up with a curse to find myself surrounded by silent, grim-faced Ghen. Ignoring my protests, they hauled me to my feet and hustled me through the studio toward the door. There were five of them, surrounding me so closely I couldn't see what was going on.

"Where are you taking me?" I cried, powerless to resist them. Of course they didn't understand Bria, but my question must have been obvious. When they ignored me I began to scream, "Help! Help!"

By now they were forcing me through the door outside the studio. The Ghen on my left slapped his hand over my mouth to silence me. I couldn't breathe. I struggled frantically to pull my head away, but his other hand was behind my neck. My movements caused him to loosen his grasp, however, so that my nose was clear and I could breathe again. I bit him until I tasted blood. He grunted, but kept his hold on me.

I felt the heat of the crowd pressing in all around us, could hear Bria voices calling out my name and Kirabbis's, but they were blocked from my view by the bodies of the Ghen. Would they even know I was here, and needed their help? Creator of Wind, what did these Ghen want with me?

The Ghen, tightly encircling me, forced their way through the crowd as quickly as possible. When I stumbled trying to keep up, their grip on my arms pulled me forward. The crowd of shouting Bria was moving too, staying with us, and for that I was glad. Surely the Ghen wouldn't murder me in the very midst of so many Bria.

I recognized the Council building ahead of us, but could hardly believe they were taking me there until they actually propelled me up the steps and through the door, closing it firmly behind them. Inside they released me and stepped back, the one nursing his bleeding hand.

Briarris rushed forward, throwing his arms around me. Over his shoulder I could see Brock'an's grimace of relief. What was he doing here? He was supposed to be on the wall.

"What's going on?" I demanded, releasing myself from my parent's embrace. "What are these bullies up to?" I gestured angrily at the Ghen who had roughhoused me here.

"Oh, I can't believe they'd actually have hurt you!" Briarris cried.

"Well, they came close," I rubbed my bruised arms.

"Not the Ghen, the Bria!"

"The Bria? What are you talking about?"

"You didn't see them? Hundreds of Bria shouting outside your studio and you didn't notice?" He was almost laughing; not a happy sound, more a mixture of relief and exasperation.

"I was busy. I heard some voices. It was you who told me to concentrate on my work, remember? What did they want?"

"You! They are calling you a false leader."

"A leader?" I had never wanted to lead others. Mostly I wanted them to leave me alone to work. To admire my discoveries from a respectful distance. "What do they mean?" I asked.

"They say you have promised something that cannot be done. Haven't you been paying any attention at all?"

"But I see them! Every day they come to my studio, begging me—"

"Those are the young Bria, the ones who aren't yet joined, who are waiting for you to fulfill your promise. It's their parents who call you false."

"They *want* their offspring to bear Broghen?"

Briarris sighed. "They want grandchildren, Pandarris."

"They want to stop my work?"

"They say we need faith to lead us through this, not your discoveries."

"Rubbish." But I said it with less force than I once would have. My parent did not respond. "You agree with them?" I demanded.

"That we need Faith? Yes. I need all the faith I can muster now, as do we all. That your work is wrong?" He sighed. "I don't know what's right or wrong. I'm Council Chair, and I don't know what's right or wrong!"

Surely this wasn't my parent; my parent was never indecisive. "You have to know," I said. How could he suddenly doubt my work? What if he ordered me to stop? He was Council Chair.

"My work isn't a lie! It's knowledge that they're fighting," I said urgently. "I'm not making it up, I'm learning it. But it's true, whether we know about it or not. Let me learn, and then you can decide what to do with it."

"The knowing and the doing can't be separated. Knowing changes us, changes everything."

"For the better."

"Knowledge doesn't solve problems; it just changes the problems."

"Then what is the solution?"

"I told you, I don't know." He sighed. "There's more."

The way he said it made me certain I didn't want to hear. When he paused, I remained silent. But he wasn't waiting for me to ask, he was trying to find a way to say it. "Kirabbis…"

"Where is Kirabbis?" I asked when he didn't continue. I looked at his face and fear stole my breath.

"He's dead, Pandarris."

I swayed. Brock'an hurried over with a chair and I sank onto it. The Ghen who had brought me here had already deployed themselves about the room. The rest of the councilors moved away, giving my parent privacy to comfort me. I didn't want comforting. "Tell me," I said.

"It isn't only Bria parents who are upset. Some of the Ghen also question your attempts to stop the birth of Broghen."

This was insane. Ghen were the ones who killed them at our walls to protect us.

And what had that to do with Kirabbis?

"Tell me," I repeated.

"A number of Ghen disapprove of your work. They want things to remain as they are. Igt'ur says they are saying, 'Today they won't bear Broghen;

tomorrow they won't bear Ghen.' They sound a little like Anarris, actually," he grimaced.

"They killed Kirabbis?" I whispered, afraid to say it out loud. It was inconceivable that Ghen would harm a Bria to save Broghen: a reversal as unlikely as the sun rising at night.

"It wasn't intentional. They meant only to keep him—and you—in the forest until stillseason, and then escort you back to your homes. To prevent you from continuing your research."

"They took him to the forest?" Kirabbis was so timid. They'd forced on him all his worst fears—being alone with Ghen, the dark night, the forest…

"He died of fright." Briarris confirmed my unspoken thought.

"Why didn't they take me instead?" I wailed, thinking of Kirabbis's eager curiosity, his humility, his brilliance.

"They planned to take you both."

"Why didn't they? I would have kept him alive! He wouldn't have been so frightened if I'd been there."

He put his arms around me and I leaned against him. "The ones who did it have been punished," he said.

It brought me very little comfort.

⁊

The crowd of Bria stood outside Council Hall for several removes before they finally left. I offered to go outside and talk to them, but Briarris forbade it.

"Seeing you will only incite them further."

"They wouldn't harm me," I said, "and if it appeared that they might…" I nodded at Brock'an and the other Ghen still positioned around the Hall.

"That's exactly what I'm afraid of," Briarris said. "The last thing we need right now is a confrontation between Ghen and Bria."

"Yes," I agreed, "it's better to keep them united against me."

He looked at me, about to deny it, until he caught my grin. There was nothing funny about the situation, but we both laughed until we wept.

⁊

When the crowd had gone, I wanted to return to my studio, but again Briarris forbade me. "I'm not in danger anymore," I protested.

"My whole city's in danger right now. And you're the spark of lightning that could set it off."

"How long do you mean me to stay here?"

"Until stillseason. Bria will stay in their houses then, and you'll be safe. Although, with your house so close to the wall…"

"We've been over that before," I said firmly. "I have work to do. What have you decided?" I tried to appear calm while waiting to hear his verdict. Surely he wouldn't try to stop my research?

"I've decided there's no turning back. No standing still. Continue your work. But you'll have to do it here, where you're safe. Keep me informed of everything you learn. And only me. That will take us to the next corner of this labyrinth. Perhaps there'll be a sign when we get there." He shrugged wearily.

⁊

Brock'an brought my younglings to me after storytime and again after school. He also brought sleeping mats. At night my younglings and I slept on the floor like Ghen, in the small room that was used for closed-Council. It had a fan, but no windows. Brock'an and his youngling slept there with us. I set up my enlarging tube in a separate room with a window into the courtyard.

It was obvious where I was staying, but a triad of Ghen guarded the main door, day and night. No more crowds of Bria formed. I expect they were ashamed; especially when Briarris announced in Council that Kirabbis had died of fright. He didn't give the circumstances, but let the Bria think it was their fault; meanwhile, Igt'ur made sure the Ghen knew it was theirs. The radicals on both sides were temporarily subdued.

Igt'ur and my parent were a formidable pair as Council Chair and Chair Ghen. If anyone could get us through this crisis, it would be them.

Living in Council Hall was inconvenient, but I'd never been particularly attached to my house or the studio. It was only my enlarging tube that I cared about, that and my samples.

Not that they had anything new to show me. Always the same two organisms; always two of them joined and the others died off. If only Kirabbis

263

were here with his unusual insights. I tried to imagine what he might have suggested now. That the Broghen seed already lurked inside our wombs, like our Bria offspring? If so, I would never find the solution. I couldn't cut open a living Bria as I had the mangarr'h.

If I didn't find the answer soon, every Bria who refused second mating would miscarry. An entire year of Bria would bury their infants and never be parents. It was a horrible thought, but my mind returned to it, try as I might not to think of it. I dreamed of them at night, and when my eye grew weary staring down through my enlarging tube I thought I saw their faces, mouths wide in silent entreaty.

They were waiting for some miracle from me. Their Ghen mates were being patient, but for how long? When stillseason arrived, and they feared their younglings might die, what then?

క్ర

Yur'i and Tibellis came to visit me. I suspected my parent, having noticed my lack of sleep and appetite, had sent for them. They were a welcome diversion from my stalled research. I had not been allowed to attend Kirabbis's funeral and asked about it.

"If he lived, he might have found a cure for the burning sickness," I told them.

"He is a wind that others will ride on," Yur'i replied.

He was right; young Bria were already beginning to specialize in his field. I hoped they would add his name when they were published.

"Do you still believe that Broghen come from Ghen?" Yur'i asked.

When had I told him that? Or had he assumed it from what the Ghen were saying about me?

"I don't know," I said. "My research is not going very well." I watched his face as Tibellis translated but he, too, was non-committal. "How is your truth-telling going?"

"Not very well." He grinned a little. I found myself grinning back at him.

"Which is the best solution for our people?" I asked him, still grinning as though it were a trivial question. "My truth or yours?"

"There is only one truth," he said. "When a door is closed, the wind blows through a window."

"You think Wind is blowing through me?" I laughed. "You're beginning to talk like Savannis."

Tibellis grinned as he translated that, but Yur'i shrugged. "I am now the Voice of Wind," he replied.

"They don't agree with you." I gestured out toward our city.

"There have been too many changes. They are confused."

"Confused?" They had threatened me with violence and Yur'i called it confusion? "What do I do to become less 'confusing'?" I asked sarcastically. "Hide what I am discovering?"

"Never. If it is being shown to you, you must show it to us. You have no choice."

"I have a choice."

He looked at me, smiling sadly. "Pandarris, you are the one who has been shown these things because, for you, there is no choice but to tell what you see."

⌘

"What if you didn't co-join?" I asked Brock'an that evening. He had brought our dinners to my room in the Council building.

He put his food down. "No Ghen younglings," he signed.

"But still two Bria infants?" I waited as he took another mouthful.

"I don't know."

"Why not co-join on second mating?"

"There would be two Broghen."

"You know this?"

"That's what we've been taught." He looked up at me and sighed. "After dinner?"

I had little appetite and Brock'an lost his under my stare. Soon he was guiding me to the room with the birth records again.

"You're right," I signed after we'd examined the first few pages recording births that occurred in the early years after Dayannis's and Heckt'er's infants were born. "But why? Why does it take the seed from two different Ghen to produce one youngling at first mating? Why would two seeds from the same two Ghen at second mating produce two Broghen, instead?"

"We may never know," he signed.

In a rage I slammed the book shut and pounded on the wooden table with my fists, screaming, "I must know! I will know!" Brock'an allowed me to expend my fury until I crumpled, sobbing. He caught me as I fell and held me. We sat there, beside the book that held all our knowledge and gave us no answers.

℘

It was almost stillseason when Tyannis came to see me. He brought two vials, one of his breast fluid and the other of Saft'ir's mating fluid.

"You never told me what you saw in Cammis's breast fluid," he said, "but it had you upset enough to come to my house in stillseason."

I sighed, and put some of his breast fluid onto a glass. Under the enlarging tube I located the tear-drop organisms I'd seen in Cammis's fluid.

Tyannis looked at them, amazed. "These are the same as in first-year mating Ghen," he said at last. "Why haven't you told us about them?"

"Because it doesn't mean anything. We smear them on our belly rash." I thought of Kirabbis's blood organisms and their contest with the burning fever organisms. "Maybe they're good-health creatures."

Still looking down the tube, Tyannis reached for the vial with Saft'ir's sample. "What if we put them together, the way you did with the first- and second-mating samples?"

"But one's Ghen and one's Bria…" My voice trailed off as I remembered the tufts of Bria hair on the little Broghen in Tibellis's statue, on my own infant Broghen. I felt ill. So obvious, and I had missed it.

Because it wasn't the answer I was looking for, the one I wanted.

Already Tyannis was pouring some of the fluid onto the glass which held his own sample. I didn't want to look. It was all I could do not to stop him.

Kirabbis would have thought of this days ago. Kirabbis had been bound to the truth.

Tyannis's cry of surprise was no surprise to me.

"They joined," I said, when he looked up to tell me.

"You knew?"

"Not until now."

"It's the Broghen."

"I think so."

266

"How do they get into our womb?"

In unison we looked at his belly rash. Without a word, he lay down on the floor in front of the window while I found an enlarging glass and held it over his belly. He winced when I accidentally touched his rash. I hesitated, feeling a little silly, but he motioned me to continue.

I was used to looking at specimens through an enlarging tube. It took a while to angle the glass correctly over his belly to show anything. When the rash became visible, it was no longer a solid flame of red, but a cluster of scarlet circles. I moved the glass closer. Each circle was a tiny opening, large enough to admit the Bria embryos, each opening surrounded by a pucker of red skin, like wounds cut into the center of his abdomen.

❦

Briarris and Igt'ur came to see me the next day. I told them what I had seen and what I believed about the organisms in Ghen fluid, as well as the mystery of Bria breast fluid. They heard me out in silence.

"Write up your findings," Briarris said. "We'll tell the Bria who are ready for second mating that they can prevent Broghen by not soothing their rashes with breast fluid. Keep a record of those who agree. They'll believe in records. Tell them it's safe to mate, then."

"I can't know for sure if that's the Broghen seed," I protested. "It may be a Ghen, or even a Bria. The Broghen seed may be entirely different, something I can't even see with my enlarging tube."

"Tell them anyway."

"And if I'm wrong?"

"Right now, the most important thing is that our civilization continues to exist. We have to make the pregnant Bria see past their own fear and go to Festival Hall to mate."

"We tried that once, combating fear with lies."

"This isn't a lie," he said. For a moment he faced down my stare, then he grimaced. "It is a slight distortion."

I did not answer.

"I admit it's only a partial answer," he said. "Do you think you're going to achieve all knowledge in your lifetime, Pandarris? Even you can't be that arrogant."

267

"It won't work."

"It has to. It's all we've got."

"Why don't *you* tell them, if you want to?"

"They'll believe you. They're counting on you because of your foolish promise."

"I promised the children, not those already joined. I need more time!"

"You don't have more time. What do you think will happen to my city when stillseason ends and those Bria begin to miscarry? You think you saw an angry crowd before? Wait till we're burying babies."

Beyond The Wall

Igt'ur

B rock'an and I escorted Briarris and Pandarris to every house in the city, to tell Bria the news. We could not risk a public meeting, with awkward questions and accusations from Anarris and his followers. Pandarris brought his findings for the Bria to read, and a ledger to record the names of the second-year mating Bria, declaring they would be the first who would not birth a Broghen. He spoke with such confidence that most agreed not to exchange breast fluid.

We brought with us a soothing paste from the mountain plants Tyannis had brought back with him. Our healers had found them useful and had cultivated them for the past three years, but we had nowhere near enough to cover this great a demand. They would have to endure constant, intense discomfort. We also brought cloth pads to tie over the rashes, warning the pregnant Bria against soothing themselves in their sleep.

For the sake of their future younglings, they wanted to believe. Their desperate hope almost undid Briarris. But they would not promise to come to Festival Hall. Those who should have their first mating and those who were not yet joined also listened, but it was clear they did not intend to mate.

Yur'i began visiting the unjoined Bria with us. "We were never meant to create monsters and unleash them on Wind," he told them. "Perhaps this is what the Creator meant, telling us to civilize Wind. Perhaps He really meant, civilize ourselves."

They listened to him but still promised nothing. We did not have time to stay till we convinced them; there were too many houses to visit and stillseason was nearly upon us.

Ghen who were living with Bria returned to the Ghen compound on my orders. I was determined to allow no forced matings except in the case of third-year mating Bria, to prevent them from being killed by the Broghen already inside them. The third-year forcings bothered me but I had too much else to worry about, such as the resistance I saw growing among the Ghen, not only to letting their unborn infants die for lack of second-year mating, but even to the idea of taking preventative measures against creating Broghen. Mick'al was at the root of the problem. If he had spoken in favor of eradicating the Broghen, no Ghen would have dared to oppose us both.

He didn't quite go as far as to speak in favor of Broghen; they were our fiercest adversary on Wind and we killed any who returned to us. I believed that was the issue, though he never said so. They tested our mettle, and in so doing, kept us strong.

Mick'al wasn't about to advocate violence against the Bria. He was as unhappy about what had happened to Kirassis as any of us. But his silence regarding the concerns of those who had done it spoke loudly. He should have joined me in condemning their position. The fact that he didn't frightened me more than anything else that was happening in our city.

I went to talk to him.

"I need your support," I told him, "to prevent our city from being torn apart."

"I have not opposed you. You are Chair Ghen."

"I need more than that. I need you to support the eradication of the Broghen."

"I can't do that."

"You must: for the sake of all Ghen."

I had never openly argued with him before, and I think we were both surprised when I used the command only Chair Ghen could give. I knew him to be sincere in his spiritual leadership, if sometimes too rigid, and he knew me to be a pious and respectful Ghen. But neither of us had convinced the other.

એ

Stillseason descended upon the city. Festival Hall, with its fans and streamers, stood empty.

I called a meeting of Ghen on the field behind the Ghen compound. I explained what the Bria hoped to accomplish by resisting the urge to sooth their belly rashes with breast fluid, and encouraged the Ghen to be patient. This wasn't news, of course. I was merely getting everything out in the open, and frankly, trying to buy some time.

"What use is a warrior without a worthy opponent?" someone cried out. As though that had released their tongues, others called their agreement. A large young Ghen pushed his way through the crowd until he stood beside me. I recognized him as Mick'al's apprentice. Why hadn't I thought to charge him with my injunction when I had done so to Mick'al?

He bowed respectfully, then turned to face the mass of Ghen. "Birthing Broghen teaches us humility," he said. "Holding them back at birth makes our younglings fearless. Releasing them safely teaches us compassion. Watching for their return keeps us vigilant, and killing them if they do teaches us duty."

Many Ghen stamped their approval as he returned to his place on the field. Saft'ir hurried forward.

"Ghen boast about the ferocity of their Broghen offspring," Saft'ir cried out, "I don't call that humility. My womb-sibling, Yur'i, and others like him, are shamed all their lives for something that isn't their fault. Being sensitive to the Bria's fears would show whether or not we had learned compassion, and doing what's best for all of Wind is our duty!"

Only a scattering of stamping followed his words. Mant'er approached the head of the field next. He walked forward slowly. When he had turned to face the crowd he asked, in a low but carrying voice, "Are you proud of your Broghen?"

Something in the tone of his voice, a heaviness, a weariness, hushed them.

"I was proud when my youngling subdued the Broghen that shared his womb," he said. "I was proud of the fierceness of the Broghen my mating produced. And when we freed them in the south, I was proud to think my offspring, however deformed, would be the master of that land.

"I am not proud now. The Broghen of the mountain Ghen destroyed my youngling, and many other fine youths. I find myself wondering if the Broghen I created has found its way to another settlement of Ghen and Bria, to prey upon their young."

There was a deep silence, until defiantly, a young voice near the back called out, "We are warriors! Without the challenge of Broghen, we would grow weak."

"Were we a hunting party of weaklings and fools?" Mant'er roared. "No!" He paused until he had subdued the rattling of his spine ridge. "Many fine hunters and youths died on that trip. Their loss does not strengthen us, it weakens us."

"We have courrant'hs and liapt'hs to battle," I said, as Mant'er moved back to his place on the field. "We don't need to create more predators."

Koon'an came forward then.

"We are warriors," he agreed.

No one could deny that he was one of our best fighters, if not the best among us. I could feel the crowd's interest in what he had to say.

"But we are also world-builders. Our ancestors built this city. What have we built lately?" He looked around, giving them time to think about his question.

"Now is the time for another kind of warrior. Now is the time to fight for civilization. I took the best warriors we have into the mountains. Who will go into the forests and mountains, over the plains and perhaps even over the oceans, to forge links with other settlements of Ghen and Bria? Who will help me build a civilization to encompass every corner of Wind?

"Unless you would prefer to hide within these walls from monsters you have chosen to create!"

There was a long silence after he sat down. Then the drumming of feet began. Slowly it spread across the field, gathering momentum. He had appealed to their pride, their courage, to all the best within them, and had given them a purpose to capture their very breath.

As soon as the stamping died down enough for me to be heard, I intended to call an end to the meeting. There was still much to do. Resolving the issues that faced us would be long and difficult work. But I felt we were on the way. Yes, I believed we could do it, if the Bria would meet us half-way.

Then I saw Mick'al making his way to the front.

If I had seen him first, I would have adjourned the meeting at once. But by the time I noticed him his intent to speak was obvious, and Ghen were quickly quieting to hear what he had to say. If I refused to let him speak, the conflict between us would be obvious and Ghen would be forced to choose between their spiritual leader and Chair Ghen.

If I let him speak, he might destroy everything I had gained at this meeting. I opened my mouth, raising my arm in a motion of adjournment…

Mick'al caught my eye. Slowly my arm lowered. Mick'al was also my spiritual advisor; I had to hear him out.

"I have always believed there was a reason why we have Broghen," he said, "but I have sometimes wondered what it was. Until today, however, I have never wondered why we have that wall. It was to keep the Broghen out. To protect our younglings, and the Bria who depend on us. To create an area of safety within which we may turn our minds to higher thoughts.

"Today, Mant'er has reminded us how shallow that sense of safety is, and Koon'an has reminded us how little we know of Wind.

"What have we done?" He paused, staring at the attentive crowd. He had them still, spellbound, when he opened his mouth and roared: "We have given Wind to the Broghen, and built ourselves a little cage to live in!"

There was utter silence. I let my breath out softly. It left me like a prayer. Mick'al had caught Koon'an's fire and was building a vision to lead us all forward. I was no visionary, but I could see that this was what we needed.

"The Bria built walls of silence and we felt superior, because we did not need to hide from the truth." Mick'al stared from face to face, daring any to disagree.

"What else have we been doing behind these walls, but hiding?" he shouted. The scales down his back rattled in the absolute silence that greeted his accusation.

"There will be walls to guard for a long time yet, from the white Broghen, from our own Broghen offspring.

"But we were not created to guard the walls of a single city." His voice thundered over the field. "We are the guardians of Wind!" Ghen feet began to stamp. More and more joined in, and over the stamping, which shook the very ground we stood on, and the rattle of Ghen scales and the pounding of Ghen hearts, over it all Mick'al's voice roared, "We are its guardians and the Bria are its heart! Let there be no more walls between us!"

The ground shook and the air reverberated with cheers and stamping. When the noise began to die down, I stepped forward to adjourn, but once more I was interrupted.

"Igt'ur! Igt'ur!"

I heard the high-pitched Bria voice before I saw him struggling toward me. The Ghen shifted, bumping against one another to let him through. Briarris ran to me and fell against my chest, shaking. I took his shoulders to raise him so I could sign to tell him it was all right, the Ghen would not use force against the Bria. But when I lifted him, I saw that he was laughing!

"Ocallis brought them," he signed, using Yur'i's signs instead of our own, so many of the Ghen could understand. "Ocallis walked out into the streets shouting, 'Where is the heart of Wind? Where is the brave heart of Wind? Bria, be brave!' Then Tyannis came out of his house and shouted, 'Bria are brave!' and then Tibellis joined them.

"They walked through the streets calling 'Bria, be brave!' and the doors of the houses opened and the Bria came out shouting 'Bria are brave!' They took his hand, and others took their hands and they walked all together through our city shouting 'Bria are brave!'"

In stillseason? I could hardly believe it. "Where have they gone?" I asked.

He laughed at my stupidity. "To Festival Hall!"

He blew into my face for all to see and I blew into his, and the hot, still air filled with the cries of Ghen as they repeated, "To Festival Hall! The Bria have gone to Festival Hall!" Then there was a noisy scramble as those who were joined and those who wished to join rushed away to meet them.

And even though it was stillseason and I do not believe in signs or miracles, I felt the mighty presence of the Wind blowing over us all.

Acknowledgments

I am exceedingly grateful to all the people whose knowledge, time, interest, and enthusiasm have contributed to the writing and publishing of this book: My husband Ian for his careful line-editing, daughter Amanda for her critiques and suggestions, and daughters Tamara and Caroline, my Beta readers; My important early readers and critiquers, Linda and Peter Barron, Lori Christy, and Sue Moses; and my teacher and early mentor, Robert J. Sawyer. Thank you all for forcing me to write better, encouraging me to keep on, and believing in this story.

I also want to thank all the excellent people at Expert Subjects: William Sudah, Marija, Cath and Patrick, for the artistic and technical expertise that turned my story into three e-books and this beautiful print book.

To My Readers,

Thank you for joining me in the world of the Ghen and Bria on their planet, Wind. I hope my story has entertained you.

If you have enjoyed reading Walls of Wind, please consider posting a review on Amazon or Goodreads. Your review will help others find this story. Every review matters, and is valuable to me, no matter how long or short it is. I would love to hear what you thought – and I do read every one.

To find more of my stories, or send me a message, visit my website and blog at http://www.janeannmclachlan.com or visit my author's pages on Amazon and Goodreads.

May the breath of Wind blow gently over you!

J. A. McLachlan